TOO MANY SUSPECTS

There were so many names to keep track of, but I wrote them all down with notes about what we had learned from each person we spoke to.

Mayor Rod Jeffers, fuming mad at the prank that had been played on him, had looked at the security camera footage of the parade the day before Lars died. That was suspicious. However, he refused to believe that Lars Jorgenson was behind the prank. Could it have been a ruse? I put a *maybe* by his name and moved on.

Daphne Rivers had a little more going for her as a suspect. She'd been suspicious of us from the moment we met her. She was also certain that Lars was behind the goat-napping and seemed to know him pretty well. Another black mark by her name was because she was named as a person of suspicion by Grayson Smythe regarding the spectacular demise of his glass sculpture. Who else was she mad at? Could she be the prankster? I put a star by her name with a note to talk with her again.

Then there were Stanley and Felicity Stewart. They hadn't appeared angry at the goat debacle that had ruined Mom and Kennedy's fashion show; they just appeared exhausted. Even if they had an ax to grind against other members of the festival committee, which I didn't believe they did, they were working too hard during the festival to even pull off one prank, let alone poison an old man. I put the word *no* by their name and moved on . . .

Books by Darci Hannah

MURDER AT THE BEACON BAKESHOP

MURDER AT THE CHRISTMAS COOKIE BAKE-OFF

MURDER AT THE BLUEBERRY FESTIVAL

Published by Kensington Publishing Corp.

Murder At The Blueberry Festival

Darci Hannah

Kensington Publishing Corp.
www.kensingtonbooks.com

For Dave Hilgers,
beloved father, mentor, and friend,
in loving memory

ACKNOWLEDGMENTS

Every time I sit down to write about Beacon Harbor, I'm not only filled with happiness to be visiting one of my favorite fictional places again, but I have a deep sense of gratitude for all the people and the little adventures along the way that have led me here. For *here* is a wonderful place to be. And while just about everyone I meet in some small way shapes the stories I write—be it a lively conversation, a word of inspiration, a description of a place I've never been, or an interesting turn of phrase that delights me—there are those who have gone above and beyond in helping me along the way. I'd like to thank my lovely agent, Sandy Harding, for not only taking a chance on me, but for being a dear friend while helping me navigate this crazy world of cozy mystery writing. I would also like to thank John Scognamiglio, my savvy, hardworking, and delightful editor at Kensington for championing the Beacon Bakeshop Mystery series. John is the reason this series exists, and for that I am forever grateful. I would also like to thank the lovely Larissa Ackerman, who not only shares a love of Newfies with me but is also the hardest-working publicist I've ever met. And a huge thanks to Rebecca Cremonese and her team of editors for making these pages look so good. And to everyone else at Kensington who works so hard on my behalf, thank you!

I would also like to thank my friends at the Howell Carnegie District Library who have put up with me and my writing for the past ten years, and who never fail to support the books that I write. I miss you guys! And to my dear friends, Robin Taylor, Jane Boundy, Tanya Holda, Sue Hanson, and Margaret Bigham, for the stimulating conversations, laughter, and good coffee! And an additional thanks to Margaret Bigham for letting me use her name in this book. You will always be my favorite librarian!

I would also like to thank my incredible family for their endless love and support. To my wonderful parents, Dave and Jan Hilgers, for being the best parents a child could have. To my brother, Randy, for the laughter and the phone calls. To my nieces, Dana and Jenna, for being like daughters to me. To my sister-in-law, Brenda, for being the strongest person I know. To my wonderful husband, John, and our three amazing sons, Jim, Dan, and Matt, for filling my life with love, wonder, joy, laughter, and happiness. And to the newest member of our family, my daughter-in-law, Allison (Wysocki) Hannah. She knew how crazy our family is and still agreed to marry Jim! Many blessings to you both. I would also like to thank all my wonderful in-laws, whom we don't see nearly enough but love all the same—Matt and Monica Hannah and family, Becky and Scot Specht and family, Steven and Lilia Hannah and family, Clare and Merrill Krabill and family, and Rick and Meredith Hannah and family. And to Bob and Barbara Hannah, my heartfelt thanks.

And a huge thank-you to all the readers out there who have taken a chance on these mysteries that I write. As always, I hope you enjoy your visit to the Beacon Bakeshop!

CHAPTER 1

Having lived in an old, refurbished lighthouse in Michigan for over a year, I had come to realize a few things. The first was that I loved falling asleep to the sound of waves: Be they gently lapping on the beach or crashing onto the rocks, waves had become my lullaby. The second was the realization that the first lightkeeper, Captain Willy Riggs, although dying on the job in the late eighteen-hundreds, had never really left the lighthouse. Not much I could do about that. The third was that I had a smoking hot neighbor, Rory Campbell, whom I was slightly obsessed with. Okay, more than slightly, but our relationship was still a work in progress. The fourth thing that was blatantly obvious was that my giant Newfoundland, Wellington, had a perpetually wet-dog smell that lasted all summer long. He loved the water. And since we lived right on the shore, it was nearly impossible to keep him out of the darn lake. My solution, barring a leash, was a nice-smelling doggie deodorizer. The fifth thing, and by far the most important, was that I loved the freedom of running my own business. Sure, there were easier businesses to run than a bakery. The early-morning hours could be daunting for the average person, but for me, owning and operating the Beacon Bakeshop was a perfect fit. Heck, my own dad liked to remark that I had a knack for making dough. This was a play on my former Wall Street career as much as it was on my new vocation of baker. But Dad was undoubtedly correct. I did have a knack for making dough, only these days the dough I made had to be baked before it could be enjoyed.

There was one more thing about living in a lighthouse on the shores of Lake Michigan that was hard to deny, and that was the fact that August in Michigan was spectacular. The lake was warmer, the weather dryer, and hordes of happy vacationers and tourists flocked to the village of Beacon Harbor. August was also the time when Beacon Harbor held its largest and oldest-running festival of the year, the Beacon Harbor Blueberry Festival.

This year I was especially excited because, thanks to Betty Vanhoosen, head of the Chamber of Commerce, owner of Harbor Realty, and head of the town gossip mill, I was on the festival committee along with nine other *lucky*, overworked townspeople. And, thanks to Betty and her antics of last Christmas during the town-wide Christmas cookie bake-off, I had been excluded from entering a pie in the highly competitive blueberry pie bake-off that was to be held on Saturday. This was because I owned a bakery and was considered to be a professional. I wholeheartedly agreed with the committee's decision. I'd been making blueberry pies all summer long, much to the delight of our customers. One look at their faces as they took their first bite of the flaky, buttery crust bursting with warm blueberry filling that was the perfect balance between sweet and tart, and I knew that I had already won the only pie contest that mattered.

However, I wasn't to be let off the hook so easily. Instead, because I *was* a professional, I had been tasked with baking lots and lots of blueberry pies, not to sell by the pie or the slice as we already did at the Beacon, but because on Sunday, the final day of the festival, the Beacon Bakeshop was to host the rip-roaring blueberry pie–eating contest on the lighthouse lawn.

As a member of the Blueberry Festival Committee, I was planning and executing the pie-eating contest. It was sure to be a raucous, messy affair. Space was limited to the first twenty contestants, eighteen and older, who filled out the entry form and signed the waiver, which warned that eating a whole pie in one sitting could be dangerous. (No joke!) Also, they acknowledged that they were doing so at their own peril. That being done, each contestant was to get a whole, freshly baked blueberry pie to devour as fast as they could. The first one to finish their pie without the use of hands or utensils was the winner.

I never understood the appeal of eating contests, but judging from the race to enter the contest, I was in the minority. It was already Friday morning and all twenty spots had been filled, with twenty-two more on the waiting list! It looked like my weekend was going to be filled with lots of prep work and baking, not only for the gluttonous pie-eaters, but for the Beacon Bakeshop as well.

Given the setting of my bakeshop—right on the shore of Lake Michigan and a stone's throw from the public

beach—and given the beauty of the season, the Beacon
Bakeshop was busier than ever. I had also recently
opened a pup café on the patio for those visiting with
dogs. It was on the patio where we gave out free Beacon
Bites, which were essentially day-old donut holes that the
dogs loved. I used to reserve my donut holes for Welly
until Ryan Wade, one of my intrepid employees, had
suggested that other dogs might enjoy them too. I wholeheartedly agreed. Besides the Beacon Bites, we also made
a Welly-approved treat of the month. Honestly, Welly
would approve of any treat, being a dog who wasn't
above nibbling on rotting fish found washed up on the
beach. However, we strived to do better than that by making a delicious dog biscuit of the month. This month's
dog biscuit was flavored with dried blueberries in honor
of the festival.

Unfortunately, using so many plump, fresh, delicious
blueberries since they came into season, I had taken for
granted that I'd have plenty on hand for the festival.
However, after a week of baking a prodigious amount of
blueberry baked goods, I realized that we had used the
last of the blueberries. In short, I was having a blueberry
emergency!

"Those look delicious." I had just plated a plump,
blueberry-filled donut for a tourist, when Ginger Brooks,
my friend and owner of Harbor Scoops, the town's famous ice cream shop, came strolling up to the bakery
counter. She cast the middle-aged man a winsome smile,
which caused him to fumble with his wallet.

"Came to town for the blueberry festival," he said, re-
gaining his composure and his control of his wallet. He
pulled out some bills.

"Well then, you'll be wanting one of those too." Ginger pointed to the tray of warm, giant blueberry muffins that Wendy had just brought from the kitchen. I could tell it was the baked good she had her eye on this morning. And, as a single mother, she might have had her eye on the handsome tourist as well.

The man, put on the spot, nodded. Smiling, I added a giant blueberry muffin to his order. He paid, said good-bye, and took his plate and coffee out to the patio and the morning sunshine.

"Way to upsell, Ms. Brooks." Tom, our head barista, cast her a smile. "The usual?" he asked.

Ginger nodded. "You know me, Tom. I like my coffee like I like my men: strong, rich, and hot."

Wendy and I, having heard variations of this line nearly every morning that Ginger came in, giggled, none-theless. She slayed us every time with her sassy coffee order.

Tom handed Ginger her usual cup of freshly brewed house coffee. "Good," he offered with a nod. "Because if you said bitter and weak, I'd have to send you down to the gas station. Come back before the parade today, and I'll make you our special blueberry-pie cold-brew latte." Tom, with his sun-streaked light brown hair, light brown eyes, athletic build, and charming smile, had a way with the ladies. To be fair, he also had a way with coffee. He and Elizabeth, the Beacon's other talented barista, often put their heads together to come up with specialty coffee drinks. The blueberry-pie cold-brew latte was like drink-ing a scrumptious slice of caffeinated blueberry pie. Aliana, the shortest of the bunch, with her chestnut hair and sparkling green eyes also had an artistic flourish that we all admired. I had put her in charge of our menu board the moment I discovered it. Last night she had added the specialty latte, including an eye-catching drawing of what the blueberry-pie cold-brew latte looked like. She had also embellished the board with lovely, hand-drawn blueberries for the festival.

"That sounds sinful," Ginger said. "Maybe I will, but for now just this and one of those warm, yummy muffins."

I took a sheet of bakery paper and plucked a giant blueberry muffin off the tray Wendy had just put into the bakery case. "Here," I handed it over to her, paper and all. "Try it and let me know what you think?" Ginger took hold of the warm muffin with dancing pleasure.

"It's bursting with blueberries. I can already tell I'm going to love it. Bet you're having a hard time keeping these on the shelves."

"We are," Wendy replied with a troubled look. "That's already the second batch of the morning." Turning to me, she added, "Lindsey, what's the news on the blueberries? Our last quart went in there. And don't forget that your mom ordered two pies for Sunday."

Ginger's head snapped up. "You're out of blueberries? Already? And when does Ellie Montague Bakewell eat blueberry pie?" This was said with a slight mumble due to the sizeable chunk of muffin in her mouth.

Wendy, a year out of high school and one of my first employees, was intrigued by Ginger's last remark.

I shrugged. "When all aging models do, I guess. Late at night when she thinks no one is watching."

A little giggle escaped Ginger's lips. "Wicked," she admonished, grinning. "It must be hard for a former eighties fashion model and icon to have a daughter who bakes."

"Typical of you to take my mom's side," I teased.

"What about me? My livelihood relies on sugar and butter, and she moves to town and opens a high-end clothing boutique? What kind of message does that send?"

"You're terrible." She rolled her eyes as she said this, but she grinned all the same. My mom's clothing boutique was across the street from her ice cream shop. "Ellie and Company sells adorable flouncy tops and chic pants with elastic waistbands. Your mom has both our backs."

She was undoubtedly correct. I also loved the fact that my parents had recently moved to Beacon Harbor to be closer to me. Dad, although claiming to be retired, helped in the bakeshop three days a week. More when I needed him. We were still looking for an assistant baker, but with Dad and Wendy helping me in the kitchen, we were managing quite well. Mom, also having retired from modeling years ago, got the itch to get back into the world of fashion. She had opened her flagship clothing store, Ellie & Company, right on Waterfront Drive, also known as Main Street. Her business partner was none other than my best friend, Kennedy Kapoor. Unbeknownst to me, the two had cooked up the idea one day. I had to admit, they were doing quite well. Kennedy, still one of the country's hottest influencers, split her time between New York City and Beacon Harbor. However, thanks to Tuck McAllister, one of Beacon Harbor's finest men in uniform, our little town in Michigan was winning out.

"But what about the blueberries?" Wendy pressed.

"Don't worry. I put Rory on it. A former Navy SEAL should be able to handle a little blueberry reconnaissance mission. Just in case, however, I gave him directions to the Kendall farm early this morning. He should have all we need for the weekend." No sooner had I spoken than Wendy pointed to the front windows, where a black pickup truck was heading up the lighthouse driveway.

"Looks like mission accomplished," she remarked. "Mr. Campbell's a man you can depend on."

"He is, indeed," Ginger mused with a sigh. "I wish I had a Rory." She winked, then took her muffin and her coffee out the front door.

CHAPTER 2

"**Y**ou are a lifesaver," I said, running over to Rory, who was just emerging from his truck.

Rory Campbell was the type of man women craned their necks to get a better look at—and I should know, having dated him for over a year. He stood six-foot-four, his espresso-colored hair was smartly cut and just the way I liked it—short on the sides and longer on top—and, in my humble opinion, his eyes rivaled the color of the Caribbean Sea. Given all that, including his passion for fitness, his best feature by far was his kind, generous heart. I had never dated anyone like him, and truth be told, I was still trying to figure Mr. Rory Campbell out. Ironically, he was my nearest neighbor at the lighthouse. When I had first met him, he told me he was writing a military thriller. Having recently retired from his service as a Navy SEAL and finding himself the owner of a log home on the shores of Lake Michigan with nothing but time on his hands, writing a work of fiction seemed like the thing to do. Bless him, he actually was writing a book! He was also still involved in service to his country, as I later found out.

However, Rory was now finally done chasing down bad guys. What I'd never realized until two months ago was how difficult the transition to civilian life had been for him. That was because in June, Rory had finally let me read his so-called military thriller. I had stayed up late into the night, sitting up in the old light tower poring over the pages beneath an old oil lamp. Rory's novel depicted stomach-churning terror on foreign soil, and the heart-wrenching antics of a brave warrior named Ricky Camel. I must have dozed off at some point because I remember waking up at dawn with a vivid, terrifying dream still swirling in my head. I had smelled pipe smoke as well, an indication that I had not been entirely alone in the old light tower. I use the word *entirely* because, although I *was* alone, the light tower, as I had also learned, was still the domain of the first Beacon Harbor Lighthouse keeper, Captain Willy Riggs.

Oh, Captain Willy was long dead, but his eternal soul was still attached to his duty, which was keeping Beacon Harbor safe. I admired his pluck. And he admired mine, I believed, as well. At least I assumed that was why he liked to meddle in my affairs from beyond the grave. Captain Willy was harmless, but he'd been trying to tell me something that night. It took me a moment, but I finally understood what it was. The captain was a military man, like Rory. And what he'd been nudging me toward was the fact that the fictional Ricky Camel of my dream looked and acted exactly like the Rory Campbell I was dating. Confused, and with terrible thoughts pinging around in my head, I had left the lighthouse and went to confront Rory at his cabin. Once I'd arrived, Rory finally admitted that although he wanted to write a fictional military thriller, his memoir just kind of popped out instead.

"What!?" I had cried, trying to keep my inner New Yorker at bay. It was useless. My nerves had been stripped raw. "You said it was fiction! That . . . that was all *real*?" And then I burst into tears because it was both terrifying and heartbreaking at once. Hiccupping, I added, "A . . . all that time you . . . you spend alone in the woods? Now . . . now it all . . . makes sense!"

I believe my reaction had frightened him. And although he should have warned me that he'd written a memoir, I did come away from the experience with a better understanding of who he was and what he had been through. His eighteen-month sojourn into writing might have been cathartic for him, but publishing the book was out of the question. I was pretty darn certain that Rory had divulged some highly classified information in there.

That left me with my current predicament. I had finally found Mr. Right, only Mr. Right was in the middle of an identity crisis. Rory admitted he was struggling to find meaning in his life after such a harrowing, adrenaline-rush-filled career. He wanted to make a difference, but he wasn't sure how.

Honestly, I didn't know how to help him. Finding meaning was a personal journey. Oddly enough, I had found mine in a lighthouse bakery. Although I didn't have an answer for Rory, I had vowed to myself to be support-ive—and to keep him busy. The moment I heard the Blueberry Festival needed someone to head up the annual

Blueberry 5K run, I nominated Rory. Thankfully, he agreed.

I peeked into the bed of Rory's pickup truck and saw it was loaded with crates of blueberries.

"Since Chuck Kendall has a stall at the festival that he needs to stock, this was all he'd sell me. Will it be enough, do you think?"

"Unless we get fifty more orders for blueberry pie by tomorrow, this should do just fine." I stood on my tiptoes and gave him a kiss on the cheek. A wry smile appeared on his lips.

"I drive out to a blueberry farm at the crack of dawn, and all I get is a peck on the cheek? Oh, Bakewell, you're going to have to do better than that."

He was right. Although my apron was covered in flour and he was wearing a form-fitting black tee, I wrapped him up in a big hug. We were just about to kiss when Wellington appeared out of nowhere, launching his 150-pound frame at Rory and me. It was like being hit by a hairy NFL tackle running at full speed. The impact threw us apart. Rory, bouncing off his truck, remained on his feet. I landed on my backside on the hard gravel of the parking lot.

"WELLINGTON!" I cried, seething at my dog. I then realized why he was spooked. Someone had tried to put clothes on my dog. I say "tried" because the coat he was wearing was hanging off his side, and the floppy-brimmed squall hat was covering his eyes. On one of his giant back paws was a blue Wellington boot. While I appreciated the irony of Wellington wearing what the English refer to as a *Welly*, my pup wasn't having any of it. The poor dog was frantically trying to shake the hat off his head, batting at the strap under his jaw with his paw.

"Are you seeing this?" Rory grimaced as he pulled the hat off Welly's head, as if it demeaned them both. "Who in their right mind—"

"Welly. Here, good boy. Where did you run off to?"

At the sound of the familiar voice, Welly glanced back across the parking lot. Fear blazed in his intelligent brown eyes. Although Rory had ahold of his collar, Welly bucked and wriggled, trying to escape to safer quarters.

"That voice makes me want to head for the lake too," Rory admitted to my dog. To me, he added, "Now we know what spooked him."

"Well done, Sherlock," I teased before turning to the sound of chunky heels stomping on gravel. Kennedy, always the fashionista in a floppy hat, large designer sunglasses, a flowing, floral-inspired Ellie & Co. dress, and holding Wellington's leash, waved at us. Although my friend still owned an apartment in New York City, she lived with me in the lighthouse whenever she was in town, which, for the record, had been all summer.

"Hi, Linds. Sir Hunts-a-Lot." This she added with a cheeky wink, using her favorite pet name for Rory. "I see you've found Welly."

"Actually, he found us," I told her. "I thought he was napping in the lighthouse. Why is he wearing a raincoat?"

"A blueberry raincoat," she corrected, pointing to one of the tiny dark blue fruits on the light blue fabric. "And, to answer your rather obvious question, because Wellington is walking down the runway with you."

What my friend was referring to was the Blueberry Festival Fashion Show she and Mom had talked the committee into letting them put on Saturday afternoon on the stage at the brat and beer tent. Being an aging yet still attractive eighties fashion model, Mom wasn't used to hearing the word *no*. And the committee didn't disappoint her, either. Actually, thanks to Mom's minor celebrity and Kennedy's marketing genius, tickets for their fashion show had sold out in two hours. Hearing that, they were inspired to start hunting for models.

Of course, being Ellie Montague Bakewell's daughter, I had to participate in the event, even against my better judgment. There was no arguing there. Then Mom had sweet-talked Wendy, Aliana, and Elizabeth into modeling for her as well. Not only were my employees young and adorable, but they were also positively giddy to be a part of the sure-to-be-famous fashion show. I couldn't tell them not to participate. Instead, I'd agreed to shut down the Beacon early so we could all get ready for the big event. That way Ryan, Tom, Rory, and Dad could watch the spectacle as well. And a spectacle I was certain it was going to be, because wherever Mom and Kennedy went, there was always a swirl of drama that followed. And now my poor dog was caught up in it too. The nerve of them trying to make my giant, dignified pooch a fashion accessory!

I stared at Kennedy a beat too long, then shook my head. "Did you tell me he was modeling with me?"

The look she gave me relayed the fact that I was being ridiculous. "Of course, I did." Kennedy, a beautiful woman of English and Indian descent, gave her silky black hair a quick flip with her hand. Refocusing on me, she pursed her lips, adding, "Well, maybe not in so many words. But you agreed to model for Ellie and Company. Excuse me if I assumed you knew that we make clothing for both humans and their dogs."

"Kennedy, my mom's been dressing in matching outfits with her dogs for years." This, unfortunately, was true. She had even named her two Westies, Brinkley and Ireland (collectively known as the models), after her runway rivals. "It's what had inspired her to start Ellie and Company, so that others could partake in the same folly. It's what *she* does, not what *I* do."

"Lindsey's right. Besides, I didn't see Welly signing any contracts," Rory added, sticking up for his favorite canine.

Kennedy manufactured a frown. "Didn't Ellie tell you? She had that raincoat custom made especially for Wellington. Even you must know, owning this handsome guy"—she swept her hand in an arc that purposely encompassed both Welly and Rory—"that one cannot buy extra-extra-large doggie outfits off the rack. These were specially made for Wellington, and clearly he loves them."

"Clearly," I said, dripping sarcasm. Born with a doubly thick waterproof coat, Welly wasn't the type of dog who needed a raincoat. In fact, swimming in ice water didn't seem to faze him much at all. That Kennedy and Mom thought it would be appropriate was a bit comical. Although Rory was still glowering at the idea, I realized I had already lost the argument.

"Alright," I relented, letting Kennedy clip the leash on Welly's collar. "If you think you can dress him in this and get him to trot across a stage without him flipping out, I'm game. For now, however, I suggest you take off the raincoat. Take my word for it, Mom will flip out if it gets ruined before the big show."

"True. And I will. Linds, you're not going to regret this," Kennedy said, ruffling the fur on Welly's head. "Your dog is going to be the hit of the show."

CHAPTER 3

While Welly reluctantly trotted back to the lighthouse with Kennedy, Rory and I set to work unloading the blueberries. The moment they were safely in the cooler, Rory glanced at his watch.

"If you don't need me any longer, I'm going to rescue Wellington and take him out to the patio with me. Don't want to keep the boys waiting."

"Right," I said, noting it was nearly nine o'clock. *The boys* he was referring to were members of a group he had started in an effort to find meaning in his civilian life. "Before you go, take these with you."

With an appreciative look at the goodies I had prepared for him, he took the tray.

Standing behind the bakery counter, I watched as Rory and Wellington made their way to the patio with the two loaves of warm, lemon-blueberry breakfast bread I had made for them. The bread, a lovely lemon quick bread laced with fresh blueberries and topped with icing, would be the perfect treat for the men. The early arrivals had already pushed three empty tables together. Bill Morgan, a Beacon Bakeshop regular, was making his way up the walkway with Dan, his yellow Lab, bounding beside him. Rory was still holding the tray when Welly, his busy tail waving joyfully, lunged on the end of his leash. Rory let go just in time to save the bread. *Good move*, I thought, and watched as Welly and Dan greeted one another nose-to-nose. Then, smelling another friend, both dogs turned, tails swishing the air like two feather dusters in the hands of a manic maid. Jack Johnson and his golden retriever, Libby, approached. Jack and his wife, Ali, owned the Book Nook, the town's wonderful independent bookstore. Ali was obviously getting ready to open the shop, while Jack and Libby came for their Friday morning meeting.

I admit I'd had a little something to do with inspiring this friendly Friday morning group. After reading Rory's tragic memoir, I realized it was literally going to take a village to give him the nudge he needed to fully embrace civilian life once again. Sure, he loved hanging around the Beacon Bakeshop when he wasn't up north hunting or out on the lake catching his dinner. I had naturally assumed, like any other sane New Yorker, that hunting was a woodsman's hobby—albeit one I didn't understand. Then, however, I had read the infamous memoir. After that, I began to realize that hunting wild game was more of a way for Rory to lateral out of hunting enemies of the state. Those poor wild animals! Knowing he was at a loss for what to do, I suggested he ask a couple of men from the village out for coffee once in a while. Rory countered with an argument that he already drank coffee every morning with Tuck McAllister. That was because every morning both Rory and Officer Tuck came to the Beacon for coffee around the same time. True, they were becoming good friends, but I felt he needed something more.

He had mulled over my suggestion for a few weeks. Then one night over dinner he shared an idea with me. Being a veteran himself, he thought it might be a good idea to encourage other men who had served their country to meet somewhere and share their experiences.

"A support group, you mean?"

He raised his dark brows, then nodded. "Yeah, something like that. Though nothing formal. Just a casual meet-up once a week to check up on each other and talk about things."

My heart lifted with joy. "That's a fabulous idea. You could meet at the Beacon."

And that's how it all started. Every Friday morning, rain or shine—barring hunting season and monthly fishing excursions—Rory and his group of military veterans met at the Beacon Bakeshop. I supplied the baked goods and coffee; they supplied the fellowship and war stories. On sunny days, the dogs came, too, prompting me to bring out a plate of Beacon Bites as well.

So far only men had joined Rory's group. They ranged in age from their late twenties to their early eighties and had served in wars ranging from Afghanistan to Korea. Sadly, as Rory had told me, the one living World War Two vet from Beacon Harbor was in the nursing home. I always found it a bit heartbreaking to realize that this great generation was swiftly leaving us.

One of the younger members of the group, a strapping,

blond former marine named Anders Jorgenson, had been born and raised in Beacon Harbor, and had recently moved back within the last few years. This was a blessing in disguise. Anders was near Rory's age, he had served in Afghanistan as well, and the two were becoming friends. If Rory got nothing else out of the group but Anders's friendship, I'd say it was a success.

To me it seemed like anyone who attended the Friday morning group was benefiting. While women tended to gather in groups and go out for coffee together quite often, men, I mused, needed a little extra nudge. And the women of Beacon Harbor were nudging their men bigtime. I had no idea so many residents of the village had served their country. Mayor Jeffers attended, as did Doc Riggles. Anders had even begun to bring his father to the meetings, an older man in his late sixties with the same broad chest and square jaw as his son. Old Lars, the locals called him. Although he didn't say much, Lars had a pleasant demeanor. He also liked to laugh. I know this because his laughter often carried into the bakeshop.

While Alaina, Elizabeth, and Tom worked the counter, serving the line of hungry customers, I was preparing a tray of coffee for the men. I had just filled up a carafe of our popular breakfast blend when I heard a familiar voice directed at me.

"Heard you were out of blueberries." I turned from the coffeemaker and saw Winifred Peters. Winifred was also on the Blueberry Festival Committee. As the reigning champion of the Blueberry-Pie Bake-Off, she was heading up that event as well as the blueberry bake sale. A plucky older woman with the ruddy complexion of a farmer, Winifred was as knowledgeable about blueberries as she was capable of making pies. I smiled at her greeting and saw her husband, Randy, standing behind her with a small bushel of blueberries.

"Oh my gosh," I exclaimed. "Did you bring those in for me?" I was touched.

"I did," she admitted with a nod. "Chuck Kendall called early this morning and said you were out at the bakery. And during the Blueberry Festival, no less!" Beneath her brimmed straw hat was a look of admonishment. "We have a small patch out back. Mind you, they're a special variety I've cultivated for my winning pie, but since you won't be entering a pie in the contest, I felt it was safe selling you some of mine."

I hadn't quite realized how competitive blueberry pie making was, nor had I realized Winifred had her own blueberry patch. "I did manage to get some blueberries," I told the couple. "But I'd be happy to buy yours as well. Can't have enough blueberries—especially this week," I added with a smile. The couple didn't smile back. This was likely because they felt that their blueberries were special. I didn't know a thing about farming, so I played along. "However, these look like a particularly delicious variety." That won me two grins.

Winifred's blueberries went for a modest price to which I included two coffees and two cinnamon rolls. As I plated the cinnamon rolls for the couple, Randy leaned over the counter and asked, "What do you have to do to get into that club?" He pointed out the window at Rory's Friday morning group.

Before I could answer him, another man leaned in. "The League of Extraordinary Gentlemen, do you mean?" This voice belonged to Grayson Smythe, a stylish and slightly eccentric local artist who was also on the Blueberry Festival Committee. "Serve your country, Randy. Almost makes me regret going to art school. Almost." Grayson tossed him a grin.

Randy bristled. "Old Lars is there. Didn't know he served."

"Did you ever ask him?" Grayson gave Randy a pointed look. "I'm sure that if you went over to the table to say hello, they wouldn't bite."

"Well, I'm about to bring out their coffee and some Beacon Bites for the dogs. Why don't all of you follow me and say hello?"

The moment I came out the front door with the others, Mayor Rodrick Jeffers paused in his narrative long enough to declare, "Coffee's here!"

War stories be damned. The conversation this morning was all about the blueberry festival. As I served coffee, Winifred, Randy, and Grayson exchanged pleasantries with the table. Then, once he had his coffee, Mayor Jeffers picked up where he'd left off before he was interrupted.

"As I said, the float is ready to go, and my choir from St. Michael's has been practicing for weeks. This will be my fifth year as the grand marshal of the Blueberry Parade, can you believe it? Got the boys from the reserves carrying the flags, followed by the high school band playing a Sousa march. Then there's old Wade and his antique tractor club. We've got horses, dogs, classic cars, club sports, the marching fly fishermen, marching bands—beware of the middle school band. They're still learning—and most importantly, a float loaded with adorable little school children with giant blueberry hats, in lieu of the formerly traditional Blueberry Queen. Man, have times changed." Mayor Jeffers shook his graying head, lamenting the fact that there would no longer be a float carrying an attractive young lady wearing a sash.

"Amen, brother," Doc Riggles offered with a sympathetic look. "But those youngsters are quite adorable. I doubt anyone will notice the change."

Mayor Jeffers nodded. "Our float will follow theirs. Always a bit of a letdown for the crowd, but my choir will be singing a peppy rendition of Bette Midler's 'Blueberry Pie.' I think we'll win them over this year."

"Don't count on it, Rod," Jack Johnson teased. This caused Lars Jorgenson to laugh, inspiring the others to follow.

"Well, I wouldn't miss it for the world," Bill Morgan said with a grin. "Molly and the grandkids have already staked their claim on the sidewalk. Hope you're throwing plenty of candy. They always look forward to that."

Mayor Jeffers took a bite of his lemon-blueberry bread and set it down again, his face registering an *aha!* moment. "That's what I forgot! Candy! I'll swing by the store the moment I leave here."

"And speaking of swinging by . . ." Doc Riggles, still holding his coffee, stood from his chair and stared at a point in the distance. A screeching sound made everyone else look in the same direction. "I think that's Betty," he remarked. "And she's just drifted through that turn like a rally car driver!"

Sure enough, a white BMW skidded sideways through the one intersection in town, narrowly missing an oncoming car. It then regained traction and continued at an imprudent speed toward the lighthouse. A moment later, a police car appeared behind the BMW and flashed its lights. Undeterred, the white car continued up the lighthouse drive, pulled into a spot, and parked. The door flew open, yet instead of a wild-eyed, twenty-year-old wanna-be rally driver, a plump, middle-aged, brightly dressed woman appeared. The flowing ensemble she was wearing was the color of a ripe blueberry. And there wasn't a hair out of place in her stylish platinum blond bob. In fact, aside from the scowl on Betty Vanhoosen's preternaturally cheerful face, she looked relatively normal.

Ignoring the flashing lights of the police car, she yanked open the rear driver's-side door and hauled out a large metal *For Sale* sign. Betty was a Realtor, so that wasn't a surprise. What was surprising was that she was marching the thing right up to my lighthouse.

A stab of panic hit me. Had something gone wrong with the sale of my lighthouse? Had I forgotten to sign some papers? Was I losing my home? Why the *For Sale* sign?

I didn't know. Apparently, none of us did. And yet my heart began pounding away in my chest like a war drum.

CHAPTER 4

"Betty! Ms. Vanhoosen," Officer Tuck McAllister cried, chasing the Realtor up the walkway. "You were speeding. I clocked you going fifty in a thirty-five zone. That's recklessly dangerous."

Betty ignored him.

Although a Beacon Bakeshop regular and Kennedy's current man-crush, I wouldn't go so far as to say Officer Tuck's appearance was comforting. But he did look determined. However, his progress was hindered by the onslaught of dogs that ran to greet him. The poor pooches had been spooked by Betty's ire and her sign, skipping the Realtor in favor of the cop.

"Betty!" Tuck cried again, bending to greet each of the dogs. Once the dogs were appeased, he stood and continued to follow in her wake.

"Put it on my tab, McAllister!" the angry blueberry

hollered back, clip-clopping up to the Friday morning group.

"Betty, my dear, what's this all about?" Doc Riggles asked with genuine concern. Doc and Betty, both widowed, were dating.

"What does this look like to you, Bob?" she snapped, looking at him.

"It looks an awful lot like a *For Sale* sign, Betty," Bill piped up with a grin. "Being a Realtor, I would have thought you'd be familiar with those by now."

"Funny," she snapped and glared at him. "It *is* a *For Sale* sign, Bill. From RE/MAX. I own Harbor Realty! You can tell my signs because my picture is on every one of them. Do you see my picture on this sign, Bill?"

A collective dour shaking of heads followed before Doc ventured, "Betty, what is your point, my dear?"

"What's my point, Bob? My point is that I found this on my lawn this morning, along with forty-nine other *For Sale* signs."

Doc looked confused. "Are you selling your house?"

"Of course not! What I'm trying to say is that I woke up this morning to the sound of honking cars. I live on a quiet street. I didn't know why the cars were honking. However, the moment I looked out the window, I saw why. Some idiot had blocked off the road in front of my house and placed barriers up, forcing the traffic to use my circular drive as an alternative route! Imagine that!"

Unfortunately, Old Lars Jorgenson could, and what he imagined caused him to burst out in a fit of deep belly laughter. Lars's laughter, much to Betty's chagrin, was contagious. The entire table, including Randy and Grayson, were doubled over in fits at the clever, though devious use of innocent road barriers.

"Oh, laugh all you want, you fools," she told them all, looking miffed. "Your driveways weren't congested with rush-hour traffic at dawn! And that's not all!" She took a steadying breath, her face unnaturally red as she continued. "On my lawn are fifty *For Sale* signs—from every real estate agency in the tri-county area. Plucked from the lawns of homes and farms that really are for sale. See this here?" Again, she pointed to the sign she was holding. "It says, 'For Sale, 80 acres of farmland.' I own half an acre, and I'm on the water. Where did this sign come from?"

"A farm?" Rory offered with a straight face. This remark caused Tuck McAllister's forcibly neutral demeanor to crack, revealing a smile of remarkably white teeth.

"Of course! And do you know the worst part of it all?" Betty, growing wiser, answered her own question before anyone else had the chance. "As the cars were honking on my driveway, laughing and gesturing at my signs, I received a call from Pepper Danes, my nemesis from Empire Realty. Apparently, she felt slighted because she didn't see any of her signs on my lawn. She said, and I quote, 'Betty, if you're going to sell up, I thought you'd at least have the courtesy to ask me to list your house.'" Betty shook her head as if to expel a demon. "Can you imagine that? Why, I told that uppity slapdash house peddler that if I was going to sell my house, which I am not, that I would be my *own* listing agent. And I certainly wouldn't need fifty *For Sale* signs on my lawn to do it, either!"

Doc stood up and began clapping. "That's my girl. You sure showed her!"

The rest of the League of Extraordinary Gentlemen, as Grayson had coined them, followed suit. Betty exhaled forcefully, purging all her pent-up indignation. Finally seeing the humor in her unique morning, she allowed herself to smile.

Doc Riggles pulled out his chair for her and begged her to sit down. "Betty, my dear, I think you've been pranked."

I quickly poured her a cup of coffee and put it in her hands.

"I think you might be right, Bob," she agreed and took a cautious sip. She set down her mug, a question pinching her pleasant face. "It was . . . surprising, to say the least. Now, however, I'm left with the task of trying to figure out where all those signs belong. Who would do such a thing?"

Tuck, ripping a ticket out of his book, stepped forward and set it on the table before her. With a deadpan, ironic delivery, he offered, "Pepper Danes? She sounds like a monster."

This remark elicited quite a few grins.

Ignoring the ticket, Betty asked, "Do you think so? Will you look into this matter for me, Officer McAllister?" So hopeful was she that I almost believed she was about to bat her eyelashes at him.

"Sorry, Betty. That's above my paygrade. And that there"—Tuck pointed to the ticket—"That's only a warning. Fifty *For Sale* signs on your lawn, while undoubtedly surprising, does not require a high-speed race through town to the Beacon Bakeshop. Drive the speed limit, please." He ran his jaunty blue eyes around the table of friends. "As for those signs, I'm sure a few of these fine gentlemen will help you sort them out."

"Where are you rushing off to, McAllister?" Mayor Jeffers asked. "Sit down and have a natter with us."

"I'd love to, sir. But if you'll remember, I have to shut down Main Street this afternoon for your parade. After that, thanks to the sergeant, I'll be directing traffic."

CHAPTER 5

It was a clever prank that someone had played on Betty, but the answer was who? Who would have gone to such trouble to collect so many *For Sale* signs? Poor Betty was dogged by that question all day. As intriguing as the prank was, everyone agreed it was bad timing. The Blueberry Festival was about to begin, and most of the men in the Friday morning group had their own preparations to make for the busy weekend. Rory, also a committee member, was the exception. Organized to a fault, his Blueberry 5K run didn't require his immediate attention. The signup had been conducted online, and all the T-shirts had been preordered, including extras. Regarding the route the run would take, Rory not only had it mapped out, but he'd been running it himself every morning. This level of preparedness had left him time to help Betty with her sign problem.

"Nice of you to volunteer." I cast him a smile as I prepared another tray of blueberry-filled donuts.

Following me out of the kitchen, he grinned. "Am I the only one who wants to see this epic prank with my own eyes?" Tom and Elizabeth, working on coffee orders, and Ryan, prepping his sandwich and salad station on the back counter, had heard him. Apparently, my entire staff was itching to go with him. Unfortunately, I couldn't spare any of them. The line of customers was nearly out the door.

"Don't worry," Rory told my hardworking crew. "I'll be sure to send pictures when I get there." This was met with echoing smiles and a thumbs-up from Ryan.

To me Rory asked, "I was wondering if James would like to join me. I could use a hand, and since you won't let me steal anyone from the Beacon, he's the obvious choice. I know he's not working here today, which means he's at the boutique with Ellie and Kennedy. You know my motto. Leave no man behind."

Rory looked over my head and tossed Tom and Ryan a bro-nod.

"Good thinking," I said. "I'll call him now."

Rory had been right. Dad picked up on the first ring. "Sweetheart. Need a hand at the Beacon?" He sounded so hopeful. I briefly explained Betty's predicament and asked if he'd be willing to help Rory gather the signs so they could be sorted out and returned to the proper real estate agencies.

"I'd love to. Tell Campbell to swing by the boutique on his way out of town." Dad lowered his voice. "Can't get here soon enough, I tell you. I've been in the back room all morning, unloading boxes. Honestly, Lindsey, if I have to hang up one more blueberry sundress with matching dog vest, I'm going to stick my fist through the wall." Apparently, it was an item Mom was pushing at the festival.

With Rory and Dad gone on their sign-collecting mission, I was able to concentrate on business once again . . . well, almost.

While we worked through the lunch rush, serving up sandwiches, quiches, iced lattes, and our special blueberry-pecan-spinach salad, Rory kept texting us pictures from Betty's house. I had to admit, the circular drive prank was a special kind of genius. Betty hadn't bothered to remove the roadblocks before she'd left. Apparently, all the traffic on the sleepy lane was still using her alternate route until Rory and Dad removed the barricades, restoring the driveway once again. Then there were the pictures of Betty's front lawn. I literally gasped when I saw it. It had the appearance of a cemetery that had used *For Sale* signs in lieu of headstones—some with her picture on them, no less. No wonder she had raced to the Beacon Bakeshop with a pounding heart. My favorite shot of the day, however, was one Rory took of a Harbor Realty sign among a sea of competitors. The sign, with Betty's smiling face on it, was capped with the word *sold*. We all laughed a bit at that one.

While we worked, each of us behind the counter was trying to puzzle out who would have done such a thing to Betty's lawn. Tom suggested it was the work of a disgruntled client. Honestly, Betty was so beloved in the town that I didn't think she had a disgruntled client.

Ryan insisted Doc Riggles was behind the prank, arguing that maybe he secretly wanted Betty to sell up and move in with him. He received a playful swipe of Elizabeth's cleaning rag for that boneheaded suggestion. However, we all agreed that Wendy's theory was most likely the correct one. She believed it was the handiwork of bored high schoolers.

Thanks to the Blueberry Festival and the giant crowd that was pouring into town, it was one of the busiest Fridays we'd ever experienced at the Beacon Bakeshop. By the time we closed for the day—just in time to make it to the parade—we had sold out of nearly everything. It was a great feeling. Thank goodness Dad would be helping me bake in the morning.

Everyone was ready to head out the door and make their way to the crowd-lined parade route when Wendy asked, "Lindsey, are you going to the brat and beer tent tonight?"

At the mention of bratwurst, my mouth began watering. "I am," I replied. "I'll be there with Rory, Kennedy, and Tuck, that is, once he's off-duty. I bet the whole town's going to be there tonight, thanks to the delicious food, beverages, blueberry pie from the Beacon, blueberry ice cream from Harbor Scoops, and live music. Which reminds me, most of you are too young to drink beer."

"They have root beer there, too, and ginger ale," Alaina offered. "It's the perfect place to carb-load before the big run tomorrow morning. Right, Lindsey?"

As I nodded, Tom piped up, "Are you running the 5K?"

"We all know you're running, Tom," Elizabeth chided. "It's all you and Rory have been talking about. But Alaina and I are running too." She indicated to Alaina. Both Tom and Ryan looked surprised.

"Don't look at me," Wendy said. "I'm not running. I'm working so Lindsey can run."

"And I appreciate it," I told her with a wink.

"Since Rory's in charge of it, we thought we'd give it a try," Alaina added. "After all, us girls are modeling tomorrow. Doesn't hurt to burn off some calories before we go onstage."

"Have any of you been training? You can't just show up and run the thing cold." This came from Ryan, who obviously thought that running a 5K without practicing was a bad idea.

As my staff continued their playful banter, I headed for the bakery door. I felt a pang of guilt at the mention of training. I knew Elizabeth and Alaina had been training for the run a few days a week after work. They had told me about it. Since I had volunteered Rory to organize the Blueberry 5K event, his one condition had been that I be the first person to sign up for the run. And I was the first person. Kennedy was a close second—because I had signed her up too. I felt that since I was modeling for her fashion show, she should join me. Truthfully, she hadn't hated the idea. And we did try to train for the run. But our enthusiasm had petered off due to work and rank laziness. Tomorrow morning was going to be a bit of a shocker, especially since I'd have four hours of baking under my belt before the run started. My current plan was to pound down a cup of coffee and a frosted donut right before I left the bakery kitchen. Nothing like a caffeine-sugar buzz to provide that extra boost. It had served me well most days, and it would have to do for tomorrow's run as well.

"I'm going to lock up and grab Welly," I told them as they headed out the front door. "If I don't see you at the parade, I'll see you under the beer tent."

Judging from the foot traffic on Main Street, the Blueberry Parade was a popular event. Crowds lined the street on both sides, and in some places the press of people stood four rows deep. Maneuvering through such a crowd was hard enough, but with Wellington, it was nearly impossible.

We were making our way to Ellie & Company, where Mom and Kennedy had placed folding chairs on the sidewalk for our little group earlier in the morning, saving us a prime spot for the parade. It wasn't a far walk from my lighthouse, but every few feet along the way we were stopped by people wanting to pet my dog. Of course, Welly loved the attention. He especially loved it when little kids with ice cream cones came to pet him. While they were focused on him, he was focused on their ice cream. I dropped my guard for a second, and one little girl's vanilla ice cream entirely disappeared from her cone. Welly was so adept at stealth cone licking that I had to warn parents ahead of time.

"Lindsey!" Mom cried the moment I found our little group. Brinkley and Ireland, Mom's two little West Highland white terriers, greeted both Welly and me with tail-wagging delight. Brinkley with her pink diamond-studded collar, and Ireland wearing an identical one in emerald-green, were both dressed in doggie outfits that matched Mom's eye-catching, blueberry-inspired sundress. It must have been one of the sundresses with a matching pup option that Dad had been complaining about earlier in the morning. Aside from the fact he had to unload and hang them up, Mom and the models really did look adorable.

"What took you so long?" Mom asked as I took the seat next to Rory. Ireland jumped in her lap. Brinkley jumped in Dad's. Welly, with a wistful look in his eyes, stood in front of Rory. As if figuring out that his whole body would take down the flimsy lawn chair, he opted for pressing his giant head against Rory's chest instead. It was a sigh-worthy moment.

If it wasn't for the fact that Welly was blocking the sidewalk as he tried his best to fit in Rory's lap, I had to finally tell him to lie down. Reluctantly, my dog did as he was told, curling his large, fluffy body at our feet. I waved to the rest of the group, consisting of Mom, Dad, Kennedy, Rory, and Doc Riggles. Betty, heading up the Blueberry Festival Committee and owning the only real estate office in the village, was driving an antique pickup truck in the parade that had belonged to her late husband. Paige, her assistant, was driving with her; the two were advertising their business.

"Busy day at the Beacon," I told them, giving my excuse for being late. The parade had already started.

"Busy day everywhere," Kennedy remarked. "Look at this crowd! We had so much foot traffic in the store today that our summer line is flying off the shelves."

"That's fabulous!" I said with a huge smile. I was so happy for them.

"It helps that it's on sale," Mom demurred, although I could tell she was proud of the fact that shoppers liked her clothing line.

Doc, sitting at the end of the row, leaned across Dad and Rory. "Thanks to these two, Betty's lawn is safe again." The men had been talking about the *For Sale* sign debacle. Although it was quite humorous, Doc had a point when he hoped the prank had been a one-off. After all, Betty was in the parade.

"It's a parade," Rory told him. "There are thousands of people here watching. Nothing is going to happen to Betty, Doc."

I applauded his confidence.

There is something charming and nostalgic about a small-town parade, especially one that revolves around a blueberry. I'd lived in New York City, where parades were a spectacle, loaded with eye-popping floats, giant cartoon balloons, celebrities, and bands comprised of professional musicians. All that glitz and glam went straight out the window in a small town. Yet the results were, well, just as eye-popping.

The sound of a drum pierced through the chatter of the crowd. I was certain that no other high school band in the state had such an enthusiastic drum line as the marching drummers of Beacon Harbor High. Sure, the horns were slightly out of tune, and the marching wasn't exactly in perfect step, but the zeal with which the band played was inspiring. Everyone clapped as they marched by.

Over the next twenty minutes, we were treated to a continuous stream of decorated flatbed floats carrying candy-throwing riders, advertising businesses or clubs. Between these floats pranced horses from equestrian clubs, or agility dogs jumping over little barriers placed in the streets. Children tumbled. Clowns walked on stilts. A group of men marched down the street in waders, flicking their fishing poles, which already had rubber fish attached to them. They made a show out of reeling these rubber catches in. One flatbed truck carried a giant American flag constructed entirely out of chicken wire and crepe paper. There was a pickup truck covered in blue balloons and green crepe paper resembling a blueberry patch. Blue balloons seemed to be the choice of the day.

Speaking of blueberries, Betty's antique truck drove by, a lovely old 1950s, perfectly restored Chevy. Betty smiled and waved out the window. In the bed of the truck

was a giant papier-mâché blueberry. The truck was decorated with streamers and banners advertising her business. Spying us, she waved and launched a handful of candy
in our direction, all of which was scooped up by excited
children swooping in like candy-starved seagulls.

"As far as pranksters go, Betty looks safe to me," Rory
remarked, eyeing her antique truck wistfully as it drove
by. "Wish that thing had a *For Sale* sign."

I cast him a teasing eye roll.

Betty's truck rolled past us without a hitch. Then came
the little blueberries, the float that had supplanted the fabled Blueberry Queen. The kids were adorable, resembling little blueberries in a patch as they ate more candy
than they tossed.

"I have to admit," said Doc, leaning toward us, "it just
doesn't pack the same punch as a blueberry queen."

"Dirty old man," Kennedy teased as a beautiful chorus
of voices hit our ears. We all turned to see Mayor Jeffers
standing on yet another tricked-out flatbed trailer covered
in blueberry-blue balloons and pulled by a pickup truck.
The sign on the float read, *Blueberry Parade's Grand
Marshal, Mayor Rodrick Jeffers, and the St. Michael's
Presbyterian Church Choir*.

As the joyful union of voices belted out, "*Blueberry
Pie, he walks on by, and I don't know what to do with that
Blueberry Pie, but I'm gonna try . . .*" I knew this was the
fabled "Blueberry Pie" song Mayor Jeffers had told us
about.

To our delight, the float pulled to a stop in the middle
of Main Street. The choir, wearing hats that looked like
large blueberries on their heads, swayed and clapped in
time to the music as they belted out the catchy tune. Mayor

Jeffers stood before them, directing his choir with the flourish of a true professional. The crowd loved it. Then the mayor turned to the crowd and waved.

That was when the first water balloon struck, hitting the mayor square in the head.

"My heavens!" Mom exclaimed. "Wherever did that come from?" But before anyone could answer, blue balloons seemed to fill the air, coming from both sides of the street.

And every one of them was heading straight for Mayor Jeffers and his choir.

CHAPTER 6

We were all on our feet, craning to see the action, when Dad asked, "Is this part of the show?" He looked just as confused as the rest of us as the spontaneous bombardment continued.

Remarkably, only the mayor's float had been targeted. The blueberry pie song, having started with gusto, had been sabotaged by loud gasps, yelps, and a mad scramble for cover. Since there wasn't any cover to speak of on the float, the choir instead chose to huddle behind the parade's grand marshal, Mayor Jeffers.

"I doubt it," Rory answered, staring at the chaos with an unseemly grin. "My guess is that the culprits behind the water balloons got wind of that song. Can't say that I blame them for trying to stop it."

His remark caught me by surprise, making me laugh. Kennedy, also stifling mirth, tipped her elegant, dark head in his direction. "For once, Sir Hunts-a-Lot, I heartily agree with you."

"You're new here," Doc Riggles stated with a lack of enthusiasm. "That's song's been sung every year I can remember. The people are revolting," he added, grinning at his friend's desperate antics on the float. "Maybe this will inspire one of them to write a better song about blueberries!"

"Look." I pointed, then ducked, narrowly dodging a wayward water balloon. As I ducked, Welly leapt in front of me, thinking that some great game of fetch was playing out in the streets. Being a giant breed of dog, Welly wasn't the most coordinated canine on the planet, but he did have a big mouth. And he employed that mouth with the eagerness of a retriever, catching the wiggly ball in his teeth. The moment he did, the balloon popped, splashing us all. The models barked with excitement as Welly shook off the sudden burst of water, sparing no one. I quickly scooped up the popped balloon.

Looking at my damp shirt, I remarked, "The entire crowd is really getting into it. Oh, no!" I pointed to the old men driving antique tractors that signified the end of the parade. "They're just aiming at everyone now."

"It's a full-blown water fight!" Dad exclaimed with schoolboy glee.

"What I want to know is, where are all the balloons coming from?" Rory, standing six-foot-four, scanned the rowdy crowd with a hawkish gaze.

"I say, let's see if we can find a few of those water balloons ourselves," Kennedy rallied, taking my hand. "Might as well join in the fun!"

Leaving Dad to hold Wellington's leash, Rory, Kennedy, and I left the group to investigate the untimely appearance of the water balloons. Where were they coming from? Who had started the water balloon fight? And the most pressing question: Why was the grand marshal's float targeted?

As we wove through the uproarious crowd, Kennedy spied her current man. "Look, Tuck and some of the other boys in blue are trying to control the situation."

I looked, but it didn't seem like the Beacon Harbor police had control of anything. The police officers, while not targeted, were being pelted with water balloons nonetheless. Then Rory spied something in the press of bodies that drew his attention. It was a group of teenage boys; one was ready to heave another water balloon at the mayor. Rory, moving quickly, reached out and grabbed the boy's arm just as he was about to throw it.

"Dude," the kid cried as the balloon dropped from his hand like a dead fish, landing on the ground with a splash. Displeased, he looked up and glared. "Like, what's your problem, man?"

"I don't have one," Rory stated. "I just want to know where you got that."

The kid thought he was either joking or incredibly dense. With dripping sarcasm, he said, "From the bucket."

"What bucket?"

With another look of annoyance, the kid pointed while adding, "Like, the bucket of water balloons. Duh!"

We all looked to where he pointed, but a huddle of bodies obscured the object in question.

As Rory caught Tuck's eye, waving him over to get to the source of the monkey business, Kennedy and I headed for the bucket. In her haughtiest British accent, she cried, "Make way. Press coming through." As crazy as that sounded, it worked. The balloon throwers, who ranged in age from ten to fifty, parted, revealing the large white five-gallon bucket, the kind found in both hardware stores and bakeries, and everywhere in between.

"Take a picture of me!" one little boy demanded of Kennedy, as he struck a pose for her with a water balloon.

"Sorry, darling, not that kind of press. We're the investigative kind. You might have heard of me, Lilian Finch? No? Well, obviously your parents aren't watching the right kind of news. Now, tell me, who started this water balloon fight?" The boy, with a compelling lack of respect, threw his water balloon at her head, then ran away, trailing laughter in his wake. To say that Kennedy was miffed would be an understatement.

"Great reporting, Lilian," I mocked, then elbowed my way toward the bucket, as she tried to set her wet hair and sunglasses to rights. "Can anyone tell me who brought this bucket of water balloons here?"

"Hey," a lanky teen shouted at me. "Find your own bucket. This one is ours!"

In the young man's defense, he was caught up in the moment; the joy on his face as he heaved his last balloon at the grand marshal's float was incandescent.

A young couple, who looked to be in their mid-twenties, walked over to me. "Don't know who brought them," the man said. "I didn't see anyone. But those teens over there, they told us that some guy placed these here and told them to start throwing the water balloons when the grand marshal's float stopped in the street and the choir began singing that blueberry song."

"And you joined in the fun?" Kennedy asked with dripping hair and a partially soaked shirt.

"Not at first," the young woman added defensively. "But once Chase saw the bucket and the kids throwing the water balloons, he told me he just had to join in the fun."

"Guilty as charged," the man named Chase said, grinning at Kennedy and me. "Honestly, we thought it was part of the parade. These buckets"—he pointed at the now-empty pail—"are all over the place on this block, and on both sides of the street."

"What did you say?" Officer Tuck McAllister had arrived, with Rory a step behind him. He looked at the couple we'd been talking to.

"As I told these nice ladies, Officer, this bucket isn't a one-off. We walked past at least three of them until we found this one."

"Interesting," Tuck remarked. "And do you know anything about the person who left these buckets of water balloons along the sidewalk?"

The man shrugged and grinned. "Only the obvious. Whoever did this was a total genius."

CHAPTER 7

"Genius, hardly," Kennedy remarked as we sat at a long, crowded table under the beer tent. She had changed her clothes, and now looked her usual, stunning self. "More like a wily deviant. Am I right, Officer?" She shifted her flirty gaze to the man sitting on the bench across from her.

It was dusk, and judging from the press of hungry festivalgoers, the German-inspired brat-and-beer tent was the place to be in Beacon Harbor. I had to hand it to Stanley and Felicity Stewart, owners of the popular year-round Tannenbaum Christmas Shoppe and fellow Blueberry Festival Committee members. Hosting a pop-up, banquet-styled restaurant on their lawn was a brilliant idea. No matter what time of year it was, the Octoberfest atmosphere was intoxicating—from the delicious smells of brats grilling on an open flame, to the mouthwatering scent of fresh-cut fries bubbling in hot oil, to the heady effervescence of micro-brewed beer, all of which was accompanied by live Bavarian music, performed by men and women in traditional Bavarian dress. For dessert, there were slices of blueberry pie, courtesy of the Beacon Bakeshop, topped with blueberry swirl ice cream, courtesy of Harbor Scoops. Although most of the food had been locally sourced from around Michigan, the Stewarts had insisted they incorporate some of the local fare as well, namely dessert. Ginger and I had been happy about that.

Staring across at Kennedy, Tuck set down his beer mug. He leaned across the table and whispered loud enough to be heard, "Babe, please don't call me that. I'm off-duty. I feel like a fish in a barrel as it is. I had to call a quick end to that long trainwreck of a parade, and judging from the pelting of water balloons we suffered, it wasn't a popular decision."

"Oh, posh! We were all happy it ended." She threw him an air-kiss for good measure.

Rory, harboring a mild obsession for sausage meats, was on his second of three brats. "Did you learn anything?" he asked Tuck.

"If you mean, did we learn who placed all those buckets of water balloons in that section of the parade route, the answer is no. We talked to as many eyewitnesses as we could, and even pulled a few of the teens in for questioning, but they all swore up and down they had no idea how those buckets had gotten there."

Kennedy waved a be-ringed hand. "It wouldn't be the first time deviant teens lied, Tucker dear. And I should know, being a former deviant teen myself. First rule of chicanery, never confess to the deed."

Holding the nub-end of his second loaded brat before his lips, Rory paused to interject, "While that explains so much about you, it's not helpful here." Finishing the delicious sausage, he looked at Tuck. "Did you believe them?"

Tuck shrugged. "Unfortunately, I did. Like I said, everyone we talked to didn't seem to be aware of the buckets until word was passed through the crowd to start throwing the water balloons at the mayor's float. One gentleman said he was watching the parade with his kids when somebody heaved a water balloon over his head. He turned around and saw the bucket, but by then it was like flies to honey. Teenagers caught wind of it first, and it just went downhill from there."

"Somebody had to give that order," I remarked.

"True, but in a crowd that size, and one packed full of strangers, no one seems to know who gave the order, or who placed the buckets in the crowd to begin with. Also, the teens we talked to didn't really have a motive to lie. They weren't going to get into any real trouble, just a talking-to and a prime spot on the festival's cleanup committee. Mayor Jeffers, although miffed, is taking it rather well. At any rate, by the time the water balloon fight broke out, the parade was nearly over."

He paused to finish his beer, then set the mug back on the table, shaking his head as he did so. "No, it's more the fact that Sergeant Murdock wants to get to the bottom of this. She thinks the water balloon prank might be tied to Betty's *For Sale* sign debacle."

"How interesting," I said, perking up at the suggestion. Until Tuck mentioned it, I hadn't really given a thought about the two pranks being related. I then remembered Wendy's suggestion that the *For Sale* sign prank sounded like the work of bored high schoolers and found myself visualizing this suggested group of bored teens, sitting on the beach while brainstorming some devious summer fun. I had to agree, it didn't take a huge leap of the imagination to blame it on them.

I took another bite of my delicious, grilled-to-perfection brat before speaking again. "Let's say the two incidents are related. What does it mean?"

Tuck shrugged. "Honestly, I haven't a clue. One thing's for sure, it's going to keep us on our toes."

We spent another hour under the brat-and-beer tent, visiting with friends, coworkers, and neighbors. Mom and Dad were eating with Betty, Doc, and Ali and Jack Johnson. My staff, along with a large group of their friends from the village, were already on the dance floor having a blast. After a bout of dancing and small talk about the water balloon fight at the parade, Rory, Tuck, Kennedy, and I headed back to the lighthouse for dessert. Although I loved blueberry pie, I had already planned on having a quiet dessert with friends. Saturday would be an early morning for me and an extremely busy day.

After the parade, and after going from no blueberries to having a large stash of them (thanks to Rory and Winifred Peters), I had been inspired to make one of my all-time favorite East Coast desserts, a Down East blueberry buckle. When I was growing up in New York, Mom, Dad, and I had taken many trips to Maine. Next to Michigan and Disney World, it was my favorite childhood vacation spot. And whenever we were in Maine, a traditional clambake was always on the itinerary. Sure, butter-dipped lobster was delicious, but the blueberry buckle was my favorite part of the meal.

I remembered the first time I ate a piece of the buttery

blueberry cake—for clearly it was a cake. I had asked the waitress why they called it a buckle instead of a cake.

The older woman, likely having answered this question a thousand times before, smiled at me nonetheless. In a distinctive Maine accent, she offered, "Well, honey, if they called it a cake, it would sound ordinary. Everyone knows that our Maine blueberries are the best in the world, not ordinary old blueberries like those found in other states. It's said that folks have been making this cake since Maine was settled. Legend has it that when they stirred the blueberries into the batter, and the cake was cooked, the cakey bits would rise when baking while the blueberries would squish and sink, creating an uneven cake top." The waitress leaned closer, adding, "One that looked buckled instead of even. Folks then started sprinkling on the crumbly topping to hide the bumps, but that just made it even more delicious."

I agreed. In fact, I agreed with nearly everything the old waitress had just told me, except for her insistence that Maine grew the best blueberries. Until a year ago I might have believed her, but I lived in Michigan now and knew better.

Blueberry buckle, like most cakes, was not hard to make. Unlike most cakes, however, it was perfect for breakfast too. Since I knew I'd be running early Saturday morning, and although I had planned on running with a caffeine/sugar buzz, I thought it wouldn't hurt to eat a piece of blueberry cake instead of a donut—that was, if I had any left.

After coming home from the Blueberry Parade, I had changed clothes and fed Welly his dinner. Then I went to my personal kitchen in the lighthouse and began gathering ingredients while I waited for Rory to come pick us up for dinner.

I creamed together a stick of butter with three-quarters cup of sugar (everything delicious starts with butter and sugar!), then added the eggs, one at a time. Next went in the vanilla extract. With my butter/sugar base sufficiently blended, I next sifted the flour and baking powder together. After a quick stir with a wooden spoon, I then added my dry ingredients to the mixer in half-cup increments, alternating the flour with the milk. The moment the flour was in, I turned off the mixer. I then stirred in two and a half cups of fresh, plump blueberries. Transferring the batter into a prepared pan, I set to work on the crumble topping.

Crumble topping is a cinch to make and so delicious when baked on a cake. My crumble topping consisted of a half cup of flour, a half cup of brown sugar, a half teaspoon of cinnamon, and a half stick of butter (a quarter of a cup). That was it! After stirring the first three ingredients together, I then cut the butter into the flour mixture until a fine crumb mixture formed. This was evenly sprinkled on top of the batter, then the cake was put into the oven. Forty minutes later, it was perfectly baked and springy to the touch. Unfortunately, Rory had walked into the kitchen just as I was pulling the buckle out of the oven. Like Wellington, he was begging for a piece.

"After dinner," I had told him, and placed the buckle on top of the refrigerator. This was because leaving food on my countertops was akin to an open invitation to Wellington to have a snack. Rory, bless him, had eaten three brats, an order of fries, and two beers to tide him over for dessert.

"Finally," he declared with a grin as he walked into my kitchen the moment we were back at the lighthouse. He reached on top of the refrigerator and pulled down the pan of blueberry buckle. "I was so hungry after smelling this, I might have overeaten a bit at the beer tent."

"*No*," was Kennedy's sarcastic reply. "It's entirely normal for one man to order a family-sized meal."

"They were great brats," Rory defended. "Besides, I'm carb-loading for the big run tomorrow, which means I'm going to need an extra-large slice of that buckle."

"It's a 5K, Campbell," Tuck chided, "which is a little over three miles. I thought you military guys ran that in your sleep."

"We did," Rory admitted. "I just want a big piece of cake. Also, I'm not actually running in the 5K. I'm running the event. But I plan on cheering Lindsey on."

"So, the carb-loading you claim to be doing is just because you want to eat a lot?" This I said while placing a pot of herbal tea on the table.

"Pretty much. But in my defense, I decided to run to the start of the race in the morning. That way I can catch a ride home with Lindsey." He shot me a cheeky smile as he said this. "Also, I'll be running back and forth, cheering the runners on and making sure everyone is doing okay. There will be a team of volunteers working the clock and entering finish times as well. So, although I'm not officially running, I'll be running."

"You don't have to justify your love of sausage meats to me," I teased as I poured two glasses of milk, one for each of the men. Then, noting I was the target of Welly's beseeching gaze, I also cut him a little slice and placed it in his dish. With everyone momentarily appeased, I took my seat at the table and took my first bite of buckle. The blueberries were still warm, and the buttery cake with the sweet crumble topping melted in my mouth. Tomorrow we would eat pie, but tonight I was all about blueberry buckle.

"Delicious," Tuck said. Half his piece was already gone. "You two are running tomorrow, so you'll want to get to the starting line early. I might swing by and cheer you on as well."

Kennedy and I exchanged a look. I had to get up at three in the morning and bake pies. She would get up five minutes before we left for the race. And the real kicker was, neither of us was sure we would even make it across the finish line.

I plastered on a smile of pure confidence. "I think we might surprise you."

"We'll surprise them, alright," Kennedy agreed, taking a bite of buckle. "Point in fact, you might be surprised to learn that I'll be praying for rain."

CHAPTER 8

It always seemed to me that my alarm went off shortly after my head hit the pillow. A glance at the clock confirmed that I had, indeed, slept for a whole five hours, but even Welly seemed miffed at the buzzing sound that broke our slumber. He lifted his big, fluffy head, opened one eyelid, and stared at me.

"I don't know what you're complaining about," I told him, as I hopped out of bed and headed for the shower. "It's not like you have to bake pies all morning, then run a 5K, and then model a flouncy outfit onstage. Oh, right. You are going to model a flouncy raincoat onstage."

For some reason, this made Welly wag his tail. Likely because he knew that once I got out of bed, he'd get to run around down by the lake and have his morning cookies.

After Welly's morning sniff-and-dash down by the

beach, and after my habitual salute to the darkened light-room where I imagined Captain Willy was keeping watch, we made our way to the back door of the Beacon's industrial kitchen. The great thing about having a bakery in the same building I lived in was the commute. It was about a minute, give or take pup cooperation. Although I had my own private door inside the lighthouse from which I could enter the bakery, I preferred to use the back bakery entrance in the morning. It was the door my employees used, and although Dad had his own key, I wanted to make sure it was unlocked and the lights were on when he arrived.

As I did every morning, I propped open the door to the café and brought Welly his morning treats. He was getting used to the bakery rules by now and didn't mind wandering around the café while I baked in the kitchen. Once it was time to open, Welly would go back inside the lighthouse and eat his breakfast. Since the next two days were going to be very busy, I wanted to get a jump on the baking.

I brewed a pot of coffee and started right in on the dough for both yeast and cake donuts. Donuts were a staple at the Beacon, and the yeast needed time to rise before the donuts could be cut and sent into the fryer. I quickly cleaned out the bowl of the giant mixer and started in on short crust for the blueberry pies. Since we were making a lot of pies, I calculated the amount of flour, salt, lard, and butter needed (I used a mixture of both in my crust), then added these to the mixer. I was already rolling out piecrusts and prepping the pie pans when Dad walked in.

"Morning, sweetheart. You really need to hire better help."

With my apron covered in flour and my hands wrist-deep in pie dough, I smiled up at him. "I know. I'll work on it this fall. Coffee's ready."

Wellington stood in the café doorway and whined until Dad walked over to give him a proper greeting. After petting his head, followed by a sufficient belly rub, Dad came back to the kitchen and poured a cup of coffee for himself. Then he set to work on the blueberry filling.

Blueberry pies are not only delicious, but one of the simplest pies to make. That's because you don't have to peel, pit, or slice blueberries. You just have to wash them. Each 9-inch blueberry pie we made had five cups of fresh blueberries in it, including one cup of sugar, six tablespoons of flour, one tablespoon of lemon juice, and a half teaspoon of cinnamon. Dad, working on six pies at a time, mixed up all the dry ingredients in a huge metal bowl, then tossed in the blueberries, making sure each berry was coated in the flour mixture. Then the berries were scooped out and placed into the waiting piecrust. Cutting strips of pie dough, it was up to me to make sure each pie had a beautiful lattice-top crust with an egg wash and a dusting of cinnamon sugar. Once complete, the pies went into the oven ten at a time. Our plan was to make thirty this morning, then see how many we sold at the Beacon. We'd then see how many pies we'd need for the pie-eating contest and make the remainder after the Beacon closed for the day.

Dad and I worked well together and had quite the blueberry pie assembly line going. As Dad filled the rest of the piecrusts, I whipped up blueberry muffins, carrot-raisin muffins, mini-quiches, coffee cakes, and pecan rolls. With the pies lined up on the racks, ready to go into the oven, Dad started making the donuts.

I'd been so absorbed in baking I hadn't even realized the sun had risen. It wasn't until Wendy came through the door that Dad looked up from his tray of chocolate-frosted donuts. "What time does Rory's run start?" he asked.

I looked at my watch. "Oh, my gosh! Kennedy's still sleeping! And I have to change. Do you two have this?"

"Of course," Wendy answered with a smile. "Have fun running. See you all back here after the race."

"Remind me again why you signed me up for this?" To my surprise, Kennedy had been dressed in her running clothes when I found her. We quickly grabbed a piece of blueberry buckle, got in my Jeep, and headed for the high school parking lot, hoping to get to the starting line before the race began. Kennedy glanced one more time at her sleepy refection in the mirror, frowned, and flipped up the visor. "I have a fashion show to put on. I don't need this."

"I made thirty pies this morning, and all I want to do is take a nap. But here we are." I turned and flashed her an ironic grin, then added, "You're a good friend, and your fashion show is going to be marvelous because Welly and I are helping with that too. Look," I said, pulling into a parking space, "all we have to do is run fast enough to stay with the pack. Once we're out of sight, we can walk if we need to."

"Okay. I think I can manage that."

"Thanks for showing up, ladies," Rory teased, handing us our numbers. Although we'd been running late, there were still a few stragglers making their way to the race table. "The starting line is over there. When the gun goes off, just follow the pack and the chalk arrows on the street until you arrive back here and cross that same line. Got it?" He walked around the table and gave me a kiss. "Thanks, Linds," he whispered. Although he didn't say it, I knew he meant thanks for volunteering him to head up the Blueberry 5K Run. His happiness was palpable, which filled me with joy. It was a good feeling, and I was suddenly excited to run with the pack.

We found Elizabeth and Alaina in the crowd of runners at the starting line and went to join them. Tom and Ryan were near us as well, but they had fallen in with a group of young men. Kennedy and I were sticking with the girls.

"Alright, ladies," I rallied. "We can do this!" Then the gun went off, and the entire pack sprang to life like a herd of spooked buffalo stampeding toward a cliff.

Swept up in the adrenaline of the pack, Kennedy and I made a valiant effort to reach the finish line. Elizabeth and Alaina, younger and in far better shape, dashed ahead of us and were neck and neck with Tom and Ryan. As it was, Kennedy and I settled in the back of the pack. We were running side by side, arms pumping while our feet pounded the pavement. Concentrating on the chalk arrows that directed us out of the high school parking lot, we then turned down a country lane. As we ran, the pack began to thin out.

"I hope the finish line is just over there," Kennedy cried, breathing heavily and glistening with sweat.

"I don't think we've even run a mile yet," I called back, knowing how she felt.

We followed the pack around a bend, into the parking lot of a private marina, and straight toward the lake. Some of the runners were actually in the lake swimming, which didn't seem quite right. Others had clustered near the shore, looking dumbfounded.

"Yay!" Kennedy cried, heading for the cool waters of Lake Michigan. "We've done it! Our first 5K was a breeze!"

"I don't think so," I was quick to reply, breathing just as heavily. "According to my watch, we've only run a mile."

She didn't like the sound of this, and I couldn't blame her. But the fact was, the well-marked race route had brought us straight into the lake. The route ended there, causing confusion. A few die-hard athletes were swimming out to the nearest buoy by the end of the dock. Most, however, were just playing in the waves. Some were actually running in circles like lost bloodhounds fighting to pick up the scent again.

The local fishermen, sitting offshore in their boats, were laughing at the spectacle. I couldn't blame them. Confused, I pulled out my phone and called Rory.

Five minutes later, he was at the boat launch, his handsome face dripping with a mixture of confusion and indignation.

"What happened?" he asked me, barely breathing heavily.

"Somebody must have messed with your course. It ended here." I gestured to the chalk arrow pointing at the lake.

Kennedy walked beside him and put her arm around his shoulder. "Rory, dear, I hate to say this, but I think our prankster has struck again, and this time you were the target."

"Damn it," he cursed and hung his head.

CHAPTER 9

Although some had found the prank funny—for example, the local fishermen out in the harbor wheezing from the safety of their boats—I, on the other hand, had felt a stabbing pang of anger. Rory had worked so hard on this event. Although I had talked him into it, he had risen to the challenge and had found joy in organizing the 5K run. The turnout of recreational runners was a testament to that. With a sinking heart, I realized that Kennedy was correct. The prankster had struck again, this time erasing Rory's carefully drawn chalk arrows denoting the race route. Then whoever was behind the prank had redrawn a set of new chalk arrows, directing the runners straight into Lake Michigan. I looked at the fishermen once again and thought, at least someone could laugh about it. The prank was still too raw to elicit a grin from Rory.

Without proper course markings, the run couldn't continue, and Rory was left with no choice but to direct all the runners back to the high school parking lot. Miffed, he pulled out his phone and called Tuck. Unfortunately, Officer McAllister was otherwise engaged.

Rory ended the call and cast us a disparaging look. "Looks like I'll be working solo on this. Tuck is out on some farm investigating a case of missing kids."

Kennedy's large brown eyes shot even wider. "Kids? Missing? I thought things like this didn't happen in Beacon Harbor." Although still breathing a bit heavily from our one-mile jog, her pout had more of a "put-out" look to it than genuine concern. "In case you were wondering, this is what it's like to date a cop. Always someone getting in the way of your plans. I just hope he makes it back in time for the fashion show."

With a reprimanding look at my friend, I shifted my attention to Rory. "That's just terrible—and during the Blueberry Festival. Whose kids are missing?" The fact that Rory was grinning eased my mind a measure.

"Not 'kids' in the usual sense," he clarified, "but goats. *He* called them kids." Rory paused long enough to toss Kennedy a jibing look, then continued. "Apparently, some woman named Daphne Rivers phoned the police station early this morning to report a strange occurrence. The woman said that she had woken up to a dawn that was unusually quiet. When she went out to her barn to investigate, she realized her goat pen was open and all her goats were missing. Tuck, being the officer on-duty, is at her farm investigating the matter."

"So, he's out on the proverbial back forty looking into a matter of missing goats?" This seemed to annoy

Kennedy. "It's hardly a police matter. I say someone did the old lady a favor."

Rory, with a straight face, replied, "Whenever there's a missing kid, it's no laughing matter."

"Well, aren't you a comedian," Kennedy replied. "While I'd love to stay here in this parking lot and listen to your whole set on farm animals and cops, I'm afraid I can't. I have to get back to the boutique. We have a sold-out fashion show to put on." She flipped her long black ponytail and turned toward my car.

I was still grinning from the exchange when Rory turned to me. "Would you mind very much if I borrowed the Jeep? Elizabeth and Alaina are right there," he said, waving the girls over. "I'm sure they'd take you and Kennedy back to the lighthouse."

"Not at all," I said, and handed him my keys. "You're going to find out who did this, aren't you?"

"I'm going to try," he said with a grim set to his jaw. If anyone could find this prankster, an ex–Navy SEAL could, I thought.

"Well, if they're just kids, please go easy on them."

He nodded. "Don't worry. I'll be back in time for the fashion show. And Lindsey, keep your eyes open, okay? Two pranks in one day might be a coincidence, but three in the space of twenty-four hours? I think something might be going on here."

"Do you think someone might be trying to sabotage the Blueberry Festival?"

"I hope not, but two of the three pranks occurred at a festival event. Stay on your toes, Bakewell."

* * *

After a quick shower, Kennedy headed off to the boutique, where she could focus all her influencing energies on the upcoming fashion show. After promising to bring Welly and the girls there on time, I made the short commute to the bakeshop.

"How was the run?" Dad asked the moment I came through the door. Wearing a clean red Beacon Bakeshop apron, he was helping Wendy behind the counter. Watching him chat with the customers while he filled orders never failed to lift my heart. I had felt a pang of guilt when I'd hired my newly retired dad to help at the bakery. His Wall Street career had been demanding, but working at a bakery was no walk in the park either. Dad had surprised me, though. I guess retirement meant different things to different people, and for Dad it had meant staying busy while helping his daughter run her business. I couldn't even put into words how much I appreciated his enthusiasm or his baking skills, but I also knew I was going to need to hire a full-time assistant baker soon. After all, Mom and Dad were still snowbirds, with a lovely home in Florida. The moment the weather turned, they'd be heading south for the winter.

While both Dad and Wendy were holding their own against the morning rush, I threw on an apron as well and joined them.

"The run, what little I ran of it, was fine," I told them as I rang up a dozen donuts for a family. I could see Dad and Wendy exchange a knowing glance—as if they'd had money riding on the fact that I wouldn't finish the run. I should have been insulted but wasn't. Instead, I was more charmed by their comradery. Also, at least one of them had faith in me.

"So, you didn't finish," Wendy stated. I couldn't tell

whether she was on the winning or losing end of the bet. She was covering the espresso maker until Tom and Elizabeth arrived, making a lovely vanilla latte for another customer.

"No one finished," I told them. "The prankster struck again."

With everyone at the Beacon on high alert for more shenanigans, I packed up a box of blueberry baked goods and a few of our pies and sent Alaina and Ryan down to the park alongside the marina where the blueberry bake sale was underway. At noon, under the big white tent on the lawn, the highly awaited Blueberry Pie Bake-Off would begin there as well. The competitive baker in me really wanted to watch the bake-off. I wanted to judge the pies for myself, sampling each one to see if the Beacon's blueberry pie would have won had we been allowed to enter. However, I decided it was best that I stay at the Beacon Bakeshop and take care of our customers instead. It was best to leave the judging up to the judges. Besides, I had Alaina and Ryan observing the event for me. They were to call me as soon as the winner was announced. Word on the street was that Winifred Peters, the committee member in charge of the bake-off and bake sale, was the favorite to win. According to Betty, Winifred had won first place for the best blueberry pie four years in a row now. I silently wondered if I could get her to make me one of her winning pies so I could learn her secret.

It was quarter past noon when Elizabeth tapped me on my shoulder. I had just put a tray of freshly iced blueberry sugar cookies into the bakery case (a basic round sugar cookie iced and decorated to look like a giant blueberry!) when I looked at her. Elizabeth pointed out the window.

"Brace yourself," she uttered. "Betty's coming."

Sure enough, Betty Vanhoosen was fast-walking with purpose up the walkway again. In fact, she was walking so fast this time that her ankles were actually wobbling to maintain balance on the cute, though impractical, heeled sandals she was wearing. Seeing her again, with red cheeks, disheveled hair, and blue eyes wide with some new horror, her appearance had a very déjà vu feel to it. As the bell above the door tinkled, Elizabeth whispered, "This should be good."

To Betty, I smiled. "Hi, Betty. Is everything okay?"

"No, it is not okay!" Suddenly aware there were customers sitting at a few of the café tables, she continued in a loud hiss-whisper, "Something very terrible is going on in this village."

Just then my phone buzzed. I excused myself long enough to see who was calling me. It was Ryan from the bake sale. I sent a quick text stating that I'd call him back in a minute. "I'm sorry, Betty. Now, go on. What's so terrible?"

Her eyes bore into mine like a laser as she looked across the bakery counter. "He's struck again. The prankster has struck again, and this time he's ruined the Blueberry Pie Bake-Off!"

CHAPTER 10

What had occurred under the bake-off tent was a calamity of epic proportions. Betty, whose heart was still pounding from the incident, described an idyllic scene as the contestants brought in their beautifully baked offerings, registered their pies, and placed them accordingly on the twenty-foot linen-covered table. Twenty-five pies had been entered, making this year's event one of the best turnouts of blueberry pie enthusiasts and amateur bakers. Betty, not a baker herself, but a true devotee of baked goods in general (she was a regular fixture at the Beacon Bakeshop!), was to be one of the three judges. She admitted that she was excited to taste so many lovely pies.

"Honestly, Lindsey, they all looked so delicious," she confided before taking another sip of her blueberry-pie cold-brew latte. Elizabeth had made her one immediately, hoping it might help calm her nerves. From all appearances, it looked to be working. "Well, maybe not all of them looked delicious. For instance, Glenda Perkins from Beulah brought in a pie that barely looked fit enough for a pig trough."

"Ooh, Betty," Elizabeth interjected with a grin. "That's harsh." Betty smiled in kind.

"Well, it is. But Glenda walked into the tent looking proud as a hen in heat. Heaven knows why? Her pie was literally a hot mess, as you young people like to say. The filling was sloshing around inside a crust that was pale and doughy. Bless her heart," Betty added with a practiced look of sincerity. "She tried her best. But take it from me, not everyone should throw their hat in the ring of a bake-off." Finishing her statement with a pointed look, she smiled and sipped on the straw of her iced latte.

"So, up until that point, everything was going fine?" I looked at Betty, hoping she'd get to the point. But all she did was nod and drink her latte. I pressed again. "Everything looked normal under the tent?" Another expectant look from me, and another nod from the messenger. I shook my head with slight impatience. "I don't understand. When did this prankster strike?"

She lifted a pale eyebrow at the question, then slowly shifted her attention from the fortifying drink. "Well, we didn't actually see him," she offered cryptically. "It wasn't until one of the contestants set their pie next to Winifred Peters that she noticed something strange."

"Winifred's pie looked strange?" Elizabeth, like me, was hanging on Betty's every word. She then shot me a questioning look.

"Strange, yes," Betty confirmed. "Apparently, the top

crust of her pie seemed to be moving. When the poor dear went to investigate, she let out a bloodcurdling scream, then passed out cold. Thank goodness Randy was there to break her fall." Betty gave a little shake of her head and took another long sip of her iced latte.

Losing patience, I blurted, "For God's sake! Why did she scream?"

Betty's round blue eyes shot to mine as if startled. At the same moment, the straw fell from her lips. "Didn't I just tell you? I guess I forgot." She waved a hand. "It was so upsetting that I might have blocked the image out of my mind. I mean, nobody wants to relive a horror like that."

"Betty, what horror are you talking about!?" Elizabeth, losing patience with the older woman's storytelling ability—which, to be honest, was always a tad convoluted—could not hold her tongue any longer.

"Sorry, dear. Well, after Winnie screamed, we all ran to see what had caused the poor dear to collapse. And there we saw it, a little mouse poking its head right up through the beautiful top crust of her pie. Then that little devil wriggled out and scampered down her pie."

"A mouse!?" I cried as a shiver of disgust ran up my spine. At that same moment, a thousand thoughts collided in my head, the most pressing of which was, how did a living mouse get baked into a blueberry pie? But before I could voice this thought, Betty continued.

"Not just one mouse. I mean, for a very short moment we thought it was just one. But then we noticed that the crust was still undulating. And, by Hector, if we hadn't been right! Because as soon as that first little mouse began scampering down the pie, the entire crust exploded—like Mount Vesuvius! Well, perhaps not exploded so much as imploded, but you get the picture. Before we knew what was happening, the piecrust was in tatters and the whole table was covered with mice. The pie bakers screamed. Some of the spectators were actually laughing. And the braver sort, your young Ryan Wade included, were frantically trying to wrangle the mice away from the pies. However, I'm sorry to say that not one pie was spared the indignity of mouse feet or being tossed off the table entirely."

As a mouse-phobic baker, the blueberry pie prank was just about the worst thing I could imagine. Poor Winifred Peters. My heart truly went out to her. There would be no blue ribbon for her pie this year—or for anyone's pie, for that matter. The bake-off had been sabotaged by the prankster, and apparently, half the town was laughing about it.

Word of this latest prank spread through the town like wildfire. It was the fourth prank played in two days, and I wasn't the only one willing to entertain the idea that it wouldn't be the last.

"I think we should call an emergency meeting of the festival committee," Betty suggested. "We need to do something about this prankster!"

A few minutes after Betty had made the call, the committee members who could make the emergency meeting began arriving at the bakeshop. Ryan and Alaina had come back from the bake sale as well, adding yet more observations to what was now being referred to as the mice-in-the-pie prank. Wendy was back from her break, and Tom, who wasn't on the schedule, came in regardless after hearing of the latest prank. As for me, I couldn't help but think that Mom's fashion show was the next major event of the weekend. It was two hours away, and I wanted to make sure that nothing occurred to ruin Mom and Kennedy's big fashionista moment.

"What on earth is happening in this village?" Rory asked, striding into the bakeshop. I was happy to see him, but one look at his face told me he had failed to find the person responsible for ruining his racecourse. Tuck McAllister was right behind him, dressed in his police uniform. He removed his cap and took a seat at the table.

"This is beyond me," Tuck replied, raking a hand through his short blond hair. "These pranks aren't really hurting anyone, but they're sure causing a stir. Murdock is fit to be tied. It seems that word of our clever pranksters is bringing in even more people to the festival—hoping to experience a prank themselves. As it is, the town parking lots are at capacity, and people are getting creative, making spaces where there aren't any. Bill Morgan and some of the other families on the outskirts of town are renting out spaces on their lawns as overflow parking. They're making extra money by shuttling the festivalgoers into town on hay wagons."

Betty, the head of the committee, smiled at this. "Well, that is a silver lining, isn't it? The whole point is to bring people to our town."

Mayor Jeffers, after shooting her a look that spoke volumes, replied, "While we do want our Blueberry Festival to be a success, we don't want to look like fools. And I'm afraid right now, we look like the biggest of fools. First, there were all those signs on your lawn, Betty. Then somebody encouraged a whole block of paradegoers to start a water balloon fight during my choir's song."

Rory, taking over from there, added to the mayor's list of mishaps. "I've had time to think about this. Tuck agrees. Betty is the chairman of the committee, and she was the first target of the pranksters. Then came you, Rod. You're not only the mayor, but you also headed up the parade committee. I don't think it was any coincidence that you were the target of the water balloon prank. The next event was mine," he continued, his dark brows drawn together at the memory. "Somebody purposely changed my 5K course, thinking it would be funny to send the runners into the lake."

Unfortunately, Tuck had the nerve to chuckle at this. Rory shot him a look, to which he replied, "What? I mean, you have to admit it was kind of funny."

I could see that Rory thought about refuting this, then relented. "I'll grant you that it might have looked funny to those not running. But the point is, my event was ruined."

"So was Winifred Peters's event," I remarked, jumping in. "She was in charge of the bake-off and the bake sale. It was her pie that was sabotaged. Actually, according to Ryan"—I looked at the young man in question, who grinned from his seat at the table and waved back— "it wasn't even her pie."

"That's right," Ryan said. "Alaina and I checked it out. Someone had removed Mrs. Peters's real pie and swapped it out with one that looked close to hers, but was really just a nondescript pie tin covered with a prebaked crust." Ryan, also unable to stop himself from grinning, added, "Honestly, it was pretty genius."

"Maybe," I huffed, still unsettled by the thought of mice in a pie. I then looked at Rory. "Are you saying you think the festival committee members are being targeted by the prankster?"

"It's beyond a suspicion. Unless the prankster stops or

something changes, I say that as committee members, we need to keep vigilant."

Grayson Smythe, who was still grinning a little at the mice-in-the-pie prank, sobered at the thought. "Excuse me, but do you really believe we are all being targeted?" The concern on his face appeared at odds with the bright colors of his cravat. "My unveiling is tonight, right before the fireworks display. As the committee member in charge of the arts and crafts booths, as well as being Beacon Harbor's only resident glass artist, I can't help but tell you that I'm feeling a little vulnerable right now."

Unfortunately, I knew just how he felt.

"Grayson's right," I added. "How do we prevent the prankster from ruining all of our events? I'm getting a little nervous as well. My pie-eating contest is tomorrow, and the Ellie and Company's fashion show will begin in a little over an hour under the beer and brat tent."

"That reminds me, Lindsey," Wendy piped up, casting an anxious glance at Elizabeth and Alaina. "We'd all better get going. Kennedy will flip if we're late."

"She's right," Elizabeth said, getting up from her chair. "Do you think we have to worry? Ellie Montague Bakewell and Kennedy Kapoor aren't committee members. They are both formidable women, and I, for one, pity the prankster who tries to cross them. The fashion show should go off without a hitch. Besides, it's a sold-out event. I doubt this prankster fellow could slip in without notice."

Officer Tuck McAllister also stood and placed his cap back on his head. "Well, I guess we'll just have to wait and see. Ladies," he said, then nodded to the girls and me. "Kennedy might flip if her models are late, but if I'm late, she'll likely kill me."

CHAPTER 11

"You girls look gorgeous!" Mom, so easily slipping into fashion model mode, gave us her Cover Girl smile as she ran a deceptively critical eye over her volunteers. She retied Wendy's playful floral scarf and draped it with a practiced eye around her neck and down her left shoulder. I had to admit that it now looked to be in perfect harmony with Wendy's butter-yellow top and wide leg, no-pinch-waist, crop pants in what Mom referred to as larkspur blue. With that adjustment made, Wendy received a thumbs-up. Brinkley, Wendy's canine modeling partner, wore a ruffled dress in the same material as the scarf. Mom's little Westies were used to dressing up, but this was the first modeling gig for the girls. Aside from a case of last-minute nerves, they all looked as if they'd been born for the runway.

"You three," I began, looking at Wendy, Elizabeth, and

Alaina. "You ladies are certainly going to turn some heads. I just hope that when the modeling agents come calling, you'll remember me and the Beacon Bakeshop."

They looked at each other and giggled nervously. "Too much pressure," Alaina said before scooping up her modeling partner, an adorable, fluffy white bichon frise dressed in the same material as the sporty, multicolored top she wore. Alaina, modeling active wear, also had on a super-comfy, super-soft, wide-leg crop yoga pant. "Although I have to hand it to Kennedy and Ellie," she continued, snuggling her puppy. "These are the cutest, most comfy clothes I've ever worn. And the best part is we get to keep them!"

It was true. This was how Ellie & Co. had coerced fifteen women from the town and their dogs into modeling for them. Not only were the clothes bright, stylish, and cheerful in design, but the dogs added a dash of comedy as we struggled to get them ready, and ourselves, in the tent behind the stage. Thank goodness Mom had placed Welly and me toward the end of the group. I would have thought that watching the other small and normal-sized dogs getting dressed would have inspired my pup to behave. As it was, Kennedy had fed Welly a dozen of his favorite peanut butter cookies, and we only had one of the four boots on him.

"Does he really need to wear the boots?" I scrunched my nose as I looked at her. We were both kneeling on the ground trying to coax the adorable dog rain boots onto his feet. The moment we'd get one on, he'd shake off another. As I knew from experience, any more wrangling with my dog would result in my beautiful periwinkle skirt and blueberry-embroidered tee getting covered with a uniquely unpleasant mix of dog hair and drool.

"They're Wellies," she replied with a huff. "If he doesn't wear them, he'll ruin my snappy announcement." As she talked, she pushed a boot onto Welly's back paw. The moment she did, he kicked and wiggled his leg, launching it across the floor.

"He's wearing the coat," I reasoned. "And I can snug the hat on his head the moment we hit the steps to the stage. But I'm afraid he's never going to wear these boots."

"Wellies!" she corrected again, growing annoyed with us both.

"Look, you're the dog commentator. People are going to love hearing you talk about dogs and their clothes. Just say something like, 'And in the blueberry raincoat we have Wellington, who obviously ran out of the house today without his Wellies,' okay?"

She thought about it a moment. Then, recognizing that she was on the losing end of the argument, she rolled her eyes in surrender. "Fine. I just thought you and your dog would be more cooperative, like the rest of our models."

Ex-models, fashionistas, and influencers, I thought, were a far more difficult breed to deal with than the Newfie any day of the week. Yet they were also loveable, too, in their own way. Having had plenty of experience dealing with them as well, I said, "Kennedy, my dear friend. Have I ever let you down? Trust me. Wellington will be the star of the show."

"Ready, ladies?" Mom asked, brandishing her most charming smile. "Shoulders back and smiles on! You've got this!"

From my perspective backstage, the show was a resounding success. The models and their matching pups were a huge hit, and the crowd laughed and clapped accordingly. It was nearly enough to ease my backstage jitters. I could hear Mom and Kennedy, both with microphones onstage, commenting on the outfits that were being modeled. Mom handled the human models while Kennedy added color to their canine counterparts. Kennedy, being an influencer, a podcaster, and a partner in an up-and-coming line of fashion, sounded as at home on the stage as Mom did. Listening to their professionalism and the reaction from the crowd, I was extremely proud of them both. Of course, never one to miss a marketing opportunity, Kennedy was live-streaming the event on her Facebook page. Kara Stewart, Felicity's daughter, had been hired to operate the camera.

Elizabeth, Wendy, and Alaina, having come offstage with their dogs, were glowing from the excitement. "Lindsey, that was so much fun!" Wendy said, looking surprised. "The crowd loved us!"

"Don't freak out or anything," Elizabeth warned, "but there are a lot of people out there."

"Gee, thanks, ladies," I said, smiling through my nerves. I had never been very comfortable in the public eye. That's why I had chosen banking over modeling. "Okay," I said to my gorgeous dog, "we're up."

Welly and I hit the stage as Mom announced our arrival. "Up next is our very own Lindsey Bakewell, my lovely daughter," Mom added proudly for the onlookers, "and the owner of the Beacon Bakeshop. Modeling with Lindsey is her handsome Newfoundland, Wellington. These two are ready for a fun day at the Blueberry Festival, regardless of rain or shine . . ."

As Mom talked, Welly pranced onto the stage as if he were competing for Best in Show at Westminster, and not a model on display wearing a ridiculous raincoat and hat. As he walked beside me, his silky black fur, brushed to a glistening sheen, moved in soft ebony waves beneath the raincoat. I had to admit, he was a gorgeous boy.

Kennedy's voice came over the speakers next. "Welly, wearing our premiere blueberry raincoat, has a heart as big as his head. Yet even with a head that big, it looks as if he ran out of the lighthouse today without his Wellies on."

The crowd laughed at the pun. Welly, hearing his name and quite possibly the insult, suddenly stopped walking.

Right in the middle of my best imitation of a *model* turn, I only got halfway around before I was flung backward, due to my obstinate dog. The crowd laughed. I tried to smile and brush it off, growing red as a beet, I was sure. "Welly," I hissed, tugging on his leash, but he wouldn't budge. Beneath the floppy hat, his ears wiggled as his nose sniffed the air. His focus was glued to something or someone in the crowd. That's when I spied Rory.

I tugged on his leash again as Mom uttered, "Is that a goat?"

As if in reply to this, a lone bleating sound erupted from somewhere under the beer tent.

I stop tugging on Welly's leash, the word *goat* ringing in my ears.

"What on earth . . ." Kennedy's proper English accent rang out as a cacophony of bleating seemed to come from every direction. Welly gave a loud bark and leapt off the stage, nearly taking me with him.

All chaos erupted then. Goats were running loose under the beer tent while a pack of well-dressed dogs of all sizes chased after them. People were on their feet, laughing, screaming, and jumping out of the way as the chase went on. Rory, Tuck, and a host of others were frantically trying to gain control of the animals, but it was proving harder than it looked. The goats were nimble creatures, bounding through the spectators, butting unsuspecting bottoms with their little nubby horns, hopping on tabletops, and bleating at the top of their little goat lungs. The dogs had smelled the brats. I really couldn't tell what was going on, but I knew, looking at Mom's crestfallen face, that her wildly successful fashion show had ground to an undignified halt. The Blueberry Festival prankster had struck again.

"What a mess!" Felicity Stewart cried as tears welled in her large eyes. She was standing next to Mom and Kennedy. Her daughter, Kara, at Kennedy's request, had ended the live-stream shortly after the chaos erupted. We all felt the sting of this latest prank. "Stanley and I have worked so hard to make the brat and beer tent a success, and then this happens."

"Mom, it's okay," Kara said, placing her arm around her mother in a supportive hug. Kara, a lovely girl in her early twenties, had the same bright red hair as her mom. "Look," she demanded, pointing at a spot under the near-empty tent. "The goats have been corralled."

Sure enough, once the dogs were back where they belonged, the goats had been herded into a makeshift holding pen constructed out of tipped dining tables. Welly, who seemed rather fond of the little goats, was helping to direct them into the pen. Although there was no sign of his hat, his blueberry raincoat had held up quite nicely.

Tuck, with a grim set to his lips, walked over to where we stood. "I'm very sorry, Felicity. It doesn't appear that anyone saw, or remembered, how the goats got in here."

"Well, they didn't just magically appear, Tuck," Stanley replied, coming up behind his wife and daughter. "Where the heck did they come from?" he asked, looking puzzled.

"That I don't know, sir." Tuck raised his dusky eyebrows as he pulled out his phone. "But there is one silver lining to this little mess. It looks like we found Mrs. Rivers's missing goats."

CHAPTER 12

"Bakewell, you and your friends are snoopy," Sergeant Murdock began, running her cold, dark eyes over Rory, Kennedy, and me as if we were a batch of new recruits, which we might have been. "I don't know what's going on here, but it's beginning to look like this entire town is the butt of somebody's joke. Reporters have shown up, and the crowds are growing larger with each event. And if that wasn't enough, packs of young people are springing up everywhere, giggling, laughing, looking both obvious and suspicious. I can't tell if they're part of the problem or are here because of the problem. In short, this little issue of ours has grown beyond the scope of the Beacon Harbor Police Department. That's why I'm asking for your help."

"Wow," I said, feeling honored that she had called us

over to her location at the town beach. Although Sergeant Stacy Murdock was somewhat of a regular at the Beacon Bakeshop, our relationship had gone from scary-prickly to something approaching prickly-friendly over the last year. Her attitude toward Rory was a little friendlier, and her regard for Kennedy was totally jaded by the fact that my friend was dating one of her officers. Nonetheless, for a strong, competent woman with a badass reputation to protect, asking for our help was akin to a Hail Mary pass in a losing football game. In other words, the sergeant was desperate.

Filling with purpose, I answered, "We'd love to help out. Both Rory and Kennedy have already been on the receiving end of a prank. My event is tomorrow. This event," I said, gesturing to the sea of heads dotting the vast lakeside park and beachfront, "is the last event of the day. Do you think the prankster will have the nerve to strike again?"

She shrugged. "I don't see how he would with this event being so out in the open and with so many people watching, but we can't be too careful."

"Doubtful it will happen on the barge," Rory said, indicating to the flotilla out on the lake where the fireworks would be launched from. "The fire marshal is out there with them. All the fireworks have been checked, and the boys from the Coast Guard will be keeping any approaching boats at bay."

The sergeant nodded. "The fireworks are secure. I honestly don't know what we're looking for. Just keep your eyes open and call one of us if you see anything suspicious."

"Will do," Kennedy remarked. "But . . . have you ever

considered that this is what the prankster wants? Everyone on edge . . . waiting for the next shoe to drop? What could the prankster possibly do in a crowd this large?"

"Ms. Kapoor, if I knew the answer to that, I wouldn't need your help. And to answer your next question, no, you cannot have a Taser."

While Beacon Harbor's finest were busy monitoring the crowd and directing traffic, Rory, Kennedy, and I made our way to the stage, where Grayson Smythe was anxiously waiting for his show to begin.

"Are you okay?" I asked the artist, who was sitting on a chair while nervously wringing his hands.

Grayson, both an artist and a showman, was dressed in a smart gray linen suit with a white shirt, his signature ascot in bold blue silk adding a splash of color to his ensemble. He looked great, but his face was creased with worry. He looked up at the three of us and smiled. "I feel a bit like a child turning the handle on a jack-in-the-box. I know the clown will pop up, I just don't know when."

Rory knelt beside him. "Have you checked your sculpture?" Grayson nodded. "Everything looks good?" The artist nodded again. "Good. We'll be here watching the crowd and making sure nothing happens."

The look in his gray-blue eyes was one of hope. "Thank you. You three have set my mind at ease."

We were treated to another spectacular sunset over Lake Michigan, complete with a palette of colors ranging from orange to indigo blazing across the darkening sky in a display that would be hard to beat. The crowd, waiting to see the unveiling of a glass masterpiece followed by fireworks, fell silent for a moment, awestruck by the natural wonder. Then the sun dipped beyond the horizon, and dramatic music began to play softly in the background.

Grayson Smythe took to the lakeside stage, standing beside a large, twelve-foot structure covered by a white tarp. He thanked the crowd for their attention, then talked about the arts and crafts show taking place in the park by the marina. Grayson then talked about his own craft, the art of glassblowing, and how honored he was to have been asked to create a special sculpture for the blueberry festival.

The sky had grown darker; the music played louder, and Grayson Smythe was ready to unveil his masterpiece. He flipped a switch, and the tarp began to glow with astonishing color. Everyone was mesmerized by the possibility of what lay beneath that white sheet.

With a flourish, Grayson tugged at the tarp. It took two tries before it fluttered away, revealing a giant, whimsical, under-lit sculpture of glass spheres floating on a wrought-iron frame. Each sphere was a burst of glowing color. No two were alike, but every one of them was moving, swirling on their stands while on a moving frame. It gave the impression that the balls of light were floating into the sky. This first glimpse of it was beyond anything I could have imagined.

"Oh . . . so beautiful," Kennedy uttered, awestruck. Like everyone else, her eyes were transfixed on the sculpture. And then, ever so slightly, I realized that the sculpture was swaying.

"Oh no," I said, hit with a sudden, stabbing fear. "Is it supposed to be moving like that?"

Yet before anyone could reply, the movement of the frame became larger, gyrating with each swirling orb.

And then it happened. In an unstoppable chain reaction, the giant balls of glass began to topple. One by one they hit the stage and burst into a thousand pieces. A collective inhale came from the horror-struck crowd. Grayson, too stupefied to move, stood onstage and gaped at his master-piece as it slowly destroyed itself before him. There was nothing he or anyone could do to stop it.

Then the sound of one man clapping pulled my attention away from the wreckage.

"By God, Smythe! You've done it! You've finally made a sculpture worth staring at!" The deep laughter that followed was familiar.

We all turned to see who was laughing. "Old Lars Jorgenson," Rory said, his eyes widening with something akin to fear as he stared at the older man who was part of his Friday morning coffee group. Lars was now on his feet, clapping and laughing with delight. To our horror, more people began to stand and do the same, perhaps thinking it was part of the show. I cringed at the insensitivity of it all, thinking of poor Grayson Smythe and how hard he must have worked on the beautiful sculpture.

"You two, go see if there's anything you can do for Grayson. I'm going to see if Anders needs any help with his father. This isn't good," Rory stated, then took off through the crowd, aiming for the man still laughing at the artist's expense.

"Grayson, are you alright?" I asked, thinking it a stupid question the moment it left my lips. He was not alright. In fact, he looked close to tears.

"It's my fault," he uttered, staring at the naked, lit frame that just moments ago had held dozens of glass spheres. "I checked everything. I made sure it would work, but when I pulled off the sheet, something happened." His glossy, dark eyes searched mine for an answer. My heart sank, because I didn't have one.

"I don't think it was your fault at all," Kennedy said, squatting beside the wreckage while gingerly inspecting the damage. "Look here. Someone has tied this corner of the tarp to this frame. When you pulled it off, did you feel a tug?"

Grayson's eyes shot to where Kennedy was pointing. "On that end, yes." His face darkened as he stared at the end of the tarp tied to one of the tines on the wrought-iron frame.

"That mighty tug you gave it was the straw that broke the camel's back, I'm afraid," she informed him, her eyes reflecting both concern and anger at the discovery.

"Are you saying someone tampered with my sculpture?" The thought apparently caused a flood of red-hot anger to pump through Grayson's veins, as his face began to turn an alarming shade of red. I really couldn't blame him either. In a louder voice, he cried, "Somebody tried to sabotage my sculpture!?"

Kennedy and I exchanged a look, prompting me to add, "I'm afraid, Grayson, that your stunning sculpture has been sabotaged by the prankster."

A string of expletives escaped his lips, only to be drowned out by the first fireworks burst of the evening.

CHAPTER 13

"I'm not taking any chances," I told Rory, placing the lock on the cooler door. After the disastrous past two days, in which six disruptive pranks had been played on six different members of the Blueberry Festival Committee, I knew I was next. I had no idea what was in store for me, but everyone at the Beacon Bakeshop was on high alert. After the wanton destruction of Grayson's awe-inspiring masterpiece, Rory and I had driven back to the lighthouse, where I finished baking the blueberry pies for the pie-eating contest, secured them all in the walk-in cooler, and locked the bakery doors behind me.

Kennedy had opted to stay with Tuck as he investigated this latest, devastating prank played on Grayson Smythe. Although the crowd seemed entertained by it (the spectacular nature of this last debacle hadn't disappointed the prankster's fans), those of us on the festival committee were not happy. Grayson, understandably, was beside himself with grief. Hopefully, Kennedy and Tuck would be able to track down the prankster (or pranksters) and put a stop to the chaos before tomorrow. As for me, I knew the clock was ticking. Therefore, I had inspected every pie previously baked, then baked the rest myself. All thirty blueberry pies Dad and I had made (I had made extras just in case we had some orders) were now safely in the cooler. Outside on the lawn, the tent for the contest had been erected, with the tables and chairs waiting to be set up in the morning. If somebody got the bright idea to steal the tables and chairs in the middle of the night, it wasn't the end of the world. I knew that we could come up with something in a pinch, even if we had to hold the contest at the café tables, or on picnic blankets.

"I don't blame you one bit for being extra cautious," Rory said, leading me back into the lighthouse. Welly, sleeping peacefully on his bed near the fireplace, opened a droopy eye as we came through the door. "Just in case, I'm staying here tonight," he announced as we both plopped down on the couch. Although I was dead tired, I was grateful he had decided to stay. Not only was I super attracted to him, but his mere masculine presence was a comfort. With his arm around me, I happily snuggled next to him.

"And don't forget about Welly," he teased, staring at the dog, who hadn't bothered to leave his bed after his last cookie. "I don't know if you realize this, but between Welly and me, you've got the best security team in town."

That security team was tested at some point later in the night when Welly's resounding bark woke us with a start.

Rory and I, being exhausted, had fallen asleep on the couch. Welly, springing awake, was barking at the front door.

"What on earth?" I said, getting to my feet. Rory was still rubbing his eyes. I'd taken a few steps toward the door when Kennedy walked in.

My friend took one look at me and cried, "What are you doing here?" Her voice held a tinge of hysteria; her eyes were reminiscent of a doe's in hunting season.

Miffed, I replied, "I live here, or did you forget?"

"What? No." She looked at Rory, who was now standing beside me. "What I meant was, I thought you two were up in the light room."

"Too exhausted," Rory remarked.

"Doubtful we could climb the steps after the day we've had," I added. "We fell asleep on the couch."

"Then, darlings, I have some bad news for you. There's a light coming from the light tower. It's been flashing on and off for the past five minutes."

Bad news, indeed! Rory dashed for the door leading to the hallway that led to the steps of the light tower. While he ran up the winding metal staircase, I went to check the other door. The short hallway leading to the steps of the light tower could be accessed from outside as well. The fact that this door was locked could only mean one thing. I climbed the dark steps as well and stood in the light room beside Rory. There was no light, but there was the faint, lingering scent of pipe smoke.

The hair on the back of my neck began to prickle. I imagined Rory felt the same, for whenever the first light-keeper had something to say, his presence was felt. Captain Willy Riggs had come to the light room to stand watch.

"He was here," Rory whispered, as if afraid of being overheard by the captain. "You and I both know what this means."

I reached for his hand and held it firmly, for the ghost lights of Beacon Harbor were a portent of danger. We both had the unsettling feeling that things were about to turn deadly.

After our sojourn into the haunted light room, Rory and I had eventually gone to bed. Although it was always unsettling to encounter the ghost lights, sleep finally won out over worry, and before I knew it, I had fallen into a dreamless slumber. It was still dark when I awoke with a start, thinking I'd heard something odd. Rory was still snoring softly beside me when the sound came again.

I sat up in bed. It sounded like the bleating of a goat.

Welly had sat up too. I saw the profile of his large, handsome head at the foot of my bedframe, his nose pointing at the window. He chanced a quick glance at me, then began to whine.

"You heard that too?" I asked him in a whisper. His answer was to ignore me and focus on the window. Then we heard the goat again. There was no mistaking that sound, not after the disastrous fashion show debacle. Knowing there was a prankster in our midst, and figuring that I was the next target, I gave Rory a little shake.

"Hey, are you awake?"

"No," he grumbled, and rolled over.

"I think there's a goat outside. Listen. Hear that? That's a goat. I'm not sure where it is, but it doesn't sound too happy."

"You don't know that it's unhappy," was his sleepy reply. "It's a goat." That word floated in the room for a second or two before he turned to me, understanding blazing in his night-dark eyes. He sat up and looked at the window. "It's a goat!"

Welly barked.

"That's what I've been trying to tell you."

"Christ," he growled, looking annoyed by the interruption. We both got out of bed and ran to investigate.

The moment we opened the front door, Welly bolted into the darkness. There was a slight on-shore breeze, and the sky above was clear with a bright full moon and a sprinkling of stars. I could tell by the subtle lighter shade of gray on the eastern horizon that the sun would be rising soon. The goat, wherever it was, kept calling to us. I honestly couldn't tell where the sound was coming from. The lighthouse lawn looked as it should. Nothing was moving near the bakery entrance. Was the goat in the boathouse? I wondered. But then Rory caught sight of Wellington running down the beach. We both ran after him.

Once we were clear of the lighthouse, we saw it. It was perhaps a hundred yards out on the seemingly endless stretch of water. I couldn't judge the exact distance because it was so dark. The boat itself was bathed in moonlight and silhouetted against the night sky, bobbing on the gentle waves like a rocking horse. Although it was most likely no larger than a twelve-foot craft, the shape of the sides arched from low in the center to high on the ends, with the bow and stern ending in what appeared to be a swooping flourish, giving the appearance of a carved figurehead. In fact, the modest vessel had a distinct Viking-ship feel to it, which was ridiculous, given the size of it. Also, we were in Michigan. We didn't have Vikings in

Michigan. Yet adding to that effect was the source of the noise itself, the little white goat thrusting its head above the bow of the boat and bleating with the gusto of a foghorn. Some idiot, obviously our prankster, had put a goat in a boat, and that boat was now afloat on the waves beyond the lighthouse.

"Are you seeing what I'm seeing?" Rory asked, staring out at the water.

"Ahhh . . ." I uttered. Honestly, my brain was still trying to process what my eyes were taking in. Without looking at Rory, I replied, "Unfortunately, yes. Who would do something as reckless as put a goat in a boat?" It was infuriating, even more so when I realized that I sounded a bit like a Dr. Seuss book. Then, however, I caught sight of something that gripped my heart. "Wellington!" I cried, noticing that my dog was no longer nervously pacing in the surf. My daft yet noble pup was attempting a water rescue. The only problem was, he'd never be able to get aboard the boat, not without someone helping him up from the inside. And aside from the goat, the boat appeared to be empty.

"Welly, come!" I commanded, fear tinging my voice. But it was no use. Welly was a water dog, a powerful swimmer, and he obviously thought the distressed goat required his assistance. His focus was solely on the goat; everything else fell on deaf ears.

I was in tears as I called to my dog. Then, however, I felt Rory's hand in mine.

"Lindsey." His voice was like a soothing balm to my nerves. "He'll be fine for a while. Let him swim. We'll get him with my boat."

It was a good plan, and thankfully he had thought of it. Fearing for Welly's safety, as well as the little goat's, I raced alongside Rory as we headed for the trail through the woods. It was a shortcut to Rory's log home without having to go all the way around the point, a path I used often. The moment the path deposited us near his back door, we turned toward the lake.

Rory was an avid angler and a scuba diver, and his cabin cruiser was not only equipped with fishing-pole holders in the back, but also a large back platform for easy access in and out of the water. In short, the boat was his pride and joy. I was certain that had we not been in such a hurry, he would have removed the canvas boat cover with more care and ceremony than the hefty heave he used to unsnap the tarp from the open deck. He then tossed it onto the dock.

"Climb aboard," he ordered, holding the boat close to the dock so I could step in without slipping. Then, with natural fluidity and grace, he untied the mooring lines, shoved the boat away from the dock just enough for clearance, and jumped aboard.

"There's a flashlight under the seat," he told me the moment he took his place behind the wheel and started up the motor. "We'll have the navigational lights on, but once we round the point, find Wellington and keep the beam on him so we can approach him with caution."

"Aye-aye, Captain," I said, and turned on the flashlight as the boat headed for open water.

The moment we rounded the point, I had no problem finding Welly with the flashlight. He was such a powerful swimmer that he was already at the little craft, swimming circles around it as the goat followed him as best it could. Welly was looking for a place to climb aboard, no doubt, but he wouldn't find one. As Rory cut the motor and drifted closer, I left the cabin and called to Welly. This time, thankfully, he listened and began swimming for Rory's boat. As he did, the little goat grew frantic and began calling out to him again, this time with a pitiful bout of bleating. Hearing it, Welly circled around in the waves and began swimming back toward the abandoned craft. The poor dog was getting confused.

Not liking that one bit, I doubled down and promised cookies. That did the trick. Rory was already at the back of the boat, luring Welly to the platform, where we could easily pull him aboard.

Okay, not so easily. Welly on a good day weighed a hundred and fifty pounds. Soaking wet, he weighed even more. Thank goodness Rory was with me, or I might have ended up in the water with the dog. However, after Welly took a good, water-splattering shake, I gave him a big hug, happy he was safely aboard. Then Rory steered his boat toward the frantic goat and the abandoned craft.

Leaving a space between our boat and the goat's, Rory cut the engine and disappeared into the cabin. A moment later he was back on deck with a rope in his hands. I could see that secured to one end of the rope was a small grappling hook. "I'm going to throw this around the jutting portion of the bow, then draw the boat to the back, where I can better secure it to this line. Then we can tow the craft back to my dock."

"What about the goat?" I asked, imagining how a mother must feel hearing her own baby cry. The bleats of the little goat were getting to me.

He pursed his lips, looking at me as if I was serious. Seeing that I was, he answered, "The goat stays in the boat until we get back on dry land. Okay? It'll be fine. It's sailed all this way already, Lindsey. I can't imagine that another short little trip will make much of a difference.

Now, I'm going to throw this line. I need you to shine the flashlight on the boat."

"Fair enough," I said, and pointed the flashlight at the boat. Rory hooked the prow on the first try and began drawing the lovely little boat in. My mistake was running the light over the boat. "Rory!" I croaked, panic seizing my voice. "The goat . . . it isn't alone!"

"Christ," Rory uttered, looking to where the flashlight was pointed. "I never expected this."

CHAPTER 14

My heart was pounding loudly in my ears as Rory directed me to keep the light on the partially covered form lying in the bottom of the boat. The pile of loose hay covering it was making it difficult, but just enough had fallen away to reveal the profile of a pale, bearded, waxy face below a horned helmet. There was also some type of fur covering the form, but I couldn't be certain what it was. What I *was* certain of was that the whole scene—the boat, the goat, and the body—looked suspiciously Viking, making me believe that maybe this was just another horrible, stupid prank. I mean, *really!* What idiot would take the time to fashion a lapstrake-constructed boat, carve a decorative figurehead, dress a dummy up as a Viking, and then send the whole thing onto the lake with a live goat in it? Urgh! The mere thought sent a wave of anger shooting through my body, colliding with my prickling fear. I had to admit, the whole thing looked real enough, but once again, I was having a hard time registering what I was seeing. Then the little goat did something unexpected. It leapt from its place at the bow of the boat and landed on the chest of the Viking. There, it plopped down and began nibbling the hay and the blanket. Touched, yet slightly repulsed, I looked at Rory.

"Is . . . is it real, do you think? Or is this just another stupid prank?"

Rory finished securing the rope and shook his head. "I hope to God it's not real. If it is . . ." He trailed off, looking just as dumbfounded as I was.

"If it is," I said, finishing the thought for him, "then our prankster is also a murderer."

Rory stood and took the flashlight from my hand. He then turned it off, not wanting to dwell on our recent discovery. "We need to get this boat back to the dock. Then I'll take a closer look. Alright?"

I nodded, trying my best to offer a look of encouragement. I don't believe I succeeded. This was because Rory was normally calm under pressure, yet there was something about the gruesome sight that must have really struck a nerve. I'll grant, it wasn't normal. But whatever Rory had seen had quelled his curiosity for the moment.

It was a silent ride back to the dock—well, mostly silent. The little white goat was carrying on again, inspiring Wellington to bark in return. Rory was strangely silent, offering nothing. I didn't feel much like talking either. Words had left me as my thoughts spiraled, knowing we were either towing a dummy or a dead body, and the latter wasn't sitting too well with either of us.

The first fingers of dawn were upon us as Rory secured both boats to the dock. Like me, I could tell he was trying to avoid looking directly at the Viking. His first priority had been to remove the goat from the boat; to do this he fashioned a leash out of another length of rope and tried to pull the little thing out, like a dog. The goat wouldn't budge.

"Here, let me try," I said, coming beside him on the dock. He seemed happy to hand the task over to me.

"Tie her to the deck," he offered softly. "I have some carrots in the fridge and a bone for Welly. Keep the animals there. Then call the police. The body's real, Lindsey."

For some reason I couldn't have been more shocked to hear this. My eyes locked on his, and in them I saw pain and sorrow. "You knew?" It wasn't an accusation.

He nodded. "The moment the flashlight touched his face, I knew. It's Lars Jorgenson. Anders's father. Oh, Lindsey, what the hell happened?"

My heart sank at the knowledge, and tears formed in my eyes as well. "I'm so sorry." I then gave him a hug, because I knew how much Lars Jorgenson had meant to him and his Friday morning group. "What on earth happened?" I blurted, standing back to look at him. "It has the appearance of a prank, but this is a truly sick joke. Do you think he was murdered? Do you think we were meant to find him? I mean, that boat was floating right in front of the lighthouse!" I sucked in my breath as another thought occurred to me. "The captain's warning! He was trying to tell us something. And we would have missed it for sure if not for the goat . . . Did Lars own a goat?"

Rory, patiently listening to my frightened ramblings, gave a little shrug. Then his face darkened. "I can't answer any of your questions yet, Lindsey. But I mean to. If this was meant to be a prank, it's now personal. Whoever did this to that gentle, happy soul will pay. Now, if you can, please take the goat out of the boat and let me have a look at this before the police arrive."

I had more luck luring the goat to the dock because Wellington was beside me. The little goat, if it had belonged to Lars Jorgenson, might be displaying loyalty, or maybe it was just hungry for hay. I couldn't be sure of anything but the fact that it was curious. The moment Welly jumped from Rory's boat and came up beside me, the goat leapt from its boat as well. The two animals, one large and hairy, the other smaller, with cloven hooves and curious yellow eyes, met nose-to-nose on the dock. I wasn't sure how the meeting would go. Did goats like dogs? Did dogs like goats? I knew Welly to be a friendly, easygoing pup, but he'd never met a goat before. As far as goats went, I knew next to nothing about them, since I'd grown up in the Hamptons then lived in Manhattan. I held my breath as the animals sniffed and eyed one another with suspicion. Then, however, the goat's white tail began to flick. It bobbed its head and let out a sound that could have been laughter. Welly licked its nose.

"I think you two are going to get along just fine," I said, leading both animals up to the house.

Rory, taking Lars Jorgenson's death personally, had wanted to be left alone with the body, and I respected that. After tending to the animals, I sat on the bottom step of the deck and watched him for a moment before I made the call to 911. Just after reporting the body and giving the address, my phone rang again. This time it was Dad.

"Hey, hon, I'm at the bakery. Where are you?"

"Dad!" I said, then quickly glanced at the time on my phone. It was five thirty. "I'm sorry. I lost track of time, and I'll tell you why. We found a body," I blurted out, then quickly filled him in on the scant details.

Dad was both horrified and saddened, as I knew he would be. He was also understanding. "Take your time, dear. I'll handle things at the Beacon. Wendy's here as well. Don't worry about anything here."

"Thanks, Dad. I'll be there as soon as I can to set up for the pie-eating contest."

"A man's been murdered. Do you still think we should go through with that?"

"We don't really know if he was murdered, Dad. Not yet. And I think we should hold the contest," I added, suddenly thinking of the prankster. "This weird death looks like a prank, but I'm not sure it is. We think that the blueberry pie–eating contest will be the next place hit by the prankster or pranksters. I say we continue with the contest and keep our eyes peeled. Maybe we can catch whoever has been plaguing our festival. And maybe, just maybe, they know something about Lars Jorgenson's death."

"Good point," Dad said.

I had to end the call there because just then Welly dropped his bone long enough to let out a friendly bark, heralding the arrival of Sergeant Murdock and Officer McAllister. The two came marching down the side of the house to the back lawn. The sergeant, seeing me, removed her glasses and shook her head. "Bakewell, why am I not surprised that when another body turns up in Beacon Harbor, you're involved?"

"I assure you, ma'am, I don't want to be. I blame it on the lighthouse—and this goat."

As if on cue, the goat looked at the police officers, and cried, "Blaaagh!"

CHAPTER 15

"I can't quite say that I've ever run into anything like this before," Murdock mused while staring at the well-constructed Viking craft that was now being referred to as the crime scene. "And the only reason it came to your attention was because of that goat back there?" She quirked a skeptical brow as she gestured toward the deck.

"I know it sounds ridiculous, but hear me out." I offered a hopeful smile to the unbending face of the sergeant. Tuck, giving his boss a wide berth for obvious reasons, had gone straight to the Viking boat to talk with Rory. Smart man. Now, however, the full heat of the sergeant's suspicious gaze was on me. I was slightly insulted. After all, I thought Sergeant Stacy Murdock and I were nearly friends. She was a regular at the Beacon Bakeshop, and she was in the same book club as my dear friend, Betty Vanhoosen. Now, however, the sergeant had put on her scary face, the one I was sure made baddies quake in their boots. Although Stacy Murdock was a woman in her mid-forties, with a thick build, dyed blond hair, and long, wispy bangs that grazed her eyelids, she definitely had presence. Whenever she confronted me, be it for a cookie recipe or information on a dead body that I'd happened to find, I felt the need to babble until I had no secrets left.

"After what happened to Grayson at his unveiling," I began, hoping she remembered the prank, "I put the light-house on high alert. After all, the Beacon Bakeshop is hosting the last official event of the festival—the blue-berry pie–eating contest. Given how things have been going, and that all the festival committee members have been targeted by the prankster, I knew we'd be next. I took every precaution I could think of before I went to bed. When the sound of a goat bleating pulled me from my sleep, I thought the prankster had struck."

Murdock massaged her chin as her eyes shot to the Viking boat. "From all appearances, it looks like the prankster has."

"No—well, it might have that look to it, but this is hardly a prank. And this—whatever this is—hasn't been played on me," I told her in no uncertain terms. "There's a dead man dressed as a Viking in a boat. Dead! How is putting a dead man in a boat a prank?"

"The goat woke you," she stated, as if the matter was as clear as day to her. "It floated past your lighthouse. Why would somebody put a goat in a boat if not to wake you? Everyone knows that goats are noisy animals."

I shook my head, trying to dispel her weird logic. "But the other pranks were . . ." I fought for the right word and came up empty. I cringed before admitting, ". . . kind of funny. I mean, sure they were upsetting, but they were clever. And most importantly, no one got killed. Are you insinuating that the prank played on me purposely included a dead body? That's all kinds of disturbing! Lars Jorgenson is dead! Somebody put a horned helmet on his head, wrapped him in a bearskin rug, and sent him afloat in a Viking boat.

"With a goat," she added, matter-of-factly.

"And a sword," Tuck called out, holding the large weapon aloft in his gloved hand for us to see.

"Probably to round out the look," I offered. "I mean, Vikings used swords and kept goats. Right?" This was met by her unbending, dark gaze. "What I'm saying is that this isn't a prank."

"We cannot tell that for sure, Bakewell. We don't really know *what* this is yet."

"Looks like foul play to me," Rory offered as he stood in the boat. I noticed that he also had on latex gloves. "Is Doc Riggles on his way?" Murdock gave a curt nod. "Good. I think I might know what this is."

Rory and Tuck left the boat and joined us.

"It's not obvious how Mr. Jorgenson died," Tuck told Murdock, "but there is a good deal of staining on the teeth and around the mouth, as if he'd been eating blueberries."

Murdock narrowed her eyes at him. "I should think there'd be a good deal of staining around everyone's mouth and teeth by now. It is, after all, the Blueberry Festival. How do we know Mr. Jorgenson didn't die from a heart attack while eating pie in his boat with his goat?"

"Because I think this was meant to be a Viking burial," Rory said, his dark brows furrowing at the troubling thought.

"And how would you know that? Shouldn't that be for the crime scene investigators to determine?"

"I'm not telling you the cause of death, Sergeant. What I'm telling you is that I think somebody tried to conduct a shoddy version of a Viking burial here, only Lars Jorgenson seemed perfectly healthy to me last night when he was laughing at the demise of Grayson's glass sculpture."

Sergeant Murdock's face softened as she considered this. "This man laughed at the terrible prank played on Mr. Smythe? I don't think that singled him out as a target for murder. As far as I could tell, everyone there was laughing when Mr. Smythe's sculpture imploded, poor man."

"You're not going to like this, Lindsey," Rory said, looking at me. "But I know my military history, and I assume old Lars did as well. What I'm saying is that Lars would have known that Viking chieftains were often buried in their ships surrounded by all their possessions. Covered by the hay in that boat are what appears to be some of Lars Jorgenson's possessions."

"Including the goat?" I asked him.

"Maybe."

Sergeant Murdock looked unconvinced. "And you think because you found some of his things lying in the hay that this was an attempt at a Viking burial?" Her straight, stubby nose wrinkled in either disbelief or distaste, it was hard to tell which.

"No," Rory said. "What makes this a shoddy attempt at a Viking burial are two things. One, deceased Viking chieftains were not put to sea in their boats and set on fire by a hail of fire arrows. That is a myth perpetuated by Hollywood. And number two"—he held up two fingers to illustrate—"someone most definitely shot a fire arrow at that boat."

"What?" I cried as a new wave of horror struck me. I looked at the innocent little goat grazing near Rory's deck and felt my heart fill with a surge of protective mama-bear instincts. I looked back at Rory and said, "Are you telling me someone tried to light that boat on fire?" I hadn't meant to yell, but I couldn't help it. The thought was too much for me.

"Unfortunately, yes. I found a charred arrow, some burnt paper, and some singed hay. Thankfully, there was plenty of water in the bottom of the boat to put out the fire."

"Campbell," Murdock began, nodding her head in appreciation. "Your Viking burial theory is the only thing that makes a lick of sense here. Now, however, it's time for the professionals to take over. It was a stroke of luck that Bakewell here heard the goat. Otherwise, we might never have known what had become of Mr. Jorgenson. And that reminds me. We now have the difficult task of telling his next of kin. Poor Anders. This is going to be a difficult morning."

"Let me tell him," Rory said.

Murdock agreed. "Thank you. And please have him meet us at the morgue to identify the body."

"What about the goat?" I asked.

Apparently, the sergeant hadn't thought about the goat. "I suppose we'll take it down to the station and put it in one of the holding cells. It is, after all, an eyewitness."

"No," I snapped, as if the thought was absurd. "I'm taking the goat! The poor thing has been through enough for one day, what with being put in a boat with a dead man and having a fire arrow shot at it." Before the sergeant could refuse, I stormed off across the lawn in the direction of Welly and the goat. "I'll keep it until you find its real owner," I called back.

"Attagirl, Bakewell. In this case, I'll let you."

I untied the goat's leash and turned back to face the group clustered on the dock. Sergeant Murdock was laughing. Tuck looked a bit frightened, and Rory stood there, shaking his head as if the bizarre happenings of the morning were beginning to catch up with him.

"I have to go now," I called back with a wave. "I have a pie-eating contest to run, and a possible prankster to catch." I then signaled to Wellington to follow and struck off across the lawn leading the goat. "Call me when you hear anything."

"Keep the goat, but please stay out of this, Bakewell. That's an order."

The silent words rattled around in my head as my foot hit the trail to the shortcut: *I don't take orders from you, Scary Sergeant Stacy!* Welly barked and ran ahead. The goat, tugging at its leash, bleated. And then it hit me. What the heck was I going to do with a goat?

CHAPTER 16

"Knock, knock. I have a favor to ask you." I took the liberty of entering Kennedy's room without her permission, because I knew she wouldn't answer. This was because it was still early, and Kennedy was opposed to early mornings as a rule. She was still in bed, swaddled in silk pajamas, silk sheets, and a beautiful summer-weight quilt, half-hidden by a mountain of pillows. If I hadn't known any better, I'd say she looked like the poster child for peaceful abandon. I was about to say something else to wake her when the goat beat me to it.

"Blaaaagh!"

That did the trick. After flailing in her pillows a moment, Kennedy bolted upright and struggled to remove her silk sleep mask. The look on her face when she saw the goat was priceless.

"What in the bloody hell is that thing doing in my room?" She looked both annoyed and frightened.

"Blaaagh!" the goat replied. It looked like it was smiling at my friend.

"This is a goat," I told her, stating the obvious. "It's a she-goat because she has, um, udders. I've checked."

"Good for you. You can now add 'goat gender identifier' to your résumé. But I don't care what kind of goat it is, Lindsey dear. That is a goat!" She glared at me, then thought better of it. "Why . . . why do you have a goat again?"

"It's a long story, but here are the CliffsNotes. We found the goat this morning afloat in a boat."

"That makes perfect sense." As her words dripped with sarcasm, she cast me a deprecatory look.

"It makes no sense at all, and that's part of it. This little goat—"

"—was afloat in a boat. I know. We've been over that already."

"With a dead body!"

"What?" Kennedy cried and sat up even higher on her pillows. The goat bleated at her again. Kennedy frowned, then asked, "You found a dead body?"

"Yes. In the boat with the goat."

She pursed her lips as she held up her hand in protest. "I'm still muddled with sleep, there's a goat in my room, and you sound like a cheeky children's poet. There are just too many rhyming words in this story to take you seriously. I acknowledge that this goat was in a boat afloat with a dead body. Let's just continue from there. Shall we?"

"Yes, thank goodness. The body of Lars Jorgenson was in the boat with the . . . ahem, animal. And he was dressed from head to toe like a Viking. It was this little goat that woke us up before dawn, making a racket. We thought the Blueberry Festival prankster had struck again. I'm surprised you slept through the noise."

She waved a hand. "I sleep like the dead. Oh, poor word choice. Like a baby," she corrected. "Did you say 'Viking'?" She tilted her head as her nose wrinkled at the thought.

"Unfortunately, yes. That's what makes this so horrible. Rory thinks someone was attempting a Viking burial, launching a flaming arrow at the boat."

"With that goat in it!?" she cried, horrorstruck at the thought. "Someone meant to burn a dead body and that darling little goat as well? Don't look so surprised. She *is* darling—as far as goats are concerned." She swung her legs out of the bed and came to meet the little animal in question.

"She's pure white, and her fur is far softer than I imagined." The goat was loving the attention. Had Welly come with us instead of staying put in the kitchen eating his breakfast, he would have been whining with envy.

"She's a sweet little thing," I agreed. "Welly likes her, and you know what a great judge of character he is. Scary Sergeant Stacy wanted to take her to the police station and lock her up in one of the cells until she found her owner. I couldn't stand the thought."

"Of course not. Because you're a big, old softie. You said that Lars Jorgenson's body was in the boat? Anders's father?" Now fully awake, my friend was paying attention.

"The very one. And we both know he was very much alive last night."

"True," she agreed with a thoughtful nod. "Last night when I was with Tuck, we went to have a word with the senior Mr. Jorgenson. Anders apologized for his father's untimely outburst when Grayson Smythe's sculpture came to a spectacular end. Funny, but Mr. Jorgenson Senior looked very hale and hearty to me. I can't imagine what happened between then and this morning. Nor can I imagine who would do such a thing to that harmless old man."

"I can't either. So, the question is—and I apologize in advance—why was he in a boat with a goat this morning in front of the lighthouse?"

She sucked in her breath at the mention of the lighthouse. "The ghost lights! I saw them last night, remember? At least I think it was last night."

"It was," I said, offering a knowing look.

"It was a warning. The captain was sending a warning." Kennedy shivered slightly, then ran a hand through her silky black hair.

"Doubtful it's a coincidence. This is the third time since I've come to Beacon Harbor that the ghost lights have been seen. Captain Willy must have some sense that danger is lurking near our shores."

"Of course, he does, Lindsey. He's a ghost! Ghosts have special powers . . . like turning on lights and clairvoyance." She cast me a look and waved her hand. "Everybody knows this."

"Okay, that's a lie. However, I think it's something you might want to investigate on one of your next *Kennedy's Crusades* podcasts."

"I just might," she replied as she arched a perfectly shaped brow at the thought. "So, what you're telling me, aside from the fact that you now have a goat, is that Lars Jorgenson might possibly have been murdered last night, and that somebody tried to give him a roaring Viking sendoff?" She crossed her arms as a wild thought lit her large dark eyes. "You're about to throw your hat into the ring, so to speak, aren't you? You're planning on snooping around for answers."

"I have the goat. Murdock said she is the only eye-witness we have, although, admittedly, she's not a very good one. But it's a start. Which reminds me, I'm going to need you to keep an eye on her for a while. I have a bakery to open, a pie-eating contest to run, and a possible prankster to catch."

"What? No-no-no! *You* volunteered to keep her, not me." Kennedy tried to back away from the goat, but the goat, for some odd reason, seemed to like her. She pranced forward and began nibbling on the hem of Kennedy's silk pajama top.

"Stop that, you wee beast!" She shooed the goat and yanked the yummy silk garment out of its mouth. "What do I do with a goat?" She threw her hands in the air with something like fear in her eyes.

"You are brilliant, my friend. You'll think of something. Maybe you can start by giving her a name? And she probably needs to be milked." After that remark I headed for the door.

"I'm a London girl," she called out. "London girls do not milk things!"

"I'm a New York City girl," I countered. "Don't look at me."

"And yet here we are, living in the wilds of Michigan in a haunted old lighthouse with a goat and another dead body!"

"When you put it like that, I'll admit, it doesn't sound ideal." I rubbed the goat's back, marveling at how soft her fur was. "Okay, maybe ask somebody who knows about goats."

"Sound advice. And here's a little tidbit for you. Keep on your toes, Lindsey dear. After all, a dead body is not a prank."

CHAPTER 17

After leaving the goat with Kennedy, I was finally able to shift my focus to the bakeshop once again. Heading down the stairs, I found Welly waiting at the bottom, his soulful brown eyes looking at me with question. His tail thumped as he shifted his gaze to the stairs. Funny, but I actually knew, or thought I knew, what he was asking me.

"She's with Kennedy," I said, and rubbed his fluffy head. "They'll be down in a few minutes." Welly followed me through the house as I made my way to the door leading directly to the café. "I'm afraid you're going to have to stay here awhile longer," I said, leaving him sitting there. "I'll be back shortly to take you for a walk." I gave him a kiss and slipped through the door, hoping that Welly, Kennedy, and the goat wouldn't get into too much trouble while I was gone.

Dad, Wendy, and Alaina were hard at work behind the bakery counter. They had done a marvelous job of stocking the bakery cases and opening the bakeshop while I had been otherwise detained with a body and a goat. Dad's questioning gaze met mine as I skirted around the line of customers patiently waiting for their morning coffee and whatever yummy delight they had their eyes on. It was still early, and a good deal of those who waited in line were regulars at the Beacon, with a few summer residents and blueberry tourists mixed in. I greeted my friends as I made a beeline for the bakery counter. However, my best efforts were thwarted by Betty Vanhoosen.

She was the next customer in line, and as I passed her, offering a friendly "hello," she grabbed my arm and walked me over to the self-serve coffee bar, in the manner of a principal having a word with a naughty student. I was a tad alarmed.

"I heard you found another body," she said in a whisper as loud as a fog bell.

Her words stopped me in my tracks. Because the Beacon Bakeshop was also the local hangout of those who loved their small-town gossip, all heads turned our way. Meanwhile, my head was abuzz with the annoying possibility that Betty Vanhoosen might possibly be clairvoyant. How did she know about the body? Had she seen the ghost lights last night too? Or was she in cahoots with the captain? After all, she had sold me the lighthouse knowing it was rumored to be haunted. Then I looked into her round blue eyes and remembered that Betty was in a relationship with the county medical examiner.

"Doc told you?" There was possibly a note of annoyance in my voice as I said this. After all, I didn't think it was very professional of Doc Riggles to call Betty and tell her that another body had turned up in town and that I was the one who had found it.

While pondering this, I stared suspiciously into Betty's round, guileless eyes. Then she blurted, "He got a call early this morning. We were in bed." This little fact I could have easily lived happily without ever knowing. But I knew it, and now there was no taking it back. Then, projecting her voice like an actress onstage wanting to wake up those in the back row, she offered, "All I know is that you found another body, and it's believed to be that of Lars Jorgenson."

"Lars Jorgenson!" Bill Morgan cried out and left his place in line. Roger, his son, followed him. So did Jack Johnson and Rod Jeffers. In fact, thanks to Betty, all eyes were now on us, including Dad's, Alaina's and Wendy's.

"Why didn't you say something, Betty?" Bill admonished, looking both affronted and hurt.

"Because, Bill, it's not something one blurts out in a bakeshop at eight in the morning."

"But you just did, Betty," Jack remarked.

"Okay, listen," I told them. "I do have a bakeshop to run, and we're closing down early for the pie-eating contest. Why don't you all have a seat and wait here a moment. I'm going to help Wendy take care of these fine people"—I gestured to the tourists—"and then I will tell you all I know, which isn't much."

Fifteen minutes later, I returned to the group, which had grown to eight people, and described the events of the morning.

"When we heard the bleating of a goat that early in the morning," I told them, "we thought it was the prankster. Then, when we went to find the goat, we saw that it was in a boat, floating about a hundred yards out from the lighthouse. The poor thing was beside itself with fear. Wellington began to swim out to it, so we took Rory's boat out to get Welly and tow the other boat back to Rory's dock. However, when we reached the goat's boat, we discovered a body lying in the bottom of it. Again, we thought it might be a prank because the body was dressed like a Viking, or what we imagined to be a Viking."

"A Viking?" Rod Jeffers repeated, thinking he had misheard me. I nodded, confirming that he hadn't.

"Why was he dressed like Viking?" Bill asked.

I shrugged. "That's part of the mystery. We don't know why, but I'm sure it has something to do with his death."

Betty looked horrified, and rightly so. "What on earth?"

"I thought it was a dummy," I admitted. "In fact, I was really hoping it was a dummy. Yet when we finally towed the boat back to Rory's dock and had a good look at it, I saw that it was Lars Jorgenson. That's when I called the police."

Everyone was speechless.

"Who would want to kill that dear old man?" Betty cried with a pained look on her face. "And the humiliation of dressing him like a Viking to boot!"

I held up my hand. "Betty, I didn't say that he was killed. All I said was that his body was found in the bottom of a boat."

"Afloat with a goat," Roger added, shaking his head in sorrow. "Sorry about that. It just rhymes so well." He shrugged. "Poor old Lars."

Betty shook her head. "That's a load of hooey! Honey, he might have been a few donuts short of a dozen, but he wasn't crazy. This smells like murder to me."

"Murder?" The word rippled through the café, catching everyone off-guard, including new customers coming through the door.

"We don't know that," I cautioned, lowering my voice. But my words fell on deaf ears. Betty was convinced it was murder, and the others were coming around to her way of thinking. I also knew that with Betty at the helm of the Beacon Harbor gossip mill, news of Lars Jorgenson's death would spread through the town like wildfire. It was just one more worry in a day that already had me on edge. After all, the prankster was still out there, and the blueberry pie–eating contest was sure to be the scene of the final, public humiliation of the festival. I had no idea what was in store for me. All I could do was run my event and pray for the best.

CHAPTER 18

"Bakewell!"

The sound of the familiar, yet startling voice caught me off-guard. Welly, apparently, thought it an invitation to investigate, and trotted out of the tent to greet the sergeant as she came up the walkway. I had been so busy setting up tables and chairs under the tent that was soon to be the site of the blueberry pie–eating contest that I had nearly forgotten about the body. Nearly, I darkly mused, because every customer who came out of the bakeshop had felt it his or her duty to cross the lawn, enter the tent, and question me further about my gruesome early-morning discovery. It became such an annoyance that Tom and Ryan, who were helping me, began insisting that the nosy visitors pick up a chair and unfold it while I answered their questions. I had to hand it to those industrious young men. Due to their quick thinking, we were nearly done with the setup for the pie-eating contest. However, I had forgotten that Sergeant Murdock might need to question me further about the body.

I straightened up and followed Welly out of the tent and onto the blanket of lush grass to meet Sergeant Murdock. It was another spectacular summer day in Beacon Harbor, with clear skies, low humidity, and nearly eighty degrees already. A slight breeze coming off the lake would help with the heat as the day wore on.

"Hello, Sergeant," I offered with a smile. "I hope your investigation is going well."

Welly had gotten to her before me and was receiving a much friendlier greeting from the woman than I had ever gotten. Although, admittedly, it would have seemed odd had she fluffed the hair on my head too. I'd settle for a smile and a wave. Or just a smile. I guess finding another body had really ruffled her feathers.

Murdock finally looked up from my dog. With a finger, she brushed a wispy lock of hair out of her forthright brown eyes. Unfortunately, they were still humorless. "I wouldn't say that it's going well, Bakewell, but it is going." She tilted her head in the manner people do when they have something interesting to say. "By my count, this is the fourth time you and Campbell have reported a body."

Oooh, not interesting, but accusatory. I hit her with, "Lucky for you we came along when we did, or all those bodies might have gone unreported." I had meant it as a joke. Perhaps adding a smile was not the best choice of facial expressions under the circumstances.

"Before you came along, Bakewell, most of the deaths in this village were due to natural causes."

"And most of the baked goods came from the grocery

store. Look," I said, offering a proverbial olive branch, "while I see how it might be easy to make such a leap regarding these recent deaths, it wouldn't be very professional of you to glom onto a nebulous correlation like this, especially since you already know the real murderers have been caught. I hope you're not insinuating that Rory or I had anything to do with poor Mr. Jorgenson this morning. Rory was quite fond of him, you know, and Lars was quite fond of my baking. Therefore, neither of us has a motive to kill him."

Murdock dropped her guard for a brief second, becoming almost human. "I'm sorry if I sound a bit gruff. It's just . . . this whole matter is troubling."

She ran a critical eye over the venue for the Blueberry Festival's final event and returned her gaze back to me. "I realize you have an event coming up within the hour. The reason I'm here, Bakewell, is because I need you to take me over to the exact spot on the beach where you and Campbell spotted the boat this morning."

I nodded in understanding and gestured for her to follow Welly and me as we crossed the lawn and walked around to the back of the lighthouse. Welly, happy to be free of the business side of the building where he was always put on his best behavior, trotted over to the thick weeds and wind-swept bushes on the side of the boathouse to do his business. While he wandered away, I directed Murdock's attention to the second story of the lighthouse, particularly to a couple of open windows sitting under dormers that jutted from the red-shingled, mansard roof. "Those are my bedroom windows up there," I told her. "It's been so lovely at night that I've been sleeping with the windows open. That's probably the only reason we heard the goat at all."

Murdock looked at the windows in question and made a note in her notebook.

"Those two"—she pointed to the other windows with her pen—"are those from Ms. Kapoor's room?"

"Kennedy?" I raised a brow at this. "No. That's a bathroom and another guest room. Kennedy's room faces the other side of the lighthouse." I had no idea why she'd asked this, so I chalked it up to curiosity.

Murdock, seemingly satisfied with this answer, proceeded to study the lighthouse grounds, finally settling her gaze on the sizeable outbuilding that had once been a boathouse but was now being used as my garage. Welly reemerged from the bushes to join us.

"Mind if I have a look in there?" Murdock asked.

"Not at all. But aside from my Jeep, some old lighthouse fixtures, and Christmas decorations, it's mostly empty."

"Do you own a boat?" Her hand was poised on the handle of the solid access door as she asked this.

"No. Why?"

"No reason. I just assumed that since you live in a lighthouse, you'd have a boat."

"I don't. Not yet, at any rate. I've been too busy running my business to even think about buying one. Anyhow, Rory has a boat."

"Convenient," she remarked and walked through the door.

I didn't know why she wanted to take a look at the boathouse, but I could only assume she was looking for some scrap of evidence that might link me to the crime scene. I knew enough about Sergeant Stacy Murdock to know she was as sharp-eyed as she was prickly. Unless I was totally ignorant of the goings-on in my boathouse, I was fairly confident the beautiful wooden boat the body had been found in hadn't resided on my property. However, a drop or two of panic sweat began beading on my brow. My inner critic posed the question, *What if it had and I hadn't known?* The converted two-car garage I used took up less than half of the building. The other side I didn't pay much attention to. *Oh*, I chided myself, *what a silly thought!* Of course, I'd know if there'd been a boat in my boathouse. Right? Just to be sure, I scanned the floor for traces of sawdust or wood shavings.

"Aside from that old Fresnel lens over in the corner and the pile of boxes containing your Christmas lights, this place is spotless." I detected a hint of disappointment in Murdock's voice as she said this.

"Thank you. You look annoyed."

"I am. I was certain you were a closet hoarder. The lighthouse always looks so tidy and perfect, I was sure you had a stash of garage sale fodder and random junk in here." To shock me even further, a smile touched her lips.

"I'm a single woman who moved from a two-bedroom high-rise apartment in New York City to a rambling light-house with four bedrooms and enough space for a bakery café. In short, I have more space than I know what to do with."

"Wish I had that problem. With three growing kids and Brian spending more time at my house than his, the Murdock household is getting crowded." Murdock seldom talked of her personal life. That's why I couldn't keep from smiling at the way she talked of her longtime boyfriend, Brian Brigalow.

"How is Brian?" I asked. "Any thoughts on making that relationship permanent?"

She shot me a hardened stare—a natural defense—but then let her guard down a measure.

"Don't know." She shrugged. "Thinking about it. You'll be the first to know if I do."

"Really?" The shock of it made me warm toward her even more. I had no idea our friendship had progressed beyond her professional suspicion to, well, friends.

"That was a joke, Bakewell," she added, deflating my ballooning thoughts. "But don't worry. I like you." Shifting her attention back to my boathouse, she added, "You have a lot of space in here. This would make a great place for a microbrewery."

I laughed. "Maybe in my spare time. For now, I'll keep it as an overly large garage for my Jeep."

"Just a thought," she added with a grin as we left the building.

I next took the sergeant for a walk down the undulating shoreline as Wellington bounded ahead of us on the sand. On this side of the lighthouse sat a beautiful, wild stretch of pristine beach, with the sun-kissed waters of Lake Michigan on one side, and small, rolling dunes on the other. Where the dunes ended, the forest began, growing thick in the low areas and covering the gentle hillsides and bluffs farther inland and down the coastline. Rory's home was farther down the beach and around the point, which wasn't visible this close to the lighthouse. However, it was very visible from the light room, which was where I had first spotted the home of my closest neighbor many months ago, never imagining the person who lived in the charming log home would be spending so much time with me. I pushed the pleasant thought from my mind as I came to a stop on the beach. Welling-

ton, as if remembering his predawn adventures, sniffed
the ground as he trotted through sand and surf, pulling to
a stop at the exact place where he'd gone into the water
after the goat.

"That's it," I said, walking over to my dog. "The boat
was about a hundred yards out on the lake, just there. It
was facing south, so in my mind I believed it had come
from somewhere farther up north. It hadn't yet rounded
Lighthouse Point. But I could be wrong. It could have
come from way offshore and drifted in." I shrugged, remembering the odd sight.

I watched as Murdock snapped a few pictures with her
phone, then wandered down the beach farther to see if
there were any more suspicious tracks.

"We looked for a sail in the boat, or a sign of a motor,"
she told me, as we headed back to the lighthouse. "When
the coroner's people removed the body, we saw that the
boat was fitted for a sail, but there wasn't any indication
of one in the boat. There were also oarlocks, indicating
that it could have been rowed out onto the lake, but we
haven't found any oars yet. I'm asking you to keep an eye
out for those. If you find anything suspicious, call me."

"Will do," I said, then faced the sergeant. "Do you
think Mr. Jorgenson was murdered?"

She paused a moment before answering, likely pondering how much to tell me, knowing that I had a habit of
sticking my nose where it didn't belong. However, I
could tell the manner of this death had gotten to her as
well. She finally glanced my way and relented.

"It's highly possible. However, there is some evidence
to suggest it might be suicide we're dealing with instead.
And we haven't ruled out a natural death either. In the
case of natural death, however, the fact that Mr. Jorgen-

son was found dressed as a Viking while lying at the bottom of a boat suggests there might have been somebody with him. We won't know for sure what happened until Doc Riggles examines the body. He's ordered a full autopsy and toxicology screen to be done Monday morning. Any way you look at it, Bakewell, it's sad business." She shook her head.

"I agree. But what evidence do you have that suggests Mr. Jorgenson might have committed suicide?"

"Mr. Jorgenson was a large man. He's six-foot-four and well over two hundred pounds. It's doubtful somebody took the time to dress him like that after his death. They'd either have to be very strong, or there was more than one person involved. Then there's the matter of putting the body aboard the boat. Again, not an easy task for one person. The entire scene—and I hesitate to say 'crime scene,' because the boat likely wasn't the scene of the crime—is highly suspicious. However, as we both know, anything is possible."

"True. I never thought about that." I made a mental note of all she was telling me as we walked.

"Then there's the matter of the goat," she offered, shaking her head in puzzlement. "Doubtful a murderer would put a goat in the boat with a body—not unless whoever it was wanted the body to be found. You said the goat woke you and Rory?"

"The goat woke me and Welly," I corrected. "I woke Rory. Given his military history, and his at-the-ready attitude, he's a surprisingly heavy sleeper."

"So, the goat woke *you*." For some reason she found this interesting. "Well, that's part of the reason I'm here as well. Anders Jorgenson is on his way to the morgue to identify his father's body. I've asked him to meet me at the police station when he's done. I'd like to see if he can identify the goat as well."

"Good thinking," I told her, and stared at her a bit too long.

"I came to pick it up, Bakewell. I'm going to need you to get it for me."

"Oh," I said in a very noncommittal tone.

"I thought it might have been in your boathouse. Clearly it's too clean in there to be harboring a goat."

"It's a boathouse, not a goathouse," I joked. When she didn't so much as lift a corner of her lip in response, I got the message. "You want me to get the goat now."

Murdock hit me with her dark, suspicious eyes. "Will that be a problem? Can't imagine you're already attached to the thing. It's not yours, Bakewell. We don't know whose it is, but I do need to see if Lars's son can recognize the animal."

"No. No problem," I assured her. "I'll just, ahh . . ." I cast a look at the lighthouse, hoping the goat was still in Kennedy's room. Funny, but I'd been working so hard in the bakery that I suddenly realized I hadn't heard any goat noises in quite some time. Turning back to the sergeant, I continued, "I'll just run inside and get her for you."

"Do that, Bakewell."

I left the sergeant in the rear parking lot next to her cruiser and ran to find Kennedy and the goat. I returned a few minutes later, puzzled and empty-handed. Murdock, noting that I didn't have the goat with me, leaned against her cruiser and crossed her arms. It was a very intimidating pose coming from her.

However, intimidation wasn't going to work on this big city girl. I called forth my Lindsey-tude and hit her with the obvious. "So, I have a bit of bad news. I couldn't find her."

"Her?"

"The goat is a she. I forgot to tell you. I've checked." Although I thought this was a bit of good detective work, she obviously didn't. Murdock raised a brow, or at least I think she did. It was hard to tell because her bangs were so long.

"You've checked?" The way she said it made me feel dirty. I shook it off as she added, "So, where is she?"

"I'm not sure."

"Don't tell me you've already lost the goat?" Her small, grim-set mouth puckered with displeasure. The effect caused a slight shiver to shoot up my spine.

"Oh, no." I waved a hand, attempting to put her at ease. "She's not lost. Did I say she was lost? I didn't mean to give you that impression. The goat is perfectly fine. She's with Kennedy."

"What!?"

This really got her. I hadn't expected such a violent re-action at the mention of my friend. The fact that it was so violent caused me to realize Murdock might have been a little miffed that one of her best officers had his head turned by my posh, beautiful friend.

"Are you telling me, Bakewell, that you took the goat I entrusted to you and you gave it to—to a flighty, self-centered fashion influencer to watch?"

It was exactly what I was trying to tell her. Honestly, I hadn't given much thought to what I was going to do with the goat once I had taken her back to the lighthouse. But I did know that Kennedy would look after her. I didn't know why Murdock made it sound like such a bad idea.

"Look, Kennedy is a very responsible person. She's an

industry unto herself. And she was happy to look after the goat."

"I'll take your word for it. Where are they, Bakewell?"

I shrugged. "I don't know. And I wish I had time to hunt her down for you, but I have a blueberry pie–eating contest to attend to that's about to start in"—I checked my watch and nearly had a heart attack as I blurted—"ten minutes! Call Tuck," I advised her, running for the kitchen door with Wellington fast on my heels. "If anyone knows where she is, it's Tuck. Better yet, he has her on speed-dial. Hope you find the goat!" I called back, then disappeared with my dog through the door, relieved I was no longer the sole focus of Murdock's extreme displeasure.

CHAPTER 19

"Glad you could make it," Dad teased, spotting me as I ran through the kitchen door. "Whoa, slow down, kiddo," he advised with a grin. "Everything's fine. We have it under control. The tables are all set up, Ellie and Elizabeth are manning the registration table, and most of the contestants have arrived and are already wearing their complimentary bibs and T-shirts."

"Really? Thanks. What a relief." I paused to take a breath. "Say, you haven't seen Kennedy and a goat anywhere, have you?"

Dad lifted a dark eyebrow in question. "The goat you found in the boat this morning?"

"That would be the one."

"Honestly, no. I think Ellie told me that Kennedy was managing the store this morning."

Why did that make me nervous? Oh, right. Because

she was supposed to be watching the goat, which was now crime scene evidence and an object to be identified by the deceased's next of kin.

"She didn't say anything about the goat?"

"Nope. And I haven't heard a goat either, which should make you happy. After all, besides the bake sale, beer tent, and the farmer's market, this is the last scheduled event of the festival. No goat noises means—"

"—that the pranksters have already tried that one. And mice are off the table too."

Dad, sensing that I was nervous, pursed his lips. "Lindsey, everything is going to be just fine. Your family is here to help. And your boyfriend has returned as well. You'll be happy to hear that I put him on guard duty. Take Wellington out there too. He was planning to walk the dog around the perimeter with him, as a deterrent."

"Good thinking," I said, feeling much better for knowing that Rory had returned.

"I was just coming to get the pies in case you were going to be detained further by Sergeant Murdock. How did it go, by the way?" he asked as he made his way to the walk-in refrigerator. I pulled Welly through the kitchen, shooed him into the café, and followed Dad to the walk-in.

"Murdock's still not sure what happened," I told him as I unlocked the door. The blueberry pies were all there, neatly stacked on the shelves of the rolling bakery racks, just as they had been last night when I had put them in there to cool. "It could be murder, suicide, or an odd natural death—like a sudden heart attack while rowing a boat with a goat while dressed as a Viking—only they haven't found the oars." I shook my head at the absurdity of how that sounded.

"Who are we to judge how a man spends his free time?" Dad grinned as he said this, but then another thought came to him. "Maybe he was a reenactor, you know, like those Civil War reenactors? They dress in period clothing, use period tools and utensils, and even talk like they did during the eighteen-hundreds. They really get into character."

"You know, I never thought of it. But you could be right. After all, it's pretty well acknowledged, although still debated in some circles, that the Viking, Leif Erikson, was the first European to set foot on North America—a thousand years before Columbus. The surname, Jorgenson, definitely has a Norse ring to it. I've never heard of a Viking reenactment here in Michigan, but what do I know?" I shrugged. "I'm still learning about the quirks of Michiganders. That's what they call people who live in Michigan, you know."

Then, however, I remembered the one little detail Rory had discovered, evidence that a fire arrow had been shot into the boat in what he had termed an "historically inaccurate interpretation" of a Viking funeral. Or maybe it was a reenactment gone wrong. Whatever had occurred in that boat, it was going to stay a mystery awhile longer.

"Doc Riggles should have some answers after examining the body," I told him. "Did you check these for signs of tampering this morning?" I thought to ask. After all, Dad had been the first baker in the kitchen.

"I did. Everything looked fine to me."

I personally checked all thirty pies again, not because I didn't trust Dad, but because the bakeshop had been open all morning, and the pranksters could have snuck into the kitchen while my staff was serving customers and I was outside busy setting up the tables and chairs or walking with the sergeant down the beach. However, it was just as

Dad said. The pies looked beautifully baked and thank-fully untouched, leaving me to believe that they were not going to be the target of this prank. At least I didn't think they would be.

After removing the extra pies from the bakery rack, Dad helped me roll the remaining twenty blueberry pies out of the bakeshop, with Welly following us. The mo-ment we hit the walkway, I stopped. Just like the night before at Grayson Smythe's unveiling, a larger-than-expected crowd had gathered on the lawn, covering nearly every bit of grass. The sight of the crowd sparked a sudden wave of panic to wash through me.

"Are all these people here just to see twenty contes-tants attempt to eat an entire blueberry pie?" I croaked. I was sure my eyes were as wide as saucers.

"I'd like to believe they're here for the right reasons, you know, to cheer these brave yet crazy gastro-athletes on. It is the Blueberry Festival, after all, and this is the last official event of the weekend. But, well . . ." His voice trailed off.

Dad didn't have to finish his sentence. Because at that moment Betty, who had volunteered to help me judge the event, spotted us and waved. "The pies have arrived! The pies have arrived," she shouted, making sure every head turned in our direction.

The crowd was not stingy. A loud, collective cheer went up as the pies were spotted. Dad and I waved as we continued rolling them to their inglorious doom. I low-ered my voice and whispered, "They're just here waiting to see what final humiliation the pranksters have up their sleeves for us." The mere thought kicked my Lindsey-tude to life. "What in heaven's name is going to happen to us?"

"My dear," Dad said, peering at me from the other side of the rack, "you don't have time to worry about that now. You've baked twenty beautiful blueberry pies. There's an equal number of people sitting at that table who are about to attempt to eat one in record time. Your only job is to concentrate on running this event. Leave the pranksters to the professionals."

"Which would be me," Rory said, suddenly appearing from behind me. "I've been looking for you, and Wellington." Welly wagged his tail in greeting as Rory clipped his leash onto his collar. Then he kissed me.

"You're a sight for sore eyes," I told him.

"Glad you made it, Linds. After the pie-eating contest, we need to talk."

"Yes," I replied, noting how the death of Lars Jorgenson had taken its toll on him. His handsome face looked pale and drawn at the edges, and his bright aqua-blue eyes had a hardened appearance, rimmed as they were with dark circles. My heart went out to him, knowing that he had spent the morning with Anders.

"Are you going to be okay?" I asked in a whisper.

His eyes filled with intensity. "I'm fine. But if our pranksters dare to appear here, they'll regret it."

I had no doubt that they would. Feeling safer, and filling with confidence, I turned to the contestants. "Alright, who's ready to eat some pie?"

The pies were placed before each contestant, who ranged in age from eighteen to sixty. Most were men, but there were a few hearty women in there, trying their hand at devouring a whole nine-inch pie. I wished them all good luck, letting them know that failure to devour an entire pie was not a sign of weakness, but prudence. This received a laugh from the crowd.

The rules for the contest were simple: The first person to finish their entire pie and stand up from the table would be the winner. The one caveat was that hands were to remain behind the back at all times. Failure to do so would mean disqualification. Once every contestant knew what was required of them, the bell was rung, and the timer started.

The pies were attacked with reckless abandon as teeth chomped through crust and tongues splattered blueberry filling across the table. I had never seen pigs eat but felt that even they might have been repulsed by the sight. However, the crowd loved it and cheered the epic eaters on.

"This is not going to be easy," I said to Betty, who was judging the group to my left.

"Don't worry, dear. Outright cheating aside, there's only one man up here who can eat a whole pie in one sitting. Everyone else is just doing it for fun and a free pie, you know, getting into the spirit of the contest and the festival. However, most people will stop before they vomit. I say 'most.' That large man sitting in James's section will win. Erik Owens, is his name. You wouldn't know it to look at him but trust me. He's from Empire. I've seen him eat thirty hot dogs in ten minutes during Pioneer Days."

"Oooh, that's disturbing."

She nodded in agreement as she tapped a young man on the shoulder, disqualifying him for using his hands. "It's far from the world record," she continued. "But around here, it's sure something."

"*Something* is the right word," I teased, shaking my head at the thought.

Leave it to Betty to be correct about the man from Empire. Most of the contestants had given up after eating a quarter of their pie or were still nose-deep in the process when Erik Owens stood up from the table, his blueberry-covered face looking triumphant.

"We have a winner!" Dad declared, having stopped his timer the moment the man stood. "A whole blueberry pie eaten in one minute and eighteen seconds! That's . . . amazing!"

Again, the crowd cheered. I cheered too. It wasn't until after the gift certificates and the participation medals had been given out that I realized the blueberry pie–eating contest had gone off without a hitch. Rory, having walked with Wellington through the onlookers while the contest had been in full swing, reappeared with my dog once again, shortly after the winner had been announced. He gave me a thumbs-up, which I took to mean that we were all-clear, the pranksters had never shown up. As Welly and a few other dogs came to help with the clean-up, I was still suspicious. Then, however, as the crowd began to wander away, I heaved a sigh of relief.

It was a successful end to the events of the weekend, and yet I had the feeling the crowd felt sightly cheated by the lack of chaos and drama. I, for one, was glad of it. Yet there was something about the omission of a clever prank on my event that left me feeling unsettled. I knew what it was, but I didn't want to admit it. And yet I could see that Rory had come to the same conclusion. As Mom, Dad, Betty, and my wonderful staff at the Beacon worked to clean up the mess under the tent, I walked over to Rory.

"Why do I feel a sense of doom for not being pranked?"

"The trouble is, I think you were pranked earlier this morning," he said, acknowledging my worst fear. "Lindsey, what kind of sick mind are we dealing with?"

I honestly didn't know. But the thought left me hollow and cold inside.

CHAPTER 20

With the tables and chairs under the tent all put away and ready for the tent rental company to pick up, and with the rest of the blueberry baked goods off to the bake sale in the capable hands of Alaina and Ryan, and with Mom and Dad off to their house to prepare for their annual Sunday cookout—this one celebrating the end to the blueberry festival—I was finally able to pull Rory aside for a private word. I really wanted to hear about the rest of his morning, and what thoughts he had on the death of Lars Jorgenson.

I'll admit that when I'd heard the goat so early in the morning, I thought the pranksters had struck. Since I was the last person on the festival committee, the entire town knew I was next in line to receive an unwelcome surprise. And what more unwelcome surprise could I have had than what we found in those dark moments before dawn?

I looked at Rory again. Due to his military training, he had the unique ability of remaining calm under pressure. I really admired that. However, acting wasn't a skill he possessed. Watching him help clean up the horrific mess of the blueberry pie–eating contest, he had tried his best to appear interested. He even smiled as he congratulated the pie-eating participants and exchanged small pleasantries with friends. However, the tightness in his jaw and the pinched look around his eyes told me he was really struggling with this one. And then another thought arose, one I hadn't even considered. Was there a murderer on the loose in Beacon Harbor? I cringed at the thought.

"How are you holding up?" I asked, placing a hand on his shoulder.

"That mess was disturbing," he said, throwing me off. He then grinned, and I did too.

"Disturbing all around," I agreed.

"It's undoubtedly why they talked the newest member of the Blueberry Festival Committee into hosting it. Next year just say no."

"Sound advice. I'll remember that. Why don't you come inside? I'll fix you a sandwich. I doubt you've had anything to eat today."

"Thanks," he said. "It's been a rough morning. And you're right. I could definitely use something to eat. However, I think lunch is going to have to wait a few minutes longer."

With a question on my face, I looked to where he pointed. Welly, still stuck on "sandwich," was staring at Rory, knowing he'd get at least a nibble or two from the table. I found it amazing, especially after he'd gobbled up chunks of crust and tried to lick up the blueberry goo before the sponges came out. However, the moment Welly saw Officer Tuck walking toward the tent leading an animal on a leash, he barked and bounded off to greet them.

"That's . . . not the same goat," I remarked, having a hard time reconciling what I was seeing.

"Well, it's mostly white," Rory remarked. "And Welly seems to recognize it. I suppose one goat is as good as another."

I gently slapped his arm while making a face at him. "I don't remember it having a glittering rainbow mane as long as a horse's. Nor were its hooves a shimmering pink. They've literally been painted with glitter! That's definitely not the same animal we found this morning."

"I agree. The goat we found in that boat wasn't wearing bling—at least not that I remember." Rory crossed his arms, watching his friend try to walk the goat to the tent. It wasn't an easy endeavor. "Check out that collar. Is that bell made of real silver, do you think?"

I didn't know what to think. I waved at Tuck and pulled Rory out from under the tent with me to meet him.

"Hello." Although Tuck smiled, he looked embarrassed. "Sergeant Murdock called this morning. She sent me to find the goat." He turned to the goat he was leading, "Which I have."

"Holy mother, that's the same goat?" Genuine shock appeared on Rory's face. "What the heck happened to it?"

"It's been bedazzled."

I covered my mouth and tried not to laugh. I removed my hands long enough to add, "Wow."

"Yep. It's the same goat. I hear that you gave her to Kennedy." He shot me an accusatory look. "I called her asking after the goat and she said that she had it at the store. So, I drove over to Ellie and Company and found her sitting outside at a table with this thing." He pointed to the animal in question. The goat, oblivious, was gently nudging Wellington with its head. "She was letting kids pet it and feed it carrots. She was also selling a lot of collars and pet clothes. When I asked her what she had done with the goat we found this morning, she told me that *this* was that goat." Tuck removed his cap and ran a nervous hand through his short sun-kissed hair. He had the careless good looks of a Ralph Lauren model, with a touch of midwestern farm boy mixed in. He didn't get the name Officer Cutie Pie for nothing. With the cap back on his head, he continued.

"She, umm . . . she thought it needed a good grooming, so she took it to Peggy's Pooch Salon for an emergency Sunday morning groom. I'm not sure whether you're aware of this, but Peggy's been trying her hand at competitive creative dog grooming. I don't even know what that is, but one look at this goat and I can tell that it's not normal."

"I agree," Rory mused aloud.

"I think I know what that is," I said, being the only dog owner among them. "I heard about it when I lived in New York City. I think it's when they take your dog and try to make it look like another animal—like turning a golden retriever into a lion. Clearly this goat is still a goat."

"Is it?" Tuck was a tad snappish as he questioned me. "Because Kennedy told me that Peggy is making it a horn."

"She already has horns, adorable, little swept-back ones. Why is Peggy making this goat another horn?" I cast the officer a questioning look.

"To turn it into a unicorn, of course." This was said with a heavy dose of sarcasm. "I thought that was obvious."

Rory and I looked at one another and shook our heads, trying not to laugh at Tuck's expense.

"And do you know what the worst part is?" Tuck asked.

"It gets worse than this?" Rory added with a straight face. "I can't imagine."

"I brought the goat to the police station so that Anders could identify it. Apparently, Lars Jorgenson did own a goat. However, one look at this thing here, and he shook his head. 'Nope,' he said. 'My dad wouldn't be caught dead with a goat like that.'"

"So, the goat wasn't identified?" My heart sank as a sudden wave of anger swooped in, thinking of Kennedy and her selfish scheme to turn the goat into a marketing oddity.

"Well, actually, it was," Tuck quickly informed me. "Once I explained what happened to the goat, you know, how it was taken in for an emergency grooming, he tried calling it by name."

"It has a name?" I didn't know why, but I found this an exciting break in the case. "Well, don't just stand there. Tell us!"

Tuck removed his cap again, this time holding on to the rim of it with both hands. It occurred to me then that he was in the grip of a powerful emotion. "Her name is Clara," he said softly. "Came right to him when he called her name. Anders looked relieved. He then told us that his dad had bought the goat shortly after his mother had died. Said his dad was very lonely and that he'd always had a fondness for goats. He named her Clara after his wife. Anders said he did that so that he'd never forget her name."

The thought that Lars Jorgenson had kept a goat touched

me, as did the fact that he'd named it after his wife, so he wouldn't forget the goat's name.

"She's a sweet thing," Tuck added with a fond look at the animal in question. He reached between the animal's horns and gave a gentle rub. The goat made a soft noise and leaned her head against his leg. It reminded me of the look Wellington gave me whenever I rubbed his ears. Pure pleasure!

Seeing that Clara the goat was getting more attention than him, Welly inserted himself between the goat and the officer, nudging Tuck's hand.

"Is Welly jealous?" he asked my dog. Welly's answer was another nudge to his hand. After giving both animals a little love, Tuck straightened. "Anyhow, sad business about Lars Jorgenson."

"Did Anders let on that his dad was sick or anything?" This I thought to ask, in case it had been a natural death. Maybe the goat was used to joining him on the boat?

As soon as the question was out of my mouth, Tuck shook his head. "Lars didn't have a heart issue, cancer, or anything like that, according to Anders. He insisted his father was a healthy older man. The boat also belonged to the deceased. Lars was a carpenter by trade who also dabbled in fine woodworking. However, he didn't know the boat had ever been tested. At least he's never sailed in it."

"Interesting," Rory mused. "The boat had never been placed in the water before?" Tuck shook his head in answer to this.

"And one more thing before I go." Tuck turned to me. "Would you mind keeping the goat a bit longer? Anders and his wife are understandably having a hard time at the moment. They're still trying to wrap their heads around this whole thing. He asked if the goat could stay with you."

I looked at the little white goat that had been partially transformed into a magical unicorn and thought, *Why not?* Welly seemed happy enough with her. What harm could there be in keeping a goat for a few days?

"Leave her with us," I said, taking the leash. Tuck actually breathed a sigh of relief at this. "I'm sure Kennedy will be thrilled with the news."

"She will. Although I caution you not to let her take this"—he gestured to the goat's bedazzlement—"any further. If it is murder, this animal, like it or not, is part of the crime scene. Her appearance has already been altered, which might be a problem. I hope not. Anyhow, thanks, you two. See you guys tonight at the cookout."

And with that Officer Tuck McAllister turned on his heels and left, happy, it seemed, to be rid of the goat.

A short but loud bleat brought me back to my senses. I had a goat!

"Well," Rory began with an ironic twist of his lips, "you said you wanted to keep the goat." He waved his hand in a magical gesture, adding, "Your wish has been granted, m'lady. If baking more than twenty blueberry pies and finding a body haven't been enough for you this weekend, you are now going to have to figure out where to keep Clara, the bedazzled goat."

He took my free hand and led me, the goat, and Welly back to the lighthouse. "I'm famished. You promised lunch. And I have a lot to tell you. But first, where are you planning to keep Clara?"

I shrugged, cursing myself for being such a kindhearted idiot.

CHAPTER 21

Rory was starving, and I had just the thing for him. First, however, I had to rig something up to contain the goat. Although she had been inside the lighthouse earlier in the morning, I didn't want to make a habit of that. Goats, after all, were indiscriminate poopers, and I liked my floors clean. Well, "clean" was a relative term. With a Newfie in the house, there always seemed to be a dust bunny of dog hair hiding out of reach of the vacuum or the odd puddle of drool on the floor, but goat poop was a mess too far. Rory found some rope in the boathouse. While I attached one end to Clara's leash, Rory secured the other end around the trunk of a tree on the bushy side of the boathouse. Clara would have shade and plenty to nibble on should she so choose. And the best part was, we could keep an eye on her from the kitchen window. While

Rory was off fetching a bucket of water, I returned to the lighthouse kitchen and set to work on lunch.

Ryan and I had been talking about making an epic grilled cheese sandwich to offer for lunch in the fall. I loved the fact that all my employees had a lot of input in our menu. It changed often, depending on the season and the availability of fruits and fresh ingredients. Due to Ryan's enthusiasm, and his description of a sandwich he'd once tried in Chicago, I had been experimenting with an apple yeast bread. Essentially it was an enriched white bread with chunks of cooked cinnamon apples incorporated into the dough. It was then baked, resulting in a scrumptious sweetbread that was perfect for toasting. It would also be the base of our epic Gouda melt sandwich that we were still working on. Knowing that Rory was a tried-and-true taste tester, I decided to try it out on him and see what he thought of it.

I took out a loaf of the bread in question, then went to the refrigerator and pulled out the other ingredients I needed. I took out a jar of mayo, butter, thinly sliced deli ham, and thick slices of Gouda cheese. In the pantry I found a can of cranberry sauce. I wouldn't need much of it, but I thought it would make the perfect addition to a sweet, yet tart mayonnaise spread. While my pan was heating on the stove, I sliced the bread, spread half with a cranberry-mayo combo, then placed two thick slices of Gouda on top of it. Next came a generous layer of ham and another two slices of Gouda. This was going to be decadent! With the other slice of bread placed on top, I then put a tablespoon of butter in the pan. Instead of buttering the outsides of my apple bread, I often took a shortcut and just plopped the butter directly into the pan. Once it started melting, I laid the sandwich on top of it and partially covered the pan with a lid. This was to retain more heat without trapping moisture inside the pan. Too much moisture would lead to a soggy sandwich.

Timing and temperature were everything when making grilled cheese. Although it was a simple sandwich to make, the pan needed to be hot enough to melt the butter, but not too hot to burn the bread before the cheese melted. Likewise, if the heat was too low, the bread would be pale and soggy. No, the key to a perfect grilled cheese sandwich was that crisp, buttery-toasted bread on the outside while the inside was warm and gooey. The sweeter apple bread worked amazingly well. The natural sugars in the chunks of apple created a satisfying caramelization, buttery and crisp, with a hint of sweetness. The Gouda melted perfectly while cooking, heating up the thinly sliced ham and blending nicely with the cranberry mayonnaise. I removed it from the pan and placed it on a cutting board, admiring the outcome. The kitchen filled with the fruity essence of the warm bread, the pungent Gouda, and the salty ham. Unfortunately, Rory and Welly walked in right at that moment.

"It smells amazing in here!"

Welly thought so, too, and attempted to lay his nose on the counter, which was a no-no. I gently pushed his nose off the counter and plated the sandwich for Rory. "You said you were hungry, and I have a new sandwich I wanted to try out. Hope you don't mind."

He walked over to my quaint kitchen table and took a seat. "As I've said before, use me all you want, Bakewell. That's what I'm here for. This sandwich smells amazing."

"Gouda and ham on grilled apple bread," I supplied, placing the plate before him.

"Where's your sandwich?"

"I'm waiting to see what happens to you first." I grinned.

He took it as a challenge. After the first bite, his eyes rolled back in his head as he let out a soft moan of ecstasy. The sound hit me like a cold wave washing over hot sand—refreshing, invigorating, and, yes, erotic. Was that what I'd been waiting for? Yes, yes, it was. Dangit! What was wrong with me? Apparently, Welly had the same issue, only his motivation for staring at his second-favorite human was far different than mine. Welly was so focused on the cheese oozing from the toasted bread that he was actually drooling.

"Welly!" I chided. "Lie down!" Rory slipped him a piece of bread before he did what he was told.

"Well, I suppose I'll join you."

"You won't be sorry," he said with a grin. "This is hands-down the best grilled cheese I've ever had."

A few minutes later, I joined him with my own half sandwich—just enough to tide me over until the cookout—and two glasses of lemonade. "Okay," I said. "Tell me about your morning."

Knowing what it was like to lose both his parents, Rory had requested to be the one to break the news to Anders Jorgenson. It had been an emotional morning. Anders, seeing Rory on his doorstep, had assumed the visit was a friendly one. When he and his wife, Susan, learned the real reason for the visit, they could barely comprehend the death, let alone the odd circumstances that had surrounded it. Disbelief, denial, anger—it was all there. Anders was certain there had to be some mistake. He told Rory he had taken his dad home that night after the fireworks, and swore the old man was fine. It was late. His dad liked to get to bed early. There was no way he'd take a boat out on the lake so late at night.

Regarding the small Viking craft, Rory had very little to add to Tuck McAllister's original statement. Anders said his father had built it, but to his knowledge, Lars hadn't ever taken it out for its maiden voyage. Regarding the whole Viking theme, Anders told Rory that Lars had been born in Norway, and while his dad had a fondness for Viking lore, as a matter of cultural pride, he wasn't in the habit of dressing the part.

"He told me that Lars was a stubborn, headstrong man," Rory said. "That's why when Lars's wife passed away three years ago, the family moved back here to be with him. Anders is the only child and felt it was his duty. I offered to drive him to the morgue to identify the body, but Anders insisted on going alone.

"My father struggled with cancer," Rory added. "I knew what was coming, and yet nothing prepares you for the death of a parent. But watching Anders struggle with the news of his father's death . . ." There was genuine sorrow on his face as he spoke. "It was a shock—the furthest thing from his mind. No wonder he was in denial." Rory inhaled and sat back in his chair. His intense blue gaze held mine. "It doesn't make sense, Lindsey. My gut tells me that Lars Jorgenson was murdered."

I covered his hand with mine. "We won't know for sure, but I feel the same way." I paused to take a sip of lemonade, thinking all the while. "If he was murdered, who would want him dead?"

"The prankster or pranksters. Lars must have done something to our mystery prankster to really tick them off—enough to murder the man and dress him up like a Viking."

"The whole Viking thing, it speaks of a lot of prep and planning. A lot of effort went into staging that death scene. Is it okay if I call it a death scene?"

Rory shrugged. "There was a good deal of planning and preparation that went into all the pranks this weekend. Arguably Lars Jorgenson's was the most elaborate."

"With the smallest audience," I added, thinking. "The prank played on Betty was done to her lawn. It could be argued that it was done for her benefit alone, but let's be honest. Everyone who drove by her house was affected by it."

"Had a good laugh too," he added. "Blocking the road and diverting traffic through her circular drive was a clever touch." Having finished his own lemonade, he grabbed mine and took a sip.

"I told you I'd be happy to refill your glass."

He shook his head. "I like sharing." He set down the glass and picked up his train of thought. "But Lars's death—the Viking ship? That was meant to be seen by you. Think of it. It's a well-known fact that since you've moved to Beacon Harbor, you've found three bodies and helped solve two crimes."

"Don't forget that you were with me too. And Lars Jorgenson was in your Friday morning group. There's a personal connection to you as well," I pointed out.

Stroking his chin, I could tell he was entertaining the possibility. "So, whoever is behind these pranks knows that you and I are dating—"

"Which is basically the whole village," I interjected.

He continued seamlessly. "They know we both spend a lot of time in this lighthouse. And they know we've found bodies before."

"Again, it's not a secret around here. If somebody purposely killed Lars Jorgenson with the intent of floating the body past the lighthouse to be discovered by us, it really could be anyone. Oh," I said, as a thought suddenly popped into my head. "Whoever is behind this is a local."

"Well, yes. I thought that was obvious."

I took back my lemonade and drained the cup. "Okay, but I have another thought. Before you say anything, hear me out on this. I know that Lars was an older gentleman, but what if . . . what if he was our prankster, and somebody found out?"

I felt a small welling of pride when I realized this thought had never occurred to Rory. Ha! Maybe I did have a knack for crime-solving.

My victory, however, was short-lived. His narrow-eyed skepticism sucked the wind from my proverbial sails. "Lindsey, that's ridiculous," he remarked. "Lars Jorgenson was a sweet, older man. According to Anders, Lars wasn't keeping his house up as usual. It was getting too much for him. I seriously doubt Lars would have had the strength or the stamina to pull off pranks of the scope and nature we've seen."

I only had one fact up my sleeve to back my theory. "Whenever there was a prank, I distinctly heard him laughing. You have to admit, Lars loved to laugh."

"True, he was laughing, but he wasn't the only one. That hardly makes him our prankster."

"Okay. Well, how about this. After discovering his body this morning, the pranks stopped. If you'll recall, the blueberry pie–eating contest went off without a hitch. It was the only event during the weekend to escape the hand of the prankster, which makes me wonder. If Lars Jorgenson was the blueberry festival prankster, and somebody found out about it—somebody he pranked—wouldn't that make sense?"

Loyalty ran deep in Rory Campbell. It was one of the traits that made him so attractive to me, and yet it was the very reason the poor man was having a hard time wrapping his head around the possibility that one of his beloved fellow veterans could be behind the shenanigans at the festival.

I watched as he finished the last bite of his Gouda melt in silence, slowly chewing as if he didn't want the experience to end. Then he brought his troubled blue gaze back to me. "It's highly doubtful," he said. "The pranks stopped because Lars's death was the final prank. However, because I like you, Bakewell, I'll consider your theory as well." His smile was disarming, and yet the thought he felt that my theory wasn't sound rankled a bit.

"Fine. I guess we have ourselves a real mystery here. Just what we need. As if we don't have enough on our plates already!"

He stood up from the table and walked around to give me a kiss. "I didn't think you could just sit this one out, especially since we we're the ones who found the body."

"Where are you going?" I asked. Wellington had popped up from his place under the table and followed Rory to the door. Clearly, they were up to something.

"I'm off to fashion a makeshift goat pen before the cookout. Can't leave that quasi-unicorn tied to a tree all day."

"Where are you going to put her?"

"Don't worry about it. I got this." And with that, Rory and Welly slipped out the door.

CHAPTER 22

Finding myself alone in my kitchen once again, I decided to whip up another cookout dish to pass beside the blueberry pies I had promised Mom. Although the Beacon Harbor Blueberry Festival had ended, my devotion to the small, piquant, and delicious berry was endless. Also, I had extra blueberries on hand and didn't want them to go to waste. Therefore, I decided to make my favorite blueberry salad and bring that as well. I called it my Blueberry Summer Salad—a salad nearly as delicious as a blueberry pie, yet arguably healthier. Besides, working in the kitchen always helped me relax and think more clearly. After the day I'd just had, I needed another bout of cooking therapy now more than ever!

I took down my largest glass salad bowl, then went to

the refrigerator to get out my ingredients. Since I was making the salad for at least ten people, I intended to scale the recipe up to size. To my way of thinking, unlike baking, which generally required a stricter adherence to a recipe, salads were more freeform dishes. That was the beauty of a salad. If you didn't like a certain ingredient, you could just omit it, and no one would be the wiser. Likewise, if you loved, let's say, tomatoes, and you were making a classic Caesar salad, which didn't call for tomatoes, by all means, add the tomatoes! Going rogue when making a salad was not only fun, it was also delicious!

The main ingredients in my Blueberry Summer Salad included a large bag of triple-washed baby spinach, which I put in the bowl, filling it nearly to the top. I then added two cups (and a dash more) of washed, fresh blueberries, and marveled at how pretty they looked on top of the vibrant green baby spinach. But I wasn't done yet. I next pulled out a hunk of Danish blue cheese and crumbled a cup of it on top of the blueberries and spinach. With that done, I then took a zip-lock bag out of my fridge that contained toasted pecans. I loved toasted pecans and usually had a bag of them ready for my favorite recipes. I measured out a cup of the nuts, gave them a light chop under a sharp knife, then sprinkled them on top of the salad. That was it for the salad. I covered the bowl with plastic wrap and began to make the dressing.

I really enjoyed making salad dressing. Homemade salad dressing wasn't hard to make, and it always tasted better. My Blueberry Summer Salad was no different. I took out my blender and added the simple ingredients— one green onion chopped, one teaspoon of salt, three tablespoons of sugar, one cup of vegetable oil, one-third cup of raspberry vinegar, and one cup of blueberries. Then the entire thing was blended to a smooth, rich, beautiful light purple dressing that resembled blueberry yogurt, but tasted so much better.

I had just transferred the dressing into a small container when Kennedy waltzed through the door.

"That looks delicious," she said, gesturing to the salad.

"It's for the cookout. I had extra blueberries and suddenly remembered that, as far as I knew, you hadn't volunteered to bring anything."

"Guilty as charged." She leaned against my kitchen island and cast me a pouty look of apology. "I should have offered. However, it might have slipped my mind, having assumed that you and I were looked upon as a couple, you know, you're the one who cooks, so you bring the dish to pass, while I bring the party-girl fun."

"I'm sure the entire village already knows that. I just thought, since you took such good care of the goat after I pawned her off on you, that I owed you. I made you a salad to bring."

Her smile this time was genuine. "You know, you really are the best, Linds. I have to apologize. I might have gone a little overboard on the goat-grooming incident. In my defense, the poor thing smelled terrible and looked like she could use a good grooming. Besides, I felt she was a little down in the mouth, having gone sailing the night before with a dead body. I thought a trip to the goat spa with some extra TLC would set her up nicely. It always makes me feel better."

"I never thought of a pet groomer as a spa for the animals. It's more a relief for us humans."

"True. And in my defense, it was Peggy's idea. She was rather excited to try her grooming skills on a goat.

She usually sticks to dogs and the occasional cat, or so she told me. I gave her a hundred dollars and told her to work her magic. She might have taken me literally."

"Well, the woman has skills. She turned Clara into a unicorn," I remarked.

"Clara?"

"That's her name. Unfortunately, the goat was so clean and so bedazzled that Anders nearly didn't recognize her when he was asked to identify her this morning. However, I'm told that once he said her name, she trotted right over to him. That's how they knew it was the same goat."

Her dark eyes narrowed with remorse at the thought of Clara nearly going unrecognized. "I did think Peggy might have gone a wee overboard. But I encouraged her. Then, once I picked the goat up and saw how beautiful she looked, I just couldn't resist dressing her up and parading her in front of the store. The shoppers adored her." Kennedy tilted her head then, allowing her glossy black hair to fall over her shoulder. "Clara is a beautiful name for a unicorn."

"A goat," I corrected, "but I agree. It was the name of Lars Jorgenson's late wife. I was told he named the goat after her so he wouldn't forget its name."

"No offense, but I'm not sure that naming a goat after one's wife is a compliment. Also, no one is going to believe I made that gorgeous salad."

True, I thought, on both counts.

I hadn't given much thought as to where Rory was going to construct the goat pen. Lighthouses weren't exactly barn-animal friendly, but he was a clever man, and I was certain he'd find the perfect place. Well, he had. Rory, like Sergeant Murdock before him, had believed the clean, mostly empty half of my boathouse would make the perfect temporary home for a goat. I wasn't exactly thrilled with the idea, suspecting that goats weren't nature's cleanest animals, but it was probably our best option. The boathouse had windows we could open for fresh air, and a door that locked so we didn't have to worry about anyone taking her while we were gone. Rory had cordoned off a large area, covered it with hay, and given her some stout wooden crates to climb on and a trough for water. He also scattered some carrots and apples around in case she got hungry. Clara, to her credit, seemed happy with her new home. And really, I couldn't blame her. After the long, trying day she'd had—going from a boat with a body to an overzealous dog groomer—it must have felt nice to have a quiet place to finally lie down and rest.

As we got ready for the cookout, Tuck came by the lighthouse to pick up Kennedy. I offered to drive, but with Wellington coming too, real estate in the back seat would be hard to come by, not to mention covered in dog hair. Needleless to say, my offer was declined.

My parents' lake house in Beacon Harbor was a gem. Of course, the location was spectacular, being right on Lake Michigan. The house itself was large without being gaudy; modern, yet with a nod to homes built during the turn of the nineteenth century, giving it undeniable charm. The eye-catching front door, reached by a series of wide stone steps and flanked by thick white pillars on stone foundations, was in the center of the first floor. On one side was a beautiful four-season porch of all windows. The windows continued, curving around the corner to provide a spectacular two-hundred-seventy-degree view of the lake and manicured grounds. The other side of the entrance was more typical, yet with the same spectacular curved windows, wrapping around the corner of the house.

The purchase of the house had been a surprise, one sprung on me last December. The moment I saw it, I knew how lucky my parents were to make such a find. Then I remembered that luck might have had a helper in the super-Realtor skills of Betty Vanhoosen. This was the house she had up her sleeve. The moment she showed it to James and Ellie, visions of spending their summers in Beacon Harbor with me sprang to life. Betty might have had her faults, but she sure had a knack for finding the right home for her clients. I couldn't thank her enough. Having worked in the grind of the NYC financial district, I had been so busy that I hadn't gotten to see much of my parents, especially after Dad retired and they moved to Florida. Now, however, we were practically neighbors.

We drove up the long driveway and parked behind Tuck's car. Hearing us arrive, Brinkley and Ireland appeared, racing across the lawn on their fluffy white feet to greet us. The moment I got out of the Jeep, I'd petted them both, but clearly, they were waiting for their BFF, Wellington. With our yummy offerings in hand, we followed the rambunctious dogs around back, lured by the mouthwatering smell of burgers on the grill.

"Welcome!" Mom cried upon seeing us. Always the hostess, she looked adorable in her white floppy sun hat, Ellie & Co wide-leg cocktail pants, and a sleeveless blouse. "So glad you kids made it. The burgers should be ready in a few minutes." Mom took the pie from my hand and set it on the long built-in counter, already overflowing with an array of delicious summer foods—baked beans, corn salad, potato salad, caprese salad, as well as chips and salsa. Rory placed the extra pie he was carrying beside mine and gave Mom a polite cheek kiss in greeting. Then he and Tuck excused themselves and headed straight for the grill, where Doc Riggles, Betty, Jack, and Ali Johnson had gathered.

"I'm so glad you girls are here," Mom said. Betty excused herself and came to stand beside Mom. A knowing look passed between the older women, and I knew they'd been discussing Lars Jorgenson's untimely death. "I meant this little gathering to be a celebration of a successful Blueberry Festival," Mom continued. "After all, everyone has worked so hard. But I'm afraid the festival's been overshadowed by death."

"Strictly going by the numbers," Betty interjected, "it was a success. Rod Jeffers confirmed it for me. A record number of visitors attended the festival this year. Obviously, those nasty pranks had something to do with it. People are ghouls." The face she made illustrated her point. "Never in my memory have we had a Blueberry Festival quite like this. Pranks. A suspicious death— Ooh," she interrupted herself, looking at Kennedy. "I heard about that poor goat."

"Poor goat, my Aunt Nellie's knickers!" Kennedy snapped defensively. "That goat received the equivalent of the platinum package at the puppy spa, so do not *poor goat* me."

Betty's face reddened as she lowered her voice. "I meant, you know, dear, the part about the creature being cooped up in a boat with a dead man." She pursed her lips into a little O, and shook her head, sending her platinum-blond bob swinging about her face. "It's as gruesome a scene as I can imagine. What in the world is going on in this town? No. Don't answer that," she quickly interjected, casting a look around as if to make sure no one was listening. "I think," she began in a loud whisper, "that we should put our heads together on this one. You know the old saying, it takes a village?"

"Betty, I don't think that saying is in regard to snooping around," I told her. "At the very least, if Murdock catches wind that the four of us are sticking our noses where they don't belong, she's going to flip her lid."

"Phooey. As long as Kennedy doesn't say a word to Tucker, we should be fine. Right, dear? Now, let's enjoy this cookout. Those burgers smell divine, and you just have to taste my street corn salad! It tastes like that roasted corn you buy at a festival, only without the mess. We'll meet in the kitchen after dinner for a little girl talk. Got it?"

Although the cookout was lovely, I found that I was having a hard time trying to forget the gruesome events of the morning. The image of the deceased Lars Jorgenson, dressed as a Viking, and with his dear pet goat, kept popping into my head as I tried to enjoy the delicious food and good company. In fact, it might have been the perfect evening, but I was too bothered by morbid thoughts to fully attend to the conversation. I hadn't had the chance to really discuss Lars Jorgenson's death with anyone other than Rory, and he wasn't too keen on my suggestion that Lars was somehow involved in the pranks. In fact, Rory had all but brushed the thought away, which was why I brought the notion up the moment we gathered in the kitchen with Mom and Betty.

I was transferring leftover hamburger patties into a zip-lock bag when I asked, "Do you think Lars's death has something to do with the pranks? The reason I ask is because the pranks stopped after his body was found."

"I never thought about that," Mom offered. "I was just so happy the pie-eating contest went off without a hitch."

"Well," Betty began, looking thoughtful, "I was on the committee but didn't run any events, and I still got pranked. I woke up to a sea of *For Sale* signs on my lawn. It was diabolical—"

"And quite clever as well," Kennedy added, drying the wineglass Mom had handed her. "You have to admit, Betty, gathering all those signs and then rerouting traffic through your circular drive was not only amusing, but it must have taken some planning."

Betty, sitting at the island counter while eating her second "thin" sliver of blueberry pie, pointed her fork at Kennedy. "Mind you, I'm still miffed about it, but I will admit that it had a certain flair of irony, if not humor. Damn drivers were honking as they drove through my driveway!"

"It must have been a tough morning," Kennedy offered without sounding sarcastic. She then secretly rolled her eyes at me before picking up another glass to dry.

"Was anyone laughing?" I thought to ask her.

"They were all laughing," Betty remarked without humor.

"Do you remember if Lars Jorgenson drove through your driveway?"

"Lindsey," Mom began, her arms buried to her elbows in soapsuds, "do you really think Lars could have been behind these pranks? He wasn't exactly a spry young buck."

Betty, thinking on this, took another bite of pie. "I didn't see him," she said, after swallowing. "But then again, I didn't stick around too long once I realized what was going on. But do you know? I think it was the sound of laughter that woke me up in the first place. Then the honking started." She set down her fork and looked at us. "I can't be sure, but now that you mention it, that deep belly laugh I awoke to did sound familiar."

"It could be just a coincidence, but I heard him laughing at our fashion show as well—the moment the goats ruined everything." After her remark, Kennedy's eyes flew open. "Goats! Do you think Lars had something to do with the goats crashing our fashion show?"

I had just finished putting the leftover salad in a plastic container, then set down the bowl. "Your fashion show was held under the beer and brat tent. Felicity and Stanley Stewart were on the festival committee, not you and Mom, so technically they were the ones who were pranked, I believe. We'll call it a two-for-one pranking. Regarding Lars Jorgenson, you are right. He was in the audience. He also has a goat, but it could be just a coincidence."

"Right," Kennedy said. "And was it a coincidence that he stood up after Grayson's glass sculpture collapsed and laughed?"

We had all witnessed that. Mom looked at me then. "Was Lars Jorgenson at every one of the events that got pranked?"

I shrugged. "I don't know for sure, but I think we could find out."

Mom stepped away from the sink and dried her hands. "Are you suggesting that Lars was the prankster and somebody he pranked found out and murdered him?" I could tell the mere thought was as titillating to her as it was disturbing.

"It's just a theory," I told them.

Betty piped up, "It would help if we knew for sure that he was murdered. Bob doesn't like to mix work and pleasure, but I do know he'll be conducting the postmortem sometime tomorrow. The moment I find out the cause of death, I'll make a group text and send the results."

I wasn't sure if that was legal, but I appreciated her enthusiasm on the matter.

Mom walked around the island and sat next to Betty. "Even if he died of natural causes, what sicko would dress the poor man up as a Viking and put him in that boat with his pet goat? It doesn't make sense."

It really didn't make much sense unless one considered Rory's Viking burial theory. I didn't have the heart to tell Mom and Betty that Rory believed somebody had actually tried to set that boat with Clara in it on fire. Just thinking of it made me want to strangle the idiot responsible for it all.

Kennedy was also upset. "Indeed," she replied to Mom's question. "One would think that killing the poor bloke would have been vengeance enough. Generally, I applaud such theatrics, but in this case, it has the taint of severe derangement. In short, we might be dealing with a real monster."

". . . or maybe Lars's death was natural. Maybe he was a reenactor, you know, like a Civil War reenactor, only in his case a Viking one?" Judging by the skepticism that seemed to animate all their faces, I could tell this theory wasn't sitting too well. I shrugged. "Dad suggested it earlier. I just thought I'd throw it out there."

"We'll consider it," Mom said, channeling her inner Charlie's angel and apparently taking the lead on the investigation. "Well, ladies, we have a lot of questions to sift through, but I think we're up to the challenge." A gleam rose to her eyes as she addressed us. "Well, then, it's settled. In order to solve this puzzle, we need to uncover the identity of the prankster!"

"That's . . . that's what I was saying, Mom." I looked to Kennedy for support.

Shrugging, she added, "I'm in, of course. But Tucker's not going to be happy."

Betty waved her off. "Best to keep him in the dark, dear, until we need him. Tomorrow, while I'm at work, I'm going to see if I can't poke around a bit regarding those stop signs. Somebody must know something about how they got on my lawn."

"Oh-oh!" Mom interjected, her face beaming with excitement. "I just remembered something Ali told me earlier. As you know, the Book Nook is our neighbor on Main Street, and I was asking her what kind of security she and Jack use for the store. She said they installed security cameras both inside and out a few months ago, because one of her sons insisted on it. She didn't think they needed it, but she told me she was glad they did when Rod Jeffers came by and asked if he could see the footage taken during the parade."

"Wait." I looked at Mom. "Are you telling us that Mayor Jeffers has already seen footage from the parade?" Mom nodded. "Do you know when that was?"

"Saturday evening, according to Ali."

"Mom, if Mayor Jeffers saw that footage and discovered who the prankster was, it might help us figure out what happened to Lars Jorgenson."

Kennedy crossed her arms and looked at me. "I think what Lindsey is trying to say is that the good mayor of Beacon Harbor just might have something to do with that goat in the boat with the body."

CHAPTER 23

Goats are noisy creatures. I learned this just after three in the morning, when Clara started making a fuss in the boathouse. It was eerily reminiscent of the night before, and it woke me out of a dead sleep. Welly was awake too. I then rolled over in bed, hoping to induce Rory to go out and check on her. But the bed was empty, reminding me that Rory had decided to sleep at his own house, due to a busy Monday morning schedule. Smart man, I mused and rolled over, covering my head with the quilt. That worked for a few minutes, until Welly jumped on my bed, pawed at the quilt, and began licking my face.

"Alright," I said. "Let's go see what Clara is complaining about now."

I threw on a pair of sweatpants, slipped on my flip-flops, and padded out to the boathouse, yawning every step of the way. Normally waking so early was no big deal. My alarm went off at 3 a.m. four days a week, so I could start baking. But Monday was my day off, the bakeshop was closed, and I really thought I could sleep in. Clara obviously had other plans. Welly, seemingly anxious by the noise, bounded ahead of me and waited at the boathouse door. The moment I unlocked it and flipped on the light, Clara stopped bleating. She jumped out of her water trough and ran over to greet us, apparently wide awake and ready to play.

Her crates had been tipped over and chewed, and water was all over the hay-strewn floor. Unfortunately, one of my boxes of Christmas lights had fallen prey to her curiosity as well. For the life of me, I couldn't figure out how she had reached it, but she had, and now my giant candy canes were scattered on the floor, chewed and trampled, some even partially covered with hay as if to hide the evidence. "Wow," was all I could say, looking at the mess. "I see that somebody was very busy."

Still muddled with sleep, I made the executive decision to let her out of the boathouse to play with Wellington in the cool night air. She seemed happy to be out, happy to have company, and I really couldn't blame her. I didn't know much about goats, but I could see that this one liked company.

Clara followed Welly as he explored the dark lawn. Since I was up and wasn't really certain of how to proceed with the noisy goat, I decided to walk down to the water beyond the lighthouse, knowing the animals would follow in due time.

Although I couldn't see much in the darkness, I always found the lake particularly beautiful at night. Aside from the perpetual pounding of waves on the shore, it was solemn and peaceful, the perfect background for an unquiet mind. It had been a frightfully confusing weekend, and Clara was a puzzle unto herself.

I found the large driftwood log I'd been searching for, sat down, and stared out into the darkness, thinking of the man who kept a rambunctious goat for a pet. Why a goat? Why Clara? Was she some type of service animal? This I pondered, recalling that Lars had been a veteran and therefore maybe needed emotional assistance. However, I doubted that goats made good service animals. But who was I to judge such a thing? I had spent most of my adult life chasing money, not gathering knowledge on farm animals. And yet here I was, sitting on a piece of driftwood in the middle of the night, thinking about goats. I rolled my eyes. New York Lindsey would be so proud of me. Then again, New York Lindsey wouldn't have gotten herself involved with a goat in a boat floating out on the lake with a dead body. I shook my head to clear the thought.

Clara gave a soft bleat somewhere in the darkness behind me. I knew Welly was there too, by the jingling of the tags on his collar. It was then that another name popped into my head. Daphne Rivers. Saturday morning, she had called the police to report that all her goats went missing. Her goats showed up later that day at Mom and Kennedy's fashion show. Was it a coincidence that Clara was in the boat with Lars? Was she the same kind of goat that Daphne raised? I didn't know, but I knew I needed to make a visit to the Riverses' farm, if for no other reason than to learn about taking care of a goat.

I was fully dressed and on my third cup of coffee by the time Kennedy came down to the kitchen to join me.

"Whoa! Is the goat living in the lighthouse now?" she asked with a fake smile, staring at Clara. "Because I thought she was staying in the boathouse?"

"You obviously didn't hear the racket she was making at three this morning."

"Not a peep," she remarked, gingerly petting both Welly and Clara as she made her way to the coffeemaker. "One of my many talents is that I sleep like the dead."

"Lucky you." I slipped Clara another slice of carrot as I watched Kennedy pour coffee into her mug.

She turned, leaned against the counter, and said, "You know goats live outside, right?"

"I do. But I think Clara is lonely. I'm just giving her a little freedom before I have to put her into the boathouse again. Then we're off to the Book Nook. I talked to Ali this morning, and we're all set to view that video."

"Ladies," Ali said, greeting us as we came through the door of her lovely shop. The bookstore was one of my favorite places in the village. Like the couple who owned it, it gave off a friendly, welcoming vibe—from the light atmosphere to the colorful and fascinating books, both new and used, that filled the shelves and tables. In one corner was a nook with comfy reading chairs by a little stone fireplace. There was also a section of the store dedicated to postcards and memorabilia of Lake Michigan and Beacon Harbor.

Ali continued. "So glad you're all here. As I told Ellie last night, Mayor Jeffers has already viewed the footage from the parade."

"I didn't think anything of it at the time," Mom admitted. "Not until Lindsey mentioned something about discovering the identity of the prankster."

"Very interesting," Ali admitted. "And you think that's what the mayor was searching for . . . the identity of our prankster?" As she talked, we followed her around the register desk and through a door leading to the back room. "I apologize for the mess," she said, pushing aside a large box overflowing with used books. She then brought us over to the desk and turned on the computer.

Curiosity was brimming in Kennedy's eyes. "Didn't Rodney say he was searching for the prankster?"

"No. I got a call from Christy Parks," she said. Christy owned Bayside Boutiques on the other side of the street. "She asked if we had a security camera outside the store. When I told her that we recently installed one, she told me the mayor was at her shop asking to see if anyone had security footage of the parade. All she said was that he wanted to watch the tape if we had it."

"So, you set it up for him?" I looked at Ali. She gave a little nod as she brought up the footage on her computer.

"I did. I don't know if he saw anything of interest. He left before I could ask him. I was just happy somebody had found it useful. Heaven knows it seems like having a security camera outside the door is overkill in a sleepy village like this. But maybe we're on to something. After all, you three are here too."

Once Ali set up the footage, she excused herself and left to attend to her store. With the three of us staring at the monitor, I played the footage, starting from the time the crowd had begun to gather on the sidewalk in front of the Book Nook earlier in the day. From there I sped through the timeline, watching the sidewalk steadily get more crowded, until Kennedy, spying something at the edge of the screen, called for me to stop.

"There," she said, pointing to a figure moving through the line of people. I rewound the tape and watched it again. The figure was dressed in a bulky blue windbreaker, with a ball cap partially covering his face. I say *he*, because it was pretty obvious this mystery person was a man. It was hard to tell exactly who he was, but one thing was certain, he was carrying something weighty in his hands by the way he wobbled as he walked. We couldn't see clearly but I was pretty certain he was lugging two large buckets with him. We watched as the ball-capped man went over to a group of teenagers. He appeared to say something to them, then bent down and straightened.

"Wait," I said, stopping the video. "I think he just set down two buckets. It's hard to tell, but he clearly set something down."

We then watched as the capped man gave the teens the thumbs-up sign, then walked away. One of the teens followed him. We watched awhile longer and noted that the teen returned carrying two more buckets. He didn't set them down but kept moving beyond the scope of the footage, presumably to take them to another spot.

"Are you seeing what I'm seeing?" I asked Mom and Kennedy.

"Could that man be our prankster?" I had rewound the footage again, and Kennedy pointed to the capped man. "Clearly the teens are involved too."

"I don't know who those kids are. They might not even be from this town. However, I think that man is our prankster. The only trouble is, we can't see his face."

Mom leaned forward, getting a better look at the screen. In her defense, she wasn't wearing her cheater glasses. "We can't see his face, but can you rewind that again? We might be able to tell who it is by the way he walks."

We watched the tape several more times, knowing we

had found our prankster, but frustrated at the fact that we couldn't properly identify him.

"You know," I began, thinking. "Although I can't be certain, I don't think that man is as tall as Lars Jorgenson was."

"It's hard to say," Kennedy remarked. "He looks like he's walking a tad hunched over."

"Maybe Rod Jeffers figured it out. After all, both men were in Rory's Friday morning group."

Mom stood and rested her hand on my shoulder. "Good work, ladies. I'm afraid I have to jump next door and return to the boutique. But I suggest that you girls pay Mayor Jeffers a visit. But be careful. While I'm not suggesting that our mayor is a murderer, I do find it odd that he saw this tape the night before Lars's body was found."

"Good point," I said, while thinking roughly the same thought. Mayor Jeffers might have already identified the prankster and paid him a late-night visit. After all, he and his choir had suffered a terrible embarrassment during the Blueberry Parade. Watching it play out again on the tape had driven that point home. Everyone in the crowd was laughing as the water balloons hit their mark. Everyone but Mayor Jeffers. The chilling anger that oozed from his face made the hair on my neck prickle. Was I looking into the face of a murderer?

I hoped not, but Kennedy and I were about to find out.

CHAPTER 24

After leaving the Book Nook, Kennedy and I made the short drive over to St. Michael's Church. Although Rod Jeffers was the mayor of Beacon Harbor, that was only his part-time job. His real vocation was the music director of St. Michaels Church. As I pulled into the church parking lot, Kennedy grabbed my arm.

"Are we seriously going in there?" If I had to put a finger on her expression, I'd say she looked troubled.

"Why not? Are you afraid you'll instantly combust the moment you cross the threshold?" I teased.

"Ha . . . ha." It was forced, pretend laughter. Kennedy was not amused. She narrowed her eyes and added, "I suppose next you're going to use the old, 'If God drank milk, your face would be on the carton' routine with me. If you'll recall, Lindsey dear, I was here on Christmas Eve with you and the fam. I didn't combust then, and I won't now. It's just . . . what if the mayor–slash–music director really did have something to do with Lars Jorgenson's death? I may have a rucksack of amoral tendencies compared to your micro-clutch of faults, but a killer hiding behind the cloak of God is pure evil in my book."

It was just like Kennedy to use a purse analogy, but there was some truth to what she was saying. "I agree. The thought is disturbing. But we don't know for sure if he had anything to do with Lars's death. That's why we're here—to find out."

"Right. But if we get too close to the mark, he could go after us as well. I don't know about you, but I'm not too keen on being murdered in a church, at least not a Presbyterian one."

I looked at her and rolled my eyes. Kennedy was being overly dramatic. Whenever that happened, it was usually a sign she was either trying to be funny, or she was nervous. Sitting in the church parking lot as we were, it was definitely nerves that had her on edge. Honestly, I couldn't blame her. Traipsing to the basement office of the music director in a nearly deserted church was an unsettling thought. However, we had unanimously decided to snoop around, and that's exactly what we were going to do. Snoop around and ask questions. Trying to put her mind at ease, I offered, "Look, it's probably nothing. He's the mayor, after all, and a musical man of God as well. I don't know that he had anything to do with Lars's death, but we have to find out what he gleaned from that security camera footage. Aside from Mom and Ali, we're the only ones who know that he's seen footage from the parade. It's likely just a coincidence that Lars died after the mayor saw the tape." Dangit! I had babbled a sentence too much. Judging from her caustic sneer, I should have stopped at "parade."

We followed the sound of piano music through the historic church and down a flight of stairs to the basement. There we found Rod Jeffers tinkering at his piano while flipping through religious music for next Sunday's choir selection. His door stood open, and he greeted us with his usual disarming smile the moment he saw us.

He swiveled on the piano bench as he said, "Lindsey, Kennedy, what a surprise. To what do I owe the pleasure?"

"You play very nicely," I said, thinking it best to start with a compliment. It was also true. The mayor could play. "We just wanted to ask you a few questions about the water balloon prank that was played on you during the parade."

At the mention of the prank, his smile faded. His face flushed bright red, and he looked as if he still felt the embarrassment it must have caused him. Knowing we were staring at him, the mayor abruptly stood and walked over to his desk.

"You've come about that, have you? Not much to tell, really. Everyone there pretty much saw the whole thing."

"That water balloon fight derailed the entire parade," I reminded him.

He gestured for us to take a seat in the chairs on the other side of his desk. Once we were seated, he sat down as well. Behind his glasses, his gray eyebrows drew together in troubled thought. He took a deep breath, then admitted, "It was terrible, of course. A public humiliation— not only for me, but for my choir."

"I can only imagine," Kennedy remarked. "What we want to know is whether you saw the person responsible for the prank . . ." She lifted a brow and stared at him with her level, probing gaze.

The mayor looked uncomfortable under such a bold stare. He loosened the collar of his shirt before shaking his graying head. "I did not, young lady. I was too busy conducting the choir to take note of the crowd. It wasn't until that first water balloon struck me in the head that I realized something was amiss. It nearly knocked my glasses off. Those blasted balloons kept coming. The spectators weren't only laughing—they were participating, the bloodthirsty devils!"

His anger was palpable, causing Kennedy to flash me a pointed *I told you so* look. Apparently, she thought the mayor might flip into killer mode at any minute. I ignored her in favor of hearing the mayor out.

"However," he continued, his anger deflated like a pin-pricked balloon, "like the soldier I once was, I just kept trudging on through the song, urging my singers to do the same. That, perhaps, was a mistake." He looked so glum after this last statement that I felt inclined to cheer him up.

"I found it endearing that you kept going. You were all so committed to that song. I have to admit, although I love blueberries and making pies, I had never heard that "Blueberry Pie" song before Friday evening." I didn't go so far as to say that I liked it, because that would have set Kennedy off for sure. I needn't have worried, however. Kennedy was ready to pounce.

"Mayor Jeffers," she began in her deceptively dulcet podcast voice, "you stated that you don't have any idea who was behind the prank? I assume that was before you confiscated that security camera footage from the Book Nook?"

"What?" His head swiveled between us, as if he wasn't certain which one of us to train his bulging gaze on. "'Confiscated'? It was hardly confiscated. I simply asked if—Hey, how do you two know about that?"

It was my turn to give a pathetic shake of my head. "This is Beacon Harbor, Rod. Need I say more?"

"Betty Vanhoosen!" he cried, pinning the proverbial tail on the donkey, so to speak, only in this case, he was a tad wide of the mark. "This has her written all over it." It didn't help that Kennedy giggled at the name.

"Actually, it was Ali Johnson. She told us you came by asking to see the footage. I assume you were looking for the identity of the person responsible for the water balloon debacle?" I couched this as a question, curious to see how he would answer. The fact that he didn't answer was troubling.

His face darkened, and with a grim set to his lips, he asked, "What exactly are you suggesting?"

Kennedy waved her hand, as if slapping away a pesky fly. Mustering her superior influencer attitude, she leaned forward and said, "Don't be thick. We saw that footage too. We all know that the recently deceased Lars Jorgenson was behind the pranks. We find it odd that you saw the footage mere hours before he died."

His brown eyes appeared as if they were ready to pop out of his head. "Lars Jorgenson? What exactly are you suggesting, Ms. Kapoor?"

Kennedy narrowed her eyes at him. "I think you know what we're suggesting, Rod. A goat, a boat, a Viking, and a misplaced fire arrow. It doesn't sound like a very Christian sendoff to me."

CHAPTER 25

"How rude!" It was unusual to see the unflappable Kennedy Kapoor so flustered, but that's exactly what she was as she stomped across the church parking lot toward my Jeep, her full lips pressed into a thin line and her bright yellow purse carelessly flung over her shoulder.

"We've just been tossed out of church," I said, taking long strides to keep up with her. My face was still hot from embarrassment. "It's a first for me . . . maybe not for you, but I don't like it. Why did you have to go in for the kill? Couldn't you have just asked if he had talked with Lars Jorgenson after viewing the tape, or made a visit to his house?"

"The setting was making me uncomfortable," she admitted. "Who plays piano in the basement of a church?"

"It's his office," I shot back.

"In my mind, there was no point in beating around the bush. I just wanted to make the accusation and see how he reacted."

"Well, thanks for bringing me up to speed on your plan, Ken. As I recall, fifteen minutes ago, you were terrified at the thought of confronting a murderer in a church. Then you fling the accusation at the mayor—without any real proof!"

"I thought I was on to something. He looked guilty." She paused to open the passenger-side door of the Jeep before adding, "In hindsight, I suppose I might have confused guilt with embarrassment."

I buckled myself into the driver's seat and started the engine. "Ya think?" It was pure sarcasm. "Funny that neither of us confused guilt or embarrassment with anger. We read that one correctly." I looked at my friend. "That footage of the parade wasn't at all clear or conclusive. We saw what looked to be a man wearing a baggy windbreaker and a baseball cap carrying a couple of buckets into the awaiting crowd. We never clearly saw his face. Then he got others involved. Also, it would have taken a ton of time to make all those water balloons. As the mayor pointed out, it's highly doubtful that only one person is responsible for these pranks." I paused a moment as I pulled out of the parking lot. "Aside from a friendly hello, I barely knew Lars Jorgenson. Rod Jeffers did, however. He was quick to defend the man, and clearly thought it absurd that Lars could have pulled off a prank of that scale all on his own."

"Yes," she said, while rooting through her purse. "He made that quite clear before escorting us out the door. Doubtful we'll be invited back. If God really does drink milk and my face is on the carton, I have that man to blame for it. Thrown out of the house of God!" She sounded almost affronted. Then, as if striking gold, she peeped with joy and held out her hand. "Care for a breath mint?"

I took my eyes off the road only long enough to pluck one from her hand and pop it in my mouth. Her thoughts were as slippery as a watermelon seed!

"The blame is all yours on this one, I'm afraid," I told her, glancing briefly at my phone to make sure I was heading in the right direction. "You're going to write the mayor a letter of apology, and I'm going to send him a pie. In the meantime, we need to keep searching for the identity of the pranksters while gathering more information on Lars Jorgenson. The more facts we uncover, the closer we should get to solving this mystery. You have to remember that we don't know for sure that Lars was murdered."

"It's beginning to look like we don't know much of anything. How tragic. By the way, where are we going?"

"Our first theory regarding Lars as the prankster might be wrong. Really, we were just speculating on that one. However, the man had a pet goat named Clara. Goats, if you'll recall, were also used to disrupt your fashion show and make a mess of the Stewarts' brat-and-beer tent. We also know whose goats were used in that prank."

"Daphne Rivers!" Kennedy blurted, shooting me a look of approval. "The crazy goat lady. Brilliant idea, Linds."

We drove out of town on the county road, flanked by woods-lined, rolling farmland. It was beautiful country, dotted with horses and cows. Then we came upon a sign that read, *Happy Goat Lucky Farm.* I knew we were in the right place due to the silhouette of a goat on the sign, as well as the suspiciously familiar herd frolicking in the meadow beyond the fence.

Kennedy smiled at the sign. "At least the goat lady has a sense of humor."

"I think you have to have a sense of humor to raise goats." I returned the smile and parked in the farmhouse driveway. "Remember to tread lightly," I reminded her. "We don't want to get kicked off a goat farm as well."

We were in the process of walking to the front door when the sound of a dog barking stopped us in our tracks. We turned to the barn and saw a lively black and white border collie running to greet us. A trim, fit-looking woman appeared behind him and came over as well. The woman, somewhere in her late forties, was wearing faded jeans, a T-shirt with a goat logo on it, and a red bandana that was holding back a sheaf of frizzy brown hair. She was dusting the hay off her jeans as she walked.

"Piper," she called to the dog. The dog, however, was busy greeting us with cautious excitement, sniffing our hands and swishing her silky black tail. "She's friendly," the woman called out unnecessarily. "Shop's over here." She pointed to a smaller building adjacent to the barn. "But we're not open on Mondays."

"Sorry to hear that," I said, walking over to meet her. "Are you Daphne Rivers?" She gave a little nod in response. "Beautiful place you have here. I'm Lindsey Bakewell, owner of the Beacon Bakeshop, and we're not open on Mondays either." I offered a friendly smile as I said this, hoping to get one in return. My hopes were dashed by the guarded look on the other woman's face. Undeterred, I continued. "This is my friend Kennedy Kapoor. We've actually come here to ask you a few questions."

"What kind of questions?" From the look of her narrowed eyes, she didn't like the sound of this.

Kennedy, mustering her most disarming smile, explained, "I was running the fashion show under the brat and beer tent at the Blueberry Festival. Unfortunately, it was sabotaged by your goats."

"I had nothing to do with that!" she snapped. "My goats were stolen the night before." Although she was an attractive woman with the healthful glow of one used to working the land, the mention of the goat debacle turned the fine lines of her face into ruts of pain and anger.

"We know," Kennedy told her. "We've come here to see if you have any idea of who might have pulled off the prank."

"Prank?" she said, glowering at us. "Stealing livestock is no prank, it's theft." Then, somewhere in the recesses of her red-brain thoughts, she must have realized she was taking her anger out on the wrong party. She blew out a breath of exasperation and offered, "Forgive me. It's just that the thought of such treatment to my goats still boils my blood. Those goats out there are my life, my livelihood!" Her cheeks flooded with color as she spoke. "They are not the butt of some stupid joke!"

"I agree," Kennedy said, levelly. "It quite ruined my day as well."

"Look, Daphne, none of us are happy about the pranks that were played during the festival. We're here because we wanted to see if you had any idea who could have done this to your goats."

Daphne shifted her gaze to me then. "You own that lighthouse bakery?" I nodded. "Nice. I keep meaning to visit. Heard good things." She took a deep breath, then allowed her shoulders to sag a bit. "I'm not sure why you want to stick your nose into this business."

Kennedy looked at me, urging me to come up with a good excuse. I had many. Aside from natural curiosity, there was also the fact that Rory and I had found the body. But for some reason I didn't want to tell her this. Instead, I told her plainly, "I ran the pie-eating contest. My event was the only one not sabotaged by the pranksters. We're just trying to figure out who the pranksters are."

She thought about this a moment. "Festival's over. Shouldn't matter now. However, since you've taken the time to drive all the way out here, I'll show you what I found."

"Prickly much?" Kennedy whispered as we followed Daphne to an access gate on the side of the barn opposite her store. Piper ran ahead of us and stopped short of the fence where the entire herd of curious goats had gathered, bleating happily to us.

"Here are my babies. Goats, just so you know, are inquisitive creatures." It was remarkable, but the sight of her animals seemed to shift her mood. Daphne was actually smiling with something akin to pride as her goats trotted to the fence to greet her. Kennedy, noting this as well, gave me a sharp elbow in the ribs coupled with a look that could only be described as pleasantly horrified. I passed her an eye roll in return.

"Over here," Daphne remarked, pointing to the soft dirt before the gate. "This is what I wanted to show you."

I knelt and studied the marks. "These look like tire tracks. Is that unusual?"

"Just the size of them," she remarked. "What I wanted to point out is the fact they're from a truck. A large one.

This is an access gate," she reminded us, as I got to my feet. "I drive my pickup back here all the time to deliver hay and feed, but I found these tracks on Saturday morning. They're not mine. I find that troubling."

"You think whoever made these tire tracks took your goats?"

"As you know," she began, looking at Kennedy, "all my goats went missing. Judging from the size of these tracks, I'd say whoever did this was using a large horse trailer or a box truck."

"And this person just drove right up and took them?" Kennedy, glancing at the playful, chaotic goats, was having a hard time believing this. "I assumed, given that they don't look like they're trained to follow commands, that your goats wouldn't abide marching into a strange truck in the middle of the night."

Daphne reached through the fence to pet a sizeable brown and white goat with large horns. The goat seemed to love the attention. "Goats, in general, aren't cooperative creatures. They're especially daunting if you don't know anything about them. However, the person, or persons, who took my goats knew enough about my herd to cajole the bellwether."

I tilted my head, not following. "Are you referring to a forecast of things to come?"

Daphne sneered at my ignorance. "The term *bellwether* comes from goats. In this case it means the dominant wether. A wether is the term for a castrated male," she added, clearing that up for us. "The bellwether is the dominant castrated goat, usually wearing a bell around its neck, hence the term bellwether. Goats that are free-range grazers like mine will follow the bellwether wherever he chooses to graze. If you can't see the herd, just listen for the sound of the bell and you'll find them. So, whoever took my goats, knew this guy," she said, stroking the long ears of the brown and white goat wearing a bell around its neck. "Bode-Goaty is my bellwether. They took off his bell and lured him into the truck with some food, knowing the rest would follow."

"You're saying goats aren't independent thinkers?" Apparently, this was a revelation for Kennedy.

"Not really. Goats are herd animals. They thrive in a herd."

That explained why Clara was making such a fuss at three in the morning. She really was lonely. I focused back on Daphne. "You think whoever took your goats was familiar with them. Do you have anyone else who works here with you who could possibly be involved?"

"No," she said, then added, "Danni, my daughter, helps me when she's not at school. I also employ a friend of mine, Mary Eccles, to run the store. My ex-husband used to be involved until the day he decided to slaughter one of my goats for meat."

As she said this, I looked at said goats, feeling ill at the thought of eating one. Kennedy, by the look of disgust on her face, apparently did too.

"I'm a vegetarian," she told us. "I run a dairy. My goats are dairy goats, not meat goats. Needless to say, the marriage ended due to irreconcilable differences."

"I'll say!" Kennedy offered a forced smile. "You mentioned a daughter. How old is she?"

"Danni will be a sophomore in college, but she's not behind these pranks, and neither is Mary. They both love these goats as much as I do and would do nothing to harm them."

"How about your ex?" Kennedy probed. "He's obviously not above eating your goats and would certainly know the bellwether. Sounds like a suspect to me."

"I agree. The only trouble is he now lives in Boston with his new wife." Although she offered a sneer as she said this, I got the feeling she knew more about the goat-napping than she was letting on.

Therefore, acting on a hunch, I asked, "Do you know a man named Lars Jorgenson?" Her expression was in-scrutable, but she finally nodded her head.

"I heard he passed away," she added softly, as if not wishing to speak ill of the dead. "He was a difficult man, but he was also one of my best customers."

I had never heard the term "difficult" associated with Lars before, so I asked her to explain what she meant.

"He was a bit obnoxious, you know, in the way some men are. They think they're so funny when they make a joke. Lars thought he was funny. The first time I met him he told me he'd been born in Norway and had grown up on goat cheese. He told me he was happy I was making goat cheese. It wasn't a lie. He and his wife would come here every week to buy my latest products. It was kind of them."

"Did Lars or his wife ever think of starting their own goat farm?" I asked.

She shook her head. "No way. Clara wasn't the type to embrace farming. Lars was a carpenter, but he did like the goats. I think Clara mostly humored him. However, when she died a few years back, he drove out here and asked if he could buy one of my goats."

"Did you sell him one?" I asked.

She pursed her lips and nodded. "I did. I sold him an older doe, only because he was so lonely, and the goats always made him smile. Goats do that."

"They do," Kennedy agreed, no doubt thinking about her own short stint with Clara. Then, however, she shifted her attention to me, her intense dark eyes urging me to ask the tough question we had come to ask.

I cleared my throat and ventured, "You say Lars was familiar with your goats. He would have known the bell-wether, wouldn't he?"

Daphne's face darkened at the suggestion. "Yes. And damn him, he had no right using my goats for his prank!" Her anger was back with a force.

I looked at Kennedy, making sure she had heard it too. Yep, she had.

"Lars took your goats?" I looked at Daphne. "And you're sure of this?"

"I don't have any proof, if that's what you're asking. It's more of a mother's instinct. Yet ever since my goats turned up under the brat and beer tent, his name's been rattling around in my head. I don't think anyone else could have pulled it off. Another thing? Aside from feasting on bratwurst, French fries, and whatever else they happened across under that tent, no harm befell them—not even a random nip from one of those dogs. Like the Norwegian god, Loki, Lars Jorgenson was a notorious trickster. His wife told me about it on several occasions. The poor woman had been the target of many of her husband's silly pranks. But using my goats to crash that fashion show was a prank too far!" She was shaking, she was so angry.

Kennedy, Mom, and I, having been on the receiving end of that prank, wholeheartedly agreed. Knowing we had gotten what we'd come for, a name, I was satisfied with leaving it at that. It wouldn't do any good for Daphne to grow suspicious of us. Instead of asking more questions, we told her we were taking care of Lars's pet goat, Clara. Daphne looked genuinely happy to hear it, and not only gave us some helpful tips on how to look after her, but a few bales of alfalfa hay and a bucket of grain as well. I didn't have the nerve to tell her the goat had been groomed, bedazzled, and partially turned into a unicorn. She wasn't the type of woman to smile about that. However, she had suspected Lars of stealing her goats, and now he was dead. Was it a coincidence? I didn't feel it wise to push our luck.

As Kennedy and I drove back to town, she mused aloud, "We visited two people today, and Lars Jorgenson's name keeps popping up. I find that interesting. Daphne is clearly on team Lars the Prankster, while the mayor is not."

"I agree. And they were both very angry about the prank played on them."

"The question is," Kennedy began, lifting her large fashionista sunglasses just enough to look at me, "were either of them angry enough to kill?"

I had to admit, it was the thought that plagued me the entire drive home.

CHAPTER 26

I made a quick call to Rory to see how his day was progressing. He had promised to take Dad out fishing, then after he got back, he had done a little investigating into the prank that was played on him during the Blueberry 5K as well. Since Kennedy, Tuck, and I were going to his house for dinner tonight, he thought it best to be mysterious and wait to divulge his revelations then. Hearing that, my competitive side kicked in, and I might have hinted that Kennedy and I had learned a bit more than we actually had. No doubt, the conversation over dinner was going to be interesting.

Since the day was still young, and since I had oversold our snooping abilities, I decided to put my money where my mouth was and keep probing for answers. It's what inspired me to make a sudden, swerving turn into the parking lot of the Tannenbaum Shoppe instead of continuing down Waterfront Drive.

Kennedy yelped. "Please give me a little warning before you have a sudden urge to pull into oncoming traffic! In spite of what that banner says, Christmas in August is highly overrated and hardly merits such motoring risk!"

"Sorry." I flashed her an impish grin as I roared into a parking space in the near-empty parking lot, came to a jarring halt, and turned off the engine. I had seen the rental trucks. The tents were in the process of being taken down. "You've seen my lighthouse at Christmas. Do you honestly think I'm here to shop?" It was a rhetorical question, one delivered with a pointed look. "I've been thinking about Daphne's truck comment," I told her, staring at the partially deconstructed event tent. "If a truck or trailer really did pick up those goats, we might be able to find evidence of that here as well."

She held up her hands in mock protest. "Whoa, Miss Marple. I know we've had some success sniffing out baddies in the past, but when did we cross the line into tire tracking? I, for one, couldn't tell the difference between a MINI and a lorry on that pavement. The operative word here, darling, being 'pavement'."

"True," I said, looking at the impressive parking lot. The Tannenbaum was a popular destination in the late fall, and its overly large parking lot reflected that. "But if you'll remember, the parking lot was full during your fashion show. It was a standing-room-only event." This remark brought a smile to her face, as I knew it would. "Also," I said, capitalizing on her waxing mood, "look at the rental trucks."

It hit her like a revelation. "They're on the grass!"

"Bingo. Felicity and Stanley are there as well. Let's get out and ask them a few questions."

Felicity spotted us the moment we got out of the Jeep. She smiled and waved us over, looking eager about something.

"It's sad to see it go," I remarked to the couple as we stood beside them, marveling at the huge tent that for three days had been the busiest restaurant in town. "I was getting spoiled by this place. The brats, the beer, and those fries! You two really knocked it out of the park with this one. I hope it becomes a yearly tradition."

Felicity grinned at the remark. "I'm so glad you think so. In fact, Stanley and I had so much fun hosting the brat and beer tent that we've been talking. Tell these ladies the news, dear," Felicity urged her husband with her thick-lashed eyes.

"As you know," Stanley began with a grin, "our Christmas store, although wonderful, is reduced to seasonal success."

"With a name like Tannenbaum, darling, that's a given." Kennedy flashed him a private wink. Although Stanley was faithful to his wife, it was no secret that he found Kennedy attractive, a weakness she exploited when it suited her. The man had turned bright red.

"Rrrr . . . right," he stammered, consciously shifting his gaze to me. "But hosting the brat and beer tent got me thinking. We have plenty of space here, and thanks to my software company, I have connections in the spirits world."

"Oh!" Kennedy clapped with delight, bringing his focus back to her. She was shameless. "You're finally turning the old Bavarian monstrosity into a haunted house!"

Felicity's face fell at this, yet before she could reply,

Stanley corrected, "Not those kinds of spirits, Ms. Kapoor. You know very well that I was referring to the drink kind—beer, wine, and the harder stuff."

"Of course, I did. It was a little joke." She offered a cheeky smile to Felicity as an apology. "Go on."

Felicity, thank goodness, was in high spirits and barely took note of Kennedy's teasing. "We're thinking of opening a Bavarian-styled restaurant with an outdoor beer garden right here," she announced, beaming from ear to ear.

It was wonderful news. As we congratulated the Stewarts on their possible new business venture, I decided to bring up the subject of the goats. That little incident had been the one blemish to a very successful weekend for the couple.

"Ah, yes, the goats." Stanley shook his head at the memory.

"Do you have any idea how they might have gotten here?" Kennedy asked, looking serious for once. "I doubt a herd of goats just stumbled along down the road until they smelled grilling sausage."

As Kennedy talked, I noticed that Stanley was deep in contemplation. After thinking a moment, he piped up, "Actually, I did find something suspicious this morning. I didn't see it before, but only because I wasn't looking. It's over here," he said and urged us to follow him as he walked toward the Tannenbaum. "I think this might answer your question."

We followed the Stewarts as they led us to the thick, lush lawn on the far side of Felicity's Christmas shop. Clearly the grass here wasn't meant to be driven on, unlike the grass just off the parking lot where the rental trucks were now parked.

"Whoa," I said upon seeing the tracks. Because this

time the tires had driven over healthy grass and not dusty dirt, it was impossible to see the treads, but the tracks looked wide enough to me to be from a horse trailer or box truck.

Stanley crossed his arms and frowned at the marks on his pristine lawn. "Like I said, I saw these this morning when we were in the process of taking down the tables and chairs. I was puzzled at first, thinking some of the local kids had given me a little lawn job out of spite, but then I recalled the goat incident Saturday afternoon. That makes the most sense."

"It makes sense if you think about it." Felicity gestured to where the tire marks stopped on the lawn as she talked. "Your Ellie and Company fashion show was taking place at the back of the tent." She pointed down the length of the lawn where the stage had recently stood. "All eyes were on the show. Whoever brought those goats as a prank must have pulled into the auto repair shop over there."

We all turned in the direction Felicity indicated. The auto repair shop, though not very visible, due to it being about seventy yards away through tall grass and some wild brush, was the next business down the road, sitting behind the Tannenbaum Shoppe. Felicity continued. "It looks like the truck drove from their parking lot, through that brush back there, and came between here. The Tannenbaum Shoppe would have blocked any view of the truck from the road."

Kennedy and I stared at the wide track marks on the lawn. Although I couldn't be certain what type of vehicle they were from, due to their sheer size and width, I didn't think they were from a car or an SUV. I then looked at the Stewarts and agreed. "I think that's exactly what happened. The prankster would have known the fashion show had started. All eyes would be focused over there while they pulled the truck through here. It would have been a short walk from the truck to the tent. Amazing that the goats were so cooperative."

A grim smile came to Stanley's lips. "I'm sure they were helped along on their errant quest by the intoxicating scent of grilling brats."

Kennedy bristled at the thought. After all, it had been hers and Mom's big moment that had been sabotaged. "I don't doubt that they were, the beasts." Then, with a probing look, she asked, "Say, did either of you happen to hear any rumors about who this goat-buster was? A murmur of a name or wild speculation? I'd like to know."

The Stewarts, both redheads, and both in fine form for a couple in their late forties, looked at one another. Felicity shrugged as Stanley shook his head. "If they had," he remarked, "no one has uttered a word to us."

"It has to be a man, though," Felicity reasoned. "No woman I know would think about using goats as a prank. Just as no woman I know would ruin such a lovely fashion show."

As Kennedy gloated over the flattering remark, I asked one more question.

"Do you remember if Lars Jorgenson was in the audience?"

Felicity, out of habit, pushed a lock of thick red hair off her forehead before replying. "Poor man. We heard about what happened to him. He was definitely here that afternoon. No one was laughing harder at the debacle than Lars Jorgenson."

CHAPTER 27

"We cannot go home now!" Kennedy exclaimed, swept up in the heat of our proverbial hunt. "Not while the name Lars Jorgenson keeps springing up in conversation like rogue kernels of popcorn in a kettle."

I looked at my watch and agreed. It was early in the afternoon, and we had plenty of time. I was going to make lunch back at the lighthouse, but somehow eating out sounded better. "It is suspicious," I agreed. "But we have no proof, Ken. What we do have is the mayor and the Stewarts claiming that Lars was present but couldn't have pulled off such a prank. Unlike Daphne Rivers, who thinks he was very much involved in stealing her goats. Daphne doesn't think it could be anyone else. We've also seen blurry video footage that might or might not have been Lars Jorgenson carrying buckets of water balloons. In short, I'm super confused right now."

"As you should be. They are either trying to protect his memory, or one of them did the poor bloke in. My money's on that Rivers woman. She's the only one who's mentioned the Norway connection. She also sold him a goat. And you and I both saw how angry she was. She's ticked all our boxes."

"We really don't know that he was murdered," I reminded her, gripping the steering wheel as I tried to think. We were still in the parking lot of the Tannenbaum Shoppe. "Alright, why don't we grab a quick lunch and figure out whom we should talk to next."

"I already know," she said. "Aside from goats ruining our fashion show, the next meanest prank has to be the one played at the blueberry pie bake-off. Putting mice in a beautiful pie like that is the ultimate slap in the face."

The pie-baker in me wholeheartedly agreed. "I guess that means we're off to visit Winifred Peters."

While we were at Hoot's Diner grabbing lunch, I made a quick call to Betty to see if she had an address for Winifred, the two being longtime acquaintances. *Quick* was a relative term when talking about Betty. I had rung her while she was in a chatty mood. I played along for a bit, telling her about what Kennedy and I had gotten up to without spilling too much detail. Satisfied with that, I next asked her if she had heard anything from Doc yet regarding the autopsy.

"I'm afraid Bob ran into a little difficulty this morning regarding that," Betty explained in a softened voice. It sounded like she was cupping her hand around her phone so that no one could hear her speak. "Apparently, the family didn't want an autopsy done. They tried to block it, stating something about the indignity of the process."

"They can refuse?" I found this incredulous.

"Well, dear, it's never a pleasant thing to contemplate an autopsy when a loved one passes. Since Anders is the next of kin, I believe he has the right to refuse an autopsy. However, in this case, due to the strange circumstances of the death, his request will be denied. Bob, being the medical examiner, has jurisdiction there. It's his duty to the law. Anyhow, that's why it's been momentarily delayed."

I thanked her, wrote down Winifred's address, and ended the call. I then told Kennedy, who was finishing up her Cobb salad, why the autopsy was delayed. Being the amateur sleuths we were, the thought of refusal set off a tinkling of warning bells.

Kennedy set down her fork, dabbed at her lips with her napkin, and said, "Looks like Anders Jorgenson has just made our list of possible suspects."

I couldn't deny that he had. Refusing an autopsy on a death as suspicious as his father's was beyond troubling. I didn't want to think about it, and I suspected it was the reason Rory wouldn't talk about his busy morning over the phone.

Winifred Peters lived two miles south of town, just off a picturesque road that wound through an old-growth forest that opened every now and again to reveal a homestead. The Peterses' driveway was long, and the house, when it came into view, was the essence of old country charm. The two-story, wood-sided dwelling had been painted white with dark green shutters and had a spectacular wraparound porch with steps leading to the front door. Dotting the porch were six hanging baskets overflowing with cheerful flowers. The lawn and flower beds had the distinct look of being in the care of an obsessive-compulsive gardener. But I loved everything about it.

Probably because it reminded me so much of my grand-mother's house.

Kennedy and I walked up the steps to the front door and gave a good knock. A moment later a voice called to us, dictating that we should walk around to the back. There we found the retired couple, comfortably dressed while sitting in the shade on the back patio. Winifred smiled upon seeing us and held up her frost-covered glass.

"Randy and I are just enjoying a blueberry mint julep. Would you ladies care to join us?"

Her words were barely out before Kennedy piped up, "You had me at 'julep,' my dear! But of course!" She then lowered her voice, and asked me, "Why, Lindsey, have you never offered me a blueberry mint julep?"

"Honestly, it never crossed my mind."

As Randy went into the house to make two more of the drinks, Kennedy and I sat down with Winifred and asked her about her blundered blueberry pie bake-off. The moment the subject was brought up, I instantly regretted it. Winifred, a plump woman in her early seventies, turned as red as a beet at the memory. I didn't think it looked healthy.

"I'm deathly afraid of mice!" she cried, her fleshy cheeks quivering as she spoke. "*Deathly*, and what does that idiot prankster do? He replaced my beautiful pie with one riddled with mice. I nearly had a heart attack, it was so shocking!"

Although I hadn't been there to witness the atrocity myself, the mere thought made me queasy. As Winifred went on about mice and pies, Randy thankfully appeared with our drinks.

One sip of the beautiful blue drink and I knew we were

going to be drinking them with our dinner as well. The julep was a delicious mix of the classic Kentucky Derby drink, made with a good bourbon, simple syrup, and muddled mint. However, with the addition of pureed blueberries and crushed ice, the traditional julep had been transformed into a blueberry summertime dream. I could tell that Kennedy was enjoying hers, too, by the fact that her eyes were shut, and her nose was pointing to the heavens.

"Sublime," she finally remarked, opening her eyes. "And I don't mean the mice, but this drink."

Randy nodded at the compliment. "I can't take all the credit. While I do love me a good mint julep, it was Winnie's idea to put them blueberries in the drink. Those are Winnie's blueberries in there too. She's been growing them for years. That's what makes her pies so delicious."

"It's true," she said, happy to turn her mind from the importunate rodents. "With these delicious blueberries and my own winning pie recipe, I would have won that contest again for sure! That . . . that prankster robbed me of my fifth blueberry pie victory!"

"I can attest to how delicious your blueberries are," I told her, remembering how she had brought me some when she'd heard we were running low at the Beacon. "But you can't really be certain you were going to win without having tasted the other entries."

Winifred brooded. "I've tasted most of those pies before. It's always the same. I've won it the last four years in a row, and I would have won again if not for outright sabotage!"

"Do you have any idea who might have replaced your pie with that tampered one?" I asked, before taking another sip of my delicious blueberry mint julep.

It didn't escape my notice that Winifred and Randy exchanged a troubled look. I could tell something was up, but they were obviously hesitant to say what it was in our company.

Kennedy, noticing the odd behavior of the couple as well, decided to use her English charm on them. She leaned forward and offered a conspiratorial grin. "Allow me to offer up a name. If it's not the right one, I'll make you my granny's bramble, which is essentially a gin drink with blackberry liqueur. It's delicious too." She wiggled her perfectly plucked brows, then released the name with all the finesse of a gunshot. "Lars Jorgenson."

As the name hit Winifred's ears, she sucked in her breath with force. Her frightened brown eyes held to Kennedy's. The look on her face could only be described as spooked. "Are you a witch or something?" she asked in hushed tones.

"Hardly," Kennedy replied with a wave of her hand. "Just an educated guess."

"Well, it's educated, all right," Randy confirmed. Although not nearly as spooked as his wife, he regarded my friend with narrowed eyes. "Winnie told me she believes Lars Jorgenson's to blame."

"Do you have any proof?" I thought it best to be sure before we careened headlong into the brick wall of wishful thinking.

"Do you mean, did I see him? The answer is no. But that prank had Lars Jorgenson written all over it."

"Why do you say that?" I was curious that the name invoked so much anger.

"It was revenge," she stated matter-of-factly. "Oh, alright. I'll tell you. Clara Jorgenson used to win the blueberry pie bake-off every year until she got too sick to enter it. I was always the runner-up—always winning second place—and every year that old goat would come over to me and tell me that my pie would never measure up to his dear Clara's. Hers was the best, he'd tell me. The blueberries she used were superior because he grew them for her himself. The nerve of that man! When Clara died, rest her soul, that old goat was so jealous of the fact that my pie started winning the blueberry pie bake-off that he couldn't stop himself from reminding me that if his wife was still alive, she'd win and not me. But Clara and her superior pie are not around anymore, and he couldn't stand it! Can you believe that garbage? It was harassment, I tell you!"

"Lars used to grow blueberries?" I don't know why, but I found this interesting.

"He did. I'm not sure that he still does. It was for Clara."

"But . . . you never saw him replace your pie with the other one. Is that correct?"

"I didn't need to. I knew it was him. Why, you ask? Because I could hear him laughing his socks off at our expense the moment that first mouse appeared."

CHAPTER 28

It was hot out, and my Jeep smelled like baked hay as Kennedy and I headed back to the lighthouse. It had taken some effort getting her into the Jeep after watching her down one more blueberry mint julep and one blackberry bramble, the making of which she had coached Randy through. The Peterses had been quite taken with her. While Kennedy continued to charm them, I continued thinking about Lars Jorgenson. His wife had been a champion pie baker. Nobody had told us about that before. We had also learned that he had grown blueberries especially for Clara and her pies, which I found very touching. Could Lars really have been jealous enough of Winifred to sabotage the entire bake-off just to keep her from winning? It was a puzzling thought. One thing was certain, however. Both Winifred and Daphne had named

Lars as the prankster, and both had been visibly upset by the pranks that had been played on them. Even if Lars had been the prankster, could one of them have been angry enough to kill him, dress him up as a Viking, and then put him in a boat with a goat and send him off into the lake? As I drove back through the old-growth forest, I shook my head.

"No. No, you're quite right. You're going the right way," Kennedy piped up, lifting her head off the headrest with a sloppy smile.

"I'm not lost. I'm thinking."

"Ouch," she uttered lazily, pressing her fingers to her temples. "I can't think. My head is spinning too much."

Ignoring her, I continued. "It's just that I don't believe Daphne Rivers would ever put a goat in a boat and send it afloat with a dead man!"

"Well, I've got one for you! There once was a fisherman named Fisher who fished for some fish in a fissure. Till a fish with a grin, pulled the fisherman in. Now they're fishing the fissure for Fisher." She grinned. "I'm not *that* drunk."

"What the heck are you talking about?" I took my eyes off the road long enough to flash her a questioning look.

"I thought we were doing tongue twisters."

I wrinkled my nose at her. "No. I'm thinking about who might have killed Lars Jorgenson. It's not Daphne Rivers."

Her eyes were still closed, and her fingers were still pressing into her temples when she replied, "We don't know that he was murdered. Remember? And I think the goat lady is absolutely nutters enough to have done it . . . if he was murdered. Think about this. She spends her days milking goats and making goat cheese and naming them things like Bode-Goaty. That is not the behavior of a sane woman."

I disagreed but didn't want to get into it with Kennedy while she was still on her blueberry mint julep high. Instead, I reasoned, "Daphne loves her goats. She'd do nothing to harm them, therefore she wouldn't have put Clara in the boat with the body."

"Have you ever heard the phrase *culling the herd*, darling?" She cracked open an eye to look at me. "Don't fool yourself. Animal husbandry is a cruel business. The weaker ones always get snuffed out first, and although Clara is a sweet thing, let's face it. She's not dealing with a full set of horns."

"Probably because you tried to make her into a unicorn," I teased.

Kennedy's eyes were closed again when she acknowledged the deed with a smile and a wiggle of her fingers.

As I drove, I had to agree that Daphne seemed angry enough to cause harm. She was also strong and could have easily shoved a boat with a body in it out into the lake. She also could have shot a fire arrow at it had she wanted to. That being said, however, I still didn't think she'd do something so cruel to a goat. Just as I was mulling over these troubling thoughts, Kennedy's eyes flew open, and she suddenly lifted her head off the headrest.

"Or maybe that was the point of it! She's crazy for goats, so no one would expect her to put one in a boat. Clara is her scapegoat, pardon the pun."

I considered this. "Or maybe Lars really did die of natural causes while floating in a boat with his goat, while dressed as a Viking." I took a slow, deep breath and let it out as I turned down Waterfront Drive. The Beacon was in view, with the lake shimmering in the sunlight beyond it. It was a sight that never failed to lift my spirits.

"I'm really hoping Rory and Tuck can shed a little more light on what happened to that poor man."

The moment we got to the lighthouse, I realized we were pinched for time. Not only did I have two animals to attend to now, but I also had a dessert to make and a couple of side dishes to throw together as well. Kennedy, far from being sober, wasn't going to be much help in the kitchen. The truth was, even when she was sober, she wasn't much help in the kitchen. I was mentally planning how it was all going to come together in time, when Kennedy surprised me by volunteering to take care of Clara and Welly while I, to use her own words, toiled away in the scullery.

I headed to said scullery while Kennedy stayed in the boathouse with Clara. Once inside I was greeted by an excited Wellington. After giving him a big hug, and a *happy to see you* treat, I turned to let him out the screen door when I realized that a unicorn was staring back at me. Thinking Clara had gotten out, I went to grab a leash until I spied Kennedy waving her arms.

"Welly and Clara are going to play on the lawn for a while. I'll just sit right here and keep an eye on them. Go," she shooed, backing under the large oak tree. "Go make food."

I didn't need to be told twice. After washing up, I started on dessert first. Still in the throes of a blueberry obsession, I decided on a blueberry treat, but one that was incredibly easy to make. My mom's creamy Blueberry Delight fit the bill. It was not only delicious, but a cinch to make. I preheated the oven to 350 degrees and took out a nine-by-thirteen-inch pan. Although I could have gone with a graham cracker crust, I decided to up the flavor and make a crust from store-bought Pecan Sandies instead. I put the whole pack in the food processor and ground them to a nice crumb. I then transferred the crumbs to a bowl and stirred in a third of a cup of melted butter. I then pressed the crumb mixture into the bottom of the pan and sent it into the oven for ten minutes. While the crust was cooling, I beat together a brick of cream cheese, a cup of powdered sugar, and an eight-ounce tub of Cool Whip. This common mixture, when spread over a cooled crust, tasted amazing! However, to make it even more amazing, I took out a bowl of my blueberry pie filling (a store-bought can of blueberry pie filling would work just as well), stirred in a cup of fresh blueberries, then spread it over the cream cheese mixture. I next sprinkled a cup of chopped pecans over the blueberries and topped the whole thing off with another layer of Cool Whip. That done, I covered it with plastic wrap and sent the Blueberry Delight into the refrigerator to chill. I was then ready to start on my next item, roasted new potatoes.

I loved using tiny new potatoes for a quick side dish because they were so full of flavor and cooked relatively quickly. I took out a bag, washed the potatoes, quartered them, and put them in a mixing bowl. I then coated them in olive oil, adding salt, garlic, and fresh dill to taste. Once every piece was coated, I spread the potatoes on a foil-covered baking sheet and placed them in the already-heated oven until they were roasted to a light, golden crisp.

While the potatoes were cooking, I cleaned a bunch of asparagus with the intent of roasting them as well; adding

bacon and a sprinkling of Parmesan cheese. I knew Rory
only tolerated asparagus, but with it gently tossed in olive
oil and sprinkled with flavorful cheese and chunks of delicious, cooked bacon, I had a feeling the roasted asparagus was going to rise to the top of his *veggies I'll eat* list.

Once we'd gotten all cleaned up, and with dessert and
side dishes packed in a handy carrier, Kennedy and I
headed down the wooded path to Rory's log home with
the smell of grilling fish leading the way. Of course,
Wellington, newly addicted to grilled fish, bounded ahead
of us with his bushy tail held high. Apparently, he believed he was going to score some fish too. Clara, with
the instinct to follow her leader, came to a jarring halt at
the end of her leash a mere eight feet away. Kennedy
nearly toppled over from the shock of it. However, it had
been her idea in the first place to put one of Welly's old
harnesses on the goat and take her with us. We both recalled what Daphne Rivers had told us about goats wanting to be in a herd. Welly was definitely not a goat, but
Clara seemed to accept him as her bellwether, being content to follow him wherever he went. We felt that bringing her was a better alternative to leaving her in the
boathouse, where she'd just make a racket and try to eat
more Christmas decorations.

"Ladies," Rory greeted us with a smile the moment he
spied us making our way to the back deck. His face fell
when he saw the goat. "You brought a . . . unicorn to a
cookout?"

"And dishes to share," I added, holding up the insu-
lated bag.

Tuck, standing beside Rory at the grill with a beer in
his hand, clearly didn't know what to make of it. He
looked at Rory, then back to Kennedy and the goat. "What

you've done to that barnyard animal should be a crime. I honestly don't know if I'm at a cookout or a little girl's princess party."

"Don't be so dramatic, Tucker," she chided. "Little princesses don't eat grilled lake meat; they like chicken nuggets. Think of this unicorn as a witness protection disguise. Besides, you should be thanking us for taking such good care of her. We'll just secure her lead to the deck, and all will be fine. Now, let's eat. I'm starving, and we have so much to tell you."

We ate our delicious feast on the deck, enjoying the spectacular view of the lake and the fine weather. Welly, after scarfing down his own delicious meal of fish, went under the table and curled at my feet. Clara, taking her cue from him, also went under the table, napping between Kennedy and Tuck. With two large animals under the table, there wasn't much room for legs, but the pets were quiet, satisfied to sleep beneath our busy forks and the heated discussion.

"You ladies were busy," Tuck remarked briskly after hearing about our day. "Talking with the mayor, Daphne Rivers, the Stewarts, and the Peterses!" He shook his head as he looked at us. "You do know that if the sergeant finds out about this, she's going to come down on you?"

Kennedy furrowed her brows at him. "We're simply trying to sniff out the prankster. We're pretty certain it was Lars Jorgenson."

"That's ridiculous!" Rory clearly didn't agree with our theory. "After James left, I called Anders. Honestly, I felt bad even mentioning it, and with good reason. Lars's death wasn't only bizarre, but it was out of the blue. They never expected it. Anders was quite firm on the matter that his father had nothing to do with any of those pranks."

"Well, he would. He's clearly defending his father's legacy," I was quick to point out. "We heard from Betty that Anders refused an autopsy. The way I see it, he's only prolonging the process. The ME has an obligation to determine the cause of death."

"What?' Rory set down his fork. I could tell he found the matter troubling as well. "I wasn't aware that Anders did that. Do you know why?"

"Betty alluded to the fact that it was to spare Lars the indignity of the process."

I could see that Tuck was listening to this closely. He leaned across and looked at Rory. "Do you believe him?"

"What are you suggesting?" Rory asked.

"Look," Tuck began, setting down his beer, "until we know the official cause of death, I say nothing. However, you and I both know that Lars Jorgenson was most likely murdered. What do we know about Anders's relationship with his father?"

Rory's face darkened. "He was a good son. He loved his father!"

I could see that this line of questioning was really getting to Rory. I placed my hand over his and changed the subject. "Look, this is such a troubling matter, made more so by the fact that Rory and I discovered the body. This morning Kennedy and I were working off the suspicion that Lars's death was an act of revenge. The only problem with that theory is that while Daphne Rivers and Winnifred Peters named Lars as the prankster, Mayor Jeffers did not. And the Stewarts distinctly remember him sitting in the audience laughing when the goats crashed Kennedy's fashion show. And if he was in the audience, he couldn't have released the goats."

"No," Tuck said, looking at me. "But what if he wasn't alone? What if someone was helping him, like his son?"

"But what is the point of that?" Rory asked, challenging Tuck. "Why would either of them ruin the Blueberry Festival?"

"I have to agree with Sir Hunts-a-Lot here." Kennedy flashed Rory a conspiratorial grin. "What is the motivation? *I think I'll ruin the Blueberry Festival with childish pranks and then kill my father!* I don't think Anders Jorgenson has the motivation to do that. However, I do think Daphne Rivers would be mental enough to kill. Hold on," she said, thinking. "Maybe the mayor is as well. After all, he threw us out of the church." Looking at her face, one might have thought she was innocent of any wrongdoing, but I knew better.

"That was because you accused the man of murdering his friend."

"Well, he seemed angry enough that his parade had been ruined by water balloons. I took a chance!" Anger tinged her voice as she spoke.

"It's okay, Kennedy," Rory soothed. "I took a chance, too, today. After a few blissful hours fishing on the lake with James, I decided to do some snooping around as well. If you'll remember, my event was sabotaged by the prankster. My race route for the 5K had been washed away and replaced by new chalk arrows. I figured the culprit had to use the same type of spray chalk that I used. I went to the hardware store I originally bought it from and asked if anybody else had recently purchased a can of spray chalk. Oddly enough, Grayson Smythe purchased three cans last Wednesday."

"Grayson Smythe," I repeated, thinking. "We haven't talked with him yet."

"I didn't get to either. His studio was closed when I stopped by. He should be in tomorrow."

"Why do I get the feeling you three are going to pay Grayson Smythe a visit tomorrow?" To call Tuck's expression suspicious was an understatement.

"Don't look at me, Tucker dear. I will be working."

"I have to work too," I said, when his eyes shot to mine. Of course, I was going to visit Grayson tomorrow the moment the Beacon closed.

Tuck, resigned, took a deep breath. "Look, I know I can't stop you three from poking around. All I ask is that you please keep me posted on what you find. The strange death of Lars Jorgenson is haunting us all."

CHAPTER 29

Before I left Rory's, I made him promise he'd wait to visit Grayson Smythe until I could go with him. After a long, passionate kiss, he agreed. Dammit, but I had half a mind to spend the night at his place. However, if that happened, I knew for a fact I wouldn't get up for work in time. However, the death of one of his fellow veterans weighed heavily on Rory, and it had disturbed me as well. Staying the night was tempting, but in the end, Clara and her piteous bleating made it quite clear that I had to get back to the lighthouse. After all, it would never do to leave a goat on the back deck unattended all night long.

Kennedy had left with Tuck, which shouldn't have bothered me at all. Yet somehow, I felt unsettled returning alone to the lighthouse after such a day, with only a goat and a dog to keep me company. As I walked through the dark, forested path to the lighthouse, I thought about my former life in the city, and how odd it was that with so many strangers teeming around all the time, I never really felt alone. As if to remind me that I wasn't alone, Clara uttered a soft *blaaah*.

Welly and I brought her to the boathouse for the night, and I added a fresh bale of hay to her bedding and made sure she had plenty of water. I stroked the vibrant pink hair between her horns. "I really wish you could talk," I told her, as she rolled her eyes back in goatish ecstasy.

As if understanding me, she answered, "*Blaaah*."

Welly, feeling left out of the conversation, whined excitedly.

"It's just that, well, you saw everything the other night," I continued, moving my hand down her rainbow-colored neck and along her spine. "You were in the boat. You saw the person who put you in the boat with Lars. And I bet you know who killed him too . . . if he was killed," I quickly added.

She craned her neck to look at me and answered, "*Blaaah*."

"It must have been traumatic for you."

"*Blaaah!*"

"Okay, I get it. I don't understand goat-speak, so I'm just going to have to figure this one out the old-fashioned way. I just wish I knew how to do that." I gave her one last backrub and said, "Sweet dreams, Clara."

"*Blaaah*," she called back as Welly and I left her in the boathouse for the night.

Talking with a goat was far more frustrating than talking with a dog. Welly, at least, could understand me. He could also tell me when I forgot to do something, like get him his night-night cookies. He trotted over to the cabinet where they were kept and sat down. His intense gaze was on me as he started to whine. I didn't need to be told twice. I gave Welly his cookies, then sent Rory a text to let him know we were home safe. We flirt-texted back and forth for a while, until he ended it with, *Say good night to the captain for me.*

Ooh! Why did he have to say that? He was trying to make me regret my decision to leave him. I shook my head at Welly, and said, "Men!"

Knowing I was in for an early morning, I locked up and headed upstairs, with my valiant pup leading the way. I washed up, got into my pajamas, and felt I'd be asleep the moment my head hit the pillow. But in this I was wrong. My mind was too plagued with thoughts of all the possible ways Lars Jorgenson might have been murdered, and the many suspects who were piling up. I was trying my best to mentally unravel a possible thread that might lead me to the person responsible for the gruesome scene we had encountered Sunday morning. Lars Jorgenson, lying in the bottom of that boat dressed like a Viking, wasn't something I was soon to forget, if ever. Wellington, knowing I was in a weakened state of mind, jumped up on the bed and snuggled beside me. He was right. I wasn't about to send him to his own bed on the floor. Instead, I pulled him closer and stroked his soft fur as I thought about each of the people we had talked to during the day. It took a while, but eventually I exhausted myself and fell asleep.

A part of me was conscious I was dreaming when I saw the familiar Viking ship again. This time its large red sails were set, and it was riding on a wind-blown sea, moving through the choppy waves with rugged grace. In the bow stood a thick-set man, adorned in blue homespun and swaddled in fur. I knew him at once as a Viking.

The seafarer laughed with challenge at the wind and the spume that pelted his bearded face. His long blond hair trailed out behind him like a sprung sail, looking as wild and reckless as the laughing man himself. I thought him young, and glorious, and utterly immortal, until the wind shifted. The once-lovely hair slowly became more thin and gray with each rippling gust. The beard fluttered away too, and the round flesh of his face sank in measure, becoming thin and rutted with lines where there hadn't been any before. The man was old and familiar, yet he still stood tall in the bow, defiant and laughing. He was eating blueberries by the fistful, staining his lips blue as he laughed. Then a white goat appeared beside him crying, *Blaaah, blaaah, blaaah!*

I smelled the sweet, woodsy tang of pipe smoke then. The goat smelled it too and trotted off the ship, leaving the Viking to sail alone. The goat followed the smoke, trotting down a wooded pathway until it came to a bright red door. The goat stood before it, whining to be let in. Its whining grew more insistent. *Whining?* I thought, growing confused. Did goats whine? But it didn't matter. The red door clicked, then creaked. I realized it was opening slowly.

It was a ghost, I thought as terror seized me. I stared at the door as my heart pounded in my chest. What would I see behind the door? Dear God, what would I see? Pipe smoke tickled my nose, demanding my attention. As I filled with fright, my eyes flew open, and I stared into the darkness. That's when I realized Wellington was whining, not a goat.

I half believed I was about to see Captain Willy Riggs,

but the room was still dark, and the scent of pipe smoke that had pulled me awake was now gone. I must have imagined it, I thought, and sat up in bed. Welly was sitting by the open window, whining at something unseen in the dark. I swear that above the whining of my dog, the faint sound of footsteps climbing up the light tower stairs hit my ears. I fought to listen again, but the whining was too distracting. I believed the captain had visited me, but why? Unfortunately, the strange dream was already fading from my memory, dissipating like spun sugar in a tub of warm water. I wanted it back, but all that was left were bits and pieces.

"Welly," I called to my dog. He turned his big head, and I imagined he was looking at me. "What is it?" Welly didn't answer, but the goat did. I could hear her muffled bleating above the wind and the constant whoosh of the waves. Clara was awake at this God-awful hour and apparently wanted the world to know it. I exhaled sharply and looked at the time on my alarm clock. It was set to go off in half an hour. Great. It was no use trying to go back to sleep. I was too disturbed by the dream I couldn't fully remember, and so I got out of bed.

I splashed my face with cold water, got dressed, and followed Welly out of the lighthouse. He sniffed around, did his business, then trotted off in the direction of the boathouse.

The dim light in Clara's stall revealed that the goat was standing in her water trough again, pawing at the water with one glittering hoof, and dunking her head in up to her muzzle. The crates had been knocked around, and the hay was scattered and covered with droppings, reminding me that I needed to sweep up the floor and put down some fresh hay. Aside from all that, the goat was so happy to see us that she jumped right out of the trough and bounded over to the makeshift fence. Staring at her brightly colored mane and glittering hooves, I suddenly remembered the white goat from my weird dream. As Clara and Welly greeted one another, with sniffs, nudges, and head bobs, I stared at the goat, wondering if she had somehow communicated something important to me through my dream. The white goat had trotted up to a red door. What did it mean? Was it literally just a red door, or did it mean something deeper? I shook my head to clear my thoughts as I silently scolded, *Lindsey, you're losing your friggin' mind*. As if to drive this thought home, I looked at the bedazzled goat once again.

"*Blaaah*," she said. "*Blaaah, blaaah, blaaah!*"

"I agree. This place is making me crazy too," I remarked, then opened the gate, letting her out on the lawn with Wellington.

CHAPTER 30

"Morning, Dad," I said, greeting my father as he came through the kitchen door. After feeding Welly and tending to Clara, I had gone straight to the bakery kitchen and was working out my frustration on dough. Baking always helped me clear my head.

Dad, taking one look at the worktable and the racks along the wall now filled with cooling Danishes, mini quiches, muffins, and cake donuts, remarked, "Somebody's been busy this morning." He came over and gave me a kiss, then went to greet Welly, who was waiting anxiously by the door. "I heard the goat when I drove up," he remarked, tying on his apron. "Any word on how long you'll be keeping her?" Dad raised an eyebrow at me while pouring a mug of coffee.

I had just painted melted butter onto a sheet of rolled-out sweet roll dough and was shaking a mixture of cinnamon and sugar over it, when I shrugged. "The Jorgenson family is in mourning right now, and they have enough on their plates. And the police are still trying to figure out what happened. Tuck asked me to keep her a little longer. Hopefully, they'll figure this one out soon. I don't think I'm cut out for goats."

Dad grinned. "I distinctly remember telling you that you should get a boat, not a goat."

"And yet here I am, boatless but not goatless." We both smiled at that. As Dad got to work, rolling the cart of raised donuts over to the donut fryer, I added, "She might look like a unicorn, but there's nothing magical about what she's doing to my boathouse. Did you know that goats are indiscriminate poopers? No? Well, it's true."

"Lindsey dear, that's exactly the reason people don't keep goats in boathouses. Call that boyfriend of yours and tell him to build you a proper goat pen."

"I won't be keeping her that long," I reasoned, hoping it was true.

Dad cast me a sly look over his shoulder. "That's what your mother said about me, and here we are, going on thirty-nine years of marriage. Famous last words."

He might have thought he was being funny, but the thought of keeping a goat at the lighthouse permanently frightened me nearly as much as the strange dream from last night, only I really couldn't remember much about it but the fact that it was disturbing.

As we baked and began loading the bakery cases, I brought Dad up to speed on what Kennedy and I had learned the day before. Dad looked impressed.

"I thought you'd take it easy on your day off, especially after the weekend you've had."

"Well, Dad, finding a body and a goat changed things

for me. We learned a lot yesterday, but nothing, unfortunately, conclusive. One thing I'm almost certain of, however, is that Lars Jorgenson was either the prankster or was somehow involved in the pranks. But I can't quite figure out why."

Dad was dipping a tray of fresh-out-of-the-fryer donuts in decadent maple frosting and sprinkling them with bits of bacon when he looked at me. "You said the goat lady, whatsherface, was certain Lars was behind the temporary theft of her goats, but couldn't prove it. And that pie-making Peters lady was convinced Lars was the one who sabotaged the blueberry pie bake-off as well, but she didn't have any concrete proof either. Is there a way you could find some proof?"

I thought about this a minute before answering him. "There might be. Daphne Rivers showed us a set of tire tracks in the dirt by her goat pen. She thinks her goats were loaded onto a horse trailer or a box truck. I supposed I could have Tuck send the tire tracks to a lab and see if they can find out who owns or rented a vehicle with those exact tires."

"Sounds complicated."

I nodded. "There is one more member of the festival committee who was pranked that we haven't talked with yet, Grayson Smythe."

"The artist?"

"Yes. Rory and I are going out to his glassblowing studio after work today. I've been thinking about the pranks all morning. Although they were all cleverly disruptive, there was a common thread weaving through them all. They were each designed to infuriate the targeted committee member. Betty, a Realtor, got signs on her lawn. Rod Jeffers, the mayor and church music director, got bombarded with blue water balloons while directing his choir during the Blueberry Parade. Apparently, the choir sings the same song every year, 'Blueberry Pie'."

Dad was loading up a donut tray for the bakery case when he piped up, "They got what they deserved. That song was terrible." Although he was only partially joking, I silently agreed.

"Next was Rory's 5K run. Since I signed him up for it, I don't think the pranksters targeted him personally, but it did make him angry. Former military professionals take their exercise very seriously."

"And in his case, it shows. Am I right?" He wiggled his eyebrows at me as he said this.

"*Dad!*" I wanted to sound serious, but a silly little giggle escaped. I couldn't help it. I liked Rory, and Dad, who delighted in teasing me, knew it. The truth was, he liked Rory too.

I cleared my throat and continued. "Then we have Winifred Peters, the reigning blueberry pie champion. She had her pie replaced by one filled with mice. Very disgusting. Glad I wasn't there to see that one, or I might never eat another blueberry pie again. Then we have Stanley and Felicity Stewart, who had their food tent crashed by goats during Mom and Kennedy's fashion show. Again, not directly personal, but it was infuriating for all parties involved. Then, however, we have Grayson Smythe, a gifted artist whose glass masterpiece was publicly destroyed in front of thousands of people. That wasn't just personal—it very likely hurt him financially as well. The man makes his living selling his art, and his art was publicly destroyed. Worse yet, Lars stood up and clapped— loudly—when it happened. I'm very anxious to see what he has to say."

"Well, don't be disappointed if he doesn't confess to murdering Mr. Jorgenson, my dear. I've met the man. He's a decent sort, hardly the type to seek revenge. Grayson is refined, civilized, and overtly mild-mannered."

"You've talked with him?" For some reason this surprised me.

"Not since last night. We chatted a bit while your mother shopped at the arts and crafts booths before his unveiling. Apparently, Ellie loves blown glass. All I can say is that I'm half glad that glass monstrosity of his didn't survive the night, or else it might have ended up in my backyard. Imagine the worry of having to mow around that thing!"

I laughed with him at the thought.

The Beacon Bakeshop was back to its normal weekday pace, a fact we were all happy about. The usual customers came in for coffee and sweet rolls. There were vacationers hankering for a novel coffee drink, and beachgoers longing for sandwiches and cookies they could enjoy lakeside. Dad left at noon as usual, to hit some balls at the driving range. Although Rory was teaching him the ropes regarding fishing, it wasn't about to supplant Dad's love of golf. Wendy, after making and decorating a batch of adorable beachball cupcakes, spent the afternoon outside at the pup café with Wellington, handing out Beacon Bites and offering coffee refills. Clara took a spin out there as well and was an instant hit with the children. Rory came in an hour before closing time and was shooting the breeze with Tom.

"Hey, Linds," Tom said, flipping a dishcloth over his shoulder. "Elizabeth and I have this. We'll close the Beacon. Rory says you're going to talk with Grayson. I say go now."

"He's right," Elizabeth said, coming up beside him. "You should go."

Of course, during our quick morning meeting before we'd opened, the day's agenda was pushed aside in lieu of the progress Kennedy and I had made on our mission to snoop around. The strange death of Lars Jorgenson was on the tip of everyone's tongue. It was all anyone could talk about . . . well, that and all the obnoxious pranks played over the weekend. As we worked, my young staff had come up with all kinds of theories and scenarios, some of which were highly entertaining but unlikely. What we were all missing was the true grit of facts to keep our wild guesses afloat. Therefore, my staff was urging me to hurry up and solve this mystery. I was honored by their optimism, and, quite frankly, inspired by it as well. Ryan, for giggles, had even started a death pool in the kitchen at a dollar a guess.

"Seriously, Lindsey," Elizabeth continued, staring at me with her large blue eyes, "Grayson is the only person pranked that you haven't talked to. Although Clara the unicorn is the current favorite guess in the pool as the killer, we're all on pins and needles to see what Grayson has to say."

"Really," I chided. "We still don't know that Lars was murdered."

"My money's on crazy Winifred Peters," Ryan added with a grin.

"For me, the jury's still out," Rory remarked with a grim set to his lips. "Ready, Linds?"

I took off my apron, said good-bye to my staff, and headed out the door with Rory Campbell.

CHAPTER 31

Grayson's Glass Studio was two miles north of town, residing in a charming old Victorian that had been repurposed into an art studio. Although the parking lot was empty, the grounds were lush and immaculately kept, full of trimmed hedges, mature trees, and bright flower gardens, each one containing a stunning piece of glass art as the focal point. Giant glass flowers, oversized hummingbirds, and stunning butterflies created a sense of whimsy as Rory and I walked up the winding brick walkway to the studio. The entire way, I was silently marveling at the skill it must have taken to create such remarkable images out of glass.

"One thing's for sure, Grayson is really talented."

Rory gave a little nod. "I agree. The sculpture of those glass spheres was the only piece I had seen of his. But this garden is something else."

If the garden was whimsical, the showroom inside was a vision to behold. Just like the sculpture he had created for the blueberry festival, his work was sublime. Translucent glass of every color adorned the many shelves— from delicate stemware, glassware, serving bowls, and vases to fragile ornaments and intricate sculptures of animals and ships. I was so overwhelmed by the scope of his work that I failed to hear him approach until he was standing right next to me. I jumped at the sound of my name.

"So sorry," he apologized. "I didn't mean to sneak up on you like that. I heard the bell when you walked in."

"This place is wonderful," I told him. "I can't believe this is the first time I'm visiting your studio."

"I'm a bit off the beaten path," he admitted, "but I like it that way. I get more work done. Besides, thanks to the internet, I can now ship my glasswork anywhere in the world."

"Sounds dangerous," Rory remarked, running his fingers along a lovely fluted champagne glass with swirls of seafoam green in it. "These pieces look so fragile."

Grayson smiled. "Packaging glass for shipping is an art in itself. A lot of trial and error, I'm afraid. Also, a big bright sticker with the word *fragile* written on it helps. Can I show you around?"

I was about to say yes when Rory shook his head. "Actually, Lindsey and I have been meaning to pay you a visit. We've been thinking about your unveiling Saturday evening that went horribly wrong. It was heartbreaking to watch."

At the mention of the disaster, Grayson closed his eyes as if pained, while his lips formed a thin, troubled line. "The memory is still very painful, I'm afraid," he finally said, opening his eyes once again. "Glass is a fragile medium to work in. Pieces break all the time when I'm creating in the studio. It comes with the business. Still, all those hours of work, sweating away at the glory hole, only to have it all be destroyed in a matter of seconds! I feel a bit ill recalling the sound of all that exploding glass."

"I can only imagine," I said, sympathizing with the artist.

Rory, looking more puzzled than empathetic, asked, "What exactly is a glory hole?"

A thoughtful smile crossed Grayson's lips. "It's the term we glassblowers commonly use for the reheating furnace. The incredibly high temperature in the furnace melts the sand, changing its molecular structure into glass. It is over this hot furnace where the glassblower is able to shape and work the molten glass into art. It's quite a process."

"You are obviously very gifted at it," I remarked. "As you know, we were all so puzzled and angered by the pranks that were played during the festival. The identity of the prankster or pranksters still eludes us. Rory and I were just wondering if you have any idea who might have played such a mean-spirited prank on you and your glass masterpiece?"

Grayson's face darkened as he thought about it. "Come," he said, and beckoned us with a wave. "Why don't we sit in the garden while we discuss it."

The garden we were brought to this time was out back, nestled in a secluded spot between the shop and a gray-painted barn our host used as his glassblowing studio. It was possibly even more beautiful than the gardens out front, with a pleasing brick patio and an area under a pergola that housed a table and a built-in outdoor kitchen. The lawn here was thick and perfectly manicured. It was defined by a myriad of trimmed hedges, lush plants, interesting shrubs, and raised garden beds. I imagined this was his private haven, a space he enjoyed and where he entertained guests. He brought us to the cushioned wicker furniture on the patio and offered to get us a drink, which we both declined.

"Any thoughts on who would have wanted to destroy your sculpture?" Rory prodded.

The artist sat in his chair while his face clouded with troubled thought. At length he finally replied, "I hate to even say it, but it could have been Daphne Rivers."

Rory and I exchanged a look. I'd never expected that name to pop up in a glass studio. I looked at Grayson and asked him why.

He huffed and hung his gray head, cradling it between his hands. He then looked up and said, "The short answer is that I insulted her goats by calling them smelly, useless animals. This was in response to her bringing one of them over to my studio and letting it smash one of my glass butterflies to pieces. She then called my art ugly and useless as well." He looked up with a grim smile. "This incident, however, was in response to something that, on my part, I felt was quite innocent, but that might have led to the breakup of her marriage."

"What?" I blurted. I could see that Rory was also surprised by this news. "How did you do that?"

Grayson turned his palms to the heavens as he shrugged. "We were all at a holiday party thrown by the Chamber of Commerce. Derik Rivers and I were both standing around the meat platter, filling our plates with thick slices of prime rib, when he started complaining to me about his wife being a vegetarian and how he craved meat. I looked at him and said, 'You raise goats, correct?' to which he nodded. I then proceeded to tell him about the most delicious, curried goat stew I once had in Morocco." Grayson pursed his lips at the thought. "You see, I might have planted the seed that inspired him to slaughter one of his wife's precious goats. It was not only the death knell of that poor goat and my lovely butterfly, but their marriage as well."

The fact that Kennedy and I had heard about the grue-some incident from Daphne gave a lot of credibility to what Grayson was telling us. Still, I argued, "But you weren't the one to actually slaughter that goat, right? You just made a tasteless comment."

"Tasteless?" He lifted a brow in mock question. "I just pointed out the obvious. Many cultures raise goats for meat. Like I said, I might have planted the seed, but Derik acted on it at his own peril."

"If you ask me," Rory began, holding the artist in a level gaze, "the marriage was likely in trouble long before your comment. So, what you're telling us is that Daphne holds you responsible for her husband's actions?"

Grayson nodded. "That woman has a screw loose! However, I'm not saying she is responsible for destroying my sculpture. All I'm saying is that if I had to point my finger at anyone in Beacon Harbor, it would be at Daphne Rivers. She'd love nothing more than to see me make a fool of myself in public."

"What about Lars Jorgenson?" I asked. "I hate to mention it, but he was the person who stood up and began clapping when your spheres began to topple."

"I think he said something along the lines of, *You've finally made a sculpture worth staring at*," Rory reminded him. "Did you have an issue with Lars as well?"

Grayson's naturally pale face grew a shade lighter at the mention of the name. Clearly, he was upset, but even he couldn't deny that Lars Jorgenson had publicly mocked him as his sculpture fell. The artist exhaled and slowly shook his head. "I heard about what happened to him, you know. So sad. So shocking. Lars Jorgenson was a good man, and if my collapsing art provided him with his last moment of joy on this earth, then I can live with that. I don't like it, mind you, but there's the silver lining in my tragedy."

"Did you know him well?"

A wan smile appeared on his lips as he looked at me. "Old Lars and I go way back, all the way to grade school, in fact. Although I've only been back in Beacon Harbor for a few years now, what you might not know is that I grew up here. I remember the day Lars was the new kid in school. We were all so fascinated with him because he spoke another language. He had come from Norway with his parents and was only beginning to learn English. We had never seen his like before around here, I'll tell you. Quite the celebrity on the playground." A wave of nostalgia took him, and he shifted his gaze to the garden.

"So, you and Lars were friends." Although I had seen them together at the same table on Friday morning at the Beacon, they didn't appear to acknowledge one another. Maybe I had missed it.

Grayson answered my question. "I wouldn't call us friends. As you can tell, we were quite different people. Lars was big, brash, and popular. He was the star of the football team, fell in love with a beautiful girl, and married her. I, on the other hand, never quite fit in, being artsy, sensitive, and uncoordinated. Even back then, the kids knew I was different."

Although no one ever talked about it, we all knew that Grayson was a gay man. It didn't matter, because it wasn't a big deal in the world today. However, I couldn't even imagine how he must have felt growing up in a small town like Beacon Harbor, protecting such a secret. I leaned forward, feeling quite protective of this sensitive, gifted man. "Did Lars and his friends tease you? Were they bullies?"

Rory's icy-blue gaze shot to mine as I asked this. It was an unexpected line of questioning, but he understood why I was asking it.

For some reason this made Grayson smile. "The brute teased me unmercifully, but only about my glassblowing. That was because I teased him about his woodworking. Lars was a carpenter, you know. However, back in high school he was always polite to me. We weren't friends, but we had known each other a long time. It was more a matter of mutual respect. Anyhow, Lars stayed in Beacon Harbor. I went to college, traveled the world, and opened a glass studio in San Francisco. It was only when I started yearning for the country life that I came back here." He gestured to his beautiful surroundings, adding, "I'm not sorry I did."

"So, you don't think Lars was behind the prank that sabotaged your masterpiece?"

Grayson closed his eyes and shook his head. "No. However, no one can deny that he enjoyed it. How is his son doing, by the way?"

Rory and Grayson talked about Anders for a while, then Rory stood up to leave. "I have another question," he said, looking at the artist. "Do you, by chance, use a lot of spray chalk?"

Our host looked surprised. He also stood, leaned forward, and asked with a grin, "Describe *a lot*."

"I used it myself to mark out the course for the Blueberry 5K," Rory explained. "I went to purchase another can and was told that you recently bought some as well."

I marveled at how glibly my boyfriend could lie. However, I don't know if Grayson was buying it.

"I did buy some the other day," the artist admitted. "I use it to mark out my larger projects. Glass is a fickle medium to work in, Rory. I always draw out what I'm going to make before I start blowing the glass, including the colors I'm going to use. It's part of the process. Sometimes I use the chalk paint on my lawn. It washes away quite nicely once I'm done."

"Cool," I said with a grin, and popped up from my chair. It was getting late, and Grayson was no fool. Being one of the committee members, he knew about Rory's disastrous 5K. We didn't need him growing offended by the fact that Rory had checked up on spray chalk. The last thing I wanted was Grayson calling Scary Sergeant Murdock to report our snooping. "I love a good can of spray chalk. I'm thinking of having Alaina put some chalk art on the lighthouse walkway. She's a very talented young lady."

"That's a marvelous idea," Grayson said, walking us through his shop. "However, might I suggest using regular sidewalk chalk? It's far easier to work with on a sidewalk."

"Yes. Good point. Well, thank you for your time, Grayson. You have a lovely place here. By the way, my mom is quite a fan of yours. She loves your work."

His face brightened, and a genuine smile burst forth. "Ellie Montague Bakewell admires me? I've died and gone to heaven! Lindsey, please tell your lovely mother to come visit. If she does, I'll give her a private tour of the workshop."

We were in Rory's truck, ready to pull out of the parking lot, when he turned to me with a grin. "Funny, but he didn't offer you a private tour of the workshop."

"That's because I'm not Ellie Montague Bakewell. I'm just her daughter. It's like being two whole notches above chopped liver."

"Just two notches?" Rory teased. "Babe, you're nothing like chopped liver. And you have no idea how happy I am that you are *not* your mother."

CHAPTER 32

As Rory drove back to the lighthouse, we were both still puzzled by the conversation we'd had with Grayson Smythe. If what he said about Daphne Rivers was true—and we had no reason to doubt him—then maybe we needed to take another look at her. She had pointed her finger at Lars Jorgenson as the man who stole her goats. Rory, like Kennedy, floated the possibility that it all could have been a setup to throw suspicion on Lars Jorgenson, although the reason why Lars was the target of her anger still remained a question. But what if Daphne was behind the theft of her own goats? Her call to the police station on Saturday morning could have been part of the plan. What if she had already loaded them in a horse carrier and drove them to another part of her property before Tuck had arrived to take her statement? Daphne wasn't at the fashion show, but Lars Jorgenson was. She could have driven her truck between the Tannenbaum Shoppe and the brat and beer tent and released her own goats before driving away, relying on the good Samaritans under the tent to make sure her goats were corralled and safely returned. After all, as Rory had reasoned, we already knew whose goats they were the moment they stormed the fashion show. As Rory and I tossed around possibilities, I even wondered if Daphne could have been the person I had seen in the security footage of the parade. I had assumed it was a man, but Daphne could have thrown on a large windbreaker, tucked her hair under a ball cap, and carried buckets of water balloons into the crowd. With the help of her daughter and her friend that worked in her cheese shop, it was possible. Daphne was a fit, strong woman. And she had a hefty amount of anger.

Also, I reasoned that since she lived on a farm, she likely wasn't afraid of mice either. She could have sabotaged the pie bake-off and the 5K. And she most definitely could have snuck up to Grayson's masterpiece when no one was looking and tied one of the corners of the tarp covering it to the frame of his sculpture. Grayson had told us she had it out for him, but what about everyone else? Did she have an issue with Mayor Jeffers, Betty, or Winifred? I was fairly certain she didn't have anything against Rory. How could she, when she didn't even know him? Then again, maybe it was the whole Blueberry Festival she was opposed to? When Kennedy and I had talked with her, she hadn't mentioned anyone other than Lars. But she was certain he had taken her goats. And now he was dead. Did she kill him because he supposedly took her goats? Or was she the prankster and had framed Lars for some deeper, more sinister reason? Then again, there was always option number three: She could merely be what she appeared to be, a prickly, goat-keeping mama bear with attitude.

"Lars," Rory remarked, pulling my attention from Daphne and her goats. Rory, I noted, was shaking his head. Then, struck with a sudden thought, he made a not-too-legal U-turn and headed in the direction we'd just come from.

"We're going back to the glass studio?" I asked. For the life of me, I couldn't think why. Then, as if to answer my question, he made another turn, this time heading in the direction of the expressway.

"Doc Riggles was doing the autopsy today. If he's found anything, he might be inclined to share his findings with us."

"Is he allowed to do that? I mean, Betty usually spills the beans to us, so to speak. I kind of rely on it. Although . . ." I added, thinking, "I'm sure Tuck would tell us, when he knows anything."

"True, but we're a mile away from Memorial Hospital. And, to answer your question," Rory said, flashing me a sideways glance, "under ordinary circumstances, if an autopsy is ordered, the findings are only shared with the attending physician and the next of kin. If the next of kin feel like sharing the findings with family and friends, that's up to them. But, as you know, this situation is quite different. Lars's death was suspicious. The next of kin didn't want an autopsy done at all, but the police did, so one was done anyway. In this case, the autopsy findings are shared with the police and other authorities." At the word "authorities," a sly smile appeared on his lips.

"*Oh*," I said, understanding where he was going with this. "In this case, we are 'authorities.' Gotcha!"

This time the look he flashed me wasn't sly. "No. You're

a baker, Bakewell," he reminded me with a remarkably straight face. "However, I'm ex-military and have done my share of contract work with the Coast Guard. We found the body on the water, and the boat the body was found in was towed to my dock. Although we're not *officially* investigating this case, both Doc Riggles and Sergeant Murdock know we have thrown our hat into the ring as well. All we're after, Lindsey, is the cause of death . . . if one has been determined. I think we'd both like to know whether Lars Jorgenson was murdered or if he died of natural causes."

"That would be nice. I mean, there's always the chance we could be snooping around for nothing."

Rory turned into the main entrance of Memorial Hospital, then shot me a sideways glance. "There was nothing ordinary about Lars Jorgenson's death. Whatever information Doc Riggles is willing to tell us, we need to keep it quiet. Tuck and Murdock have been investigating this case as well, but from a different angle. Tuck told me they've been concentrating on the pranks and interviewing the high school kids. Remember, the cause of death is still unknown."

It was the way he looked at me that caused me to ask, "You know something, don't you?"

His shoulders lifted slightly as he parked his pickup truck.

"Before we go in there," I began, eyeing the small but mighty hospital that served our little village and the surrounding area, "I'd like to know what you think he died of . . ."

With the engine turned off, he put his hands on the steering wheel and sighed. "Definitely not the fire arrow. No scorch marks on his body. My gut instinct tells me he was most likely poisoned."

"Ooh, a woman's preferred method of killing, statistically speaking, that is." I tilted my head from side to side as I said this. "Maybe our Daphne Rivers theory isn't that crazy after all."

Doc Riggles's office was in the basement of the hospital, next to the morgue and the rooms where the autopsies were performed. I had never been to the basement of the hospital before, and I felt a little unsettled as I walked down the maze of deserted hallways, praying all the while that the recently deceased were safely out of view. Since coming to Beacon Harbor, I had stumbled across a few dead bodies and was still emotionally scarred from each one. Finding Lars's body floating aimlessly in that beautifully carved boat was something I wasn't soon to forget either. In fact, it was the source of my recent unsettling dreams. I didn't think I could handle seeing another as we followed the sign directing us to the morgue.

As we turned the corner, something white popped out of a doorway. I yelped at the suddenness of it before realizing it was Doc Riggles in his lab coat.

"Heard someone coming. Hope I didn't scare you, Lindsey?" Although his tone was apologetic, he was grinning.

My heart was still pounding a bit as I lied, "Not at all."

"Did Murdock send you?" he asked, looking puzzled at our sudden appearance.

Rory shook his head. "We were in the neighborhood. Lindsey and I were wondering if you were able to determine a cause of death for Lars Jorgenson?"

Doc Riggles looked up and down the empty hallway before ushering us into his office. "I was just finishing up for the day. The official report's not done yet, but I have contacted Murdock with my findings." As if weighing something in his mind, he suddenly shrugged. "You were undoubtedly going to find out tomorrow." As he spoke, he lifted a very technical-looking paper off his desk and wiggled it. "Just got this thirty minutes ago. Very curious, indeed."

"What does it say?" I was on pins and needles with anticipation. Rory was, too, only he was far better at hiding his emotions than I was.

Doc looked at Rory. "We talked earlier at your home when you and Lindsey brought the boat, the goat, and the body back to your dock. I know you had your suspicions then. Care to walk us through them again?"

I assumed the job of a medical examiner was morbid and lonely, and looking at his office in the bowels of the hospital, I believed I was close to the mark. Therefore, with an unusually captive audience, it seemed the doctor couldn't resist building a little suspense before the big reveal. Rory, thankfully, played along.

"The body didn't appear to have any physical signs of a struggle. Aside from the whole Viking getup, he looked peaceful, at rest. The silly objects found with him in the boat looked intentionally placed, except for the charred arrow and the burnt bits of hay. Seeing that made me think we had stumbled on a bizarre, ritualistic funeral." Rory paused here, and the doc encouraged him with a nod to continue. "Right, well, Lars's face, due to death, was pale and bluish. The color was particularly strong around the lips and mouth. I thought maybe he'd been eating blueberries, but then I was struck with the thought that maybe he was poisoned." Rory crossed his arms and leaned an elbow on his chair to indicate he had come to the end of his observations.

"Good man," Doc Riggles praised. "What a sad, confusing scene to come across. However, it appears that on two accounts you are proven correct. This paper here states that Mr. Jorgenson was very likely poisoned. He had unnaturally high levels of atropine alkaloids in his body, including scopolamine and hyoscyamine."

I leaned forward in my chair. "What does that mean in English, Doc?"

"Well, Lindsey, those toxins are commonly found in the plant atropa belladonna, more commonly referred to as deadly nightshade."

"Belladonna!" The word caused me to sit up in my chair. "I've heard of that one. Isn't that the plant women used to use a long time ago to dilate their pupils and make their eyes seem larger? Apparently, men of yore were into that look."

Doc Riggles gave a little nod. "Belladonna historically has been used for its medicinal qualities as well as an odd sort of cosmetic. However, it also has a long history of use as an effective poison."

"So, you think somebody injected him with poison extracted from the belladonna plant?" Rory stroked his chin meditatively as he thought about this.

Doc shook his head. "No, not injected. The plant was ingested, or more specifically, the berries of the plant were. When I examined the stomach contents, I found that he had eaten quite a bit of them too. Which brings me to your next observation, Rory. You said that his lips were blue, which is a sign of deoxygenated blood. However, there was also staining around the lips, mouth, and tongue from blueberries as well. We found the presence of both in his stomach, leading us to believe he might have confused the berries of the poisonous nightshade plant with blueberries."

"So, are you saying that he was murdered or not?" I asked, feeling very confused.

Doc, looking tired, removed his glasses and massaged the bridge of his nose. He set his glasses on his desk before replying, "Although we now know what caused his death, I'm afraid the findings are inconclusive. It might have been accidental, it might be purposeful, as in suicide, or he might have been murdered by someone disguising the belladonna berries with common blueberries. It's hard to say which scenario we're looking at here. We know that the berries of the plant are very poisonous and are known to cause delirium, hallucinations, and eventually death. The delirium and hallucinogenic qualities might explain the fact that Lars was dressed as a Viking. He was of Norwegian descent, after all, and his son has confirmed that his father was obsessed with Viking lore."

"But . . . but he was found in a boat!" I exclaimed a bit too loudly. I lowered my voice, adding, "Rory just said it looked like somebody attempted a Viking funeral. How is that not considered murder?"

"Well, my dear, we're medical people, not criminal investigators. All my office can tell you is the cause of death. The police know the results, and now you do too. While I have every confidence that Sergeant Murdock will be working hard on this matter, I also know that you two have, shall I say, a *knack?* for this type of thing. I'm hoping you will work with the police to put the pieces of this troubling mystery together and figure out once and for all what happened in the moments leading up to that fatal boat ride."

CHAPTER 33

Still reeling from the inconclusive nature of the find-ings of the toxicology report, we headed back to the lighthouse. I knew we were going to have to put our heads together on this one, so, against Rory's better judgment, I was getting ready to send Kennedy a text, when I realized she was already back at the lighthouse playing with Welly and Clara on the lawn.

"There's just no escaping her," Rory said, parking his truck by the boathouse. "I thought we could sneak up to the lightroom alone for a change."

"Ooh," I remarked playfully. "So, we can drink a little wine and talk about romantic things like murder?"

"You have a point, Bakewell." He flashed his most knee-weakening grin and got out of the truck, making me regret that remark.

Welly, the leader of the Rory Fan Club (which had

now expanded to include a bedazzled goat), was right there beside the truck lavishing praise on his second-favorite human in the form of tail wags and slobbery kisses. The moment I appeared, Welly shifted focus and bounded over to me with the same happy energy. It made me feel good to know that I was loved too. I gave both Welly and Clara a big hug, then headed for Kennedy.

"It's been a long day at the shop," she informed us. "I'm starving and thought dinner would be ready. Since you weren't home, and kitchens aren't my thing, I thought I'd play with the pets for a while."

"Good thinking. We've just come from Doc Riggles's office."

"No!" she said, bubbling with intrigue. "You must have a lot to tell me."

"We do. If you and Rory will take care of Clara, I'll feed Welly and whip up something for us to eat. Let's meet for dinner in the lightroom in half an hour."

Wellington followed me to the kitchen and ate his yummy kibble dinner while I set to work on a quick, portable dinner that would be fun to eat in the lightroom. Since I had plenty of Blueberry Delight left over from the other night, dessert was a no-brainer. Dinner, however, was another matter. Spying two loaves of French bread that I was going to use as a side for spaghetti later in the week, I decided instead to make some delicious French bread pizzas and a caprese salad to go with it. I turned on the oven and went to work, cutting the French loaves in half lengthwise, then dolloping a generous amount of pizza sauce on each half. Then, after pulling some veggies from the fridge, along with a pack of Italian sausage, I began prepping my pizza toppings.

Making French bread pizzas was not only easy, but fun

as well. After the pizza sauce, I sprinkled on the mozzarella cheese, then layered on slices of cooked Italian
sausage and sautéed veggies. Since Kennedy and I loved
our veggies, I sliced up a large tomato and chopped some
black olives to put on top of our loaf as well. I placed the
pizzas side by side on a parchment-lined baking sheet and
sent them into the oven for fifteen minutes—just until the
cheese was nice and bubbly. I then sliced some soft, buffalo mozzarella and layered it in a shallow dish with
sliced tomato and fresh basil leaves. I then drizzled a little olive oil over it, some aged balsamic vinegar, and
sprinkled on a little salt and pepper. I had just finished the
caprese salad when the oven timer went off. Dinner was
ready!

We sat up in the old lightroom, nestled on cushioned
white wicker chairs beneath the soft glow of strung Edison lights. We nibbled on the delicious French bread pizzas and sipped our favorite drinks as we watched another
spectacular Michigan evening unfold. The wind had
picked up, and a thick layer of clouds had moved in, casting the water in shades of blue and gray as light slowly
faded from the sky. It was a moody evening, a fitting
backdrop for our macabre discussion of the life and death
of Lars Jorgenson.

"I'm writing it all down," I told Kennedy and Rory as
I grabbed my fake leather-bound logbook from the captain's desk. My old boss had given me the notebook as a
gift when he heard I was moving to Michigan and was
going to live in an old lighthouse. I loved the gesture and
had used the notebook before as a makeshift suspect
board. It felt a little like déjà vu as I opened the logbook
again and wrote down the name of the case we were
working on.

"What's your heading?" Kennedy asked.

"*The Curious Death of a Viking*," I told her.

"You should have just put *Viking Murder*. I'm a professional. It's short and to the point."

"Professional?" I gave her a well-deserved eye roll. "News alert—Instagram posts and half-formed tweets hardly make you a professional writer. Besides, this is *my* logbook, and I think my title captures the essence of our mystery better."

"Viking. Murder. It's all you need." If she thought her proper English accent was going to give more credence to her stupid title, she was wrong. She even cast Rory a conspiratorial grin, but Rory was strategically remaining neutral, preferring instead a fourth slice of French bread pizza.

"Look, my title stays for one very important reason. We don't know that Lars Jorgenson was murdered, but we're going to figure that out. Once we do, we can change the stupid heading. All we know is that somehow he ingested the berries from the deadly nightshade plant and was found drifting in a boat with a goat dressed as a Viking!"

"Fine. Viking Death. It's still short and to the point."

I picked up my pen, crossed out the small words, and wrote, *Curious Viking Death*. I then showed the revised title to Kennedy. "Happy?"

"It's a fair compromise," she agreed, and gave me a wineglass salute.

Rory set down his empty beer bottle with enough force to wake the captain. "Are you two finished?" he scolded. This was met with stunned silence. "Good," he remarked. "Now, let's get to work!"

There were so many names to keep track of, but I

wrote them all down with notes about what we had learned from each person we'd spoken to.

Mayor Rod Jeffers, fuming mad at the prank that had been played on him, had looked at the security camera footage of the parade the day before Lars died. That was suspicious. However, he refused to believe that Lars Jorgenson was behind the prank. Could it have been a ruse? I put a *maybe* by his name and moved on.

Daphne Rivers had a little more going for her as a suspect. She'd been suspicious of us from the moment we met her. She was also certain that Lars was behind the goat-napping and seemed to know him pretty well. Another black mark by her name was because she was named as a person of suspicion by Grayson Smythe regarding the spectacular demise of his glass sculpture. Who else was she mad at? Could she be the prankster? I put a star by her name with a note to talk with her again.

Then there was Stanley and Felicity Stewart. They hadn't appeared angry at the goat debacle that had ruined Mom and Kennedy's fashion show; they just appeared exhausted. Even if they had an ax to grind against other members of the festival committee, which I didn't believe they did, they were working too hard during the festival to even pull off one prank, let alone poison an old man. I put the word *no* by their name and moved on.

The Peterses were another story.

"The pie baker," Rory said. "We know she grows her own blueberries, and you told me how mad she was at Lars. She believed he was the prankster."

"She did," I agreed.

"Perfectly resented him," Kennedy added, refilling her wineglass. "Lars's wife, Clara, was the town's champion blueberry pie baker. Winnie only won because she's no longer in the competition. The mice-in-the-pie prank really threw the old girl over the edge. Maybe even enough to poison her former rival's husband. On a side note, Randy Peters knows how to make a killer blueberry mint julep."

I inhaled sharply. "You said 'killer.' Do you think he could have made one and added some poisonous deadly nightshade berries to the mix?"

Kennedy sobered a measure. "He certainly could have. With the burst of mint and the amount of Kentucky bourbon in that drink, it would be hard to detect."

"I'm putting a star by their name as well." I looked up and asked, "What about Anders Jorgenson? Maybe his relationship with his dad wasn't quite the feel-good father-son relationship we think it was?"

Rory bristled. "No. Don't put his name down."

"But he refused the autopsy," I reminded him.

"Seriously, Linds, he's not a suspect." After Rory said this, Kennedy and I exchanged a look. Although I felt differently, I knew enough to trust Rory's instincts. Nonetheless, I quickly scribbled down the name *Anders Jorgenson*, and moved on.

"Okay, that leaves us with Grayson Smythe."

"He's known Lars the longest," Rory remarked. "They met in grade school."

"Right," I said, writing the information down. I looked up, adding, "However, their relationship was respectful at best. Lars was a big, bold, manly-man while Grayson is in many ways his polar opposite; slight, sensitive, artistic."

"He also didn't think Lars was the prankster," Rory added. "Instead, he had good reason to point his finger at Daphne, having instigated the demise of her marriage, so to speak."

"True," Kennedy remarked. "Yet wasn't it Grayson who also bought a few cans of chalk paint this week? Is that just a coincidence, do you think, or could he be the one who rerouted your racecourse?"

"I'll put a *maybe* by his name." I finished writing and set down my pen. "Well, we've written down what we know, which, looking at it on paper now, I realize isn't much. We still don't know whether Lars was the prankster, and if he was, did somebody find out and poison him, or was his poisoning an accident?"

Rory held me in his thoughtful gaze. "Those, I'm afraid, are questions that are going to require a little more fieldwork."

I shook my head, thinking that my brain was actually hurting, trying to ponder the mysterious manner of Lars's death. "What do you suggest we do?"

Rory narrowed his vibrant gaze in thought as he looked at us. "I suggest we pay a little night visit to the empty house of Lars Jorgenson."

"The home of a dead guy!" Kennedy's large, dark eyes glittered with intrigue. "Sounds spooky. I'm in."

"Me too," I said, gathering the empty plates and the tray of leftover pizza. "Besides, it's getting late, and I don't want to keep Captain Willy waiting." At the mention of his name, the Edison lights began to flicker.

"Dammit, Lindsey!" Kennedy chirped, jumping to her feet. "Why do you have to keep reminding me this place is really haunted?" All bravado and bluster, my dear friend still had the fortitude to grab her empty wineglass and the bottle before bolting down the circular tower stairs, leaving us in the lightroom with an echoing reminder of, "Uncool!"

"Are you sure she's going to be okay with this?" The grin on Rory's face was unnaturally wide and a tad mischievous. He was a handsome man on a bad day, but when he smiled at me like that, I believed I could do anything—even go on a spooky night visit to the home of Lars Jorgenson.

I grinned back, adding a breezy, "She'll be fine. We'll take Welly with us just in case she gets traumatized by a rogue Viking ghost and needs a comfort animal. Besides, I think Welly's been feeling a little left out since Clara came along."

Rory took the tray from my hands and headed toward the stairs. "It's hard to compete with a goat who looks like a unicorn," he said, and shook his head at the ridiculousness of it all.

CHAPTER 34

Rory had never been to Lars's home before, but thankfully he'd been given the address from Anders the day before. Kennedy had informed us that Tuck had already been to visit the home on Sunday morning, but we didn't think anyone had come back since the toxicology report had revealed the cause of death.

Like most houses in the surrounding countryside, Lars's home was tucked away off a series of dark, barely visible dirt roads that wound through the heavily wooded hillsides. In the daylight, it would have been a challenge, but not impossible. However, at night, having never been there before, the going was slow as we tried to sniff out the way with the bright lights of my Jeep and a little help from Google Maps. The only trouble was that some of the roads weren't even on the map.

Kennedy, sharing the back seat with Welly, crossed her

arms over the front seat. "It boggles the mind who would even want to live all the way out here. It's no better than a rabbit warren."

Rory, my copilot, took his eyes off the wooded tunnel of road long enough to furrow his brows at her. "It's quiet. It's a paradise," he added. "And in case you hadn't noticed"—he paused to tap the map on the nav system—"we're a stone's throw from the lake."

"We're heading directly for the lake!" I cried, slamming on my brakes. Welly yelped as the Jeep skidded to a halt. The road had ended at a gap in the trees that opened to reveal thirty feet of sand and the dark, rippling waters of Lake Michigan. I threw the Jeep in reverse and backed down the road a quarter of a mile. "Let's try this again," I said, determined to find the darn place come hell or high water. "The driveway should be off to the right."

With our night eyes peeled, and with the help of the handy flashlight I kept in the glovebox for emergencies, we finally found a little mailbox on a split-log post that was partially hidden by weeds, not fifty yards from the dead end of the road. Rory aimed the light on it, revealing a dangling wooden plaque that read "Jorgensons."

"Bingo," Kennedy remarked with a lack of enthusiasm. "Can't wait to see what's back in these spooky woods."

We followed the winding gravel drive to the end, where the woods opened to a clearing that revealed a surprisingly cozy-looking two-story home. The house, sitting on a fieldstone foundation, looked to be constructed out of wood that had been stained such a dark brown that it nearly appeared black in the darkness. If it wasn't for the bright red windows, and the two dim sconces by the front door, I might have missed it altogether, going straight to the other building on the property, which was a barn.

Welly, getting a whiff of some unseen animal in the dark, leapt out of the car and dashed off the gravel drive and into the thick ferns that lined the woods.

"Where the devil did he go?" Kennedy's voice sounded more spooked than annoyed, which prompted Rory to stoke that fire.

"He's either spooking the spooks away," he teased, "or bears. Either way I think we're good to proceed."

"HEEL!" I commanded to the wiggling ferns as I walked with Rory to the front door. Kennedy, choosing the safety of the pack instead of staying back alone in the Jeep, slammed the door and hurried over the gravel to join us.

"Ooh, this place definitely looks haunted."

"Honestly?" I chided, staring at her pensive face. "We are here to investigate a possible murder, not a ghost. Relax and stay observant."

"Mightn't I remind you that the last time we entered a house uninvited in this village we found a body?"

"Kennedy!" It was Rory's turn to admonish her. "If you don't want to come in, go back to the Jeep and wait for us there."

On edge, she turned to go back to the Jeep, but stopped short at something in the darkness. She then let out a piercing, "*AHHH!*"

We turned in time to see Welly leaping out of the black night, narrowly missing her, to join us at the front door, his bushy tail wagging with pride. Apparently, Welly remembered something from obedience training.

"It's just Wellington," I hissed, pulling her with us. "Look, I doubt we're even going to get in. The door is probably locked."

As I spoke, Rory turned the knob. There was a *click*,

and then Welly, knowing the ins and outs of doors, thrust his big head against it and trotted inside. Under the dim light of the sconces, Rory gave a shrug. "Nobody locks their doors out here. Come on. Let's see what we can find."

The moment Rory flipped on the lights, my jaw dropped. I didn't know what I'd been expecting, but definitely not the textured richness of the interior décor. Instantly my mind conjured the disturbing image of the Viking lying dead in the bottom of the boat. The Norwegian crafts-manship of the room—from the dark-beamed ceiling to the honey-colored pine furniture, the intricately carved mantle of the fireplace, to the woven area rugs and the rosemaling artwork that adorned the decorative pieces—was a step in giving that gruesome scene context.

"Is it just me, or does anyone else feel as if they've just stumbled upon one of Norway's UNESCO world her-itage sites? This place has the lived-in feeling of an old Norwegian mountain cabin." Kennedy walked over to a chair and picked up a handmade blanket covered with beautifully crocheted flowers in bright colors. "How ghastly!"

"Ghastly?" Rory repeated, not bothering to hide the annoyance in his voice. "Look at the workmanship in this place. This furniture is handmade. I knew Lars was a car-penter, but I never knew he was capable of such fine workmanship. I have a whole new respect for the man." With a look of awe animating his strong features, Rory then went over to the far wall to examine the contents of the exquisitely carved built-in shelving. He flipped a switch that turned on a multitude of built-in lights. The objects they illuminated were a collection of artwork and pieces from Norwegian history, including those distinctly remi-niscent of the Viking era. Rory moved his fingers gently over a few of the pieces, until landing on a footlong replica of a Viking ship. He gently lifted it from its cradle.

"What does this look like to you?" he asked me.

I inhaled sharply. "It's so similar to the one we found his body in. This must have been the model for that boat."

"I agree," he said, then continued to study the shelves. "Look here." Rory pointed to some empty spaces along the shelves. "Nobody's dusted for a while. There are pieces missing."

Kennedy was sitting in one of the cushioned chairs, mindlessly stroking Welly's lustrous fur, when she suddenly looked up. "Do you think this is about a robbery?" It was a good question.

Rory shook his head. "I could be wrong, but I don't think it was. There were artifacts lying next to the body in the bottom of that boat." He shook his head, puzzling over what we had discovered. "I think somebody placed those objects next to him."

"Which would indicate that Lars was dead before he was put in that boat." I looked at Rory. We both fell silent, taking in the room while trying to make sense of the scene we had discovered early Sunday morning. Bits and pieces were starting to fall into place. The sound of Kennedy's voice pulled us back to the present.

"Well, I'll leave you two in here to ogle the wonders. I'm going to check out the kitchen." She stood up and disappeared down a hallway.

"She's right," I told him. "We should look around."

While Rory went to investigate the second floor, I saw the light on in the kitchen and went to join Kennedy. I walked in to find her beautiful face aglow from the light of the refrigerator. She peeked around the door, grinned, and pulled out a blueberry pie.

"This looks delicious," she said, grinning as wide as a cream-licking cat. "I bet it's his wife's recipe. I heard all about it sitting on the Peterses' patio this afternoon. According to Beacon Harbor at large, Clara Jorgenson's blueberry pie was the gold standard of pies."

As she backed out of the refrigerator with the pie in her hand, a sudden image from the strange dream I'd had that morning popped into my mind. It was of the glorious Viking, eating handfuls of blueberries as he sailed on the high seas. Had the captain been sending me a message? I wondered again, staring at the pie. Yet before I could say anything, Kennedy peeled back the plastic wrap and stuck a finger in the thick, blueberry filling. The dollop of filling was poised before her open lips when I suddenly slapped her hand away, sending the pie filling airborne.

"Nooo!" I cried. "Don't eat that!"

Horror-struck, she gave me her best *How dare you!* look, as the blueberry filling landed with a splat on her new, sleeveless, blue-and-white-checkered linen shirt. I cringed, knowing that blueberry, like black coffee, was the bane of fine linen everywhere.

"Look!" she said, anger shooting from her eyes. "When I asked you to be my diet buddy, I didn't think you'd take it so literally. Look at me!" She waved her hand down her flawless figure. "I ate one slice of veggie pizza tonight! *One!*" she exclaimed, totally omitting the three glasses of wine she had enjoyed with that one slice of pizza. "It's not as if one bite of blueberry filling is going to give me an acute case of cottage-cheese thighs."

"Kennedy!" I shot back. "This isn't about your imaginary diet! This is about poison, and blueberries! Don't you get it? There could be poison in that pie!"

"What!?" she cried and looked at the pie cradled like a

baby in her free arm. She yelped as if scalded. Thank goodness the pie wasn't a baby, because she dropped it like a hot potato, and we watched it splatter on the floor. Welly, solely focused on the pie and not our argument, lunged at the blueberry mess with tongue dripping.

"NOOO!" we both cried, grabbing for Wellington. Two skinny girls, one in sensible shoes and the other in chunky heels, were only a slight deterrent for a food-crazed Newfie. Yet we were both determined. Using teamwork, we heaved him away from the blueberry mess with struggled force. Welly, with all four paws clawing the pine flooring, was fighting us every inch of the way. Thankfully, Rory had heard our screaming. Wherever he had gotten to in the house, he had raced to the kitchen and came flying through the doorway in the midst of our struggle.

"What in the world—" Clearly, he hadn't been expecting the sight that confronted him.

"We found a blueberry pie," I cried, fighting for breath. "In the fridge."

"Then what's it doing all over the floor?" he questioned, looking at us as if we were actually fighting over the pie and not trying to protect it. Clearly, he was missing the important bits.

"Deadly nightshade. Blueberries. Baked into a pie! Can you hold Wellington back while we get the pie off the floor?"

"Christ!" he blurted and lunged for Wellington. With Rory on the job, the situation was swiftly brought under control. Welly, understanding only the driving need of his belly, was forcefully escorted to the kitchen door and shooed outside. It was a split-second decision, yet I had a gut feeling that my dog was safer on the other side of the door at the moment.

While Kennedy washed her hands and blotted the stain on her blouse, I pulled up a picture of the deadly night-shade plant on my phone. "Look at this," I told them. "These berries could easily be mistaken for blueberries. While there are definitely blueberries in that pie, as a baker I know how easy it would be to boil down a couple cups of these poisonous berries and mix them together with blueberries to make a flawless filling. With enough sugar, I bet it would be nearly impossible to taste the difference."

"You think the poison that killed Lars could have been delivered through this pie?" Kennedy's voice sounded a little strained as she asked this.

"Both berries were found in in the contents of his stomach," I told her. "As we've been told, Lars loved his blueberry pie. I'm not sure if this pie is the murder weapon, but since it's here in his kitchen, we have to check it out."

Kennedy shut off the water and turned from the sink. Beneath her tawny skin, her face looked remarkably pale. "I'm rather certain he ate a piece," she remarked, lifting a little dessert plate from the other side of the sink. "I found this. There's a fork in there too. Before I dropped the pie, you saw as well as I did, Lindsey, that there was a large slice missing."

Rory was chewing on his bottom lip, a sure sign he was anxious. "We're going to have to notify Murdock. That pie needs to be tested."

"I'll send Tuck a quick text," Kennedy said and pulled out her phone.

"No," Rory snapped. "Not yet. Not until we finish looking around."

As Rory and Kennedy discussed the best way to alert

the authorities without making it obvious we were in the Jorgenson home snooping around, I was doing just that. More snooping. The kitchen was another fine example of craftsmanship, from the tall, honey-colored pine cabinets that reached to the ceiling, to the green granite countertops. I opened a cabinet out of pure curiosity and paused. I opened another, just to be sure.

"Hey, does anyone else find it odd that these cabinets have labels stuck to them?"

"That depends on what the labels say," Rory remarked, coming over to where I stood.

"Look," I said, pointing to a white label on the outside of the cabinet. "It says *glasses*, and voilà!" I opened the cabinet to reveal the shelves of glasses inside. Some of the shelves even had labels too. "I didn't notice it before, because we were stuck on that pie, but all the cabinets here are labeled."

Again, I watched as a troubled look crept over my boyfriend's handsome face. I knew how the death of this man had weighed on him, but as another possibility percolated behind his crystal-blue eyes, I could see he was mentally berating himself. I gently stroked his arm, resisting the urge to wrap him up in a fierce, protective hug.

"You're thinking what I'm thinking, aren't you?" he said in a quiet voice. "Could I have been so blind as to miss the signs?"

"What are you two whispering about?" Kennedy had come over to the cabinet we'd been staring at. "Labels. They do that for the pensioners who are getting a wee bit barmy. What?" she said defensively. "It's true." She then sucked in her breath as the thought finally penetrated her thick head. "Could it be that old Lars Jorgenson was losing his memory?"

"I remember Betty casually remarking about it, saying something like he was a few donuts short of a dozen, but that he still had a sense of humor." I gave a sad shake of my head at the thought.

"It was hard to tell," Rory remarked. "He never said a whole lot. The man was undeniably pleasant, but often he'd just smile and nod. He also laughed. Come to think of it, Anders usually talked for him."

"Well, we don't know anything for sure, but now we have another item to add to our list. Could Lars have been suffering from memory loss?"

"Winifred said Lars had a blueberry patch," Kennedy offered. "His blueberries, she said, were what made his wife's pie so remarkable. Maybe that pie is just fine, and instead Lars mistook the purplish berries of the wild deadly nightshade for blueberries?"

"It could be," I said. "If that pie turns out to be the source of poison, and Lars didn't make that pie, then we can assume he was murdered. However, if the pie is clean, and we find deadly nightshade growing in his blueberry patch, we might be able to prove that his death was an accident."

"Would you ladies mind checking out the blueberry patch by yourselves?" Rory asked, still looking upset. "I'm going to take a look at the barn."

With the aid of a flashlight and the app on Kennedy's phone, we left in search of the blueberry patch. Thanks to Wellington and his newfound love for blueberries, he sniffed the air and trotted across the backyard to a little pathway hidden between the hedges. We followed his dark, shaggy form as he pranced through the bushes and trotted along the path until finally bringing us to an opening that could only be the famous Jorgenson blueberry patch. Inspecting the patch with our flashlights, we saw that most of the blueberries had either been picked or the entire bush had been nibbled to the nub, bringing to mind Clara the goat. However, what we didn't find near the blueberry patch was any trace of the deadly nightshade plant. It could be growing in the woods, but we hadn't a clue where to begin looking for it.

"I could be standing on this deadly nightshade and be none the wiser." Kennedy aimed her light at me as she spoke, causing me to shield my eyes. "It all looks the same to me," she admitted and moved her light again, this time aiming it at the dark woods bordering the blueberry patch.

"I'm hardly an expert either, but I don't see any poisonous berries growing near these blueberries. Let's call it a night."

Kennedy agreed, and we followed Welly out of the blueberry patch and back the way we had come. My dog, as usual, bounded ahead of us. We found him a moment later sitting before a door in the side of the barn. He was whining. However, the moment I came up beside him I pulled up short, sucking in my breath.

"What is it, Linds?" Kennedy whispered, standing beside me. "You look as if you've seen a ghost, but we're outside, so that can't be it. Ghosts don't live outside." She uttered this fallacy as if it were gospel truth. I didn't have the heart to set her straight. In fact, I was suffering another odd flashback from my dream.

"That's a red door." I pointed to the door in question. "You're going to think I'm mad, but I saw this door in my dream last night. This exact door!"

Her perfect features twisted in consternation. "I don't know what I find more disturbing, the fact that you remember your dreams, or that you're dreaming of doors instead of that grumpy Paul Bunyan you're dating."

"No, I mean, I have those dreams too. But last night I had a truly strange dream. I saw a white goat standing in front of this red door. I'm not sure what it means. I think that maybe the captain somehow influenced my dream, and he was trying to tell me something."

Her eyes looked as if they were ready to pop out of her head. "I don't like that one bit," she hissed. "I don't want any creepy ghost popping into my dreams uninvited. Do you really think that's what's happening here?"

"I don't know," I said. "But I think we should open it."

The door was unlocked. The moment I opened it, my mind swirled with thoughts of Clara, giving me the feeling that this was her world. The moment I turned on the light, these feelings were confirmed. There was no doubt that the little white goat had lived in this barn. In fact, half of the space inside the barn was dedicated to her pen. The floor was strewn with hay, and there was a handcrafted manger near the wall, a food and water trough, and what was essentially a large dog door cut into the barn wall that led to an outside pen. However, the most eye-catching feature was a large climbing structure, constructed out of wood, that had been built in the middle of the indoor pen.

"Now, this is a goat pen," Kennedy remarked, and followed Wellington as he sniffed at the climbing structure.

Although I didn't immediately see Rory in the woodshop part of the barn, the moment I called his name, he poked his head above a pile of wood at the other end of the building. He motioned for us to join him.

"Look at this gate," I remarked, walking to the swinging doorway in the low wall that divided the goat pen from the woodshop. "How clever is this? Clara could push it open and join her human in the woodshop, or if Lars was busy, he could lock it."

Kennedy and Welly followed me through the swinging gate. Kennedy looked back at the goat pen we had just left and said, "Lars must have really loved his goat."

"Come have a look at this," Rory said, coming over to the workbench to meet us. "This place is amazing. It's a woodworker's dream. If I had to make an educated guess, I'd say that Lars made that beautiful boat he was found in right here. Look at all the wood shavings on the floor. This is the same wood used to make that boat. He'd obviously been working on it for a long time. Anders knew about it, but never talked about it. If my father had made a boat that beautiful, I'd likely tell the world."

I gently rubbed his arm, knowing that he missed his father. "We forget that Anders grew up here. His dad was a carpenter. Maybe to him the boat wasn't that special."

With a grim shake of his head, Rory remarked, "Maybe. But I don't think a boat like that would slip his mind. I think he's hiding something."

"Like the fact that his dad was losing his memory?" I questioned. "Didn't he move to Beacon Harbor to be closer to his father? Maybe he didn't want anybody to know about that?"

We'd seen enough in the barn. As we were heading back to the house, Welly started whining. When we noticed he wasn't with us, we found him sniffing around a huge object covered by a tarp. Whatever was under the tarp had sparked Welly's interest. My first thought was that some poor animal was hiding under it.

"Whatcha doing?" Rory asked, walking over to the dog. To us, he said, "It looks like a truck is under here." Sure enough, when Rory lifted the tarp, we saw a logo on the side of it that read *Jorgenson Carpentry*. "This is Lars's work truck."

Kennedy inhaled sharply. "Is it a box truck?" Her large eyes, expressing an *aha!* moment, shot to mine. "Daphne told us that such a truck could have been used to steal her goats."

"Oh dear, that's the smell I've been smelling." As I spoke, Rory lifted the back gate. The moment it was up, we were hit with an unmistakable scent of goat.

"Bloody hell!" Kennedy swore. "This is the truck! Daphne was right! Lars Jorgenson did steal her goats! The proof is in the goat droppings . . . that are literally all over this truck."

Kennedy had seen enough and brought Welly back to the Jeep with her. Yet there was one more place that drew my attention. Rory, as if reading my mind, nodded, and together we walked over toward the beach.

Walking through the loose sand to the private pier, I had the very real feeling that this was the scene of Lars's death. Perhaps it was the chill in the night air, or the sound of the wind coming off the lake and rattling through the trees. Whatever it was, my skin was covered in goose-flesh.

It was hard to deny that the beautiful Viking boat had been launched from this very spot. It would have been heavy, and there were deep enough ruts in the dark sand to suggest it had been pushed into the lake beside the dock. I even saw the distinct pattern of goat prints, which gave me a start. They were familiar, made from Clara, who had been bleating for her life in that damn boat.

Tears came to my eyes as I thought of the poor, helpless goat. What was her role in this tragedy? Thank goodness Welly had heard her when he did, or we might never have found her or Lars's body. Doing a quick mental calculation, I believed that my lighthouse was just above four miles south of this very spot. Traveling four miles in a drifting boat would have taken a long time. It made me appreciate how brave that little goat had been.

"Are you alright?" I asked Rory. He was standing at the edge of the dock, staring out at the black lake. I came beside him and took hold of his hand. Although I knew he was stoic to the core, I could feel him trembling.

"I'm sorry," I whispered. "I can't imagine how hard this has been for you."

Rory tightened his grip on my hand. "I didn't know him well, but I liked him. He was a good man."

"Then let's find out who did this to him," I said, and together we walked back to the Jeep.

CHAPTER 35

"Good morning, ladies," I said, as Mom and Betty walked into the bakeshop. It was early, but it was already shaping up to be another perfect summer day in Beacon Harbor. Our regulars, delighted with the weather, had taken their breakfast and coffee to the patio, leaving the café tables inside empty. I couldn't blame them. The lake sparkled like a sea of diamonds on such a morning. Dad was already sitting outside with Rory, both men enjoying their morning coffee while the dogs played on the lawn with Clara. The little goat was becoming a hit with the customers.

Betty removed her large sunglasses, a purchase she had made at Ellie & Co., no doubt, and fluffed her blond bob, shaping it around her face before marching up to the counter. Mom, removing a pair of the same sunglasses, was pulling off a lakeside casual look this morning, with a long, light denim skirt and a white top studded with cottage-garden flowers. Both ladies looked like they were on a mission.

"Betty's got some news for you," Mom casually informed me, leaning an elbow on the counter in what I believed she thought was a slick, informant-type move. "I think you're going to want to hear this, dear. Oh, and Tom"—she broke character to wiggle her fingers at my barista, who was busy with a stack of drink orders—"I'll have my usual skinny cappuccino, dear." She tossed him a wink before bringing her attention back to me. "And a blueberry muffin, Lindsey. They're to die for."

"Got it. And Betty?" I smiled at the Realtor who stood next to Mom, trying to pull off the same air of mystique.

"Deadly nightshade," she uttered.

"Excuse me?"

"The poison found in Lars Jorgenson's blood. Deadly nightshade." Betty hit me with a round blue-eyed stare to make her point. I found it disconcerting.

"Ya don't say?" I tried to look surprised by what she was telling me.

"Oh," she added with a lift of her voice, "and I'll have a skinny cappuccino too, Tom. And one of those lovely caramel pecan rolls. I'm feeling a little nutty today."

Ooh, there were so many replies to that comment, but I held myself back and simply replied, "Ya don't say?"

"I would have called you last night with the news, but it was late, and I knew that a few short hours wouldn't make a difference."

Those few short hours, as Betty had called them, had inspired us to rummage around the deceased man's home in the middle of the night. I was still trying to process all we had learned. Mom, trying to look casual, shoved her phone under my nose.

"This," she whispered, pointing to the picture of the poisonous plant in question, "is what killed him."

"Wow," I replied, attempting to look impressed. "I'll make a mental note of it."

"Here's the thing." Betty leaned her platinum head over the counter, adding, "Bob still can't determine whether Lars was murdered, or he poisoned himself by accident. However, we all know he was murdered, don't we?"

As Betty spoke, I could see Tuck and Murdock through the front window making their way to the bakeshop door. Knowing it would be best to move the middle-aged sleuths along, I appeased them with, "Well, we still have to prove it. Ladies, good work. We'll have to meet soon and compare our notes. Hopefully, we're getting close to solving this mystery. And Mom, I'm supposed to tell you that Grayson Smythe would love to give you a tour of his glassblowing studio."

Mom's face lit up with joy. "How wonderful. I'll ring him when we get outside and make an appointment. I've always wondered what it would be like to make glass."

"Me too," Betty agreed. "It looks fun."

"Betty," I interjected, thinking of something else. "Were you aware that Lars Jorgenson had memory issues?"

"Yes," she replied breezily, as if I had just asked her about the weather.

I lowered my voice. "How . . . serious was it?"

"I think it was pretty serious. Last year he forgot my name—just dropped out of his head while he was talking to me. Nobody does that around here. However, if you want more information on that, you should probably ask his housekeeper."

Alarm bells went off in my head as I practically hissed, "Lars had a housekeeper?"

"Well, of course, dear. He was getting forgetful."

"Why didn't you mention this to me before?"

"It must have slipped my mind." She looked at Mom and shrugged. "Maybe I'm the one losing my marbles. Anyhow, her name is Fran Lightfoot. She used to clean my house, too, before she became more of a caregiver and struck off in that direction. I'll send you her contact information."

I thanked the ladies, gave them their baked goods, and told them that Elizabeth would deliver their cappuccinos to the patio.

Mom and Betty stopped Sergeant Murdock as she came through the door. I cringed, hoping the ladies wouldn't babble on about deadly nightshade, but there was little I could do to stop them from behind the counter.

Tuck, sneaking away, came over to have a private word with me.

"I heard you found a blueberry pie in the Jorgenson home last night."

I nodded. Last night we had discussed how best to handle the discovery of the blueberry pie we had found. Everyone agreed Tuck needed to know about it, but we equally agreed he wouldn't be happy when he learned how we found it. However, since the man was smitten with Kennedy and had a man-crush on Rory as well, poor Tuck really had no choice in the matter. We had called him on the phone and told him what we had done. He promised to be as discreet as possible.

"Don't say a word to the sergeant that you were there," he warned. "Now that we know the cause of death, I'm heading to the house this morning. I'm going to take the pie over to the lab and see if Kennedy's instincts about it containing deadly nightshade are correct. That woman's uncanny," he remarked, shaking his head in wonder. He was also smiling. That dang smile had earned him the nickname Officer Cutie Pie, and for good reason. Officer Tuck McAllister was one fine-looking man.

However, I was still stuck on the fact that he thought it was Kennedy's instincts that stopped her from eating the pie. Swallowing the objection that was dancing on the tip of my tongue, I choose instead to issue a warning. "That pie is not in the best condition. We might have dropped it. Bet Kennedy didn't tell you about that."

"What?" He looked around to see if the sergeant had heard him, then lowered his voice. "You dropped the pie?"

"Me?" I was slightly offended he'd jumped to that conclusion so quickly. "No, Kennedy dropped it. Look, it's not important. If Murdock asks why the pie looks so mangled, just tell her you had a bumpy ride on your way back to the station. Okay? Also, we found Lars's work truck covered with a tarp. There's a ton of goat poop in the back of it. We think it was the truck used to steal Daphne Rivers's goats."

He lifted a questioning brow. "But Lars had a goat too. Couldn't the poop have come from Clara?"

"I'm no expert on the subject, but I think that what we found in the back of that truck was a little bit more than what one goat could produce over the course of a year." I shrugged, then realized Murdock was nearly upon us.

"And would you like a coffee to go with those donuts, Officer McAllister?"

"Yeah. Black, please." He gave a nonchalant smile and reached into his trouser pocket for his wallet.

Murdock, I noted, looked to be in a slightly better mood than usual. She ordered her latte and sweet roll, before asking, "Did Tuck tell you we've learned the cause of death on the Jorgenson case?"

I offered my warmest smile as I lied through my teeth. "No. Actually, it was Betty who spilled the beans on that one. She's what you might term 'close to the source.' Do you have any idea how it might have been done, you know, how the poison was delivered?"

Although usually tight-lipped about her investigations, Murdock decided to humor me. "We think the poisonous berries may have been mixed with blueberries, perhaps even baked into a pie. You didn't sell Lars Jorgenson one of your blueberry pies recently?" Her deep-set brown eyes nearly disappeared in the folds of her skin as she hit me with her best scrutinizing look.

"Ahhh," I stammered until I realized that this was Murdock's attempt at a joke.

"If you actually laced your baked goods with poison, Bakewell, I'd already be dead." She gave a little laugh as she took her latte and sweet roll to the patio. Tuck, offering a nod of approval, followed her out the door. I watched as they walked over to the table with Mom, Dad, Betty, and Rory, and sat down to join them. Welly, Clara, and the models had finished playing and were at the table, too, shamelessly double-teaming Tuck with their begging eyes.

Rory, I knew, was going to be busy today. He'd been a little tight-lipped when I'd asked him what he had planned for the day. I knew that after breakfast he was taking Dad fishing on his boat. However, after that adventure, all he told me was that he was looking into a possible business venture. Knowing Rory, this new business venture could involve anything from secret government work to taking more old men out on his boat for a fishing expedition. Whatever he was looking into, I knew he'd tell me in his own time. I knew he was feeling a bit lost and troubled these days, so I thought it best to give him space. Therefore, I pulled out my phone and sent Kennedy a quick text.

Tuck is going to take the pie to the lab. Also, we have a new lead, Fran Lightfoot. She's Lars's housekeeper. Want to join me after work?

I'm at Ellie & Co until noon, she replied, *then I'm going to the beach with Clara and Welly to do a photo shoot with a sassy new line of sandals from Stomp House. Will swing by the Beacon when I'm done.*

Perfect! I replied. *Save a pair of those sassy sandals for me!*

Betty, true to her word, sent me the contact information for Fran Lightfoot. I headed back to the kitchen to work on the afternoon treats, including more blueberry pies, some decadent brownies, a few varieties of cookies, and cupcakes. Although my hands were plenty busy, my brain was plagued by visions of Lars Jorgenson eating slices of blueberry pie.

CHAPTER 36

"Ready?" Kennedy asked, sauntering through the front door. I noticed she was wearing a new pair of very chic ankle-strap sandals. Welly and Clara, waiting patiently on the other side of the glass, had their faces nearly pressed against it as they stared inside, begging to come in. They looked adorably pathetic.

"I have another hour of work left, then we can go," I told her, pouring her a glass of blueberry-lemon iced tea. I had just made a pitcher, and Wendy, Alaina, and I were enjoying it immensely. I snapped on a clear plastic lid, added a straw, and handed it over to Kennedy. "Here," I told her. "You look like you could use this about now."

"This looks refreshing," she said, eyeing the iced drink. "It's hotter than Hades out there." She delivered a pointed look before taking a long sip. Her head rolled back in delight. "Delicious!" she declared. "It's just the thing to revive the senses after they've been melted on the hot Michigan sands and trampled over by a dog and a goat. Working with animals is so exhausting."

"You're the one who insists on using them," I reminded her.

"Because people on social media adore them. Oh!" she exclaimed, suddenly remembering something. "I forgot to tell you. Tucker called. The lab results on that blueberry pie came in."

Wendy and Alaina, who were working with me on the slow afternoon shift, leaned in. Kennedy had tossed out the bait, and we were practically salivating to hear what Tuck had told her.

"Well?" I prodded. "What did he say? Was there poison in that pie?"

Kennedy gave a curt nod. "Linds, you might have saved my life last night. You've got great crime-solving instincts, my baking friend. That pie had enough deadly nightshade berries baked into it to drop an elephant. Just think of what would have happened if I had eaten that bite?" Her lovely face wrinkled with concern.

"At the first sign of trouble, I would have taken you to the hospital and had your stomach pumped," I told her, walking around the counter to give her a big hug. She looked like she could use one.

"I knew it!" Wendy said, casting Alaina a pointed look. "Looks like the Blueberry Pie Prankster struck one last time. Poor Mr. Jorgenson." She shook her head, giving her long blond braid a good swing.

"Well," Kennedy began, trading her pouty frown for a smile. "I have a little thank-you present for your quick thinking last night." As she spoke, she reached into her giant tote bag and pulled out a pair of the same adorable sandals, only in shades of blue and deep raspberry. "I had the company send me a pair in your size too."

They were super adorable. I wanted to squeal with delight but refrained for the sake of my reputation as a responsible adult. As the girls inspected this new pair of sandals, Kennedy offered to have a few more pairs sent to the bakeshop.

"Perks of the job." She grinned and took another sip of her iced tea.

"So, you now know that Mr. Jorgenson was poisoned with a pie. What's next?" Alaina asked, crossing her arms as she took in this news.

"Well, that's why I'm here. Lindsey received another hot tip for us this morning. We're going to have a little chat with the housekeeper. Interestingly enough," she continued, holding the girls in her expressive gaze, "I've only read two mysteries in my life, and in both those books, the housekeeper did it. So, ladies, I'm thinking we may get lucky today."

"I'm hoping you do," Wendy said, flinging the towel she'd been using to wipe down the counter over her shoulder. "The sooner this prankster-creeper is caught, the better!"

Kennedy leaned an elbow on the counter and held Wendy in her large brown gaze. "We are giving it our best efforts, darling. Which brings me to my next question. Do you two mind very much if I borrow your boss early today? If you two ladies can hold down the shop, we can have a word with this mysterious housekeeper."

"Of course!" Wendy was quick to agree.

"We totally have this." Alaina tossed me a grin. "We've been slow this afternoon, and we close in an hour. Go"— she mock-shooed us—"and keep us posted, okay?"

"Ladies, I can't thank you enough," I said, and headed for the kitchen. Once there, I took off my apron, put on my new sandals, packed a half-dozen blueberry muffins in a bakery box, and grabbed my purse. A few moments later, I was heading out the front door with Kennedy, where Welly and Clara were delighted that we had finally come out to play with them.

Unfortunately, our playtime with the pets was short. Clara was put back into the boathouse with a fresh pail of water and a scoop of goat chow. Welly had taken that as a good sign and headed for the Jeep. Unfortunately, it was hot outside, and if, by chance, he'd have to wait in the car, it would be a disaster. Besides, having a nice rest in the cool air-conditioned lighthouse would do him good after a tiring photo shoot on the beach with a demanding blogger-diva. With both animals taken care of, Kennedy and I headed for the home of Fran Lightfoot.

Fran Lightfoot lived outside of town on a rural road that was dotted with small, tidy houses on two-acre lots. Fran's home was no different, only her house was painted beige instead of the usual white. Although everything was neat enough at first glance, a closer look at the weed-filled garden, the overgrown walkway, the slightly chipped paint on the house, and the dead branches on the old, drooping trees, gave the impression that whoever lived inside was either careless, or too busy to care. I believed the caregiver fell into the latter category.

"I hope she's home," I told Kennedy as I gave a knock on the front door.

"You didn't call first?" She looked miffed that the thought had slipped my mind.

"Relax. I have muffins." I lifted the red bakery box in question and winked. "If she's home, she'll talk with us.

No one will slam the door in our faces today with these blueberry yum-nuggets in my hands." I had just finished speaking when the front door opened, revealing a small, slender, middle-aged woman with the loveliest head of salt-and-pepper hair I'd ever seen. It was thick and pulled into a long ponytail that fell to the middle of her straight back. The older woman looked lively and in good shape. I imagined that her demanding job had a hand in that.

"Fran Lightfoot?" I asked.

The woman's questioning dark eyes fell to the bakery box in my hands, then scanned our faces for some sign of recognition. When none came, she asked, "Do I know you?"

We shook our heads and introduced ourselves. "We heard that you worked for Lars Jorgenson. It must have been hard for you to learn of his death. I . . ." I paused and offered a wan smile. "I was the one who found him. Well," I corrected, "I should say that my boyfriend, Rory Campbell, and I found him. It's not much, but I thought you might like some muffins."

"Oh, honey!" Compassion rose in her kind eyes as she thanked me for the treats. She then invited us to come inside. We followed her to a cozy little kitchen in the back of the house. There she set the box of muffins on the counter and began heating a kettle of water for tea while she offered us a seat at the equally cozy kitchen table. Although it was hot out, I truly believed there was something about a pot of hot tea that soothed the soul in difficult times.

"I hope tea is okay?" she thought to ask. "I could make you instant coffee instead, if you'd prefer?"

Kennedy and I were both quick to assure her that tea was fine. We then encouraged her to tell us about her time caring for Lars Jorgenson.

"I couldn't believe it when I heard the news," she told us, tears welling in her eyes. She dabbed at them with a tissue and apologized. "I'm so sorry. It's just that I've been working for him for over two years now. I really got to know him, you know? Such a dear man. Very kind. Not a mean bone in his body, which makes this so troubling. I keep thinking about who would do something like that to that poor man?" I could see this woman had genuinely cared for Lars due to the stream of tears trickling unchecked down her cheeks. She grew embarrassed, thinking it a sign of weakness to show so much emotion, but Kennedy and I were touched by the level of care that Fran Lightfoot had for her client. She poured the water into a teapot and brought it to the table.

"We have no idea," I told the woman. "That's part of the reason we're here."

Kennedy leaned in, adding, "You think somebody had a hand in this? You don't believe Lars could have crawled in that boat with his goat and had a heart attack or something?" Although we knew Lars had been poisoned, Kennedy was trying to see how our hostess would react to the question.

We watched her pour three cups of tea before she answered. "When I heard the news, dear, there was no doubt in my mind that he was murdered."

"How can you be so certain?" Kennedy raised an eyebrow at her.

A sneer of pure skepticism crossed the housekeeper's face. "Really? Dressed as a Viking and floating dead in a boat with his pet goat? That's the most sad, absurd thing I've ever heard."

"So, what do you think happened?"

"I really have no idea. It's up to the professionals to figure that one out."

Kennedy cast our hostess her most charming smile. "You might have already heard through the grapevine, but Lindsey and I have a bit of a reputation around here for solving crimes. Since Lindsey found the poor man and his goat, she's already involved, for better or worse."

"You two are trying to find the person who did this to Lars?" It was hard to tell whether she was happy about that or not. Her face showed nothing but skepticism. Then she must have thought better of it, because her eyes narrowed as she said, "Very well. He deserved better than he got. So, what is it you two would like to know?"

Kennedy shot me an *It's all yours* look. That was my cue. "One thing we'd like to know is whether you thought Lars was having memory issues?"

She nearly choked on her tea as a ripple of derisive laughter escaped her. "Honey, the reason I was hired in the first place was because the family knew Lars was slipping, only they were trying to hide it. They never said a thing to me about it either. When I was hired, all I was told was that they needed someone to come in and do light cleaning, shopping, laundry, and things like that. Lars, to his credit, was very good at hiding the little slipups at first, but eventually the disease takes hold, and no matter how good you are at deception, there's no stopping it. Whenever I confronted the family, they were very understanding but insisted that we never talk about it, especially to Lars. Heartbreaking is what it was." She shook her head, causing her long ponytail to swing like a pendulum across her back.

Kennedy asked the question on both our lips. "What disease are we talking about here, Fran?"

"Alzheimer's, dear."

Although we had seen the labels on Lars's kitchen cabinets, hearing the word was like a shock wave rippling through my emotions until finally rattling around in my brain. I was sorry to think I had more questions than revelations, but there was no denying that this new bit of information was somehow an important piece of the puzzle. I didn't know much about Alzheimer's disease, but for the fact that it was devastating for both the patient and family.

"So, that's why there were labels on all the kitchen cabinets." I looked at our hostess for confirmation. She took a sip of her tea and nodded.

"That poor man had become so forgetful that I'd ask him for a mug, and he'd bring me a plate, stating that he didn't have any mugs. He had a cabinet full of mugs! He just couldn't remember which cabinet it was. That's what sparked me to label his cabinets. It made life a bit easier for him."

"That was very nice of you," I told her and took a sip of my tea. It was nice and strong, just the thing for a difficult conversation like this.

She nodded, looking off into the distance. "He often talked of his family history, what he could remember of it. Lars's memory was failing him, but he remembered things from his childhood easier than things that happened five minutes ago. That's not uncommon with memory issues like his. Lars liked to tell me little things about Norway. I do know he had a Viking helmet and a cape. He also had a fine sword in his collection. But why he was dressed like that when they found him is beyond me."

I was still shocked that none of us had detected the fact that Lars had memory issues, including Rory, who had known him far better than Kennedy or I had. Last night, spotting those labels had been a revelation. Fran talked a bit longer about her client and his memory issues, and then I asked her about the blueberry pie we'd found in the refrigerator.

"That was his favorite. He never forgot about his love for blueberry pie. I heard all about how his wife, Clara, made the best pie in the whole county. I even saw all her blue ribbons. The secret, Lars would tell me, was in the blueberries. He was proud of his blueberry patch. Working in it always seemed to give him a sense of peace. But this year he just couldn't remember to keep it up. Honestly, it still looked fine to me. We would go there nearly every day with his goat, Clara. Our game was to pick the ripe ones as fast as we could before Clara got to them. That goat loved blueberries. Sometimes she would get out of her pen, and I'd find her in the berry patch, eating to her heart's content."

"Did you make Lars a blueberry pie recently?" Kennedy slipped the question in while looking at our hostess with polite inquiry.

Fran looked surprised. She shook her head again as she took a sip of tea. "Now, that's a skill I don't have. I can whip up a fast, nutritious supper, or straighten up a house in no time, but I cannot bake to save my life."

"Do you know who brought him that blueberry pie in his refrigerator?" I asked.

"What pie?" She looked confused.

"A beautiful blueberry pie was found in his fridge. We were curious about how it got there." I didn't want to tell her it was the pie that had killed her client. We wanted to see how much she knew about it.

"I'm afraid I can't help you there. The last day I saw him was Friday afternoon, before the parade. If there had been a blueberry pie in his refrigerator, I would have seen it."

"Do you think he could have made it himself?" Kennedy asked.

Fran shook her head. "Honey, that poor man couldn't make a pie even if he had wanted to. His days of following a complex recipe like that were beyond him."

"So, pulling off pranks like the ones played at the blueberry festival were out of the question for him as well?" I studied our hostess as I asked this.

"It's doubtful he could have played those pranks. Not on his own, at any rate. However, that man still had his sense of humor about him. That was a blessing." Fran smiled at some fond memory. "He loved to laugh," she remarked as her mood shifted to maudlin once again. "I'm . . . just so sad he's gone. He was my favorite client."

"We're sorry for your loss," I told her sincerely. "But before we leave, do you have any idea who might have baked Lars a pie?"

Fran shrugged, then seemed to be struck with another thought. "How silly of me to forget. I'm sorry, this whole terrible situation has me quite shaken. But now that you mention it, Susan could have brought him a pie. Susan," she offered, answering our questioning gazes, "is Lars's daughter-in-law. She was always kind to him and quite a good baker. You might want to ask her about the pie."

CHAPTER 37

"What does it say about a person when they're actually okay with dining under a wall studded with the heads of murdered animals?"

I smiled at my fashion-forward friend as she breezed through the doorway of the Moose, Rory's favorite Beacon Harbor restaurant. Sure, he felt at home in a room that felt like a hunting camp and was dedicated to the North Woods hunter. But the food was undoubtedly why he came, particularly the fried perch. Tuck was also a fan of the iconic restaurant, which meant that Kennedy was required to make an appearance at the restaurant a few times a month and belly up to the table like a local. She was getting good at it, too, which I found slightly unsettling.

"You're either in love, or you're desperate for a good meal," I teased as I pulled her to the table where Rory and

Tuck were waiting for us. "I haven't quite figured out which."

As Kennedy sat next to Tuck, I took the seat next to Rory and gave him a kiss. "Good idea, this," I said, gesturing to the room at large. "How was your day?"

"It was good," he assured me with a confident grin. Noticing that Tuck was about to say something, he quickly added, "I'll tell you about it later."

Tuck looked at me from across the table. "So, I take it Ken told you about the pie?" I nodded. "I would have told you directly, but I figured you were busy with the bakeshop."

"It was a busy morning," I agreed. "And Kennedy did tell me. I guess our suspicions were confirmed. Still, what a terrible way to go," I remarked, glancing at the menu. Rory's hand touched my arm, and I looked up.

"Seriously? You really need to look at the menu? You order the same thing every time we come here."

"You do, too," I parried with a smile and set down my menu. Rory was correct. I already knew what I was going to order. We both ordered the same dinner every time we came to the Moose—their famous fried perch. I silently cursed myself for being so predictable and made a mental note to order something different next time, just to wipe the knowing grin off Rory's face. But I loved that knowing grin. I then shifted my gaze to the young police officer again, now in fashionably tight jeans and a slim-cut Polo in a shade of blue that matched his eyes.

"I don't know much about belladonna poisoning," I admitted. "But I really hope Lars didn't suffer much."

Tuck lifted his shoulders. "Hard to say. I doubt it was pleasant. Death never is."

There was really nothing to say to that. Thankfully,

Karen, our usual waitress, came to take our order. She sauntered up to the table, dropped a basket of hot rolls and butter between us, and said, "Well, well, if it isn't Beacon Harbor's own team of Super Friends. I have to ask, have you found the prankster yet?"

"Working on it." Tuck gave her his best stone-cold-cop look, which wasn't entirely convincing due to his boyish good looks.

"Karen," Kennedy jumped in, gracing our waitress with a fake smile. "You flatter us. Be a dear and bring us a bottle of wine." She indicated that I was going to share it with her. "Tucker will have a rum and Coke, God only knows why, and Rory, who is suffering a breakout of antler envy, will have your best scotch over ice."

After Karen scribbled our drink orders on her notepad, she looked up. "I might as well take your orders now. The usual?" She scribbled a bit more, then added, "I heard a rumor and want to know if it's true. Someone said that old Lars was killed by a slice of blueberry pie."

Tuck grimaced. "We're trying to keep that quiet for the time being, but since you seem to know, it looks like we've failed. Yes," he said with a begrudging nod. "The rumor's true."

"That's ironic," she remarked while staring at me a beat too long. "I'll be right back with your drinks. Oh, and I should warn you, tonight's dessert special is blueberry pie. Any takers? I thought not." She made one more note on her pad, pursed her lips in sardonic delight, and went to get our drinks.

Once our drinks were delivered, our lighter conversation turned once again to the matter of Lars Jorgenson. Rory picked up his scotch and swirled the liquid in his glass, "So, Linds, before you got here, Tuck told me that you and Kennedy went to talk with Lars's housekeeper today. I honestly didn't know he had one." Although he offered a kind smile, I could tell he found the thought troubling. Rory had spent a good deal of time with Anders, and apparently the subject of a housekeeper had never come up. Was it mere oversight or a cause for suspicion?

"We talked with Fran Lightfoot today," I told them. "The poor thing was very broken up about the unexpected death of her client. She seemed like a kind woman. Kennedy and I both agree that her sadness regarding her client was sincere. She also told us a few interesting tidbits that might help us put the pieces of this puzzle into place."

Both men leaned forward. "Like what?" Tuck asked.

Kennedy picked up a dinner roll, stared at it, then put it on a side plate. She looked at Rory. "I find it remarkable that you didn't know that Lars Jorgenson suffered from Alzheimer's disease."

Rory nearly spit out the sip of whiskey he'd just taken. "What? Lars had Alzheimer's?" Although we had suspected Lars might have had memory issues, due to the labeled cabinets found at his home, somehow hearing the name of the disease was quite another matter. "Where did you learn that?" he asked Kennedy.

"Fran Lightfoot," we both replied.

"But that's not all, Rory." I took hold of his hand as I continued. "She told us there wasn't a pie in his refrigerator Friday afternoon, which was the last time she'd seen him. But she did tell us that Susan Jorgenson could have been the one who baked that pie."

I believed a slap in the face would have been kinder and easier for him to handle than this news. I watched as some terrible inner turmoil clouded his handsome face as he struggled with the implications of what we were telling him. Then, however, the soldier came through, and he looked resolved and ready to face whatever was to come. "I've met Susan. She seemed kind. Are you suggesting she might have knowingly poisoned her father-in-law?"

"We don't know," I was quick to reply. "But her name came up as someone who liked to bake for Lars. Fran didn't know the pie found in Lars's fridge was the murder weapon. We thought it best to leave that information out during our talk. We also learned that Lars was clearly beyond baking for himself. It could be possible that Susan Jorgenson took that pie to her father-in-law's house at some point after Fran left and before Lars was found by us early Sunday morning."

"True," Rory said, thinking. "But what's her motive for doing so?"

Tuck set down his rum and Coke and offered, "Maybe it was as simple as the fact that he was becoming a huge burden on the family? Or maybe the younger Jorgensons stood to inherit a good deal of money? We've obviously talked with the family. They seemed genuinely shocked by his death, but on some level it could all be an act. They're hesitant to say too much, but everything they have told us checks out. However, there's the issue with the autopsy. Refusing it only served to prolong the cause of death. It could be a sign they were trying to hide something. I'm not sure about the inheritance angle, but we do know that Lars Jorgenson did own a good deal of prime lakefront property."

Rory's face darkened. "Anders isn't rich by any means. They're hardworking people with two little children to raise. Could it really be about money?"

"Do we know anything about how Susan Jorgenson really felt about her father-in-law?" I offered.

"I'll visit the family again tomorrow," Tuck said, fondling his half-empty glass. "Maybe there's a good reason why they didn't mention Lars's memory problems. I'll also look for clues to see if Susan baked that pie."

Rory took a sip of his scotch and cradled the glass between his hands as he reminded us, "There's still the matter of the prankster. If all Lindsey and Kennedy learned was true, clearly Lars wasn't our prankster. However, there are still two committee members who believe he was, namely Daphne Rivers and Winifred Peters. Need I remind you that Winifred is a champion pie maker?"

"Rory's right," I said. "Also, Kennedy and I can attest to the fact that Winifred seemed angry enough to bake such a pie."

"True," Kennedy chimed in. "But let's not forget about the deadly nightshade. Who has access to that plant? We now know that's what killed him. I say, we find the plant and we find our killer."

"Kennedy." Rory lifted his glass to her. "That might be the single smartest thing you've said all day."

It was hard not to think of the puzzling death of Lars Jorgenson, but thankfully my work at the Beacon Bakeshop kept my hands and my mind occupied. It wasn't until the lunchtime rush was over that Rory came to pick me up for our planned outing. Although my staff was perfectly able to handle the bakeshop, Dad had insisted on staying while Rory and I made another visit to the house of Winifred Peters. Winnie had been high on my suspect list. We knew she could bake a pie, just as we knew she had her own blueberry patch. However, what had become obvious from our first visit to her house was that Winnie and her husband, Randy, had no love for Lars Jorgenson. Rory and I had brainstormed the possibilities last night.

Winifred and her husband could have delivered the pie. Then, once Lars had been poisoned, the two of them could have staged the whole Viking burial scene to throw the cops off their scent. With two people working together, they could have dressed Lars and gotten him into the boat. It didn't take a huge leap of the imagination to link them to the murder. Afterall, Winifred had motive and means, but did she have the murder weapon? That was something Rory and I were going to find out.

With Welly already in Rory's truck, we drove out to the Peterses' lovely home once again. As we pulled up the driveway, I said, "We don't want to appear obvious, so while I talk to Winnie, why don't you secretly send Welly into her blueberry patch, then make a show of going after him? Once you're there, start looking for signs of the deadly nightshade plant."

"That's your plan?"

"It's all I've got. It might not work, but at the very least it will get you into her blueberry patch."

"Devious, Bakewell," he said with a teasing grin. "But do you really think our canine partner is up to the challenge?"

"Let's find out." I looked into the back seat and held up a blueberry Beacon Bite. "Does Welly want a Beacon Bite?"

Getting a whiff of the cookie, Welly sprang up from his seat and licked my face, hitting me with a slobber bomb. What did I expect? I wiped my cheek as I gave Welly his cookie. "Good thing I brought plenty of these."

I held up a zip-lock bag filled with Beacon Bites. "All you have to do is lob a few of these babies into the blueberry patch and Welly will go after them. But please be careful. If you spot any sign of poisonous nightshade, call him back and get him out of there. I'll press Winnie to see if I can get her to confess to making that pie." I held up my cell phone. "If she does, I'll have proof."

"You're turning me on, Bakewell." Rory leaned over and gave me a knee-weakening kiss. Thank goodness I was already sitting down. Welly, smelling the cookies, started to whine, prompting Rory to reach into the back seat and open the door. Welly jumped out and began trotting off into the woods. "Stay on your toes, Linds," he whispered. "I'll be keeping an eye on you from the blueberry patch."

"No, I did not bake that man a blueberry pie!" Winifred cried, as if the mere thought was the height of revulsion. I watched as her jowly cheeks flushed red with anger. "Besides, that man was a pie snob. His dear Clara made the best pies," she mocked. "He'd no sooner eat one of my pies than I would make him one. Besides, I wouldn't waste my precious blueberries on him!"

I stared at her as her tirade against Lars and his pie snobbery continued, catching all her self-righteous anger on my phone's recorder.

"Winnie," her husband chided. "The man's dead. Cut him some slack."

Winifred huffed and tried to appear civil, but the affront to her blueberry pie bake-off was still eating away at her. "It's just that I'm a very competitive woman," she remarked, trying to justify her anger to me. "You're a baker, Lindsey. You know the joy of baking something special and having your friends gush over it. Well, I'm a good baker too. I've been doing it a heck of a lot longer than you, missy, and I just wanted the recognition that's due me. But that blasted man robbed me of it!"

"Well, we don't really know that for sure," I reminded her. "It appears that Lars Jorgenson was suffering from memory issues. His housekeeper told me he didn't have the mental capacity to pull off such involved pranks."

"Phooey!" she huffed. "Maybe he wasn't working alone."

As Winifred talked, I looked over her head at her blueberry patch. While Rory was walking the perimeter, Welly was smack-dab in the middle of it, nibbling on something.

Winifred continued. "As I've told you before, those childish pranks have Lars Jorgenson written all over them." She was about to add something when her eyes narrowed. She looked at me, then spun around before I could stop her.

She let out a screech at such a high pitch, I jumped with fright. "There's a . . . a bear in my blueberry patch!" she cried, and bolted in the direction of Wellington, waving her arms frantically as she ran.

Rory, kneeling at the far end of the berry patch, suddenly stood up, causing a new wave of panic and outrage in Winifred.

"There's a bear *and a man* in my blueberries! Randy, get your gun!"

Randy grimaced, eased himself out of his chair, and started for the back door of the house.

"Get out of there, you heathens!" Winifred cried. "Those are my prized blueberries!"

Rory and Welly, both fast on their feet, dashed out of the blueberry patch and into the bordering woods, where they vanished. I wasn't about to wait around either. With Winifred gone, I made a beeline for the pickup truck. I jumped in the driver's seat, started the engine, and drove down the road where Rory and Welly were emerging from the dense woods. I pulled the truck over and picked them up.

"Well?" I asked.

Rory shook his head. "I didn't see anything that looked like atropa belladonna back there. But I'm afraid that Winifred is correct." Rory opened his hand to reveal a handful of plump, juicy blueberries. "She really does have the best blueberries in the county. These things are delicious."

CHAPTER 38

The fact that Winifred Peters didn't have any obvious signs of poisonous nightshade growing on her property didn't fully exonerate her. She had plenty of anger for the deceased man, and so she remained at the top of my suspect list. However, as we drove back to town, Rory surprised me by asking me to take the next road, which headed away from town and the lake.

"Where're we going?" I asked.

"I was up all night thinking about what you and Kennedy said about Susan Jorgenson. We know that Winifred Peters is a champion pie baker, but I'm not convinced she baked a pie for Lars. Sure, she's angry enough to harm him, and a bit crazy too, but I don't think she'd ruin the reputation of her precious blueberries by blending them with poisonous ones. Remember, Lars wasn't her rival— Lars's wife was. Lars was just displaying his fierce loyalty to the woman he loved. Randy Peters would do the same if the tables were turned. It's an endearing flaw that we men have, I'm afraid. We champion the women we love."

My heart was beating a tad wildly as he spoke. I looked at him as I continued to drive his truck, and asked, "And, umm . . . what about *my* blueberry pie?"

"Babe," he said, putting his arm around my shoulder and gently caressing my cheek with his fingers, "there isn't a pie in the world that can compare to yours, and I mean that."

My heart fluttered. His praise of my baking skills acted as a powerful aphrodisiac. I was about to lean over and kiss him, when he said, "Here! Make a right here!"

I nearly missed the road but made the sharp turn, causing the truck to wobble a little on the gravel road. "Whoa!" I exclaimed. "You can't say such things about my baking when I'm driving. Save it for the bedroom."

He laughed, kissed my cheek, and directed me to the home of Anders and Susan Jorgenson.

As we drove up the driveway of the new, modest-sized home, Anders welcomed us with surprising warmth. Susan had been in the kitchen with the children when we arrived, but once they heard that Welly had come with us, she and the two children came running to the back deck to meet my huge, lovable dog. Welly loved children and was more than happy to play with them in the yard. They tried to make him retrieve their ball, but fetching was a skill we were still working on. Nonetheless, the children giggled and chased after him as they played a competitive game of keep-away.

"So nice to meet you," Susan said to me. "I was in the kitchen making cookies with Hans and Gretta," she explained. "This has been such a sad time for us. If I'm not keeping busy, I'm crying."

"I understand," I said, and we talked a little about baking while Anders went to get drinks.

We sat on the back deck in plastic Adirondack chairs. Rory and Anders were drinking a beer while Susan and I stuck with bottled water. After all, I was driving. Rory was the first to broach the subject of Lars's memory issues.

"Yesterday Lindsey spoke with Fran Lightfoot, Lars's housekeeper. Fran mentioned that Lars had been diagnosed with Alzheimer's disease. I've never heard a word of that before yesterday. Is this true?"

It was obvious the question was an uncomfortable one for the Jorgensons. The couple sat in silence, looking to one another as their faces blanched in turn. Then Susan's eyes filled with unshed tears. She hastily excused herself and went back into the house. Anders, watching his wife leave, finally broke the silence.

"I'm afraid it's true," he said, and hung his head. A moment later he looked up, and I could tell this stoic man was on the verge of tears as well. Rory looked into his friend's eyes and gently squeezed his shoulder, urging Anders to continue.

"My father was the epitome of a tough man, you know?" he began, sniffling and wiping his eyes. Embarrassed, he cleared his throat and took a swig of his beer. "Susan and I . . . started noticing little things around the time my mom got sick, but we all brushed it off as normal signs of stress and aging. Then, shortly after Mom died, I got a call from an angry homeowner, one of Dad's clients who was relying on him to finish a custom kitchen job. He told me my dad hadn't shown up in weeks. Dad wasn't answering his phone. That prompted me to drive up from Kentucky that afternoon as all sorts of terrible scenarios were playing out in my head. When I got to his home, I found him in his woodshop working on that damn boat of his."

"The little Viking boat he was found in?" I asked. Anders nodded.

"He didn't recognize me when I came through the barn door. That's when I realized something was going on. His normally tidy house was a mess. Food was left in the pans and on the kitchen counters. His clothes were scattered around every bedroom upstairs. It was heartbreaking to see."

"I can only imagine," Rory said in his steady, unwavering voice. The unspoken comradery between the two men was evident in the way they regarded one another. This was a side of Rory I seldom saw, and it touched me, making me realize what a special man he was, not only to me, but to those he cared about. It caused my throat to constrict uncomfortably with emotion, and I happily let the men continue.

Anders looked up at Rory with pain and sorrow inhabiting every line of his face. "I took Dad to the doctor that weekend. That's when he was diagnosed with the disease. I remember the day well. He was so angry about it. I wanted him to move in with me, but he refused to believe that anything was wrong with him. That's when I hired Fran Lightfoot to help him around the house. We also decided that since he wouldn't leave his home, Susan and I would have to move to Beacon Harbor."

Just as Anders mentioned her name, Susan returned to the back deck carrying a tray of cookies.

"Please forgive me," she said, setting the cookies on

the outdoor table. "The pain is still so raw. He was such a dear man and watching him suffer with that terrible disease—slowly losing a lifetime of memories and his ability to take care of himself . . ." She shook her head and sobbed. "I know it sounds terrible, but I truly believe he's at peace now, reunited with his dear Clara."

My eyes caught Rory's as she said this. I knew he was thinking the same thing I was, but he shook his head nonetheless, silently telling me to hold my pressing questions for the moment. It was hard to do, because the thought that Susan might have assisted her loving father-in-law into the afterlife with a pie was becoming a real possibility. My mind reeled with the facts as Anders continued to speak.

Susan often baked for Lars, so he would trust her.

Poison as a murder weapon was historically used by women.

The couple had tried to hide Lars's declining condition.

The couple had tried to decline the autopsy.

Yet most importantly, the burden of caring for such a stubborn loved one had altered their lives, causing them to have to pick up everything and move to a different state. Their aging parent had caused a difficult predicament for them.

"Susan's right," Anders continued. "My dear father, the old Viking, is at peace now. I truly believe that. But like the Vikings he had studied and worshiped, he was as stubborn as he was proud. We agreed, for his sake, to hide the fact that he had the disease. We decided, as a family, that we would do whatever we could to make sure he lived as independently as possible until . . ." But here Anders paused, choking up again. When he had control of himself, he added, "Until the time came when we would have to put him in a home. That time had come," he said to Rory. "Susan and I had to make arrangements for him with a home that specialized in memory care. They would have taken good care of Dad, but the thought of leaving his home made him angry and depressed."

"You were going to put him in a home?" As Rory said this, his clear blue gaze shot to mine. "What happened?"

"That's the thing. We think . . ." Anders paused again to look at his wife.

"We think," Susan repeated, picking up where her husband left off, "that Lars took his own life."

"But . . . he always appeared so happy," I remarked.

Anders nodded. "He loved to laugh. And he was a happy man by nature, but he was also deeply depressed. He knew, on some level, what the disease was doing to him. I remember the day, not long after he was diagnosed, when he picked up a picture of Mom and didn't know who she was. At first, he told me he didn't believe that he'd been married to such a beautiful woman. Then, when I showed him more pictures—pictures of their wedding, of me when I was little, of our vacations—he grew so sad and frightened. He drove off that very day to some farm and came back an hour later with a goat. I thought he was crazy. I was about to return the goat back to the farm where he bought it, until he said, 'I'm naming her Clara, so that I never forget my wife's name again.'"

"He . . . named the goat after your mom so that he wouldn't forget *her* name?" This was a revelation to me. We'd thought the goat was named Clara so that Lars wouldn't forget the goat's name, not the other way around.

Somehow that depressed me more than I cared to admit, and my heart went out to this family and all they had been through.

"You said that your dad was driving?" Rory asked, stuck on this little detail. "Did he still drive?"

"Actually, he was still driving up until a few months ago. He was a decent driver and still seemed aware of the rules of the road. But the trouble was, as the disease progressed, he just couldn't remember how to get home anymore. That's when we took his keys away."

"What about his work truck?" I asked, knowing that someone had recently used it. "Did you take the keys to that too?"

Anders looked puzzled. "How do you know about that truck?"

"I didn't," I lied. "He was a carpenter. I just assumed he'd have a truck." Quick recover, Bakewell!

Anders shrugged. "I leave the keys in it. Once we moved to Beacon Harbor, I essentially took over my dad's business. I used to bring him with me, but after a while it just got to be too hard working on the job and keeping an eye on him. Dad wasn't happy about that, but there wasn't much I could do about it at that point."

Rory leaned in and asked his friend, "The police found a blueberry pie in the refrigerator with one slice missing. They think that was the last thing Lars ate before he died. I have to ask, did Susan bake Lars that pie?"

Anders looked at Rory, his brow furrowing with suspicion. "That young police officer, McAllister, was here earlier today asking the same question. What are you suggesting, Campbell?" Rory, staring at his friend with an unwavering gaze, didn't flinch.

"I liked to bake for my father-in-law," Susan jumped in with a smile, trying to break the sudden flare of tension. "We used to pick blueberries, too, but I didn't make him a blueberry pie, not recently at any rate."

"When was the last time you baked him a pie?" I asked, trying to hit a friendly tone. But the couple was on to us.

Susan shrugged. "A couple of weeks ago. But we all ate it, Anders, Lars, and the kids." Susan looked at her husband for confirmation. Anders nodded, indicating that it was true.

"Look," Anders said, "I'll be honest with you. I go to my father's home every night to put him to bed. On weekdays, I drive to his house, get him out of bed, get him dressed and fed. I park my car there, then take his truck to work. When I'm done with work, I return home, eat dinner with the family, then drive the truck back to his house. Fran makes him dinner, but I put him to bed, every single night! I was with him during the fireworks at the Blueberry Festival. Susan took the kids home while I drove Dad back to his house. I opened his refrigerator to get him a glass of milk. He always drank a glass of goat's milk before going to bed. I was the last person to see him, and I can tell you with absolute certainty, Campbell, there wasn't any blueberry pie in that fridge on Saturday night!"

It was hard to tell if Anders was lying, covering for his wife, or telling the truth. However, giving him the benefit of the doubt for the moment, if he really was telling the truth about the pie, it meant that somebody else had visited Lars's home after Anders had left and had brought the pie. That still left the window open for Winifred and Randy Peters. Then again, Fran Lightfoot would have known that Anders tucked his father into bed every night as well. Puzzled, I looked at the couple, and asked, "Do either of you know how that pie got there?"

"Not a clue," Anders said, shaking his head. "Everything was fine when I left him. Then the next thing we know, we're being woken up at the crack of dawn, by you, Campbell. You were the one to break the news that my father was found dead in the bottom of his own boat, dressed as a Viking, and with his damn goat in there too! I wish to God that somebody could tell me how the hell that happened!"

CHAPTER 39

"I hate myself for saying this, but I don't know if I believe him." Rory cast me a look as we drove back to the lighthouse.

Welly was lying across the entire back seat, panting heavily from the exhaustion of playing with two young children. How good it would be to be a dog, I thought. Dogs weren't bothered with pressing questions, like what the heck happened to Lars Jorgenson. Nope, my dog's only concerns were food, cookies, playing with friends, and sleeping. I looked at my boyfriend and offered, "It is suspicious, the way they've been hiding everything to protect their father. Anders said he believed his father might have done this to himself. Do you think that's possible?"

"Sure, he could have eaten the pie, gotten dressed up as a Viking, and climbed into his boat with his goat for one last ride on the high seas. But again, here's the problem; somebody made him that pie."

That dang pie, I thought, and pulled into the lighthouse driveway. I was surprised to see Dad sitting in the back-yard under a tree with a drink in his hand and Clara neatly folded beside him, sleeping peacefully.

"Now, that's a sight you don't see every day." I smiled at Rory and parked his truck. "A former Wall Street ty-coon snuggling up to a bedazzled goat. It nearly melts the heart," I teased and got out of the truck. The moment I opened the door for Wellington, the goat sprang up and trotted over the lawn to greet us.

"Thank you for closing the Beacon," I told Dad.

"The young people did all the work while I did a little prep for tomorrow. Mom will be over soon, along with Betty and Doc. You do remember inviting us all over for dinner tonight?" Dad smiled, figuring that I had forgot-ten.

"Dad," I admonished. "Of course, I remembered. I was planning on fish tacos, but since you and Rory didn't have much luck today out on the boat, we're having my backup meal of barbecue chicken with corn bread, green beans, and a fresh berry fruit bowl. I've had the chicken marinating all day, just in case."

"Smart girl," Dad said and gave me a kiss.

Dad helped me set up for dinner on the Beacon's patio. I hadn't gotten around to having a private deck built around back yet, so when the weather was this perfect, I used what I had.

We pushed the tables together, opened the red umbrel-las, and were good to go. Rory was out back working his magic on the grill with Welly and Clara to keep him company. Every now and then, Dad and I caught a whiff of the grilling chicken, making our mouths water. While Dad worked on making a few pitchers of his famous sangria, I made the corn bread, washed and prepped strawberries, blueberries, blackberries, and raspberries for my berry bowl, whipped the cream, and steamed two pounds of farm-fresh green beans. Kennedy and Tuck arrived just in time to help set the table. Betty and Doc came shortly after they did and joined us. With the side dishes ready to go, and the pitchers of sangria already on the table, Kennedy looked up and grinned.

"Ellie's here," she said, and pointed at the lighthouse driveway.

I turned and saw Mom pulling up the lighthouse drive in her red convertible. Her famous, tawny blond hair was kept at bay by a designer silk scarf, and she was wearing her big, vintage, Audrey Hepburn movie-star sunglasses. The models were with her, too, both little dogs in their harnesses and buckled into the back seat, their little black noses sniffing the rushing air from their respective sides of the car.

Kennedy shook her head in wonder. "That woman sure knows how to make an entrance."

The moment the models were unbuckled, they darted from the car like fluffy white streaks of lightning, heading for Welly and Clara. Mom, with her giant purse over her arm, came clip-clopping up the walkway to the patio to join us.

"Darlings!" she said, beaming with delight, "I just had the most wonderful time. I was given a private tour of Grayson Smythe's glassblowing studio."

Betty looked impressed, and, if truth be told, a little

disappointed as well. "Wow. Not everybody gets a private tour of the famous glass shop." Doc rubbed Betty's shoulder in a show of support.

"It's so fascinating," Mom said breezily, removing her scarf and taking the glass of sangria Dad handed her. "Grayson is such a talent. I never realized how much work goes into glassblowing. He showed me all around his studio, even that furnace the glassblowers call the glory hole. It's incredible when you think that with enough heat, the right tools, and a lot of talent, one can turn ordinary sand into beautiful works of art."

"It is a wonder," Doc agreed. "It makes the prank played on that poor man all the more ghastly. Did he talk about that at all, Ellie? Or was he too smitten with you to bring it up?"

"Oh, Doc," Mom demurred and waved him off. Although Grayson was undoubtedly smitten with Mom, she knew how to handle the situation to her advantage. When one was a former model, it came with the territory.

Just then Tuck and Rory came from around back with a platter full of beautifully cooked barbecue chicken, three dogs and a goat following in their wake. The chicken smelled as delicious as it looked. Everyone took a seat at the table while Mom continued telling us about her tour of the glassblowing studio.

"Back to your question, Doc, we did talk about that terrible prank. Although I could see that it still bothered him, Grayson assured me the broken glass could be recycled and blown into something new. He had collected it all and had already separated it out by color. Anyhow, I asked him if he could make something for you, dear, and he did. I watched him do it."

"What did he make, Mom?" I was just dying to know.

Mom tossed me a cheeky grin. "I'm not telling. It's a surprise, but I know you're going to love it. He promised to drop it off at the Beacon tomorrow. And I have another surprise," she told us, then paused to take a bite of the chicken thigh she was holding. Mom knew her table manners, but they were no match for the tangy, sticky barbecue sauce that got all over her face as she ate the chicken. We all waited with bated breath while she chewed, then dabbed her lips with her napkin.

"Ellie, chew faster. We're all on pins and needles here," Dad teased with his deadpan delivery.

"Oh, James," Mom admonished with a silly grin. "My surprise is that Grayson has agreed to let us sell some of his smaller pieces at Ellie and Company. Isn't that marvelous?"

Kennedy's eyes lit up at the thought. "That's wonderful. Say the word and I'll start blogging about them. Hope he's up for the challenge."

Dinner was progressing nicely. Kennedy was on her third glass of sangria, Welly and the models had all been given bits of chicken under the table, and Clara had trained Doc into feeding her strawberries. Tuck had just come out of the lighthouse carrying a tray loaded with pints of hand-scooped ice cream from Harbor Scoops, an ice cream scoop, and some dishes when Betty cried out, "Oooh! This food has been so delicious that I almost forgot to tell you some very interesting news I learned today."

"What's that, Betty?" Rory, who was always mildly entertained by Betty's bubble-headed outbursts, was trying his hardest not to crack a grin as he stared at her from across the table.

"Well . . ." she began while holding the container of

Rocky Road ice cream. It was as far as she got into her story because she was attempting to scoop the rock-hard ice cream into her bowl. Her first attempt flew off the scooper and landed on Doc's plate, prompting him to take the pint and scooper from her, while urging her to continue. Betty obliged. "Well, as I was saying, I was in the car with Margaret and Rick Bigham, showing them the old Vanderveld house in town, you know, that darling cottage with all the gingerbread work on Forrest Avenue, a block from the beach?" Apparently, due to the blank looks from the table at large, we didn't quite have our fingers on the pulse of the Beacon Harbor housing market like Betty did. She gave a flip of her hand and continued. "Well, they're in their seventies now and getting tired of their big house in the country—"

"Betty, if this is about a house sale, I'm going to be sorely disappointed," Doc told her.

"Well, I haven't sold it yet, dear," she admitted. "But to my point, Margaret has lived in Beacon Harbor all her life. She's the head librarian over at the county library, so she's a smart cookie. Anyhow, on the drive over to Forrest Avenue, I was telling her about the annoying prank that was played on me the day of the Blueberry Festival, with all those darn *For Sale* signs on my lawn. I thought it was a highly original prank, but then Margaret surprised me by telling me that the same prank had been done before."

"What? When was this, Betty?" Rory asked, now gracing the older woman with his full attention.

"Well, that's just the thing, dear," Betty said, looking at him. "It was done a long time ago—way back in the seventies, according to her memory. She wasn't sure if the prank played on me was done at the same time, but she clearly remembered that some of the very same pranks we experienced last weekend were also done at one of the earlier Blueberry Festivals, creating a bit of chaos back then as well. Of course, nobody back then had turned up murdered. But Margaret did seem to remember that some of the local high school kids were responsible for them."

"Betty," I began, looking at her pleasant round face, "if what you are telling us is true, then this information might lead us to the pranksters."

"We've already been talking to the high school kids," Tuck chimed in. "Although they've all laughed and giggled while we've questioned them, not one kid has cracked or admitted to planning those pranks."

"Maybe one of them got ahold of an old yearbook, or heard stories from one of their parents or grandparents?" Kennedy offered. It was a good point.

It was curious. If the same pranks had been played at an earlier Blueberry Festival, then there would be a record of it. I really wasn't sure how all these pranks, old and new, connected to the murder of Lars Jorgenson, but there was something about the fact that they had been done before that begged to be investigated. Since Tuck and Murdock had been concentrating their energies on the high school kids, and even their parents, I felt it my duty to find out all I could about the original pranks, and the devious high schoolers who had pulled them off. If there was a link between the two, it just might help us figure out who was responsible for the murder of Lars Jorgenson.

CHAPTER 40

"Everyone knows that poison is a woman's art, therefore I think Lindsey's right. A woman is responsible for the . . ." Wendy, suffering from some odd disease that made her faint when confronted by gruesome issues, like death, paused over her word choice, and offered, "pie. A woman baked the pie," she exclaimed, wiggling her rolling pin at Elizabeth for effect, "which means it's either Winifred Peters, the daughter-in-law, or the housekeeper."

Wendy and Elizabeth had come into the bakeshop early to help me bake. Wendy was becoming an excellent baker and liked coming in early, but this was new territory for Elizabeth, who usually came in right before we opened. Wendy, I had learned, had talked her into coming in early by telling her about all the fun we had while we baked. And since both girls knew I was trying to solve this latest mystery, they were eager to talk about all the possibilities with me. I really appreciated it, because with so many loose ends I felt that I was going crazy.

I let the girls pick the music, which was interesting. I wasn't a fan of rap or house music, and I didn't know any of the words, which made me feel old, but some of the songs got me dancing. We banged out the donuts and our usual morning pastries and quiches, placing them directly into the bakery cases. We were now in the middle of making a variety of delectable pies, which we would showcase during our lunch rush. I felt a slice of triple-berry pie would pair nicely with Ryan's gourmet sandwiches, particularly the turkey and avocado, which was our hottest seller. We were also making blueberry pies, strawberry rhubarb, cherry, and peach. Elizabeth suggested apple, which Wendy and I were quick to shoot down. "Girl, we're in the height of summer," I teased, wiggling to the beat of some artist called Deadmau5. "Summer pies mean berry, and cherry, and peach. Once the apples start to ripen, we'll wow them with our apple pie. I'm counting on you to come in and help us with that. But for now, we're sticking with summer favorites."

"That's how we roll in the kitchen, Elizabeth!" Wendy added with a grin.

With a mound of pie dough before us, and delicious fruit fillings cooling in pots on the stove, we picked up our rolling pins while we continued to discuss my suspect list.

"What about Daphne Rivers, the goat lady?" I asked the girls. "Clara came from her farm. And we all know how angry she was about her goats being used in a prank."

"You told us that Betty said the pranks had been done before?" Wendy thought about this as she gently placed her rolled-out pie dough into a pie tin. "My younger brother is in tenth grade. He said everyone he knows was happy to throw the water balloons during the parade, but nobody knows how they got there. Rumor is, it was an adult."

"Yeah, I heard that too," Elizabeth chimed in.

"It just seems so odd that an adult would pull such pranks. High schoolers, yes, but a responsible adult?" I shook my head, struggling with the same question that had been plaguing me since the festival began. "And how do all these pranks tie into the death of Lars Jorgenson?"

"Maybe they don't," Wendy offered. "Maybe they're two different things." The thought had crossed my mind too, but in my gut, I felt they were somehow connected. I just couldn't see how yet.

"One thing's for sure, you should totally go to the library and talk with Miss Margaret," Elizabeth advised, using the name she'd been calling the librarian ever since she was a child. I thought it was adorable. "Miss Margaret has been working there since the dawn of time. If there's anything you want to know about this town, talk to Miss Margaret."

It was exactly what I planned to do.

I had taken off my apron and was outside, chatting with our last table of customers, a couple and their two young Labradors, who were lingering over a fresh cup of coffee while enjoying the view. Welly and Clara were with me, making new friends with the dogs. After a cautious introduction to Clara, who was eye-catching with her magical unicorn colors, the dogs were friendly and playful, inspiring me to give out another round of Beacon Bites before letting the animals play for a bit on the lawn.

It was the end of another busy day at the Beacon, and I

was waiting on Kennedy before heading off to the library to talk with Miss Margaret. Kennedy had been working at the boutique with Mom all day and was obviously detained. I was about to put Welly in the lighthouse and bring Clara back to the boathouse, when I spied Grayson Smythe walking up to the patio. He smiled and waved when I saw him, reminding me that Mom had said he was coming by to drop something off. That something, I mused, was in the footlong white box he was carrying.

"I must apologize," he began. "I was running late. I wasn't sure you'd still be open. I came to give you—" The dogs and the goat, playing in the side yard, must have heard the newcomer's voice. The motley herd ran around the corner, led by a bedazzled Clara, and made a beeline for the artist.

"Aaaaah!" Grayson cried, his eyes nearly popping out of his head as the animals charged. He tossed me the box he'd been holding as he dashed for the bakeshop door. Thankfully, I caught it. I then set it on a table as I went after the dogs.

The couple sprang from the table too, and attempted to correct their giant puppies, but it was no use. The dogs were in the heat of the chase, led by Clara. I was trying to do the same. Welly, after all, knew better. However, he must have thought it was a new game. I made a grab for his collar as he galloped past me, and I was pulled with him a couple of paces until he came to a halt.

Clara and the Labradors evaded capture. The Labradors got there first and jumped on Grayson, knocking him against the door and lavishing him with puppy kisses. Then came Clara. However, she did something then that I'd never seen her do. She lowered her head and rammed the panicking artist in the rear with her swept-back horns.

Grayson yelped again and spun on the goat, not quite certain what he was looking at.

"What the hell is that thing?" he cried, rubbing his behind. "So beguiling and painful in the same breath!"

I grabbed Clara by her collar and pulled her back as she told him, "*Blaaah! Blaaah! Blaaah!*"

"I'm so sorry." I was sure I was turning red from embarrassment. "This is a goat, a very naughty goat."

"I thought so," he remarked, narrowing one eye at Clara. "Fickle beasts. I didn't think you kept one here."

"I don't usually. I'm just keeping her for the time being. This is Clara, Lars Jorgenson's goat."

"Oh!" he said, recognizing the name. "Poor thing. No wonder she's a bit fractious. Love what you've done to her fur." Had the remark come from any other man, it would have sounded sarcastic, but I believed that the artist meant it. He rubbed his bruised backside with a hand and added, "Anyhow, I'll leave you to it." He gestured to the goat. "Enjoy the little gift, and please tell your lovely mother that she's welcome at the studio anytime." With that, the artist turned and fast-walked down the walkway to his car.

I looked at the goat. "What was that all about, Clara?"

"*Blaaah! Blaaah! Blaaah!*" she told me and pranced back to Welly's side.

I picked up the white box Grayson had brought and opened it. I didn't know what I'd been expecting, but my jaw dropped all the same. Inside was the most beautiful, intricate, delicate, glass lighthouse I had ever seen. The man really was a talent.

* * *

We found Margaret Bigham in the library sitting at the reference desk. She looked up from the computer monitor she was staring at and smiled. "Betty told me to expect you, Lindsey. You must be Kennedy," she said, smiling at my friend. "So nice to meet you both. After talking with Betty yesterday, I started snooping around and found something that might be of interest."

We followed Margaret to a private room labeled *Local History*. I had been in this room once before, when I had been searching for information about Captain Willy Riggs, my ghost, and the first lightkeeper of the Beacon Harbor Lighthouse. From all the materials I found in this room, I was able to piece together what had happened to the captain so long ago that had caused his untimely death. I was now back for a similar reason, to find out who the original Blueberry Festival pranksters had been, and a possible link to the most recent tragedy, the murder of Lars Jorgenson.

Margaret had been kind enough to pull all the relevant materials we'd been looking for, including a high school yearbook from 1972, and printing off an old newspaper article she'd found while going through the relevant microfilm.

"You found all this stuff?" I said, looking at the librarian in wonder. "I can't believe it. Thank you."

"My pleasure, ladies," she replied. "It's been a slow day. Here's something interesting," she added, opening the yearbook to the bookmarked page. Kennedy and I looked at the picture she pointed to.

"My goodness!" I exclaimed, looking at the old picture of an attractive young man with hair a tad too long, and wearing clothing that would now be considered vintage. "That's a young Lars Jorgenson!"

"Righto," Kennedy remarked, taking a look. "Don't take this the wrong way, girls, but what a dishy bloke!"

Margaret, a pleasant woman in her seventies with graying hair and chic, red-rimmed glasses, giggled. "He is . . ." She cleared her throat and corrected, "or was. I was two years ahead of Lars Jorgenson in high school, but I remember him well. All the girls used to stare at him—with that gorgeous blond hair of his, and those compelling blue eyes—and blush when he'd walk by. He broke a lot of hearts, that one did."

"I can only imagine," I said, suddenly hit by a welling sadness that the handsome young man from the old yearbook was no longer here. My throat tightened, and I swallowed a bit painfully. "Is there some significance to the year nineteen-seventy-two?" I asked the librarian.

"Yes," she said, pulling out a few pages of the article she'd copied for us. "That was the year of the first Beacon Harbor Blueberry Festival. When I was talking with Betty, I couldn't remember the year, only that the pranks seemed familiar. I decided to start at the beginning, which was a good idea. That's because it was during the first ever Blueberry Festival that the pranks happened. Here," she said, indicating the copies she'd made, "take a look at this article."

Kennedy and I studied the old newspaper article from August of 1972. The headline, "Pranksters Strike Beacon Harbor's Blueberry Festival," seemed eerily familiar. However, it was the headlining picture that nearly stopped my heart. "That's Lars Jorgenson!"

"Damn right it is," Kennedy remarked with a grin. "Thanks to that old yearbook, I'd know that dreamy face anywhere. And look, he's with four of his devious little friends. According to this article, Lars was the brains behind the pranks. It looks like we found the identity of our prankster after all."

I looked at my friend. "When we found his body in that boat with Clara, I had a gut feeling that he was somehow behind the pranks. But now I'm not so sure. The man suffered from Alzheimer's disease, Ken. Do we really think he could have pulled off such intricate pranks?"

Kennedy shrugged. "Maybe he was on some miracle drug that gave him clarity for the weekend . . . or maybe he had help."

"Maybe one of these other lads was his helper?"

"After talking with Betty, I'm going with the theory that he had help," Margaret chimed in, pointing to the picture in question. "As I've told you, I was two years ahead of Lars in high school. I'm not familiar with these boys here, and I don't recognize the names in the article. I don't think any of them still live in Beacon Harbor anymore. However, I suppose any one of them could have come back for the festival with a hankering to relive their glory days."

"Dear heavens," I breathed, having never entertained the possibility before. We thanked Margaret, took the article she had copied for us, and left the library, a little wiser and yet no closer to discovering the identity or the motive of the murderer.

CHAPTER 41

We met the fellas at Hoots Diner, our favorite low-key restaurant three miles out of town and right off the expressway. Hoots, with its pine paneling, slightly outdated woodsy décor, and green pleather-covered booths, had a nostalgic "up north" feel that was as comforting as their unchanging menu.

Rory and Tuck were already there, nursing their soft drinks. I slid in the booth next to Rory, gave him a kiss, and slapped the copy of the article we'd found on the table. "You'll never guess what we found out at the library today."

Rory lifted a dark brow in amusement. "I don't need to guess. It's right here." He picked up the article and read it. When he was done, he handed it to Tuck.

"I don't believe it!" Tuck exclaimed when he was done. "It's all here. Lars Jorgenson pulled off a series of pranks almost identical to the ones we experienced last weekend, way back in nineteen-seventy-two. That's fifty years ago!"

"They're similar," Rory agreed, "but with slight differences. The *For Sale* sign prank was played on the mayor back then, not the town's favorite gossipy Realtor. Water balloons were thrown at the Blueberry Queen, not at a float carrying the mayor–slash–church music director."

"Maybe that's because there is no Blueberry Queen anymore?" I suggested.

"Right. The town and the festival have definitely changed in the years since that first Beacon Harbor Blueberry Festival," Tuck agreed. "There were mice in the pie at the blueberry pie bake-off, but the goats were released at the pie-eating contest, not under a brat and beer tent during a fashion show. There was a three-mile run instead of a 5K, which is essentially the same thing, but during both, the course was tampered with."

"But I didn't get pranked," I pointed out. "My pie-eating contest went off without a hitch."

"Because the prankster was already murdered by then, darling," Kennedy pointed out.

Tuck, struck with a thought, leaned forward on his elbows. "Wait. I don't think that was the reason. Lindsey's pie-eating contest was on Sunday, but the goat prank had been purposely moved up to Saturday under the beer tent. All the pranks happened on either Friday or Saturday, making us all assume that Lars Jorgenson was behind them. He turned up dead Sunday morning, and the pranks stopped. The murderer wants us to believe it was him behind the pranks, but we now know that Lars couldn't have pulled them off, due to the Alzheimer's disease."

"Which his family was hiding—including trying to stop the autopsy," I added.

"For personal reasons," Rory countered with a pensive look. "They were trying to hide it for their father's sake. He was a proud man."

"We also have these other men to consider," Kennedy reminded us, pointing to the other boys in the picture. "Look, I'll bet a pair of my favorite Louboutins that Anders Jorgenson knew about his father and these pranks. In my family, such pranks would be legendary. What if Anders and some of these other men helped Lars with these pranks once again, for old times' sake?"

"And then what?" Rory probed. "Poison him afterward with a pie? It doesn't make sense. Nothing here makes sense, and that's the problem!"

It was true. We were all racking our brains over the jumbled facts and confusing circumstances surrounding Lars's death. Rory, I knew, was taking it particularly hard. His fear was that if he delved too deep into this murder, he might discover something he didn't want to know about his fellow veteran and friend. Fear and guilt collided within him, and for that reason I begged him to spend the night with me at the lighthouse, which he happily agreed to. Welly was also happy with the arrangement.

It happened again. I woke up in the middle of the night with my heart pounding from the strange, vivid, surreal dream that lingered in my head like heavy lake fog. I had seen the Viking again, only the dream wasn't about him, it was about another who looked out at him from a shadowy place. This other man, barely visible, was fragile and

waiflike compared to the warrior, but his eyes were familiar, only I couldn't place them. I awoke with a start,
thinking of those haunting eyes, knowing that somehow
the captain was trying to send me a message.

Not wanting to wake Rory, I carefully got out of bed,
grabbed my phone off the night table, and tiptoed to the
door. Amazingly, Welly remained sound asleep in his bed
too. Some watchdog, I mused as I headed for the light
tower stairs.

I needed to see the old newspaper article again. I believed the eyes that haunted my dream were somewhere
in that old photo of the original pranksters. One of them
was here, I was certain of it. After dinner, Rory and I had
gone up to the lightroom for a nightcap. I had taken the
old newspaper article with me and had placed it in the
pages of my logbook, along with my list of suspects. I
was a stickler about keeping all my information in one
place. Now, with the aid of my flashlight app, I reached
the quiet room at the top of the circular stairs, surrounded
by 360 degrees of clear glass. To my left, the complete
darkness was broken by the lonely streetlights of Beacon
Harbor. Stars filled the night sky above, but the lake just
beyond the lightroom was indiscernible. If it wasn't for
the relentless cadence of waves hitting the shore, I
wouldn't have even known it was there.

As I entered, the familiar scent of pipe smoke tickled
my nose. I had the strangest feeling that the captain was
here, too, but I wasn't afraid. Although I couldn't see
him, I regarded him as a kindred spirit. By entering the
lightroom in the dead of night, I had broken our unspoken
code, but I had the feeling that Captain Willy understood.
This thought was confirmed when I saw that the article
that I was looking for was already waiting for me on the

desk. I knew I had placed it in the logbook. The fact that it was here now was a subtle, if not eerie sign that Captain Willy was helping me from beyond.

"Thank you, Captain," I said to the room at large, then shined my light on the old photo.

I looked at the young men standing next to Lars, studying their faces and searching their eyes, but to no avail. Nothing familiar jumped out at me.

"I don't understand?" I uttered aloud. As if answering my ignorance, a rogue breeze swept into the room, fluttering the papers and scattering them on the floor. Annoyed, I picked them up again, realizing the moment I did that I'd been looking at the wrong picture. On the second page of the article was another picture, this one depicting a strapping young Lars Jorgenson, grinning from ear to ear as he hurled a water balloon at some unseen object from his place in the crowd. Most of the people standing behind him were focused on the parade . . . most, but for one young man. His hooded, expressionless eyes were laser-focused on Lars. It was hard to be sure what he was thinking as he stared at the large, lively, boisterous person before him. However, one thing was certain: His were the eyes from my dream. The face, although it was much younger, was unmistakable. Here was the connection I'd been looking for, only it had never dawned on me until now.

"Thank you! Thank you!" I said to the captain, then picked up the picture and raced down the stairs.

"Rory. Rory!" I shook his shoulder, waking him from his peaceful slumber. Welly, hearing me come through the door, was fully awake and staring at me as his head rested on the bed.

"Lindsey?" he uttered, opening one eye. "You okay?"

"I think I know who is responsible for the murder of Lars Jorgenson."

This woke him up. His thick black eyelashes fluttered as he struggled to fully open his eyes. He then eased himself higher on the pillows. "What . . . are you talking about?"

"This," I said, showing him the picture in question while shining my light on it. "There's a person in here whom you and I both know, and it got me thinking."

He squinted at what I was pointing to. When he understood what I was saying, he leaned back on the pillows and exhaled forcefully.

Since he was fully awake, I reached over to my night table and turned on the lamp. "Okay, don't judge me too harshly, but it came to me in a dream. When I woke up, I went up to the lightroom to have a look at that article again and saw this. When I saw him standing there, I remembered that there was one prank played at this year's Blueberry Festival that wasn't in this article. Every other prank had been done before, but this one."

"The one played on Grayson Smythe," he answered, and raked his hand through his disheveled hair. "Jesus, Lindsey."

"I think Grayson is our prankster. He knew Lars. They went to school together. He's right here in this picture, standing in the background, observing, possibly longing to be a part of the action. Even Grayson admitted that he was different. They knew it too. What if this is about revenge for not allowing him to participate all those years ago?"

"Do you really think that Grayson would have destroyed his own masterpiece?"

"I thought about that too, but then I remembered what

Mom said. She told us that Grayson had already sorted all the broken pieces from those spheres and planned to reuse them. They're recyclable. Sure, it took a lot of work to create that piece of art, but if he was the person behind the pranks, what better way to blend in than to be the brunt of a cruel prank?"

"True," Rory admitted, although he still looked unconvinced.

"Grayson could have easily tied one end of his tarp to the frame of his statue without anyone looking. You have to admit that his was not only the most spectacular prank, but also the most visible one. It definitely threw us off his trail. Lars, on the other hand, applauded it."

Rory thought about this a moment. "What about that blueberry pie? Do you think Grayson baked it?"

"He's never admitted to being a baker, but he's an artist. He's clever. I think he's capable of whatever he sets his mind to."

"And what about the fact that Lars was dressed as a Viking when we found him?"

"Grayson knew he was from Norway. You have to admit there was an artistic flair in the way the body was laid out in that boat. Sending him off like that could have been Grayson's last act of revenge. And there is one other thing I really didn't think about until I saw this picture. This afternoon, when Clara heard Grayson's voice, she led a charge against him. She actually rammed him with her horns! She's a gentle creature and has never done that before. I think she knows the truth!"

Rory made a sound like a grunt before he remarked, "Interesting, Bakewell, and worth investigating. We'll pay Grayson a visit tomorrow afternoon."

"I'd like to do it in the morning," I told him. With this new revelation churning through my brain, I knew I would be bursting with impatience until I talked with the artist. It could be another dead end, another red herring, but I had to check it out, regardless. This mystery was killing me.

"Can't, I'm afraid. James and I are fishing early, though not as early as your baking schedule," he remarked. "Then, when we come back, I have an important meeting."

I sat up higher on my pillows and looked at him. "Is this about your possible new business venture?"

"Possibly." His impish grin confirmed my suspicions.

"What are you up to, Rory Campbell?"

"You'll see soon enough. I tried the novelist route, but you and I both know I'm not a writer. Sitting in my spare bedroom in my cabin while staring at a computer screen was boresville on steroids. I did it once; I won't do it again. I'm a man of action, babe," he said huskily, while propping himself on an elbow. He then lowered his lips to mine, uttering, "Remember that."

"Hard to forget," I said when I could. Every nerve in my body was alive; my heart was pounding so loudly I feared he could hear it. And yet I wanted more. I smiled at his ruggedly handsome face, and said, "Now, talk to me about my baking."

CHAPTER 42

Rory had wanted to come with me to talk to Grayson Smythe. However, the longer I stayed in the bakeshop, the more I was consumed with the thought that I had sifted out not only the identity of the prankster, but possibly the killer as well. I wasn't an impulsive person by nature. Impulsivity in an investment banker would spell disaster. But for some reason I had a burning need to talk with the glass artist. My excuse for the visit was to thank him for the beautiful glass lighthouse he had delivered yesterday. After all, he'd run off before I had the chance even open it.

Then there was the fact that my staff were getting a bit impatient with me. I'd been so preoccupied by thoughts of Grayson Smythe that I was screwing up even our regular customers' orders. The clincher came when I handed Sergeant Murdock a fat-free latte and a spinach quiche.

"Bakewell, I'm a patient woman," she said, hitting me with her beady-eyed stare. "But I have to ask, are you trying to kill me?"

I realized she was joking, but immediately apologized and handed her a regular latte and a giant cinnamon roll slathered with icing. The crisis had been momentarily averted, but I was so inside my head I had no idea what was going on.

"Umm, hey, Lindsey, are you okay?" Elizabeth asked, trying to be polite, although she looked a little frightened. After all, I'd never been such a wreck at work before. That's when Wendy grabbed my hand.

"No, no, she's not," she said and walked me over to a chair, as if I were a lost toddler. After I sat, Wendy bent down and looked me in the eyes. Alaina stood next to her, doing the same thing. And Elizabeth stood behind them both with her arms crossed. Tom and Ryan, thankfully busy at their stations—Tom making espressos and Ryan prepping the sandwich counter—were also staring at me with a troubled look in their eyes.

"I'm fine, guys," I told them.

Wendy shook her head. "No, she's not. She's just saying that. This is bad."

"We've seen this before, ladies," Alaina told them with confidence. "It was the same thing last December when those cookie-nappers had her running in circles. Lindsey's trying to solve a mystery in her head while she works. Sometimes she can do it, only I think that this one is taking up more of her brain cells, rendering her unable to tell the difference between a donut and a pecan roll."

"That's bad," Elizabeth agreed.

"Is this true, Lindsey?" Wendy stood and put her hands on her hips. "Are you close to figuring this one out?"

"I really hope so," I told them honestly, and stood up from the chair.

"Who is it?" Elizabeth asked. All eyes were on me.

"I'm not going to say, but give me an hour and I'll let you know if I was right."

"An hour? Take the entire day," Tom advised with a grin.

"You guys, you're too generous," I teased, and thanked them all for being so understanding. Then I got Welly from the lighthouse and headed for my Jeep. I might have been consumed with impulsivity, but I also knew I needed to take a closer look at Grayson's vast gardens. I suspected that he was the prankster, but that wasn't enough. I needed to know if he had made the blueberry pie that killed Lars Jorgenson. Having spent much of my adult life in a high-rise condo in New York City, my experience with gardening was just slightly greater than my knowledge of ice fishing. I had the odd potted plant and a terrarium of succulents. Now that I owned the lighthouse, I was just learning about the joys of gardening, but I still had a difficult time identifying various plants. Grayson had hundreds of flowering annuals and perennials; he also had shrubs, bushes, and lots of mature trees around his property. I needed to find the right one—if it grew there. To do that, I needed to snoop around his garden, and my plan, if it worked, was to be invited to do so.

The moment Grayson saw Welly and me enter his beautiful shop, one filled with the fruits of his glassblowing labor, he dashed from his place at his retail monitor and ran over to greet us. After all, a dog like Welly in a glass shop was akin to a bull in a China shop.

"Lindsey," he said with enthusiasm. His enthusiasm

left him as he added, "And your big dog. To what do I owe the pleasure?"

"I wanted to thank you for that lovely lighthouse you brought over yesterday. That was so kind of you."

"It was my pleasure," he replied with a little bow.

I walked forward, pulling Welly with me. As my dog strained on his leash to sniff a particularly delicate-looking toasting glass on a shelf that was crowded with such pieces, I added, "I also came to tell you how much my mother enjoyed her visit. She's a big fan of yours now."

Grayson seemed to want to smile, but he couldn't quite reach the emotion due to my drooling dog and his inquisitive nose. Instead, he said, "Your mother is an angel. Far too kind. I'll tell you what? Why don't I close down the shop for a while, and we can sit in the garden and chat about your lovely, famous mother. I'll bring some tea and nibbles. Nope!" he cried, as I started walking toward the back door and the breezeway where we had entered his garden before. "Not that way. Why don't you and your big dog go back out the way you came and walk around the building? That way you can enjoy my whimsical garden creatures. But please, keep your dog on a leash. Everything out there is rather delicate."

"Of course," I said, happy to get Wellington out of there.

Once outside, we took our time investigating Grayson's intricate and expansive gardens. One thing was certain, the man had a green thumb. His roses were spectacular, his hydrangeas sublime. He had sun gardens and shade gardens, each one lush and lovely. Welly was sniffing away, pulling me in a zigzagging fashion across the flawless lawn between the gardens. Then, as we rounded the building, in the far corner of the side yard, he pulled me to a huge oak tree ringed by a bushy shrub. Welly sniffed and lifted his leg, marking what he felt was his territory, too, silly dog. However, as he piddled, I realized that this glorious oak was located in the one part of Grayson's yard that most visitors never saw. And as Welly did his male dog thing, I realized that the woody shrub he was watering was covered with green ovate leaves and dark purple berries. As my pulse elevated with the discovery, I checked my phone just to be sure.

"Heavens!" I cried and pulled Welly away from the bush. Sure enough, it was deadly nightshade, the murder weapon. I took a picture of the shrub before plucking off a branch and covertly sticking it in my shoulder purse.

We arrived on the patio just as Grayson came out the door, carrying a tray that held a pitcher of iced tea and two glasses with ice and fresh mint leaves in them. There was also a plate of lemon cookies.

I instructed Welly to lie down by my chair and remarked on his hospitality. "This looks delicious. I also must commend you. You're quite the gardener."

Grayson poured the tea before taking the wicker patio chair across from me. "Gardening is one of my passions," he said with a careless wave of his hand. "So, let's talk about something important. Ellie Montague Bakewell is a fan of my work?" His smile was so large and genuine as he said this, I felt a bit guilty for my deception. I had found what I needed and felt it best to be frank.

"Grayson, I'm sorry, but I didn't come here to talk about my mother, although she is a fan of your work. I came because I found out that you were at the very first Beacon Harbor Blueberry Festival."

He was about to take a sip of his tea as I said this, but my words caused his hand to freeze before the glass came to his lips. He set the glass back down and looked at me. "Is that a crime?"

"No. But it is a bit odd that you had witnessed all those pranks before, fifty years ago to be exact, and never said a word about it. I didn't make the connection until I realized there was one new prank played this year that had never been done before. It was the prank played on you."

He crossed his legs and stared at me with a face void of all expression. I found his silence intimidating, but I had come this far. I reached into my purse and took out the copies of the article Margaret had found for us in the local history room. As Grayson took them and read them, his face paled as his hands began to tremble.

When he finally looked up, he asked, "What . . . exactly are you accusing me of?"

"When I found the body of Lars Jorgenson in that boat with his goat, I was convinced that he was the prankster. According to that article, he was the brains behind those original pranks. It made sense. Lars was there to witness every prank, and every time the chaos happened, he laughed and laughed. My first thought was that someone found out that he was behind the pranks and got mad enough to kill him. However, as I began talking with more people—not just the committee members who were pranked—I found out that Lars couldn't have pulled any of those pranks off alone, due to the fact that he suffered from Alzheimer's disease. But I think you knew that. I think you taunted him with his own pranks—the ones he thought up years ago—right before you poisoned him with a blueberry pie laced with this." As I spoke, I pulled out the sprig of deadly nightshade in a flamboyant *ta-da!* moment. Grayson, choosing to remain silent, lifted a brow instead.

The thought that I was making a fool of myself did cross my mind. But I had come this far and was determined to drive what little dignity I had left into the wall.

"This . . . poisonous plant isn't native to North America," I told him, as if he didn't already know. "Some gardeners, however, grow it in their gardens for its pretty flowers and attractive, yet poisonous berries. I think you saw this as your chance to finally get your revenge on Lars Jorgenson, a man who had mocked you all your life."

I waited in the silence with bated breath. At last Grayson reacted, and when he did it felt as if a ticking time-bomb had gone off.

"Revenge!?" he cried, heaving with indignation.

Welly, shocked by the outburst, sprang up on all fours. I put my hand on his head to calm him as Grayson continued his tirade.

"You think this is about revenge? And here your mother went on and on, bragging about how clever her daughter is. Well, Lindsey Bakewell, you're only half as clever as you think you are. Lars Jorgenson was the love of my life!"

As he said this, his light gray eyes filled with unshed tears, making them seem as clear and fragile as the glass art he created. His admission shocked me to my core.

"What? But . . . but Lars was—"

"A straight man?" he offered. "Of course, he was. Lars was never anything he wasn't born to be, and that's why I loved him so. Ours was a complicated relationship, Lindsey. But since you've guessed the half of it, I shall confess to you the rest. Because my heart is broken, and this burden I carry is destroying me too."

I sat, a captivated audience, as Grayson told me about his relationship with Lars Jorgenson, how they had been childhood friends, but had drifted apart in high school, due to the fact that Lars was so popular, while Grayson was struggling with the fact that he, too, gravitated to Lars, but for different reasons.

"Lars knew I was gay," Grayson said. "Yet, to his credit, he never made fun of me because of it. However, after high school I knew I had to get out of this town. Lars served in the military, married Clara, the love of his life, and when he came home, he went to work for his father. I, on the other hand, went to college, studied art, then moved to San Francisco. I became a successful glass artist and married my boyfriend, Bradley. Bradley was a businessman. Through all those years, Lars and I stayed in touch. I would come home over the holidays, and we'd grab a drink at our favorite bar, just the two of us, like old times. We'd talk about our careers and our families. Truth be told, that one drink with Lars was the reason I came back to Beacon Harbor every year."

I sipped minty iced tea as Grayson told me about Bradley dying of cancer, and how lost he had been after that. Then, when Lars called him and told him that Clara had died, too, Grayson decided to sell all his assets in California and move back to Beacon Harbor.

"I came back here so I could rekindle our old friendship, one based on a lifetime of trust and familiarity. I knew it could never be anything more than friendship, but that was enough for me. We were two old men," he said and tried to smile at the thought. "It was a blessing for Lars as well. He needed a friend who understood him because he was aware he was losing his memory."

Grayson looked at me, his red-rimmed eyes filling again with tears. "He . . . he told me he didn't want to fade away like a rock thrown into a pond, its presence, like his memory, diminishing with every ripple until there was nothing left of the rock that had made the splash. He was very depressed. And then came the day when his beloved son told him he could no longer live in his home."

"Anders told me about that," I admitted. "He and Susan were planning to move Lars to a memory care facility."

"It would have killed him for sure," he remarked as a tear rolled down his cheek. "I tried to be the voice of reason, promising that I'd visit him every day, but Lars was an independent soul. A few nights later, when I came to visit, I found him in his woodshop. He was trying to hang himself, but he couldn't remember how to tie the rope."

"Oh, my God," I uttered, torn by the thought, and realized I was crying too.

"He . . . he wanted me to impale him with a sword," Grayson continued as a sad, ironic smile tried to break through. "Lars was obsessed with the land of his birth and his ancestors. He was a warrior, a real Viking, and he remembered enough to demand that he wanted to die with a sword in his hand. I told him that I abhorred the sight of blood. He insisted . . . he insisted that I end his life—or he would. When I finally agreed, the relief on his face broke my heart. Then he asked me to give him a Viking sendoff."

"So, you killed him," I said, having a better understanding of what had happened, although I didn't like it one bit.

"He was suffering, Lindsey," Grayson pleaded. "I ask you, could you watch that beautiful dog of yours suffer without doing something to help?"

It was my turn to be silent because I didn't want to contemplate the answer. I loved my dog and knew I'd do anything I could for him. The mere thought made my eyes burn and my throat go dry.

"My last gift to him was to re-create the best day of his life," Grayson explained through his tears, "that memorable day long ago at the first Beacon Harbor Blueberry Festival, where he pulled off his epic pranks and met the love of his life, Clara."

"Oh . . . Grayson," I cried. "That's why you did it? For Lars?"

"You heard him laugh, Lindsey. Those pranks brought him back to a place and a time he remembered, and he loved every minute of it. We pulled them off together."

It was astounding, and yet I was compelled to listen.

"I . . . I wanted a peaceful death for him." Choked up, he paused until he could speak again. "I remembered about the belladonna, because Lars had once told me a tale of how King Macbeth of Scotland had used it on the Vikings during a truce. The old king had a fermented drink made from it and fed it to the Vikings, later bragging that he killed them all without lifting his sword. It grew on my property, and so I knew that was what I would use. I found Clara's famous pie recipe and baked Lars a pie laced with the berries of the plant. I waited until I knew that Anders had tucked him into bed, as he did every night. Then I drove out to his house and paid him a visit, as I did every night. Just because Anders put him to bed didn't mean that Lars was ready to go to sleep. I've always been a night owl as well. Every night Lars and I would get together at his house, just two old men talking about life over a late-night snack. That damn goat was always there as well. When I walked into his house that night, I told Lars that Clara had made him a pie, and he believed me."

Grayson was beside himself with grief as he relived the last moments of his friend's life. He had somehow dressed Lars as a Viking and sat with him in his boat, cradling him until he took his last breath. Clara the goat was with them too. Grayson explained how the goat watched over her master, as faithful as a dog.

"But you left her in that boat!" I scolded as anger rose inside me, recalling the terrifying incident.

"I pulled her out of the boat!" he exclaimed. "But that stubborn goat jumped back in the moment I shoved the boat into the lake. Then she lay down on top of him as the boat drifted farther out on the lake. There was nothing I could do! It was Clara that thwarted my plans," he admitted, and he lifted the corner of his mouth at the irony of the name. "I planned on setting the boat on fire, giving Lars his Viking burial, but only one of the arrows I shot made it to the boat. I'm a terrible shot, but I thought I could do it. That boat, however, caught a current and was drifting faster than I could shoot the fire arrows. Anyhow, when one finally landed in the boat, Clara went berserk and began bleating like a fiend. She attacked it with her hooves, sending the boat rocking so violently that waves rolled in and put out the fire before it had time to spread. You see, Lars was supposed to disappear into the night without a trace. That was the plan. He wanted to be remembered for the man he was, not the helpless man he was becoming. I would just continue on, harboring my terrible secret while praying for the whole nightmare to be over. But it didn't work out that way. I killed my oldest, dearest friend because he asked me to, never thinking about what it would do to me. I was so distraught I didn't even remember I'd left the pie there."

"I . . . I have to call the police," I told him, my heart breaking for them both. I didn't even bother to wipe away my tears.

"I know," he said softly. "But let me call Anders first. He deserves to know what I did."

Chapter 43

I had solved the mystery of the Blueberry Festival pranksters; I had found the murderer of Lars Jorgenson; and yet part of me regretted I had gotten involved at all. If it wasn't for Clara the goat bleating her little lungs out on the lake in the dead of night, I would have slept until my alarm went off and then started baking, blissfully ignorant that any death had occurred. But it hadn't worked out that way. Fate, or perhaps a kindred spirit still living in the lighthouse, had other plans for me. Also, was it any mystery that Rory had gotten involved as well? All summer long he had been on a mission to find himself, and part of that process had been connecting with military veterans, like Lars Jorgenson and his son, Anders.

Learning of what Sergeant Murdock had termed an illegal assisted suicide that would come down as premeditated murder, the entire town had been affected, reeling with sadness and wonder by turns, while providing an un-yielding source for lively debate. Thank goodness we had received another delivery of sweet, plump blueberries at the Beacon Bakeshop. Once the truth behind the pranks had come out, and once Mayor Jeffers had declared Grayson Smythe banned from the Blueberry Festival Committee for life, blueberry baked goods were very much back in season. We couldn't keep enough blueberry pie on the shelves, it had become that popular.

The entire village had been moved by the story of the unlikely friendship between Lars Jorgenson and Grayson Smythe. It had come as a surprise to everyone, including Anders Jorgenson. Although Anders was struggling with the loss of his father, he admitted to Rory he was also consoled by the thought that his proud father was now at peace. After hearing the story from Grayson's own lips, Anders admitted his father could have committed suicide, but Grayson had spared him the indignity of that death and the greater indignity of the disease he suffered from. Although it was a matter for the courts to decide, the Jorgenson family reached out to Grayson. They had been blown away by a deep friendship they never realized had existed between Lars and the artist. They also knew that in a rather profound way, Grayson would forever be connected to their family. Anders realized, as most children do at some point, there was so much more to his father than he imagined. Grayson would help fill in those gaps.

On a more personal note, once Anders and Susan heard about the heroic actions of Clara the goat, and how her love and loyalty to her owner had prompted her to action by preventing the boat from burning, they agreed to keep her as a pet. They'd be moving back to Anders's childhood home, where Clara had a home too. Hans and

Gretta were ecstatic. However, for Kennedy and me, it was a bittersweet moment. We had fallen in love with the little goat, and we volunteered to watch her whenever they needed a goat-sitter. In turn they told me that Welly could visit his new friend whenever he wished. It was agreed that Clara was always welcome at the Beacon Bakeshop's pup café.

It was the Tuesday morning after a long weekend of revelations, tears, and a memorial service for Lars Jorgenson. The Beacon Bakeshop was open for business, and I watched from behind the bakery counter as Sergeant Murdock sauntered into the café. It was the first time the busy sergeant had visited since I had called her from the patio of Grayson's glassblowing studio.

"Well, well, if it isn't Beacon Harbor's own Veronica Mars." It wasn't until she grinned that I realized she was teasing me. "I never did ask, but what led you to Grayson Smythe in the first place? I have to admit, he wasn't even on our radar."

"It wasn't until Betty mentioned that the pranks had been done before," I explained. "That led Kennedy and me to the library where we found an article on the first Beacon Harbor Blueberry Festival. When I realized the prank played on Grayson Smythe was the only new prank in the bunch, it got me thinking. You know the rest." I plated a cinnamon roll for her while Tom worked on her latte.

"Bakewell, if you weren't such a good baker, I'd be tempted to put you on the force."

"That means a lot to me, Sergeant, truly," I told her honestly. "But I've had my fill of mysteries and murders. I don't think I could stomach another. From now on, I'm sticking to baking."

"Glad to hear it," she said, and took her breakfast out to the sunshine on the patio.

A while later, Mom and Betty came in for their morning coffee. Dad, after helping me bake, had taken off to go fishing with Rory again. The two had been spending a lot of time together lately, and I secretly wondered what they were getting up to. I had a feeling I was going to know soon enough. Although the initial revelation of Lars's murder had been emotional for him, as it had been for me, there was no question that he seemed happier now, lighter somehow. Things were settling back down, and we were getting back to normal again.

"Darling," Mom said, gracing me with her lovely smile, "everything in the cases looks delicious. Tell me, did your father go fishing again? I've been trying to call him, but his phone keeps going to voice mail."

"Can't get good service so far out on the lake, Mom," I told her from personal experience, and handed her a bacon and spinach quiche. She had decided on regular coffee today, after spotting our featured flavor on the self-service coffee bar. It was blueberry cobbler. For fans of coffee and blueberries, it was a delicious option.

"I'm still a bit disappointed I won't get to sell those beautiful glass sculptures of Grayson's in our boutique," she admitted. "Also, I was really looking forward to taking glassblowing classes from him."

"Maybe you should try your hand at watercolors instead, Ellie," Betty suggested. "I know this wonderful artist in Traverse City. His landscapes are truly inspired."

I saw Mom was actually considering it, when I reminded her, "But you have a wonderful clothing line to nurture and champion, Mom. And besides, I saw your sketches for the upcoming winter season. You may not know how to blow glass, but you sure know your way around fashion."

Mom smiled at that. "True. Did you hear," she began, as a look of intrigue crossed her face, "Kennedy has arranged to have Grayson Smythe as a guest on her latest podcast of *Kennedy's Crusades*. Since Grayson is cooperating and is not considered a flight risk, his lawyers have agreed to let him do it."

"I've heard," I said to Mom and Betty. "She's been recording her podcasts in the spare room upstairs, but this one will be recorded at the police station, with Officer Cutie Pie supervising." The thought of Tuck supervising the podcast in one of the small interrogation rooms made us all giggle. However, I was very proud of my dear friend for jumping at the chance to discuss the tough and controversial topic of the Death with Dignity Law. Michigan didn't have it, but some states had begun to allow terminally ill patients to request medications to end their suffering. Truthfully, the subject was too raw for me even to contemplate. But I was certain Grayson Smythe would have some interesting things to say on the subject.

"Ready, babe?" I was almost finished cleaning up for the day when I spun around at the sound of Rory's voice. He was at the back door, poking his head into the bakery kitchen and grinning at me as if harboring some great secret, which, I believed, he was. Welly poked his head inside the door too, struggling beside Rory to get even more of his large, furry body through the doorway. Rory was making sure that didn't happen.

"Where are we going?" I asked, taking off my apron.

"We're taking a little walk on the beach. I want to show you something."

We walked along the public beach toward the harbor as Welly ran ahead of us, playing in the surf. As Rory made small talk, my mind was swirling with questions, wondering where we were going. It wasn't until we came to a familiar building near the harbor that I grew suspicious. The building, an old dockside warehouse, had been the recent site of a fishing charter that had been a front for a drug-smuggling operation. Unbeknownst to me at the time, Rory had been tracking the smugglers when I had met him. I'd had a run-in with the smugglers, too, but I didn't want to think about that again.

"What are we doing here?" I asked, scrunching up my nose in distaste.

He surprised me by pulling a set of keys from his pocket and opening the door, revealing a large, empty building, albeit one with a spectacular view of the sheltered harbor and the lake beyond.

"Well," he began, ushering Wellington and me into the building. "You know I've been searching for something meaningful to do since retiring from the navy. I thought about many things, but the one thing I'm really good at is scuba diving, and I'm getting pretty decent at fishing too."

"You want to scuba dive?" was all I got from that.

"I want to teach it," he explained, filling with palpable excitement. I looked into his compelling aqua eyes as he spoke and marveled at how they mirrored the lake. "I want to take charters out to dive on shipwrecks, and lead expeditions to discover more of what's out there. Yet most importantly, when the need arises, I want to lead the search-and-rescue teams that might be required when an accident occurs, or when a body goes missing. It's not pleasant business, but it is important. Finding Lars Jorgenson out there on the lake got me thinking. What if his boat had sunk? Who would have found him then? Also, not many people are certified to do the type of diving I've done. I've been in contact with the Coast Guard, and the state and local rescue units. Also, most importantly, there isn't anyone in this town offering fishing charters anymore. Betty was the one who pointed that out to me. She also brought me here, stating that she was sad it was sitting empty and that all it needed was someone with vision. The deceptively sly woman hit on my weakness, Linds. I'd like to offer that too—the fishing. In short, Lindsey, I want to create a place on the water where I can share my passion for adventure, and where my group of veterans can work with me or hang out all day if they choose. I want a place where people like your father can learn how to fish."

I was speechless.

"And the best part?" he said, swept away with his dream. "Look out there."

I looked out the window. Across the beach at the other end of the bay was my beautiful lighthouse. A lump came to my throat as I thought about this man who was so important to me, and the fact that he had finally found something he was passionate about. I could tell he'd been thinking about this place for a long time.

"Well," he asked. "What do you think?"

I put my arms around him, pulling him into a big hug, as I told him, "I think, Rory Campbell, that you are going to need to teach me how to scuba dive."

RECIPES FROM
THE BEACON BAKESHOP

Are you craving blueberries yet? I sure hope so! Blueberries are not only beautiful and delicious, but they are also packed with so many healthful nutrients that it's no wonder these lovely little berries have an entire festival dedicated to them! Below are some of my favorite blueberry recipes, sure to bring a smile to the lips of any blueberry lover. So, get yourself a bushel and have some fun!

Blueberry Lemon Bread

Prep time: 15 minutes. Cook time: 50 minutes.
Makes one 9x5 loaf pan.

Ingredients:
1½ cup fresh blueberries, rinsed
1 teaspoon lemon juice (for blueberries)
1 teaspoon sugar (for blueberries)
1 tablespoon flour (for blueberries)
1½ cups all-purpose flour
1 teaspoon baking powder
½ teaspoon salt
1 cup granulated sugar
2 large eggs
½ cup butter (1 stick), melted
2 tablespoons lemon juice
1 tablespoon lemon zest
1 teaspoon lemon extract (optional, but it does add a nice
    punch!)
½ cup whole milk

For the glaze:
1 cup powdered sugar
3 tablespoons butter, melted
2 tablespoons (or more) lemon juice

Directions:
Preheat oven to 350 degrees. Prepare 9x5 loaf pan by
either greasing and flouring it, or lining it with parchment, whichever you prefer.

Put blueberries in a small bowl and add 1 tablespoon

of each lemon juice, sugar, and flour. Give a good toss and set aside.

In medium bowl, sift together flour, baking powder, and salt. Set aside.

In large mixing bowl, whisk sugar and eggs until blended. Gradually whisk in melted butter, followed by the lemon juice, lemon zest, and lemon extract.

Add the dry ingredients to the wet ingredients and mix, alternating with the milk, until well blended.

Stir *half* the blueberries into the batter and quickly pour into prepared loaf pan. Gently spread the rest of the blueberries on top of the batter (this will prevent them from sinking to the bottom) and place in oven. Bake for 50 to 60 minutes or until done. Remove from oven and cool for 30 minutes.

Whisk together powdered sugar, melted butter, and lemon juice. Pour glaze over cooled loaf and let sit until the glaze is set. Enjoy!

Blueberry Summer Salad

Prep time: 15 minutes. Serves 6

Ingredients:
1 cup pecans, chopped
6 cups baby spinach, prewashed
1 pint blueberries, washed
1 cup Danish blue cheese, crumbled

Dressing:
1 green onion, chopped
1 cup blueberries
1 teaspoon salt
3 tablespoons sugar
$\frac{1}{3}$ cup raspberry vinegar
1 cup vegetable oil
(*For a lighter option, a raspberry vinaigrette dressing
   works well too!)

Directions:
Toast pecans in a 350-degree oven for 10 minutes.
Remove from oven and cool.

Place spinach in a large salad bowl and top with blueberries, crumbled blue cheese, and pecans.

For dressing, place all ingredients in a blender and mix
on high until a smooth, thick dressing forms. Pour over
salad and toss well. Enjoy!

Best Blueberry Muffins

Prep time: 15 minutes. Cook time: 25 minutes.
Makes 18 muffins.

Ingredients for topping:
1½ cups all-purpose flour
¾ cup brown sugar, firmly packed
½ teaspoon kosher salt
½ cup butter, melted

Ingredients for muffins:
2½ cups all-purpose flour
1 cup sugar
1 tablespoon baking powder
1 teaspoon kosher salt
1½ cups fresh or frozen blueberries, thawed
2 tablespoons powdered sugar
1 cup plus 2 tablespoons whole buttermilk
⅓ cup vegetable oil
2 large eggs, room temperature
1 tablespoon orange zest

Directions:
Preheat oven to 350 degrees. Grease or line 18 muffin cups with paper liners.

For topping, combine flour, sugar, and salt. Stir in melted butter until mixture is crumbly. Set aside.

For muffins, in large bowl, whisk together flour, sugar, baking powder, and salt. Mix gently to combine. In small bowl, add blueberries and sprinkle with powdered sugar. Set aside. In a medium bowl, whisk together buttermilk, oil, eggs, and orange zest. Add milk mixture to flour mixture and stir until just combined. Fold in blueberries.

Divide mixture into 18 muffin cups and sprinkle topping onto batter.

Bake for 20 to 25 minutes or until muffins are done. Let cool for five minutes and enjoy!

Blueberry Buckle

Prep time: 20 minutes. Cook time: 50 minutes.

Ingredients for cake:
2½ cups fresh or frozen blueberries, thawed.
1 tablespoon lemon juice (for blueberries)
1 tablespoon flour (for blueberries)
½ cup (1 stick) butter
1 cup sugar
2 large eggs
2 teaspoons vanilla extract
2 cups all-purpose flour
2 teaspoons baking powder
1 cup milk

Ingredients for crumble topping:
½ cup all-purpose flour
½ cup brown sugar, firmly packed
½ teaspoon cinnamon
¼ cup cold butter, cut in small cubes

Directions:
Preheat oven to 350 degrees. Grease and flour sides of a 10-inch springform and line the bottom with parchment paper. This will make cake much easier to release once baked.

In a medium bowl, combine washed and dried blueberries with the lemon juice, then toss with one tablespoon of flour. This will help prevent the blueberries from sinking to the bottom of the batter as it bakes.

In the bowl of an electric mixer, cream together butter and sugar until light and fluffy. Add eggs one at a time.

Add vanilla. In a medium bowl combine the flour and baking powder. Add the dry ingredients to the wet ingredients, alternating with milk, being careful not to over mix. Fold in blueberries and immediately spread batter evenly into the prepared pan.

Make the crumble topping by mixing the flour, sugar, and cinnamon. Next, cut in the cold butter until mixture resembles a coarse meal. Sprinkle crumble topping evenly over top of batter and put in oven. Bake for 50 minutes or until a knife inserted in the center comes out clean. Cool for 20 minutes. Remove cake from pan and enjoy!

Blueberry Delight

Prep time: 5 minutes. Cook time: 8 minutes.
Refrigerate for 1 hour.

Ingredients:
1 package Pecan Sandies cookies
⅓ cup melted butter
8 ounces cream cheese, softened
1 cup powdered sugar
2 8-ounce cartons of thawed Cool Whip (not frozen)
12-ounce can of blueberry pie filling
1 cup chopped pecans

Directions:
Preheat oven to 350 degrees. Using a food processor, crush cookies into fine crumbs. You can also crush cookies in a zip-lock bag. Take out ½ cup of the crumbs and set aside. In large bowl, mix the crumbs with the melted butter and press in the bottom of a 9x13 baking pan. Bake in preheated oven for 8 minutes, then let cool.

In the bowl of an electric mixer, beat together the cream cheese, powdered sugar, and one container of Cool Whip until smooth and creamy. Spread over cooled crust. Spread can of blueberry pie filling evenly over the cream cheese mixture. Sprinkle crushed pecans evenly over the blueberry layer. Refrigerate for at least one hour or until ready to serve. Just before serving, spread the remaining carton of Cool Whip over the Blueberry Delight and sprinkle with reserved cookie crumbs. Enjoy!

Best Blueberry Pie

Prep time: 20 minutes. Cook time: 1 hour.
Rest time: 2 hours.

Ingredients:

Your favorite double piecrust, either homemade or store-
  bought
6 cups fresh (or frozen) blueberries
1 cup sugar
5 tablespoons cornstarch
$\frac{1}{4}$ teaspoon salt
1 teaspoon lemon juice
1 teaspoon cinnamon
2 tablespoons butter, to dot on top of pie filling
1 egg, beaten for an egg wash

Directions:

Preheat oven to 425 degrees. Make the pie dough and
divide in half. Roll out bottom crust and use to line a
9-inch pie plate. Set remaining dough aside.

In large mixing bowl, combine blueberries, sugar,
cornstarch, salt, lemon juice, and cinnamon. Toss to coat
blueberries evenly in the mixture. Pour blueberries into
prepared piecrust.

Roll out top crust into a large circle. To make a lattice-
top crust, cut dough into long 1-inch strips. Lay half of
the strips vertically over the pie filling. Next, fold back
every other strip, starting in the middle of the pie. Lay
one strip of pie dough perpendicularly across the tops,
and gently replace the vertical strips. Fold back the alternate strips and lay another strip perpendicularly on top of
that to create the lattice. Repeat the process until a lattice

piecrust has been formed. Trim and crimp the edges of the piecrust.

Beat the egg to make an egg wash. Gently brush the egg wash on top of lattice piecrust to create a nice golden-brown crust when baked. I even sprinkle the crust with extra sugar, for a delicious, crunchy finish. Place the pie on a baking sheet and place in a preheated oven for 15 minutes. Reduce heat to 375 degrees. At this point, I put a crust guard over the edges of the crust to protect it from burning. Put pie back in the oven and bake for an additional 40 to 50 minutes, or until crust is baked and pie filling is bubbling. Remove from oven and cool for 2 hours so filling can fully set. Enjoy!

Blueberry Mint Julep

Prep time: 10 minutes. Yields 1 serving.

For mint simple syrup:
½ cup granulated sugar
½ cup water
1 bunch fresh mint leaves

In a small saucepan, combine sugar, water, and mint leaves. Bring to a boil, stirring constantly. Reduce heat to low and cook for 1 minute. Set aside and cool completely. Remove mint leaves before using.

For blueberry puree:
¾ cup fresh blueberries
3 tablespoons mint simple syrup.

In a blender, combine blueberries and mint simple syrup until pureed. Strain mixture to remove any small seeds.

For the drink:
2 ounces of bourbon
1 ounce mint simple syrup
1½ ounces blueberry puree
Crushed ice
Fresh mint leaves

Directions:
Combine bourbon, mint simple syrup, and blueberry puree and shake well. Pour over crushed ice and garnish with a mint leaf.